Deke's Magic Kiss
Naughty Book Three

Christine Young

ISBN: 978-1-62420-760-0

Credits
Cover Artist: Designs by Ms G
Editor: Sherry Derr-Wille

Printed in the United States of America

Chapter One

Boston Female Medical College

Lights blazed in the large ballroom where the first recipients of a diploma from Boston Female Medical College danced and celebrated with loved ones. The waltz the band played was slow, making those who weren't dancing sway in time. They played a series of tunes popular at the time. The golden glow of the gas lights touched on the vibrant face of Annie Lundin as she danced in the arms of a man she seemed to know. She smiled flirtatiously as the young man whirled her around the room. He held her too close. She pushed away, a flush to her once pale cheeks bloomed as if a flower was opening to the sun. She looked nice painted in the rose color. Deke wondered what the man said to her to cause the rise of embarrassment.

By the look on her face, she chastised the man, her lips set in a grim line. Her dance partner didn't seem to care. He tugged her closer, his hand resting on the small of her back. This time she was able to dislodge herself from him. Her lips set tight, she strode from him, her back rigid. The man did not mean her well. Thinking he should intervene, Deke pushed himself from the wall where he'd been leaning, a soft curse on his breath. He thought better of his plan when another young man joined her. She laughed at something he said then turned from him moving away. What could be described as vicious, the man grabbed her arm, turning her to face him again. Her rescue came from an older man, possibly one of her professors. The tune began, the music livelier. The couple ended up at the punch bowl. As if hot or winded from the exertion, she waved her hand in front of her face, her smile infectious.

Deke Sullivan relaxed against the wall again. His arms crossed in front of him, one knee bent, his foot braced on the wall. For the time being she was safe. For how much longer he couldn't be certain. He watched. He thought of his mission, something he refused several times, declined adamantly. Jamie Lundin, her father, had paid him to escort Annie Lundin to Denver City, Kansas Territory. The journey would be difficult. She was going to be the new doc in town. What she might not understand was the fact that there wasn't a single man in the area surrounding Denver City that would come to see her. She would have a few female patients if their men folk would allow them to see a female. She didn't belong in the west. She was silk and lace, a smile to grace ballrooms not barn dances. Her features so very delicate and fragile surely, she would suffocate or die in Kansas Territory. Her soft hands would end up with callouses. That life couldn't possibly suit her.

Annie Lundin did not belong to the fierce west. She belonged in Boston or Baltimore, any city, a place with street signs. A place that wouldn't leech her beauty with the cold winters coupled with the hot summers and the hard work. There was the wind, the snow along with the ice that would cause the weakest to faint.

Geez, he thought of a woman such as this one examining him. He choked back his thoughts, his body hardening in response to the notion. With a quick readjustment to his dress pants, he tamped down the thought of her doctoring him. God, she was a fire brand. Her long blond hair expertly coiffed on top of her head showed the length of her white neck. The tendrils she artfully arranged to curl beguilingly around her face would tempt a saint. He wanted to get close enough to her to see the color of her eyes. Would they be blue, a crystal-clear shimmering blue?

Annie Lundin was dangerous to a man such as he. She could provoke and enchant create fire within that couldn't be extinguished with one taste. Her small slippered feet seemed to float magically along the floor to the tunes despite her inept partners. Hell, he had two left feet when it came to dancing. Nevertheless, he was tempted to ask for a dance. He wanted her in his arms. His hard gaze focused on the beauty of her.

The night would end. He would have to follow her through the streets of Boston to her apartment. Protect her from the threat her father described in his letter. Jamie Lundin, her father, couldn't stay for the celebrations. He'd attended yesterday's graduation ceremony where she spoke. Business called him home. He and his wife, Tira, worried about her; objected furiously when she told them she was going to Denver City. She was so spontaneous, impulsive too. Apparently, she didn't take the threats against her seriously. Either that or her father was a worrier. Deke knew Jamie Lundin. He wasn't a man to exaggerate or drum up problems that didn't exist. The threats had to be real.

Pulling out his pocket watch, Deke stared at the hour. He was bone weary. He'd hoped Annie would grow tired of the dancing hours ago. Their train west would leave early tomorrow morning, dawn. The time to rise would come all too soon. He rubbed his chin, thinking about the miles that lay ahead of them. While he understood she would have a special car to sleep and live in for the short distance they could take the train, he would have to take special care not to soil her reputation. Jamie told him his car was in front of hers. There was a living area and two bedrooms. Her father trusted him with his little girl who wasn't quite so little any longer.

He was snapped out of his thoughts by the sight of Annie, striding to the cloak room. It was about time she put a period on this celebration. He waited a moment before following discreetly. Seemingly unwilling to admit she was female all the way down to her toes, she was headed out into the darkness alone. The streets near the campus were not well lit. Four well-dressed men trailed behind her. One might call them dapper. They were drunk, swaggering yet strangely quiet. At one time each had been a dance partner. She fought with all four. Rejected each man.

Beneath his breath Deke cursed into the bleakness of the night. She couldn't have made this easy for him.

This was what her father cautioned him about, the threatening men she'd been warned against. The same ones she dismissed as harmless. Didn't she understand a harmless man didn't exist? He slipped the badge he wore into the pocket of his jacket. If it came to a fight, he didn't want these men to know he was a sheriff. His jurisdiction didn't carry sway in Boston. He would do what was necessary to protect the woman who seemed to be able to flirt and carry on leaving her male victims panting with their tongues hanging out and in need of what she so eloquently offered. If she said no, the word should be heeded even if she seduced and charmed, even if she was a sassy little flirt.

Tonight, she made several conquests. Apparently, these men meant to taste what she suggested with her winsome smile coupled with the sensual shimmer in her vibrant blue eyes. Jamie didn't understand what his daughter with her innate allure was capable of provoking in the weak male species. Just a smile's promise could get a man hard. She shouldn't be out alone in the night, in the dark without protection. He assumed he was her protection tonight as well as a host of long cold nights to come. Street lights cast a subtle glow, elongating shadows. Anyone who wished to steal away in the gloomy night could do so without detection.

The men following her didn't seem to be hiding. She must know they shadowed her. Her pace increased even while he mused once more about the inherent dangers for a female alone in the blackness. A prudent woman would have hailed a carriage. According to her doting father, Annie defied logic. She was an independent woman. He supposed any female who wished to be a doctor in an out-of-way small town high in the Rocky Mountains would have to defy more than rational thought. She would have to possess a good sense of autonomy. The west was dangerous territory. Women were few. Men obsessed over beautiful women. They either wanted them as a wife or a mistress. In either case men wanted a woman in his bed to ease his needs.

When she turned off the well-lit street, he knew the men would act. He picked up his pace, his heart pounding with energy, fighting energy. His strides lengthened. His body toned and hardened in anticipation of the looming confrontation. The shrill scream didn't surprise him. The silence afterward did.

What he saw ripped through him, blinding rage followed. She was pushed against the cold brick of the building. One man's hand covered her mouth his other ripped the cloth of her bodice and chemise. Even with the pale moonlight, he saw the white of her flesh, the pink tips that could push any man to lust. Her flailing body was caught by the faint light from the lantern on the far corner. She pounded on the man's back, screaming.

"No!"

"Ay-ee...ay-ee, ay...ay...yii..." The war cry honed from his time living with the Cheyenne never failed to send chills of fear into the opponent.

He wasn't Cheyenne. Nevertheless, he had lived with them, learned their ways. The woman he called mother was fullblood Cheyenne. He was as full blood Irish as a man could get.

The first man he encountered he leapt high, kicking him in the chin, toppling him backward. The second he tackled sending him to the ground with the force of the blow. The third man ran. The fourth, his hand thrust forward, never saw the blow that sent his head backward, blood flowing from his nose.

Deke straddled the man, his fist tucked into the cloth of his shirt. He lifted him inches off the ground. "You sorry son of a bitch." With force, he sent the man back to the ground. His head cracked when it hit solid stone. "She said no!"

He stood, dusting his hands. She'd left. All he could see now was her back, her skirt lifted as she ran. "Well, hell." He supposed given the same situation if he was female, he would have done the same. In a few seconds, he caught up with her. He walked beside her, adjusting the length of his strides to hers.

"What do you want?" She didn't look at him nor did she break stride, her rough breathing all that gave indication of the stress. One hand held her skirt high so as not to trip, the other gripped her torn bodice tight.

"Not what you think."

He couldn't help grinning. Flushed to such a high color, she was adorable. They pulled up in front of her door.

"Go away." Dropping her tight fist from her skirt to pick up her reticule, fumbling with one hand, she pulled out a key. With the door unlocked, she tried to slip through the opening without him.

"'Fraid I can't let you do that."

His hand stopped the door from shutting in his face. His foot straddled the door jam.

"Or won't?"

Striding up the steps, she ignored him. Her back rigid as a boulder, she reached the door to her apartment. Once again, he couldn't allow her to enter without him. Sometime he would have to explain his purpose.

She would object. Jamie warned him convincing her she needed him would never be easy. He would have to stick to her, not let her use her cunning to get away from him. He did have his honor. Duty first. She was his duty, a repayment of debt he owed Jamie.

She inhaled a deep breath, turning on him, her slim fingers still clutching the torn fabric. "What do you want?"

He massaged his chin for a moment, a slow grin forming on his lips, "A glass of whiskey would be nice." He grinned at the slow mercuric spread of fire he watched growing along her neck to reach her cheeks. Her eyes shimmered spitting liquid heat. Obviously, she didn't know how to handle this situation. He pushed his hat upward, lifting an eyebrow, studying her. "Too much to ask?"

"Go to hell!"

Ignored now, she set about arranging papers that cluttered her desk, still attempting to keep her grip on her bodice tight. Every now and then he caught a glimpse of rounded white flesh. A valise and a trunk were packed sitting next to the door. She was ready for the morning train. Even while she tried to put up a brave front, her shoulders shook. Beneath sooty, long lashes she eyed him, sized him up from the tips of his riding boots to the top of his hat. Deke didn't think she came up with any answers.

"You should have hailed a cab." He told her his voice taking on a soft edge. "If I hadn't been there… A safe ride home would have been prudent." He looked at his bruised knuckles. "If you'd done so, I could have avoided the skirmish. Don't like to fight though I'm damn good at it." He'd been wishing for more than a skirmish since he first set eyes upon her a week ago. Until now, she didn't know he existed.

"I didn't ask for help."

The prickly little female was bristling with outrage. She waltzed into the bedroom. A few seconds later she emerged with a shawl draped around her shoulders and tied in the front. He'd wondered when she would take care of that small inconvenience that kept her one handed.

"You needed it or…they weren't forcing you?"

Shaking her head, pointing a long slender finger at him. "Who are you?" She now stood in the farthest away corner of the small living room.

"You should have asked that a long time ago, Annie Lundin."

Her gasp of surprise didn't mean anything. He knew her father never told her about the protection he hired to take her to Denver City. Understood she was far out of her realm of expertise when it came to living in a small western town filled with miners and gamblers, dotted with a couple of whores. So high in the mountains sometimes a man had to struggle for air. The men were rough, the women easy. She didn't fit the bill. He understood protecting this woman would be a formidable task. She was a brilliant, beautiful menace.

"I'm asking now."

Deke found the whiskey bottle he knew she purchased for Jamie. The bottle wasn't packed. He poured two fingers before downing half. "Sherriff Deke Sullivan."

He finished the whiskey, keeping his gaze on her.

"You could have said so in the beginning. Will you leave now?"

"Nope to the leaving. Those men could return. Do they know where you live?"

"I'm not your concern. I've got a train to catch in the morning."

He stepped toward her, "So?"

"I've got to sleep."

"As do I." He placed his hat on the table by the door, took inventory of the apartment. The bed was too small for both of them. He chuckled thoughtfully. She didn't seem in the mood to share the mattress though he would never form the words to object if she changed her mind. "Suppose the sofa will have to do."

"Never!"

Her tiny hands fisted on her hips. She stood her ground.

"Sweetheart, I'm staying here to make certain you and I reach the train in one piece in the morning. I don't intend to sleep on the floor outside your door."

With her mouth clenched tight, she raced to him, pushed on his chest. Taken by surprise, he fell backward, bringing her with him. They landed together on the rug with a solid *oof*. He grunted with the impact. When she tried to push from him, her blue eyes blazed female fury.

"Let me go!"

With those tight little fists, she pounded on him; his chest, his shoulders. Her hair fell around her shoulders, the soft strands sliding against his face and along his hands.

Swearing softly beneath his breath, he grabbed the pummeling hands then rolled. He lay atop her, her hands held above her head. "You should stop when you're in over your head."

The shawl fell away. Her partially covered breasts pushed against his chest. The small puffs of air she inhaled to fill her lungs had to hurt. "Will you promise to keep your hands to yourself?"

This was not something he anticipated. What he hadn't expected was the fabric of her torn bodice opening, her breasts pushing against his chest, exposed. The tight pink buds invited him to taste.

Annie clenched her teeth then nodded. So many more silken strands of her coif came undone to taunt him further, sliding with smooth heat across him, catching in the stubble on his face.

"You're hurting me."

"Sweetheart, you hurt me."

"*Oaf!*"

Her breasts pushed against his chest.

"As soon as you promise, we can begin again. I'll tell you everything you need to know about me as well as my purpose here. I will also tell you why."

The press of her body next to his sent an inferno seething inside flying straight to his groin, his response so swift and hard the sensation caught him by surprise. He should remove himself from her person.

She nodded, her dark lashes briefly closing over her eyes fanning across her cheekbones.

"I need the words. Who the heck could guess what you are nodding at? Say the words, my darling."

"I promise," she spit the words out too quickly.

His lips quirked in a half-smile. He didn't trust the promise. Hell, he wasn't born yesterday. He wasn't a half-wit who would fall for her female charms. Who did she think he was? An untried boy? He stood, holding out a hand to help her to her feet.

She ignored the offer. "What are you doing here?"

"Protecting you," he said his voice bland. "From what I just witnessed you need my protection."

Dusting off her skirt, Annie stomped to the whiskey and poured herself a stiff drink. After she downed a goodly portion, she closed her eyes, grimacing, straining as the heat slipped down her throat. Her shoulders unyielding, she pointed an accusing finger in his direction, "I don't need protecting. Go find another woman to guard."

His laughter barked from his throat. "Someone important to you believes you do. At least he believes enough to have hired me. You'll get used to me. I'm easy to get along with."

"Liar!"

He tugged her into his arms intending to make his position to her crystal clear, clear as the devil inside him. Her hands on his chest, she stared at him with the bluest damn eyes he'd ever seen. Unable to stop himself, he slowly lowered his mouth to meet hers. Softly, he brushed his lips across hers, teasing, touching, caressing the fulness he encountered. Heat, enchantment, liquid fire erupted. He expected a slap to his face. Instead, her fingers rose to his shoulders then his neck her nails biting then scraping. He pushed her lips apart as he explored inside the dark sultry heat of her mouth. His hands cupped her buttocks, pulling her closer, so close she was certain to feel the heat of his heavy arousal.

Realizing he was about to take this farther than he should, he let his tongue slip from the warmth of her mouth. When he was inches away, could smell the scent of aroused woman, he grinned then winked. "I make my point."

This time the slap startled Deke. Dazed by the sensations she elicited, his mind was in a fog. He touched his hand to his throbbing cheek.

"Bastard!"

"You didn't say no."

He ignored his blinding need to show her how foolish her action was. He was angry with his stupidity. "We will leave at dawn. Best you get sleep." Through clenched teeth he grated out his comments.

Annie finished her drink, her body quivering with pent up emotions. He sat down to take his boots off then followed with his shirt leaving his clothing on the floor. His pants unfastened he rose, watching, studying her. She liked the kiss. He scratched his belly.

"What are you doing?" She stood in front of him so close he could reach out, pull her once more into his arms. If he did so, they would end up in the bed together. "Get out!"

"Going to sleep as per your suggestion."

He winked at her knowing that would infuriate her further.

"Not in my home you're not." She picked up his clothing and boots, tossing them toward him. One boot hit him square in his chest.

He grunted. "I am staying in your home. Over the next several weeks, we are going to be close, damn close. Now, my suggestion is that you retreat to the bedroom. If you don't, I'll trade sleeping arrangements with you or we could share."

Head in her hands, she sat on an old ragged chair near the fireplace. He thought he saw her shoulders shaking. Finally, she looked at him. Her eyes shimmered with the tears she refused to shed earlier. Despite her efforts, when she looked at him again, she questioned. "Who hired you?"

Damn, he hated women's tears. Time for teasing her ended minutes ago. He should have never caried this so far. In his defense, she was so damn adorable when she was angry, he had a devil of a time thinking straight. "Your father."

When she flew at him again, he was ready for her. "How dare he!"

The answer to him was obvious. She was a menace to all males everywhere with those soft white breasts, the beguiling curves of her wasp thin waist and that delectable little butt, not to mention her captivating blue eyes he was drowning in every time he looked at her. He wanted to taste and squeeze every deliciously mouthwatering part of her. "You're in need of protection from every male from here to Kansas Territory," he said unemotionally.

Her hands held once more in his, "You promised you'd keep these." He placed tender kisses on her knuckles, "to yourself."

"Oh!"

"You did." He drew in a long deep breath needing the raw restraint the air might give him. He needed to hold his temper in check.

"Sweetheart, don't like this job. You're trouble from the get go. Whenever possible, I stay away from trouble. Told your father no, until I couldn't, until he backed me into a corner I couldn't get out of."

"Are you trying to tell me it's my fault those men attacked me?"

From the beginning she sounded indignant. She had every right to be. She looked as mad as a hornet gettin' ready to sting.

"Well, honey, you flirt outrageously. Every male at the celebration panted after you. They looked at your breasts popin' out of that dress of yours..." He lifted his shoulders in a careless shrug. "What did you expect?"

He did regret the words. The attack was not her fault. He should tell her that. For some reason he didn't understand, he couldn't keep the taunting words behind his lips.

Her fists were on her hips again, her eyes flashing with heated color, ice blue fire. She pulled in a breath of air, her breasts rising as if to put a period on the point he was making. "How dare you blame something so ludicrous on a woman when a man thinks with his cock and not his head!"

She stared pointedly at his groin which was rising to the occasion.

He regarded her tiny weapons with care as well as her words. She was spittin' mad. Her audacity intrigued him. For her size she was a whirlwind of hot air. Her attacks always came out of the blue. About this she was right on all counts. He grinned at her. "Think with my cock, do I? Why, sweetheart, where did you hear such things? From that medical school of yours where you took top honors? Thought you were a lady."

"From every male on this earth!" she retorted with venom while her eyes blazed ferociously.

She looked as if she meant to fly at him again, fists blazing.

"Don't even think to hit me. I won't tolerate more than one time. You've already passed once. That slap packed a wallop. Knocked my head back a mite."

"You're not worth the effort," she gritted the words out through clenched teeth as she stomped to the bedroom again. She came out with a derringer pointed at his chest. "For the last time, get out!"

"Do you have an extra pillow or blanket for me?" After he sat

11

down, he kicked his feet onto the sofa. "Wasn't looking forward to the hard pallet on the wood floor. This here sofa's mighty comfortable for a sofa."

Her hand shook, the gun still pointed his direction. "You aren't listening. I told you I want you out of my home."

He let out the air he'd been holding since he saw the gun. She wasn't going to use the weapon. He'd stake his life on the fact. "Use the damn thing or put it away. We both need sleep. Dawn will be here early. I for one am tired of arguing. Would rather bed you than exchange more words."

"Bastard! Devil! I should…"

"Shooting me won't solve your problems. You still have to get to Denver City in one piece. Without my expertise you won't make it more 'un five miles out of Fort Laramie. As soon as you're so high in the mountains the very air you breathe doesn't reach your lungs, you'll have second thoughts."

The girl was going to be the death of him, not death by derringer, death by headache or…death by arousal. This journey would take forever if he had to listen to her rant and rave all day as well as all night. Kissing her mouth closed was one solution that he'd take more interest in than her war with words.

"Don't come in my bedroom."

She didn't walk to the bedroom but to the whiskey. Not reaching for a glass, she tipped the bottle to her lips. She drank long. Coughed. Wiped her mouth with the back of her hand, her eyes firing hotter and bluer.

He lifted his shoulders, staring at her eyes. "Bedding a viper is never pleasant. Might be able to tame the viper to my way of thinkin'."

"You've bedded a viper?" she asked sweetly, her eyes brimming with laughter now.

The about face surprised him. Caught him off guard. Her smile jammed him in the gut before his stomach twisted and his rod swelled more than he thought possible. "No."

Though he wanted to. During their conversation and struggles, her torn bodice gaped farther open. When he kissed her, it was all he could do not to test the softness of those beautiful white globes of hers.

"How old are you?" The question popped out. Even he understood never to ask a woman her age or how much she weighed not that most knew anyway.

Annie Lundin stared at him as if he lost his mind. She swiped her hands along her dress pulling the fabric lower. As if she suddenly understood what he stared at, she pulled the fabric to cover her, found the shawl that dropped to the floor earlier. He'd seen more than she intended. She was perfection. A man, this man could get lost in all those wonderful curves of hers, die and go to heaven in her flawlessness if invited.

"You're going to stay here?" She pointed a shaking finger at the sofa. "Don't you have a place of your own?"

"Damn straight. Right on that sofa unless a certain viper gives an invitation I can't refuse."

"Why?"

"Believe we've hashed over that…numerous reasons."

She disappeared again. He caught the pillow and blanket in the face. He grinned.

~ * ~

Sheets and blankets were wrapped around her sprawled legs. Sunlight poured through lace curtains leaving patterns on the floor. Her eyes burned from lack of sleep. Her head pounded in aggravation at the infuriating man in her living room. She drank too much whiskey.

A viper, am I?

I will show him viper!

Throughout the night she pounded her pillow, pushed off covers before reaching for them again when the cool morning air chilled her arms. She urged straggling damp hair from her sweaty face. The glass of water she always kept by her bed was empty. The audacity of that man. Her protector? Never. How dare her father hire a man to guard her. She was an adult. She didn't need any man to shadow her.

He did come in handy last night.

"Good you're up. I wasn't relishing having to shake you awake."

His darkly raspy voice caught her attention sending a sensual thrill down her spine. She turned to look at him. All she saw was his back. He left as quickly as he showed himself.

All through the night she hoped he was a figment of her imagination. "Go away."

Her words lacked conviction. It seemed he wouldn't go anywhere until he was good and ready, until they reached Denver City. While she understood he didn't want her in his town, he meant to fulfill the contract he signed with her father. With haste on her mind, she scrambled from the bed, hoping to put some clothes on before he barged into the room again. She slept wearing an old thin chemise that was very close to wearing nothing at all.

Dressed, feeling the protection of fabric against her body, she brushed her hair into a severe bun. She was going to disavow him from the notion she was a flirt. She wasn't. Having a good time, laughing, talking to men, was not flirting. He was from the west, a back woodsman. What did he know about balls? He shot at men to keep the peace. He was a gunslinger. How dare he assume to tell her how she acted?

When she stepped from the bedroom, he handed her a cup of coffee. "Drink up. Time's a wastin'."

Her trunk along with her valise no longer sat by the door. Her medical bag was gone. The room looked so empty. She had spent two years here, studying. At one time she thought herself in love. Two weeks ago, the man she thought would be hers announced his engagement to a wealthy Bostonian lady. The man vowed undying love the night before. Her heart ripped apart. He'd been at the celebration, danced with her. Told her he still wanted her. He'd been one of the men who accosted her. Peter Bentley was his name. Along with his friends he attacked her the same night he vowed undying love. She told him she never wanted to see him again.

Flirt, she would if she wanted. However, she'd never fall again for a man's vows of love. She was never going to fall in love, period. When she looked at Deke, she saw pure male power, fascination, strength, intrigue. Control was evident in the way he stood, by the look in his dark eyes. His broad chest, his height, the way his lips curved sensuously all spoke of male dominance. She would never allow a man to dominate her. She would never take orders from this man.

"You have time to sit, drink your coffee, have a doughnut. You do need to eat something. Gotta keep up your strength."

He sounded as if he spoke to a little girl. She wasn't. Couldn't he see that? For some reason she couldn't figure, she wanted him to see her as a woman.

Giving in to the realization that all because of her father he controlled her now, her life. She knew she couldn't get rid of him by wishing him away. She touched her lips remembering the sweetness of his kiss, the sensuously sweet way his tongue explored her, the way she melted into him became liquid heat in his arms. In hindsight, she should have slapped him harder. Instead, she clung to his broad shoulders, ran her fingers through his dark hair. The strands were silk to her fingers.

"Thank you."

The coffee was delicious, the doughnut sweet and sticky. Butterflies twitted around in her stomach sending strange tendrils of heat to parts of her she'd never actually thought of before. He leaned against the doorframe watching her. His broad arms were crossed negligently in front of him while his eyes studied her, drifting along the length of her form. She squirmed against his boldness.

Half-eaten she set the delicacy back into the sack. "I'll finish this later." She sipped the last of her coffee.

One dark eyebrow arched toward the ceiling. He pushed away from the wall. "Not hungry?"

"Can't eat a bite while you stare at me."

She sounded petulant. She didn't want to give him a reason for amusement. Apparently, she did.

Grinning, he offered an arm. She ignored him again, smiling softly when she heard the swear word follow her out the door. He picked up the sack. The sound of his boots tramped on the hard wood. At the bottom of the stairs, he caught up to her then opened the door for her. A hack waited for them. When she tried to ignore his assistance, her foot caught in her skirt. For a moment, she thought she would end up nose first on the ground. So much for her defiance, too bad she never learned from her mistakes. He caught her up before she fell, setting her on her feet.

Without mentioning her most recent fiasco, he led the way to the train cars they would share during the trip west. She rode in these cars with her family when they traveled. This was her first trip alone.

She wasn't alone.

"My bedroom is the first car. Yours the last." His husky voice behind her snapped her out of her reverie. She turned, her skirts whirling around her ankles. "We will share this living space. Did you know your father made these arrangements for you? You would have ridden in the main cars if not for his consideration."

"My father always uses these cars. This luxury is nothing new."

Now she sounded peevish. She didn't want him to realize the startling affect his presence had on her, on her nerves.

"That's what I thought. You're not going to like Denver City. The town is rough around the edges. There is no luxury anywhere in Denver City," He paused watching her closely. "Hell, the western town is rough everywhere. You should change your mind. Find a place to be a doctor here in Boston."

"I'm a doctor, Mr. Sullivan. I go where I'm needed."

"Deke."

"I'm a doctor. I'll set up practice in your rough western town. All will be fine. You'll see." Stunned by his rudeness, she scrambled for more words. He didn't have the right to assume she couldn't make it on her own. "You don't know me."

"That's true. However, in the last few hours you've shown me quite a bit about who you are."

"What did you learn?"

She couldn't help her curiosity even though she understood she shouldn't ask. Would most likely regret the question. Everything he would say would come out negative.

"I'm going to do my damndest to convince you to turn your delectable little backside around and go home. You're not a woman who is cut out for hard living. The men won't want to call you doctor. They won't drop their drawers for you to examine them. You will have no clients."

She bristled, outraged at his words. "You can't drive me away with words and threats. What about you? Would you come to me if...?"

"Well, now, oughta tell you no, however," he paused raking her slowly with his heated gaze, "Depends on your bedside manner. I could get used to your sweet hands examining me."

"Ass..." she breathed softly. Knew he heard the word.

"I'm the sheriff of Denver City." He pushed his hat back a trifle, his dark blue eyes focused on her face now. "The way I see this situation once you're in town, I'll be defending you day in and day out. Men want one thing from a pretty little woman such as yourself. It's not the kinda doctorin' you've gone to school to learn."

"Go to Hell!"

With just a few words and outrageous comments he managed to make her bristle with fury. He tapped into something she didn't understand. His dark blue eyes turned to black when he spoke of her, of her future in Denver City. He had nerve, damn him. She was terribly afraid he was speaking the truth. She was out of choices.

"Right along with you." He sat down in a chair by the window. The train was on the move. "Nice place. I'm going to enjoy this trip much more than the one I took to Boston. Though the train doesn't go far enough. Rode in the regular car with all the regular folks. Before that the stage. You're goin' to like that stage real well. After we hit Fort Laramie will be ridin' horses the rest of the way and trailin' a couple pack mule with supplies."

His legs were stretched, long and lean in front of him. The jeans he wore molded around the solid muscle of his thighs. His shirt was unfastened at the top. She caught sight of crisp dark red hair poking from the opening. He was an unyielding wall of muscle and sinew.

"Like what you see?"

His lazy drawl startled her out of her musings.

Flushed, she turned away from him. Back stiff, she marched through the cars to the last one, her sleeping chamber. A few moments of peace and quiet would be nice. He rattled all of her, every nerve stretched thin, every thought convoluted. When she entered, she saw her trunk as well as the valise. Her medical bag sat on top of the trunk. While she

17

slept, he cared for her belongings.

His hands rested on her shoulders.

"Oh!" she gasped out startled by his presence, quickly moving away from the heat of his body, from the frightening energy that possessed him. Her hand atop her chest, "You could let a person know you were there."

"I called your name twice." His voice deep and husky seemed to fill the tiny space. "You must not have heard me."

"What are you doing in here? This is my room."

She didn't want to be so close to this man who stripped her to nothingness then sent flames of fire heating her. Something about the confidence he exuded transfixed her. She'd never know a man such as this one. Even the man she thought she loved never touched her senses as Deke did. She did need protection. Guarding her heart against this man would take all she possessed.

"Checking on you."

"Stay out of this room!"

She wanted to be alone with her thoughts free of his overwhelming presence.

He tipped his hat, "As you wish." He grinned.

The man didn't move. She caught her lip beneath her teeth. "Go!"

She pushed on his chest. The mistake was obvious the moment her hands touched him. She felt the sensual heat, the pull she couldn't resist.

His large hands surrounded her waist. "When I'm ready." He paused as he seemed to think, "…or when you tell me no."

She leaned back, staring into his fathomless dark eyes. He was a man to do things his way not hers. Tell him, no? "Mr. Sullivan…"

"I've kissed you, sweetheart. Call me Deke. A man can only take so much formality with a woman he's going to become intimate with."

His face was inches away from hers. She swallowed hard, wishing for another kiss, not wanting him to touch her again. He tapped a finger on her nose. After that she watched his broad back as he sauntered through the door. She heard his chuckle from the other room.

Deep inside she seethed, her body becoming an inferno of molten liquid fire. He was the most audacious man she ever met. She collapsed into a chair, trying to control her breathing as she stared at the empty space where he stood a few minutes ago. He didn't want her in Denver City. He hated her. She tried to tell herself she despised him. She didn't. He intrigued and fascinated every sinew and bone in her body. His dark, dangerous looks, the way he didn't let his emotions show sent chills of fire down her spine. She wrapped her arms around her body as if that small gesture would smother the flames ignited by his presence. The single kiss touched a part of her she never knew existed. Her finger flew to her lips. Damn the arrogant man. She wasn't going to allow him to treat her so callously.

In haste, she decided that she would tell him his duties. He needed to understand a few rules about this journey. She wasn't going to let him walk all over her. She fixed her hair, smoothed her skirts until she felt confidence grow. When she entered the living area, he wasn't there. He left.

Damn the man.

She found the sack that held her doughnut. She ate. The food churned inside her stomach somersaulting rolling around as if it was doing his bidding. She walked from one end of the small room to the other. Back again. The train was moving faster, picking up speed. When she looked out the window, she watched the city fly by in front of her eyes as the hours dragged. Before, when she travelled with her family, they spent time in the other cars talking and laughing with the travelers. Right now, she didn't want to see anyone.

Especially not Deke Sullivan.

Especially Deke. There were rules he had to learn. She opened the door. Shut the door. She was a mass of confusion, a maelstrom of frustration.

The sun was high in the sky before he reappeared. He stepped through the door without speaking. She spent all the morning as well as most of the afternoon wondering just where he was…gambling or drinking. He might have found a woman to while away the time with. The pillow she held in front of her became a launched missile. She wanted to hurt him. To show him he couldn't treat her like so much unwanted baggage. She wasn't going to let him walk out on her.

Deke caught the projectile before it hit him. Once more, he quirked an elegantly shaped dark brow upward, "What did I do?" he asked sounding perplexed as well as a bit angry. "I left you alone as you requested. Did you want me to stay? I would have obliged you if I understood what you expected of me."

"You ass!" she bit out clearly showing him her feelings.

She was jealous and she hated the thought. The idea of a woman in his arms...

He shrugged from his jacket, tossed his hat onto the coat stand. "If I'm accused of something untoward, I'd like to know what it is."

"You've been gone." When the accusatory words left her mouth, she thought to bite her tongue. If he discovered she missed his company, he'd become insufferable. She'd wanted to be alone. He obliged her.

"True." He loosened the buttons on his shirt. "Did you miss me?"

"You're not going to undress again."

She closed her eyes. He was insufferable.

He lifted his broad masculine shoulders all the while staring at her. "Thought I would get more comfortable. You have an objection to comfort? It's a long trip. We are going to be in close quarters for a while. After we leave this train, we'll ride a stagecoach. Then…well…then we will be alone together on the trail from Fort Laramie to Denver City. Just me and you, together, alone. You're going to have to get used to me."

God in heaven what would he have to take off to get more comfortable? She didn't want to guess. Unable to help herself, she peeked at him from beneath lowered lashes. He stretched out on a chair, his shirt open to his narrow waist muscles rippling on his flat belly. Crips hair descended lower. He'd unfastened his pants. She gulped air. She remembered all the rules in her head. Now because of his insolence she added another.

"You are not to remove your clothing in front of me," she blurted, her voice shaking with pent up emotion.

Heat rushed to her face. The implication of what she said startled her.

His eyes darkened to fathomless pits. He barked a hoot of laughter as he leaned toward her his forearms resting against his massive thighs. "Anything else?"

She ran her tongue along her bottom lip. Oh God, she couldn't do this. His eyes narrowed as if she was quite insane. "Yes. I have a list of rules."

"Why am I not surprised?" His husky sigh of displeasure or fatigue didn't go unnoticed. "Go on..."

He crossed his legs at the ankles while his back now rested on the chair. His hands were folded on top of his hard stomach.

"Coming into my private room is expressly forbidden." She started to ramble more rules.

He halted her with an upraised hand. His lips quirked in seeming amusement, "I see. Nonetheless, I'm being paid to protect you. If there is danger, I will go wherever I need to be. If it's in your private space, so be it."

It seemed to her, he didn't see how his clothing or lack thereof was the problem. He didn't understand how he created unease within her. He didn't understand how his simple touch could set forth a maelstrom of emotions inside she'd never encountered. If he chose, he would do whatever he pleased. She couldn't stop the sudden outburst. Her fists clenched while her temper soared, she yelled at him, "You don't! You don't see anything!" She never yelled at people. What was he doing to her even demeanor?

"Of course, I understand. You want me so much that in order for you to keep your innocence intact, you have to demand certain things of me. You don't want me to invade your sacred space nor do you want to see me with little to no clothing. You haven't mentioned anything about sharing a bed."

"I don't want you!"

His grin sent a wave of newfound butterflies rippling in her stomach then lower to between her thighs. She caught her breath in the back of her throat. Her protest fell on deaf ears.

"Should we test that theory?" he queried softly looking as if he was going to devour her whole. "I think...if I kissed you again..."

"N-no..." She was too quick to object, her hands outstretched as if that simple gesture could hold him off. "My feelings are not an experiment or a theory to test. I don't ever want you to kiss me."

"I think testing your rules would make the trip more interesting. You see, I'm bored. Would love to make the days and nights fly by with lightning speed. With you in my bed, we could do just that. We would only have to stop to eat. You know, come up out of the sheets for air along with food."

"Why would I want to be in your bed?"

She found herself backing away. She wanted to turn, to run. There was nowhere to run.

"You tell me, sweetheart. You've men drooling and panting over you since we first met. You can be damn certain I won't drool. Nor will I pant. I saw them at the dance. Watched one man push you against a wall, his hand exploring your—"

"I screamed."

"You did. I distinctly remember the weak yell that brought me to your defense. Was the sound made from fright or sexual excitement? Did you want the man's hand on your breast, touching and weighing your soft feminine jewels? Did you want to be rescued? Or not?"

Her eyes crossed. She frowned at him, unable to put a coherent sentence together. "I don't want any man's hand there...on my..." She clenched her teeth, reasoning with this man impossible. She wasn't going to talk about her breasts with a man she didn't know.

"Should that be another rule I intend to break? Should I see if you want my hand caressing you intimately, exploring parts of you that will make you hungry as well as wild with desire? Perhaps between your lily-white thighs?" he taunted her. "There are so many places I could fondle you that would make you scream with pleasure."

Another pillow flew his way. She tried to leave. He caught her in her bedroom. He held her shoulders, his dark eyes blazing.

With a wobbling voice, she continued. "You're not going to break my rules. You're not going to test theories. You're not going to explore any part of me."

"Hmm...we'll see." His lips touched lightly upon hers. "Shall we experiment with what you want as well as what you might not want?"

His mouth was warm and soft. She held herself stiff, unwilling to allow him the sweetest of intimacies he talked about. Giving into this wicked ploy of his was not a choice. His hands drifted downward. His lips swept across her neck then found more dark secret places to explore, along her collarbone, higher to a sensitive spot behind her ear. A soft sigh rippled from her lips as she melted. She closed her eyes wishing he didn't have such a potent effect on her.

She didn't want him.

She didn't want to want him.

His kisses stopped. Her lashes flew open. Her lips parted, moist from the fervent play of his mouth upon hers. She looked into the depth of his dark penetrating eyes. "I could have you right now, sweetheart. If I wanted you, I could have you in my bed anytime. You melt for me."

He caught her arm as she attempted to slap his face again. She was furious with him. He goaded her. She fell into the game. "You cannot, not now not anytime. I will always tell you no!"

She hated him. She wanted him.

"Another theory to experiment with. Time will tell the true tale. I'm not going to rush you. You are a novice in the ways of love. While you can flirt with the best you cannot tell a man no when he wishes to make love to you. Something you need learn."

"If you're trying to dissuade me from my plans your ploy is not working."

She pushed against his chest. She wanted him to kiss her again, needed to feel the warmth of his mouth on hers.

He tightened his hold upon her. Once again, as if he understood her thoughts, his lips descended to meet hers, the taste evocative. When he pushed inside, she met him, dueled and explored wildly, gave as good as she received. She leaned into him. Heat exploded within her. A cool breeze touched upon her shoulders. He'd removed her clothing, moved the fabric down her arms. His lips explored everywhere across her shoulders, lower until she thought her knees would collapse beneath her. Still, he held her, his hands tightening around her buttocks. He squeezed. Stroked. Explored. She moaned. Purred. Sighed. The sensation was delicious. Her breath caught in her throat when his mouth closed over a nipple. She gasped at the sweetly painful pleasure. He laved then nipped softly, raked his teeth along tender flesh. She pushed against him. Her body constricted with need. She didn't understand what was happening to her.

"D-Deke..."

"What?" he asked without stopping as he turned the same heated attention to her other nipple.

Her fingers wound into his hair. She arched closer to him, giving him more access. Oh, dear God, she knew this was wrong. Understood she should tell him, no. If she didn't, he would be more arrogant than before. She didn't want him to stop. He was right. She couldn't tell him to stop. Didn't want to in any case. Wanted to learn what came after the kiss.

Suddenly, she felt the backs of his fingers brush against her. He closed her gown then set her aside. "End of experiment." His voice was raspy, harsh. "I was right. You were wrong. Pretty damn simple."

She was shaking violently, her entire body trembling with anger along with the embarrassment and the knowledge that he so easily bested her. Now he tossed her aside as if she meant nothing to him. She would have to be stronger. In the end, gaining more courage. "I've more rules!"

"Thought so." He stepped away from her, sat on her bed, stretching his legs in front of him. He patted the spot beside him. "Come relax while you spout the list I intend to ignore. Don't abide by rules set down by a woman. They're usually foolish."

His grin infuriated her. Under the current circumstances, she would have to be an absolute idiot to sit next to him. Damn his never-ending gall. "No."

"Then...there will be no more rules, Annie. From now on you'll abide my terms. Your rules, when you tell me, we can discuss the pros and cons. My terms are nonnegotiable."

Her hands clasped in front of her. "No."

She needed to make certain he understood who his employer was.

"Come sit. We can iron out all our differences in a matter of seconds."

"I'm firing you."

His grin broadened. His fine white teeth flashed in the dwindling light of the waning afternoon. "Your father told me you'd eventually say that. Won't work. You don't pay my fee. Your father does."

She wasn't going to stand in front of him and let him abuse her. Whirling, she swept out the door heading to a new destination. On the train she wouldn't go far. In this instance, she didn't get past his bedroom before she found herself plucked off the floor. She sifted in a mouthful of air then on a startled gasp the miniscule amount of oxygen she held there rushed out. He tossed her onto his bed. He followed. Her hands now above her head, he straddled her. His hard muscled thighs pressed against hers. He stared down at her. She was breathing hard. She knew what he looked at.

"Listening?" His gleaming white teeth were inches from her face. "It's well past time you listened to me. Heard me as well."

Fire raged inside her while she willed herself to calm. She didn't understand how he could raise her temperature so quickly. "We don't know each other."

"I'm willing. How about you?"

"You can't tell me what to do or not to do. Well, you can say anything you want. It doesn't matter."

"Believe me, Miss Lundin, you will comply with my wishes."

"No!"

"You've an infuriating way of not heeding to me. You can't say no to something that hasn't been spoken."

"You're hurting me."

Immediately, he let go. She struck his chest with her tiny fists. He grunted. The blow was hard, harder than he probably expected. "Why, Miss Lundin, you can't seem to keep your little hands to yourself. I can think of other things your hands could be doing that would feel infinitely nicer."

"If you weren't sitting on top of me waylaying me, I would never touch you!" Her indignation caused his smile to widen.

"Oh, but I do think you will touch me. Explore my body with fingers as well as lips, teeth, tongue." Tenderly he ran his knuckles along her cheek. "You've the softest skin I've ever had the pleasure of feeling.

Are you this soft everywhere?"

Heat flamed to her cheeks. His chuckle at her discomfort didn't suit. "No!"

"I take that as a challenge. Shall I discover exactly where you are not soft?"

~ * ~

With a turbulence of thoughts raging in his aching head, Deke sat in one of the lavish compartments of the train. He sipped the glass of whiskey the sweet little doxy serving this area set down on the table. Raking in his coins, over a thousand dollars, he sat back to watch the other gamblers. At the moment he was done. He didn't want to go back to Annie. She touched him in ways he didn't want to consider. Making love to the woman wouldn't be wise or prudent. God, how she tempted him though. Everything about her enticed him.

Hell, that was one little lady who didn't belong in the west. The little lady who bedeviled him the first moment he saw her belonged in fancy drawing rooms on the arm of a gentleman. He was no gentleman. Despite the fact Annie didn't belong with him, he couldn't help thinking about her. In less than twenty-four hours she became ingrained in his blood. What would happen over the next weeks? They would travel from Fort Laramie to Denver City alone. She would be dependent on him for every need.

He wasn't going to spare her feelings. No way in hell would the menfolk of Denver City allow her to treat them as their physician. The ones who were wed wouldn't allow a woman to tend to their wives unless it was in childbirth. He didn't know how to convince her she didn't belong in a remote western town. She was so damned determined the fact boggled his mind.

Damn, on the other hand, he didn't want to let her out of his site. If he bedded her, she would be exorcised from his head. She couldn't possibly be a virgin. She was thirty years old. Her father told him her age before he finally agreed to the job. He never thought she would become a fire in his soul. Never thought she would be irresistible. No, she was just another woman, nothing more, nothing less. He could bed her and not be touched by the fire she possessed, the response that heated like quicksilver.

He sipped his drink, cashed in his chips then headed for his sleeping car. The days from Boston passed much the same. He argued with her. He left. He won and lost cash. The journey by stage wasn't much better. He found games at the posting houses where they stopped. She sat next to him in the vehicle, sleeping, sometimes her head on his chest. She bedeviled him. Now, one day from Fort Laramie, he was ahead of the game. He would leave it like that.

He followed her rules. She'd yet to be informed of his terms. They weren't necessary yet. Once they started on the trail from Fort Laramie to Denver City, she would learn soon enough she would have to do exactly as he told her. In the wilderness, his word was law. If he said jump, she damn well better do it. If he told her to be quiet, he didn't want to hear one sound. Though she wasn't inclined to chatter.

What the devil were all his terms? There were the ones on the trail. After that, there were the rules once they reached Denver City.

He supposed the most important one was to keep her safe. She couldn't wander outside the town. She was not to leave her office unless he accompanied her. Blast it all, even in the tiny town she wouldn't be completely safe walking along the boardwalk. When passing by the saloon, she should move to the other side of the road. If there was a shootout, she would have to duck for cover. The list went on from there. On the trail, her behavior would be even more important. If he gave her an order, she couldn't argue.

This was hell. He kept his hands off her. He'd done so by staying away from her, at least until they got on the stage. The miles on the trail would be murder to his unruly body. All that was needed for him to lust after her was to look into her sultry blue eyes. She was fire in his blood. He needed to find a means to send her back to the east coast before he did something they would both regret through eternity.

Mentally, he ticked off what needed to be purchased in Fort Laramie before they left. She would need warmer clothing. The coat she brought with her wasn't heavy enough for the winter snows that would come their way if she managed to stay in Denver City until October. If she remained until October, she would be there until spring. The high country was unforgiving.

He should have spent the hours regaling her about the dangers she would encounter instead of gambling and drinking. He'd thought to find a woman to ease himself with. Whenever he looked at another lady, his mind traveled to the little viper residing in the plush cars at the end of the train.

Tomorrow would be another hell.

The next few days would be trying for both of them. Barely two words had been shared between them the last days of the trip. He ushered her on the stage in the morning then rode shotgun whenever possible sitting by the driver. When he did see her at the posting houses, she looked away. They were at the last stop before Fort Laramie. He bought a room. After looking at his pocket watch, he decided it was late enough to retire for the night.

The animosity between them would help him keep his hands to himself. He would need to sleep on the floor. A lump formed in his throat. He understood the only way to keep the distance between them was to bait her. He was just too damn tried to do so.

She turned when he cleared his throat, her clear blue eyes shimmering with emotion. She looked as if she wished to speak.

"Shouldn't you be in bed?"

He sure as hell didn't want to see her, let alone talk to her right now while he was thinking of the trip to his town, while he thought of her alone with him in the vast forests of the Rocky Mountains.

"I'm not tired. Where have you been?" Her voice sounded accusatory. Her bottom lip trembled. "I haven't seen you."

"Didn't think you wanted me around. I can be obliging when necessary. We could test some of those theories of yours."

As soon as they came together sparks flew. He saw the fire rush to her eyes, the flames igniting with the few words spoken between them.

"I never said that."

"Well, honey, I'm not one to cotton to rules set down by a woman. Told you that on the first mention. Had to stay away from you or risk your temper flaring." She was the little viper he wanted to bed. What he wanted was to wrap his arms around her, pull her against him. If he did so, she would end up tumbled on his bed. "Best you go to bed."

~ * ~

They were in the stage together. There was no room for him to ride shotgun. "What's going to happen tomorrow? We are going to reach Fort Laramie by afternoon?" She was tired of spending days and nights alone in the uncomfortable stage even if it meant haggling with Deke Sullivan to have someone to speak with. She was now looking forward to conversation. The first week of the trip, she relished the solitude. This last week she was bored to tears. She was in the mood for a good fight.

"Early morning," he corrected her while he tugged on his boots.

"What will you do?"

Pulling teeth might be easier than getting questions answered. Was he going to leave her alone in a small room while he gambled and drank? Good lord, he'd done enough of that during the trip out here.

"Need to buy supplies for the journey into the wilderness."

His reply was curt as he didn't appear to offer more information.

She bristled. He stepped forward. His hand rested on her shoulder. She felt his heat, the inferno he always generated when he stood near when he touched. She choked back the reply hovering on the tip of her tongue.

"Supplies?"

All she needed was a few simple answers.

"Food, blankets. My horse at the fort. Do you ride?"

He looked at her as if he knew the answer.

Her terror of horses was well known. Her father elaborated, understanding at some point she would have to conquer her fears. She was shaking her head, "No."

She could learn quickly. She didn't want to learn.

"Didn't think so, Boston. You need a caretaker out here. A woman who can't ride don't fit. You oughta go home. As soon as we pull into Fort Laramie, I'll set you up on the first stage headed east. We can be

29

finished with the foolishness that brought you here."

"Don't call me Boston!"

He could be such an ass. His language always changed when he wanted to make her leave. She pushed his hand off her shoulder.

Before she could blink or step back, he was holding her. His hand touched her neck. He pulled her close too near for her comfort. "That's who you are to me. You're Boston, all city girl, all fancy parlors and pretty dresses. A fancy little teacup held with your pinky sticking out. You're too soft. You don't belong in the wilderness where life can go from bad to worse in a blink."

She tried to turn. He held her tight. His lips found hers, touched, caressed, generated the magic she remembered. Heat whipped through her as if lightning struck. With his large callused hands, he framed her face. She opened for him. He groaned, the sound husky with desire. Just as always, she began to melt. His tongue delved inside, explored touched deeply into secret places. A tiny sigh broke from her.

When he pulled away, he stared at her, his thumbs danced seductively along her neck. "You're dangerous, a flirt. Too sassy for your own good or mine. You leave a man with no wits. Go to bed, Boston." He gave her a tiny nudge in the direction of her room. "Tomorrow will come soon enough. Once we're on the trail you'll be beggin' me for more time to sleep."

Dazed she stared at him wishing he would hold her again, wishing he would leave, wishing she'd never met him. She wanted to curse him. She should run as fast as she could. She wanted him to touch her, caress her as he'd done that first day. If he would hold her, the fear she felt might melt away when he set her on fire. She didn't want him to know she was afraid. She wouldn't beg him for anything.

"Annie," his voice softened. Tenderly, he ran his knuckles along her cheek. "Go to bed. Tomorrow is going to be long as well as difficult for you. You need rest, not a night of playing in my bed. Even though that's what I want."

Heat raced to her face. She needed to refute his words. "You're crude, Mr. Sullivan. I would never play in your bed."

She wanted to find out what he meant. Needed to know what he could teach her about love. Love, no, she was never going to love a man. Though she did want to know what he meant by play in his bed.

Chapter Two

Deke pushed his hat back, gazing at the building clouds on the horizon. The white billows seemed to touch the sky. He looked over his shoulder. Annie sat her horse, her lips thinned, eyebrows drawn tight to from a small crease in the middle of her forehead. She was in pain, had been for at least an hour. Hell, they still had two hours to ride before making camp. He couldn't stop here. If he kept stopping before they rode the distance, it would take a month to reach the small town high in the Rocky Mountains. Tomorrow, she wouldn't be able to walk a step. He should stop now while she still had a chance of movement. The weather was changing. Stopping was out of the question. If she faltered and was unable to ride, that would be worse.

When she reassured him she could ride, he'd had his doubts. Her first no to the question was closer to the truth. After the first five minutes all his doubts were confirmed. Giving credit where it was due, not one complaining word came from her sweetly kissable lips. She didn't ask when they would stop for the night. With her mouth closed tight, her back straining, she silently followed. Stubborn, determined little woman.

Now, looking at the building thunderheads, he was worried. On the other hand, tonight stopping early might be prudent for two reasons. She was in no condition to go farther. He could build a lean-to that would keep most of the storm from drenching her, him too. He knew a place up the road about a mile that would serve his purpose. The cave was not much of a cave. A shallow indentation into a granite boulder, the spot would give protection on three sides. Strategically placed pine boughs would further help. A crystal-clear stream flowed nearby that would provide water.

Early summer in the Rockies produced lightning shows that lit up the sky for miles around. The wind along with the rain could bite into a man's soul. He heard the slow clamor of hooves. She rode beside him. She didn't say a word. She never complained or whined. He hadn't expected that from her.

"Can you ride another mile?" he asked without turning his gaze toward her.

He waited for the answer. This little lady would never admit defeat.

"If need be," she said, her voice soft, filled with exhaustion as well as holding a hint of pain. Shadows under her eyes spoke of her deep fatigue. "I could go another hour or two."

He leaned on the saddle horn while his horse continued at the slow pace he set. He wondered if she'd be able to dismount. "There's a spot up the trail. The place will make a good camp for the night. You can rest, ease your over-taxed muscles."

"The sooner and farther we ride, the sooner we'll be there. Isn't that true, Mr. Sullivan?"

She lowered her lashes as if she didn't want him to see the weariness written clearly in the lines around her eyes. Her sigh was long and deep.

He felt the bastard she called him. She was the one who wanted to be the doc in Denver City. He warned her against the job, about the hardships that would come her way. Told her no one would come to her. There would be no patients waiting in her sitting room She would discover the truth soon enough. All he thought to do was to make the decision easier for her. He supposed she was the type of person who needed to learn the hard way. He didn't envy her the learning. He didn't like imposing role of teacher.

With his knees he nudged Pye forward. She followed, just as she trailed along behind him when he purchased the supplies for the overland trip. He pushed his hat back studying the thunderheads hovering on the horizon. The sooner he got that shelter built and food in their bellies the better.

"You know, Boston," he began his voice soft hoping to make her feel better, maybe take one more stab at his argument for her to go home, "you could make this easier on yourself. When we get up in the morning,

I can take you back to the stage. I would never hold the change of direction over your head."

Her chin tilted higher gave him her answer. "No. Nothing you can say will make me change my mind. I'm a doctor, the new doc in Denver City. I intend to do my job."

"I'll take you back anytime you give me the word," he said again as he watched her stretch her back muscles.

When she did so, her pert little breasts pushed forward in a tantalizing way. He shook his head at himself, at his thoughts, at things he didn't want to feel about this woman. She would die in this country. He didn't want to be the cause of her death. She touched him in ways he didn't want to think about.

Hell, he should hog-tie her, put her on that returning stage then never look back. He should make love to her until they were both sated. She wanted him. Never once told him no.

"Why do you hate me?" She was staring at him, her shoulders rigid. When he wasn't paying attention, she'd ridden next to him again.

So far, he'd done everything he could think of to dissuade her from staying. She equated those sentiments with hatred. Damn, he didn't hate her. He wanted to taste her, catch her sweet woman's scent when he made love to her. "You're going to die in this land. I don't want that to happen. Don't want your death on my hands. You're fragile, Boston."

"So are you…going to die," she shot back this time anger tinged her words even though she looked as if she would collapse at any time. "We're all going to die sometime. I could be hit by a carriage and die, mown down in the city by a reckless driver. There are no guarantees in this life."

"Most likely true, might even be before I'm an old man sitting on a rocking chair in front of the saloon."

He had to agree with her. At times, he courted death. He was always careful. In this land, he knew what he was about. She didn't. He didn't have another argument. His chances of surviving the elements surpassed hers.

They rode in silence. He didn't want to think of her possible demise. In his life, he took one day at a time. For her, he needed to look to the future. They needed to stop. She had to rest. The stream meandered along the trail. The water's gurgling noise deadened the sound of the hooves. A soft breeze ruffled the branches of the pine trees. A few Aspens grew near the water. The land was beautiful. He'd die here. That was a fact. He accepted the knowledge as he drunk in the crisp, clean air. He wouldn't die because he was a greenhorn in a place where he didn't belong.

He pointed ahead. "We're going to make camp over there."

Nickering to his horse he moved forward. Dismounting by the boulder, he led Pye to the stream. When he turned to help Annie, she was struggling to get one leg over the horse. She groaned, the sound one of agony. He raced forward, afraid he might be too late to catch her.

"D-Deke...!"

The thin wail sent a bolt of fear through him. She was going to fall.

"Whoa, Boston..."

He reached her before she slid from her horse. She leaned into him, her body pressed hot and hard against his. He carried her slight weight. She didn't weigh more than a minute. He set her down inside the small indentation they would call home tonight. His voice rose harsher than he meant. "Fool...stay put."

A thin veil of moisture clouded her eyes. Her small furious voice reached him as he stepped away. "I want to help! I'm not useless baggage!" She pushed the moisture away, sent him a look of determination, her lips thinned.

"You can help best by sitting where I put you. Stay out of trouble, Boston. That's one of the rules of the road."

He marched away needing the distance between them. If he stayed, he'd be tempted to...well...he'd take her into his arms. She didn't want that. Even though she couldn't say no, she didn't want to be close to him.

She was trouble, that was for certain. He admired her tenacity. He wondered how long she'd be content to lean against the rock with her eyes closed. To Deke, it didn't seem she could move one muscle let alone two. She might wish to help. He didn't think her legs would agree. They were a little more than a mile high. She was wheezing in thin air. Her body needed to adjust.

"I can gather wood for the fire. We are going to have a fire tonight, aren't we?" she asked while she stretched her legs out in front of her.

He heard the muffled whimper, saw the clouding of her eyes. She was trying to massage the muscles of her thighs. Hell, they were probably constricted in knots.

"You can't walk."

His mind took a turn, a place where he tried not to travel. He bought liniment. The ointment was meant for her. He'd known this would happen. She might let him massage her aching muscles. She might not. She would need him. Hell, this had to be another rule needing to be set in motion.

She pushed from the ground to prove him wrong. With a low moan of anguish, she crumpled back to earth. She studied her hands in front of her, examined her nails for a few seconds. When she cast her gaze his way, she sipped in a deep breath of air. "Give me a few minutes. I'll show you that I can."

From the corner of his eye, he watched her rub her thighs then her calves. She pointed her toes then flexed her feet. Once again, she tried to stand. This time, by clinging to an edge of the boulder she was able to straighten. Didn't mean she could take a step without falling. Her back bent over, she tried a first tentative step. He gave her credit. For a little mite, she had gumption.

"Well then seein' you're so agile, suppose you can start gatherin' sticks for the fire. Not going to argue with a woman over something I can't win. Make sure they're dry. Don't want no green sticks. Don't want smoke advertisin' our presence here."

"Dry?"

She still clung to the boulder. Her back was still bent at her waist. She looked forlorn, ragged around the edges as well as out of her element. Her face was too pale. The crease lines around her mouth and eyes too visible.

This wasn't Boston. She couldn't walk into the parlor then stick a piece of wood on the fire. "Dry, so there's not as much smoke. Don't like smoke in my eyes."

"How, how do you tell? I'm willing to learn. Never told you I knew everything."

She managed to push herself away from the granite. As she stepped forward, she wobbled for a moment then placed her next foot in front of her. Her actions were more a shuffle than a full out walk.

If she wasn't so damn pathetic, she'd be funny. "Break the damn piece of wood in half. If you can do so, means it's probably dry." Despite his best efforts to stop the emotion, inside amusement bubbled. "If you can't it's green."

She was trying so damn hard he wasn't about to laugh. With one hand set firmly on a pine tree in front of her to steady herself, she took a few more slow steps. They were still wobbly. She stared at him, the pain in her eyes evident. He wasn't going to say anything more to dissuade her from her mission. She could manage or not. If she found a few pieces of wood, he would commend her for the effort. He set about rubbing down the horses, settling them in for the night. They would need shelter too. When he finished, he unloaded the packhorses. The provisions they weren't using tonight were set high in the nearby trees.

After he cleared a place for the fire, he looked to her. She held a small bundle of firewood in her slender arms. Hell, she didn't have the strength to do this. The tree branches were far too big to start the blaze. They would do well for later.

As if she heard his thoughts, she spoke, "I'm stronger than I look. I used to shimmy up the masts on the clippers ships my father built. At one time, I was a little monkey. I'd go clear up to the crow's nest."

His gut twisted at her words. *Shimmy up masts?* Seems her father let her do a lot of things he shouldn't. Boston was probably spoiled and pampered, used to getting her way. "Sit down, Annie. You're tired and you've worked long enough."

"No more tired than you," she shot back at him, indignation in her voice. She shuttered her expression. "I..."

"You don't need to prove yourself to me. I can tell by watching you're not used to riding. The best way you can help me is to do what I say and rest."

He felt tenderness for her he needed to ignore.

"One of your terms?" she queried sweetly as her gaze focused on him.

It seemed she was still able to push him to anger. He stopped his seething to calmly address her question. "Yes."

He would give her her due when she deserved it. She was determined. Was ready to fight for what she wanted. As much as he didn't want to, he admired that fighting tenacity.

"You want me to sit, watch you work."

She dropped the wood she gathered by the firepit.

"Yes." He wanted to grin at her. Kept his amusement shuttered behind his teeth. He didn't want her angry just rested. "You're a tiny bit of a woman. You've no more strength in those skinny little arms of yours than I have in my little finger. Rest is what you need. Tomorrow we're going to have to make up for lost time."

She hobbled to a log in front of the fire he was going to build then sat down. "What other terms should I know about? Make the language perfectly clear so I understand all the hidden meanings. I wouldn't want to break a rule now, would I?"

"You'll know when I think of them." He heard the loud hrmph from opposite his side of the fire. "I don't have a set of rules for you. The main one though, is do what I say when I say it. No arguing. After that nothing is too all fired important to spell out."

He brought her the saddle from her mare then set it behind her. She leaned against the leather, closing her eyes. Maybe she would fall asleep. That would be a blessing for both of them. He set about making camp. By the time he finished with the fire, she was sound asleep. He wasn't going to wake her until it was time to eat and the shelter he meant to build was finished.

Striding into the woods, he cut bows. In front of the small cave, he lashed them together, tying them with leather thongs. He should have brought a tent. The weather seemed fine this morning. Though he understood the Rockies. He knew thunderstorms could rise in an instant. Rain would fall fast and hard. Stepping back, he studied the shelter. She would stay warm as well as dry no matter how much water sluiced from the skies tonight.

She moved, moaned softly. Her hands rested beneath her cheeks. Dark sooty lashes lay against alabaster cheeks. Her lips were a soft pink in color. Her nose nearly straight, had a tiny lift to the end. She was so damn beautiful, enticing. She tugged at parts of him he thought long dead. Damn, he didn't want to want her. He had from the moment he first saw her.

In the morning, she would barely be able to walk let alone sit a horse. She would never admit to a weakness, at least not to him. She would carry on as if nothing was wrong. Everything was wrong. He should stay the day tomorrow, letting her rest. They didn't have a schedule. Getting to Denver City in one piece was more important than getting there quickly.

The coffee boiled. The beans were ready as were the biscuits he made. He had to wake her. Hunkering down beside her, he touched her shoulder. She moved away from his touch brushing at his hand as if he was a pesky fly. He grinned. Her head slipped. With a startled gasp she sat up, eyes wide, shimmering in the soft glow of the firelight. For a few seconds she looked around as if she didn't know where she was.

"Deke?"

She stretched out a hand to him. Her fingers were long, elegant, the nails still clean as well as neatly clipped. They wouldn't stay that way for long. Before they finished this trip, she'd have callous on those soft hands of hers. Her nails would be filled with dirt as well as ragged. This wasn't something he wanted to be a part of.

"I'm right here. How do you feel?" He wondered if she would be honest. Beside her he sat on his haunches. His eyes narrowed, assessing.

She pushed from the ground, whimpering softly before falling back to the blanket. "I'll tell you when I feel something. Right now, all my body parts are numb."

"Thought you would hurt from the top of your pretty little head to your delicate toes. Now you tell me you're numb."

He laughed at the look she shot him. She was delicate and fragile everywhere. He had to find a means for her to understand her life here would be hell. If she remained, attempted to practice medicine, she would come to regret the decision.

"You've never seen my toes." Her words were sarcastic, meant to dissuade him from his thoughts.

"Like to though."

He needed to bait her get a rise out of her or she wasn't going to move from the spot. He'd like to see a hell of a lot more than her pretty little toes. The first night he met her, he saw the gentle curve of her breasts. Wouldn't mind a better look now. His query was crass. He didn't care. "How many men know you intimately?"

Despite the pain it must cause, her back stiffened. Her face paled. He read pain in her eyes. "You won't ever see my toes," she shot out angrily. "The rest is none of your business. There are words for..." she waved her hand in the air. "Never mind."

He arched an eyebrow. She already called him quite a few names. "Another challenge. I'm up to any tasks you might toss my way. I'll see you your toes and raise you with your ankles. Might even go higher to accept a thigh."

"A fact," she said through clenched teeth her brows creasing now in pain. "You won't be seeing my ankles or any other part of me."

He hooted, knowing he could indeed win the challenge. He wouldn't even have to set his mind to doing so. Time to change the subject to something neutral. "If you can sit up, I'll bring dinner along with a cup of coffee." He rose. Turned his back on her. A few seconds later he held out a plate then set the coffee on the ground.

She cradled the tin plate on her lap as she tried to get comfortable, her skirt holding the tin in place. "How long did I sleep?"

Her eyes were shadowed, blue smudges beneath them. She should sleep more. "About two hours. Eat it all." The words were meant as a command. She would eat everything he gave her.

"A term?" she sighed sounding as weary of that conversation as he was. "I'm not very hungry right now. I'll try though."

"No, merely something you need to do if you're going to make it to Denver City."

He dished up his plate of food. For a few minutes they ate in silence. He listened to the wind in the trees. Stared at the fire. Heard water hit on the hot stones. Felt the first drop of rain when he finished eating. The timing was better than he expected. She handed him her empty plate. He was certain he had just enough time to wash the dishes then tend the fire before the sky erupted with water.

A roll of thunder rippled across the heavens. He didn't see the lightning. Knew more would flash downward. Wind blew a tornado of dirt around the campfire sparking flames. This time the blaze of light came before the thunder.

"Sounds as if the storm is on top of us."

She scooted under the lean-to then against the boulder shielding herself from the brunt of the storm. He saw her shivers. Saw the fear in her eyes as the light illuminated her face.

He added more wood to the fire then joined her in the cozy shelter he fashioned. He would wash the dishes in the morning. Their shoulders touched. He turned to her, studying her face. "Sounds can be deceiving in the mountains. This time you're right. The storm is about a mile from us. Best we stay put until the tempest passes."

"Are we safe?"

Her voice held a thin waver. Against him, he felt her body quiver. She leaned into him.

"Should be. Are you afraid of storms?" he queried hoping she wasn't.

There were no guarantees. He didn't want to frighten her with the truth. Lightning storms in the Rockies were nothing to take lightly. He wrapped an arm around her, tugged her close hoping to keep her warm. "You're shivering."

"Where are you going to sleep?"

His soft chuckle brought a scowl to her face. "With you, inside the shelter. You thought I might sleep outside in the rain, the storm? Foolish thought."

In another circumstance he would sleep on the other side of the fire. Tonight, they would share warmth. He built the shelter. He wasn't going to get soaked through to the skin to ease her sensibilities.

"What if I tell you no?"

She pushed at the flyaway hair around her face, her eyes all too bright in the delicate oval of her face.

"My terms."

He wasn't going to explain himself. She would have to put up with his body next to hers tonight, probably every night the rest of the journey. Nights in the Rockies could be frigid. He wasn't about to let her freeze to death.

"Very well," she sighed softly seeming to give up as she pushed deeper into the small cave. "I have learned that I can't fight you."

She wasn't going to give an inch. He checked on the horses. When he returned, she was huddled next to the granite wall. She might be resigned but she pressed herself to that stone as if she could slither through the rock. She was an endearing tiny piece of baggage. For the time being she was his baggage.

He pulled the blanket over her then settled in next to her, his head on his saddle. The pine needles he spread on the ground beneath the blanket were soft and comfortable. For the longest time he looked out at the rain, the darkness, watched the fire slowly die out, embers spitting when the deluge hit. Somewhere in the hills a wolf howled, another one answered. Her body turned. She pressed against his back, her breasts soft tempting mounds. Her breath ruffled against his nape. She wasn't asleep.

The night was going to be hell. He was going to offer anyway. "How are your legs? I've liniment if you want. If I rub the healing balm into your muscles, you'll feel better come morning. You'll sleep better too."

"They are just fine and dandy."

Her teeth were chattering, her body shaking against his.

"Would you tell me if you hurt?"

"No."

He didn't expect the honesty. If he didn't do something about her cramping muscles, they would have to remain here another day. "Just for good measure, I should give them a good rub down."

Behind him, she cleared her throat. Her voice soft, "What would that entail? A good rub down?"

"You do hurt."

He was going to get the truth from her if he had to pull teeth to do so. If she thought for a second a rubdown would include his hands on the naked length of her legs, she would never admit to anything.

"In agony. Don't think I can go to sleep. All my muscles have tightened, are cramping into hard knots. Can you do something?"

He could do a lot of things, including ease the pain. "If you're going to ride all day tomorrow, you do need to sleep. You also need to be able to walk more than a step or two."

"Get the ointment...please."

"Can you roll down your stockings?" He wanted as little contact with her as possible. He wanted to touch her everywhere. Only a miracle would keep him from caressing every delicately feminine part of her. Her pain was the miracle he needed.

He would see her toes as well as her ankles. He would try not to bait her with that fact. She would come to accept the needed intimacy.

"No...I," she paused as if thinking, "No...no...don't think I can."

"Suppose I'll see your delicate feet."

He couldn't help himself. Chuckled softly when she bristled but ignored him.

With the liniment in hand, he started to work. He clenched his teeth as he undid her shoes then slid her stockings from her legs. She grimaced when he touched her, whether in pain or modesty, he didn't know.

He looked at her, grinning, smitten. "Your toes are delicate, small and pink." Slowly he ran his hand along the arch. "One challenge down."

He shouldn't bait her. Doing so would keep her mind from the pain. She would bristle. Maybe tell him to go to hell. Call him names. He couldn't help himself since she said the most outrageous things. She would think that her toes would always be concealed. He pushed her skirt to her knees.

"Ass...!"

Well, that was the truth. Rubbing the cream on his hands he started with one leg, smoothing, massaging caressing muscles strained with fatigue, knotted tightly. She was stiff. When he touched a new place, she jerked. Moaned. She was soft, silken, her muscles firm. He worked her muscles until she sighed with the pleasure. The moment the pain began

43

to ease, he knew. Tension left her body. She relaxed, her legs parting slightly. He saw more of her than she would know. When he finished, he pulled her skirt to cover her.

"Better?" he asked, watching her closely.

Her eyes widened, the blue clarity always surprising him. His erection pulsed against his buckskins.

"Much."

"Do you think you can sleep now?"

She nodded, turning over, her head once again resting on her hands. He wished he could sleep. The night would be long if he didn't figure out a way to keep thoughts of her long legs wrapped around his flanks from his mind. If she knew the power she held over him, she would never agree to any of his terms.

She snuggled into the blankets. He lay down beside her. The scent of her filled him. Her breasts brushed across his back. Once again, he stared out at the darkness of the night. The rain stopped sometime before midnight. The rolling thunder moved down the mountain. Her hand rested on his waist.

He dozed. When he opened his eyes, one of her shapely legs was sprawled over his thighs. Her head rested on his belly, her long elegant fingers nearly on top of his arousal. He stifled a groan. Tried to move her hand. She sighed softly snuggling closer to him, now touching the swelling bulge.

Damn, she was warm and soft. When she realized what she did, she would be angry with him. When she woke, she would call him more names. None of this was his fault. He didn't have his leg thrown across hers, his head on her breasts, her hand on her sweet pussy. He was tempted to flick open the buttons on her gown then take a look at the temptations she modestly presented him with.

An animal scurried by the camp. He heard the horses shifting their weight ready to travel. Dawn would come soon enough. If he had a lick of sense, he would remove himself from this situation. He clenched his teeth when he felt the softness of her breath against his cheek. All the time he spent staying away from her on the train as well as the stage rides would be negated now that he was alone in the wilderness with her.

They had days of travel left.
Anything could happen.
He needed to keep his wits about him.

~ * ~

The bed was warm and soft. She snuggled closer to the heat that seemed to flow into her. Her lashes fluttered against the hard wall of his ribcage while her fingers toyed with the hardened nipple on his chest. She ran her hand down his flat belly to the waistband of his pants. His arm tightened around her. His hand stopped her exploring fingers.

"Deke!" She jerked upright. "What are you doing?"

"Enjoying your company. How are your legs this morning?" he queried his voice ragged, husky sounding as he tried desperately to ignore what her nimble, questing fingers did to his body.

"My legs?"

Glory, she forgot all about last night as well as the massage. The way his hands felt on her legs, the liberties he took. The liberties she gave him. She moaned her pleasure during the massage. Felt the butterflies flitting in parts of her she didn't want to acknowledge. After that, dragons seemed to ignite her from the inside out.

She sat up staring down at him. One hand was behind his head. He'd been holding her with his other arm. She wrapped her hair around itself to make a bun. When she looked down, she saw that her shirt was nearly unfastened. He watched her, his eyes tense, burning, growing nearly black.

"Yes, your legs. Can you walk? Do you need help?" With the tip of a calloused finger, he touched her chin then ran his knuckles along her neck. "Did you sleep well?"

"That's a lot of questions. Suppose I should find out. What happens if I can't walk any better this morning than last night?"

She couldn't help but think about the massage, how his fingers felt against her sensitive skin. Heat flooded to her face. Deftly, she refastened her shirt.

"We stay here. You hobble around as best you can until you work

45

the kinks out. We can start out after lunch if you're feeling better. If not, we'll try for tomorrow morning."

"It's going to take forever to reach Denver City, isn't it?"

She was a burden to him, an encumbrance he resented. He'd told her so before she left Boston. Giving in to his demand that she leave wasn't tenable. She could do whatever she set her mind to.

"A mite longer than usual." He stood, extending a hand to help her. "You might need some privacy. Let me help."

The heat to her cheeks deepened. If she couldn't walk, he would have to lend her his support. She was a doctor. She would make the best of this horrible, embarrassing situation. She squared her shoulders after she stood. With his hand around her waist, he walked with her. She detested this weakness. Last night he'd seen her toes and more. How much more she wasn't at all certain.

"Thank you," was all she could think to say to him.

What else was there to speak of? Once they were near the stream she hobbled farther. The heat of his gaze seared her back. He would know what she was doing.

"Call me if you need me."

He turned his back on her, walked away while she watched. He wouldn't go far. He was being considerate.

She nodded then took care of her needs. At the stream she rinsed her face, unfastened her bodice to run cool water over her flushed skin. She drank deeply. With a groan she straightened. From the tiny effort, her heart pounded. She sat on a rock to rest not wishing to call for him. She meant to show him, she could proceed without help. She wasn't going to become a liability. He might think she was a piece of fluff and nothing more. She would show him she was made of sterner stuff.

He was there, standing in front of her his hand stretched out. "Knew you wouldn't say anything. You've got to tell me when you need me. Out here pride can kill."

"Just giving myself a breather before I started back," she whispered wishing she had more strength.

She wanted to love horses. Couldn't abide them. She wanted to prove herself to him. Was failing miserably at every turn.

His arms were crossed in front of him. He was grinning wickedly. "You're not in very good shape. We'll have to do something about that. A few more days on the trail will help somewhat."

She bristled, didn't like what he implied. On a ship, she'd be able to out maneuver him through the rigging. Despite her father's objections, she loved to climb and swing from the lines. Tira, her stepmother, called her a little monkey at times. Her father was outnumbered until he and Tira had children of their own. Her father always told her she could do or be anything she set her mind to. She wanted to be the doctor at Denver City. Also, she wanted to prove to this man she was capable.

"You have no idea. I never liked horses so..." She stopped her defense when he cocked a dark eyebrow to the heavens.

"By the time we reach Denver City, you will have a different opinion. Out west horses are as necessary as breathing. Now, would you like help back to camp? I've started breakfast. The coffee is ready."

He offered his arm, his eyes gleaming with the challenge she hoped she could ignore.

Taking his suggestion of help wasn't going to happen unless she was desperate. Each step was filled with pain. She kept the grimaces behind her teeth as she tottered forward. When she reached the fire, she looked over her shoulder, "Coffee would be nice. A big hot steaming cup would be heaven."

"I take it you would prefer to pour your own."

With freshly poured coffee in hand he sat on a nearby log observing her.

With a tiny huff of exasperation, she managed the coffee without spilling. He was giving her what she wanted, independence. She drank. Felt the spurt of energy fill her. She thought he would leave her alone when they finished breakfast.

Instead, he held out a hand to her. "You need to walk. The muscles will constrict again if you don't."

He must have seen her rubbing her legs. The muscles seemed to knot at whim. She wanted more liniment, another massage. Didn't want to feel him touch her so intimately. She wasn't going to ask. He was right. She didn't want to admit she was weak.

She tried to stand. The tiny amount of time resting must have sent her backward in her recovery. The groan erupted. He eased her up. With his help they walked around the campsite several times.

With a weary sigh, she stopped. "I need new legs."

"Your legs are just fine. What you need is another massage."

His voice turned husky, so deep the heated words sent scalding fire into her as she thought about his hands on her.

"It's daylight."

"What's that got to do with anything? The fire provided plenty of light. I saw everyplace I touched. Come, sit, and rest with your back on the saddle just as you did last night. I'm not going to rush this. Nonetheless, we need to cover a few miles today."

She didn't know why. What did it matter if they rode an hour? Right here they had shelter and warmth. He helped her. She waited for him watching his back as he rummaged through his saddlebags for the ointment. Her body heated thinking about what he was about to do. His hands would be on her as well as his heated gaze. He would think she wasn't good enough.

"I'm a doctor," she blurted softly.

She understood doctors administered. They saw people. The actions they took were never about sex. She knew that. She'd seen more than most single women.

"Right now, I'm the doctor," he murmured quietly while he stood over her, his smile disconcerting. "Do you want me to take off your shoes and stockings or can you manage?" He repeated the same question from last night.

Shaking her head, she looked at him, his blue-black eyes darkening. He was so tall, so lean. His fingers were long, his nails well shaped and clean. He would touch her again. She didn't know how she would bear the feel of his fingers.

"Christ almighty!" He crouched down. Slowly, he pushed her skirts to mid-thigh. "I saw your legs last night. This is nothing new."

"You've seen many women's...legs?" She didn't understand why she cared or why jealousy forged a place in her head.

"Enough."

Before she could protest, before she thought to tell him she was quite capable of taking her shoes off and rolling down her stockings her clothing sat beside her. "The night was dark. You didn't look at m-me."

"The flames gave me light, more than enough. I saw everything any man would want to see. Lean back, close your eyes, you can pretend a real doctor is administering to your needs. If it makes you feel better, you can pretend I'm not looking at you."

She did what he suggested. The flames he stirred with his administering fingers wreaked havoc in her stomach, in the pounding of her heart. He repeated the process, moving from one leg to the other. The caresses were not meant to be seductive. They were. A tiny purr of pleasure slipped ribbon-like from her lips. She trembled, tightened, heated. She wanted to run. Walking was impossible. "You're not...a..." she gulped air, "...doctor."

"You're going to have to get over this shyness, Boston. When you see male patients, they might be naked as the day they were born. You will have to look at them." Beneath the solemn tone of his words, he was chuckling.

"I've seen plenty of naked men," she retorted then looked to see the narrowing of his eyes the tilt of his mouth.

To her he seemed angry.

His amused bark of laughter unnerved her. His fingers tightened on her ankle. "Plenty?" He paused for a while as he worked on a knot in her calf. "How many is plenty?"

"None of your business."

Once more heat rose, flushed through her body. The naked men were corpses. She'd never looked upon a living breathing naked man.

"Bare assed? How many, Boston. Got a feelin' plenty might be one or two. You ever seen a man aroused?" He pushed and pushed.

Would he never stop? She turned her head, not wanting to answer any more questions. Her silence would mean something to most men, not Deke Sullivan. "No!" Aroused, my god, she'd not seen a man in that condition even though she'd been violated. Were they different? Of course, they were. Heat flooded her body. Disturbed, confused, she pressed her chilled hands to her cheeks.

"We appear different when we're aroused. If you see a man's erection, will you run in the opposite direction?" He questioned her mercilessly.

What right did he have to ask her something so personal? This conversation was not to her liking. She stiffened her shoulders. This was none of his affair. What happened in her past was not something he needed to know. "You're crude, Mr. Sullivan an ass..."

"So you've said before." He flipped her over, pushed her skirt so the fabric settled on her rear. She felt cool air where she should feel only warmth. "Now that's a sight I'd like to see more often." Gently, he worked the muscles, massaged and kneaded even rubbing liniment on her backside.

"Deke..." she gritted out between clenched teeth when his fingers roamed lower, touched upon her, stroked ointment between her legs. He shouldn't...

"Your butt's adorable. Anyone tell you that before?" He was still chuckling, stroking, heating her.

Her heart stopped for a moment. "No! No... God no...y-you should..."

She couldn't finish the sentence. Her body flamed, burst into fire, melted into liquid.

Finally, he tugged her dress down, turning her over again. He gave her the stockings then the shoes along with her pantalets. She dressed. Now, he pulled her to stand. "Let's see how far you can walk." He leaned against the boulder watching her. His arms were crossed as he studied her, waited for her to make a fool of herself. "Go on." He shooed her with his hands. "I'm not going to help. This is something you've got to do by yourself. If possible, I want to get a few more miles down the trail this afternoon. While we won't get a full day in, a few miles brings us closer to home."

Slanting him a baleful glare she began to walk. Her muscles seemed to work better, tension easing with each step. Each stride was no longer agony. She didn't think she would be in any better shape tonight if she rode again. When she walked around the campsite a few times, she looked at him. "Does that meet with your approval? Should I mount up right now?"

"It's a start. Two more times then you can rest. We'll start out again after lunch. If you need another massage, let me know."

He winked at her.

She glowered at him. His laughter didn't sit well. If she asked for a massage, he would take advantage. The slow deep movement of his hands on her aching muscles did help relieve most of the pain. It also sent rapid shivers of hunger through her making her too vulnerable.

True to his word, he helped her onto the saddle as soon as they finished eating the noon meal. Each walk before mounting was a bit longer. Still, her muscles tightened around the saddle. She groaned as pain shimmied down the side of one leg. Clamping her teeth together, she wasn't going to complain or give him a reason to think less of her. She was going to hang on for as long as possible. She would never show him weakness. If she did, he would pounce.

Over his shoulder he looked at her. She smiled sweetly at him while she pushed the crackling pain to the back of her head. He wanted her to tell him she'd had enough of the Rockies, to tell him he could book that stage back to Boston for her. He wasn't going to get his wishes. She was here to stay. He would have to live with that. She was a doctor, a damn good one. Given the chance, she would prove herself.

The journey took them three days longer than anticipated. Every day was much the same as the first. He massaged her legs with the liniment every evening after they finished riding then in the morning before they started again. He seemed oblivious to the fact she was half naked each time he worked on her. She got used to the thin air, breathing deeper and easier each day that passed. By the last day, she rode the entire time without extra stops. Anticipation, eagerness, flamed inside as she was eager to see her new home.

They halted on a rise above the town. He pointed out the bustling little settlement resting below them. "There it is, Boston, Denver City, Kansas Territory. One street to its name. Your dream town. Is it everything you thought it would be?" He spoke blandly.

Denver City was pretty much like every small town in the west. It boasted a main street where most of the business were located, one saloon as well as a brothel. There was a restaurant that served good home cooked meals along with a boarding house and a sheriff's office. Other places of business dotted the main road. The doc's office was near the end of main street, located across from the saloon.

When she looked down on the sleepy little town, she felt a moment of coming home. He was right. This sleepy little place was in the middle of the Rocky Mountains. She was certain at times the town could be wild and untamed. It was in the center of virtually nowhere, days from Fort Laramie. She would set up a practice here, live in the settlement become friends with the people. Oh, she didn't doubt for a minute the men wouldn't willingly come to her. She was the only doctor though. Eventually, someone would have to bite the bullet and seek her out for help. She was good at her profession. She studied hard. She knew more than most men.

"It's beautiful," she sighed giving him a look of complete awe. "Yes, it's everything I wanted and hoped for."

He pushed his hat back slightly off his forehead, "Well, now don't believe anyone's called this place beautiful before. I'll take you to your office and home. If you need anything, you'll come get me. Don't go anywhere once it's dark without me."

She followed him down the trail then along the road that ran by most of the business. A barbershop, a dress shop, the country store were all places of interest. They reined the horses in front of a two-story building. She figured this was it. Her new home.

"Residents painted your home in honor of your coming. We've been wantin' and needin' a doc for years." He lifted his shoulders, a strange expression on his face. "Now you're here, Doc Lundin. No one thought you'd be female. You might find the welcome after this a bit icy. Not what you would have expected if your gender was different. The people will believe you deceived them."

She ignored that last bit. "Shall we?" Easily she dismounted proud of herself now that she was no longer in pain. This was to be her home. She was enthusiastic. His words hit a spot of apprehension. Stiffening her shoulders, she walked forward. She wasn't about to allow him to put a damper on this moment she waited for most of her life.

Inside the first floor was the office. There were comfortable looking chairs, a small waiting room. She moved into the examining room. On the walls there were medicines. She would add to the array with some herbal remedies she learned from her relatives. Taking a few seconds she examined the bottles, deciding she would have to rearrange them in a more suitable manner for easy access. She decided to put her diploma on the wall in the front room so all could see she earned her degree.

"I see that your trunks reached here ahead of us." He leaned against the frame of the door leading into the examining room.

"Father sent them two weeks prior to graduation. He wanted me to have everything I needed when I arrived."

She whirled in a circle ecstatic with her office, her skirts flaring. It was everything she ever dreamed of. Now, she wanted to see her new home. With a deep breath, she stared up the steps to the rooms above.

She headed for the door, passing him quickly. She felt his eyes on her back, sensed the fact he was watching her. When she reached the top of the steps, she stopped. The rooms had been swept clean. In the small kitchen food bubbled on the top of the stove, the scent divine. A pot of coffee was set on the table. On the windowsill there was a pie. Clasping her hands to her bosom she spun wanting to see the look on his face.

"The townspeople knew you would be here today," he said blandly, his expression giving nothing away. "Another welcome meant for the male doctor they anticipated. Did you mislead the good townspeople, Annie?"

"How? Why do you ask such a question. Of course, not."

He was purposefully being cruel, goading her. She never told them she was female. Never gave her sex. No one asked. If the question had been put forth, she would have answered honestly.

Deke stepped toward her. He was close, too close for comfort. His hand rested on her shoulder. "Two nights ago, we had a visitor. You were asleep or I would have introduced you."

"Someone came from the town?" She was shaking, terrified of what he might say.

"To see where we were? Expected you sooner."

53

He bent to light the fire in the grate that was prepared, ready for her use. Flames quickly took a hold of the kindling. When he turned to speak to her, his gaze flicked the length of her, examining her. "They were worried about you. Thought I should have gotten here sooner with the good Doc. What they didn't know was that you were a greenhorn. I explained that relevant fact to them."

Annie couldn't help but bristle. "How did this person get here sooner? We traveled quickly the last two days."

He nodded, "You see, that's the thing. Your quickly isn't very fast. Course…" He set his hat on the hat stand by the door. "You bein' a doc and all no one thought you would be able to set a hefty pace."

This conversation was going nowhere. When she applied, she was fully aware the people would believe she was a man. Well, she wasn't. "Do you want to eat with me? Seems they left a bottle of medicinal whiskey for our consumption."

His hoot of laughter startled her. She jumped, her hand shaking.

"Medicinal? You look like a gal who likes a bit of whiskey every now and then. Want a good portion in your coffee. You might be needin' some extra courage in the next few days."

"I do. I was worried about you, Mr. Sullivan."

She poured them each a sizable glass before dishing up the venison stew that had been made in anticipation of her arrival. Feeling as if all her dreams were coming true, she sat down, a spoon in her hand pointed at Deke. "When do you think I'll get my first patient?"

She was hopeful the shock would wear off sooner than later.

He joined her at the table. Sipped his coffee as he seemed to wait to answer. "About six months from now when Mrs. Webster is due to deliver her fifth child."

Deke warned her she wouldn't have patients. People would have no choice except to come to her if they were sick or injured. Damnation, if she kept telling herself that, maybe it would come true. "You don't have to keep up the ruse. Patients will come my way. I'm certain of it. They won't have a choice," she bit out, angry with him for continuing to downplay her achievements.

"It's no ruse, Boston. The men who are hurt will go to the barber.

54

He pulls their teeth, has set broken arms and legs. He gives them the best whiskey this town has to offer to ease the pain. They're not going to drop their drawers for a woman unless it's the local whore in Riley's tavern. Betsy's her name."

Her body shook. "Did I ask you to share the meal? Well, yes, I did but now you can consider the invitation null and void. I wouldn't share food with you..."

He grabbed her arm, turning her. "I'm telling this tale as I see fit, as I know the truth. If my words sting your tender sensibilities, I apologize. Hell, Boston, do you think I want to see you hurt? Soon you're going to have to come to terms with the fact that you're female."

"I know I'm a woman! Yes."

She tried to jerk her hand from his grasp. He held tight. Pulled her closer. She found herself staring into his dark eyes, fathomless eyes. Her stomach fluttered, turned topsy-turvy.

His face was inches from hers, his voice soft, whiskey smooth as he spoke. "I don't wish to see you hurt. What I want is for you to thrive, to go to parties and dance in beautiful ball gowns. You should be attending fancy dinner affairs those six fork dinners you city folks are all fond of. This isn't the life for you. You're too delicate, too fragile for the west." His lips brushed softly against hers once then twice.

She should tell him no. Not since that time in the train...he kissed her then... His lips were warm, his mouth soft as he touched her smile. Tenderly, he prodded her lips, asking her silently to open for him to allow him access to her. Annie understood if she let him deepen the kiss she would melt in his arms. Did she want that? She didn't know.

Unwilling to let her withdraw, he drew her hard against him, caught her chin between his fingers and thumb. He kissed her, very hard, open-mouthed with shocking, scorching hunger. She thought she should struggle, to somehow let him know this wasn't something she wanted. She could take his attentions or leave them. She set her hands against the strong wall of his chest meaning to push him away. She couldn't do so. Couldn't breathe, she was losing consciousness, sanity, reason, her touch with reality. She felt the wet heat of his tongue and lips, so seductive, ravaging her mouth moving with her then against the friction of her tongue. Felt his hands as if they touched her bare flesh, sliding over her body creating an erotic conflict through the sheer linen that only seemed to enhance his slightest touch. She should have worn more clothing. All that was between them was the shirt she put on this morning and his.

A small sound broke from the back of her throat. She pressed against him again, pushing then pulling him closer unwilling to break the contact but knowing setting him away from her was what she should do. Her desire to free herself from him faded with each passing second. She'd never felt anything so haunting, the liquid heat of his fingers, the fire of his strong form so close to her. The muscles of his thighs pressed against her legs. Her fingertips remained against his chest, toying with the buttons on his shirt as if she meant to unfasten them. She wanted to feel the solid wall of his chest, the soft fur of the dark hair that grew there. Her lips parted freely to the sweet, raking of his tongue, the touch of searing wet fire that seemed to follow everywhere his lips explored. He tilted her head, tasted her more fully his tongue ravaging every part of her. His fingers moved over her breasts, cupping one fondling the other, toying with each. Her nipples hardened in anticipation of what? She didn't know.

Then his head lifted. His lips hovered just above hers. The moment just ignited by him, faded.

"Boston?"

The slap she should give him came to her when he backed away. When he looked at her as if the kiss was somehow her fault. She let him seduce her, sweet-talk as well as charm. She was all kinds of a fool.

Annie turned away, humiliated once again, shamed by her wanton thoughts. He insulted her in so many ways. She tried to compose herself, straightened her bodice, smoothed her skirts, shaking them out. To pretend his kiss didn't affect her in any way was foremost in her mind.

When she turned to confront him, her voice rang with determination. "I'll prove you wrong," she told him convinced that once people got to know her, her practice would thrive.

"That is my most fervent wish," he said huskily.

~ * ~

56

"Heard tell the new doc ain't really a doc," Henry Tubbs said as he shuffled the cards a glass of whiskey to his left on the table, a cigar hanging from his bulbous lips while he spoke.

"Who's going to see her?" Art Stewart asked as he sat back watching Henry shuffle. He sipped his drink, let the liquid roll around inside his mouth. "Not me, not goin' to any female for what ails me. Never goin' to drop my pants unless she wants to give me something extra." He waggled his bushy white eyebrows.

"Hell, I'd like to see all of her. Sherriff spent weeks alone with her. First in a fancy train then on the trail, took them twice as long to get here from Fort Laramie than it should have. What da ya think they was doin'," Seth Masters asked as he nodded toward the bar asking for a second drink. "I know damn well what I'd be doin' with the pretty lil' thing. Saw her when they pulled up in front of the building."

"Lucky bastard," Henry muttered. "Heard she was a real looker, all wheat-colored hair just as ripe as the plains."

"Ripe for pickin'. Bet ol' Deke picked her clean. Probably wore her out. She won't have no energy for the likes of us."

"Heard tell he got real close to her. Pauli saw them kissin' in the upstairs of her office first night they got here. Sure to be doin' more than kissin'."

"Rumor has it they'll be expectin' before winter if she isn't already," Pauli said standing behind Henry. He laid the cards he dealt face down on the table. "That was some kiss I saw. If it wasn't somethin' leadin' to a little play in that bed of hers, I don't know what would be. Ol' Deke had his hands everywhere. She was letin' him, no protestin' from her skinny body."

Henry thought he would mosey on over to her office one of these days. He had sent back east for another doc to fill her spot. She wasn't going to last long in these parts. A woman doc, hell what was she thinkin'? One of the Webster kids broke his arm. The old man hauled him to the barber for patchin' up. So far nothing life threatening happened. He supposed if and when it did, they would have to go to the female.

"No one here in Denver City wants a female pokin' and prodin' him to see what's what," Art said as he asked for two more cards. "If

57

anyone's goin' to be pokin' it's me into her."

"Time will tell. I for one would rather go to a female for any kind of examination than some old fart of a doc. Men don't know anything about women problems and that's a fact," Pauli put in her two cents then sashayed her pretty little butt to the bar where she picked up another order of drinks.

Henry tossed in his cards. "Going to see this little woman right now. If the sheriff ain't going to claim her, a man should. When the new doc arrives, she's going to need protection, a safe place to settle down. She won't have a dime to her name. We aint' paying her until the new doc gets here."

"You're the man to give her shelter in the cold winter? You're a married man, Henry. You goin' to keep her all fancy in another house? Your wife will hit you over the head with her rollin' pin and that's a fact." Art asked, one eyebrow tilted upward. "What about the sheriff? He might have something to say about you seein' her. Seems to me you might be infringin' on territory he's already laid claim to. If Pauli is right, he set his stakes around her a few weeks back."

"No reason why I can't try. She might like a man who doesn't risk his life on a daily basis. Sullivan leads a hard dangerous life. I can offer security. Won't be dyin' on her from a bullet from one of Belt's gang or some no-account drifter who thinks he's a fast gun."

Once outside, he stepped toward her house. Wondered if he should knock on her home door or the office. Nah, he'd never been patient. He would go to her home, introduce himself then see what would transpire. He hitched up his pants. The hour was well passed closing time for the doc unless there was an emergency for her to see to. Seemed to him, the emergency would have to be bad for anyone to knock on her door. Could think of nothing except a major disaster.

His hands were sweaty when he rapped on the wood. Drying her hands with a dishtowel, Annie opened the door for him. "Henry Tubbs?" she asked smiling peering around him. "Welcome, what can I do for you? Are you hurt or does someone else need help."

She was eager. He would give her that. With his sweat-damp hands clasped behind his back, he rocked on his heels. "Nope, no one's hurt. Just thought I would give you a friendly welcome to Denver City. You're a beautiful woman, Miss Lundin."

"Doctor Lundin," she was quick to correct him.

"Doctor," he said.

"That's nice of you to want to welcome me. Can I get you a cup of coffee?"

She whirled around, the skirt lifting off the floor enough for him to field a glimpse of her slim ankles. *Mighty fine ankles.* Her hips swayed delightfully when she moved. *Mighty fine hips. All of her was mighty fine.* Hell, he needed a woman other than the town whore who cost ten dollars a poke. He could have this little gal for free. Any woman who wanted to be doin' a man's profession wasn't a lady. She'd seen naked men. Doc Lundin would be free for the takin'. With her back still to him, he rubbed his hands together in anticipation. Hell, his manhood was swellin' hard and fast just lookin' at her fully clothed.

She still had her back to him, pouring coffee. He snuck up behind her, held her tiny waist in his hands, squeezed. Held her still when he jerked her against him.

"Mr. Tubbs! No!"

Hot coffee spilled, splattered on the floor, dipped down the side of one of her hands.

He tugged her against his burgeoning arousal. The soft scent surrounding him nearly caused him to swoon. Her sweet fanny felt delicious against his jutting erection.

The boiling hot coffee she tossed at him seared his face, dripped down his chin. With a roar, he let go sputtering and wiping the liquid away. "You'll regret that, missy." He was shaking his finger at her, sputtering the words. "You've burnt me. You little whore." He swore, his anger as boiling hot as the coffee.

She stepped back from him well enough away she could run for the door if he tried anything else. "If you'll behave yourself, I've a burn ointment in the office." She didn't make a move down the stairs.

"Don't need no doctorin' from the likes of a whore!"

"No, you just thought to have free sex. I'm not a whore, Mr. Tubbs. I'm not for sale. Best you remember that or you'll get worse than scalding coffee in your face."

Chapter Three

When Sherriff Deke Sullivan walked into Riley's saloon, the music was loud and the smoke a dense blue fog. There were two poker games at tables near the back of the room. Spilled ale stained the floors. With swaying hips, Pauli was delivering drinks to the regulars. When she saw him, she sent a wink his way.

Over the last few weeks, he heard the rumors circulating about him and Doctor Lundin. He cringed with each new tale of their budding romance. He was the last male she needed in her life. He didn't want or need a wife. Once what seemed a lifetime in his past, he was married. She wasn't suited for this life he led. Opposites, the two women were opposite in every way except the delicacy of their bones, the haunting beauty each carried regally. His wife had not been suited for this life either. She should have stayed in the city. He insisted on her living with him, in the cabin on the ridge. She perished, not in childbirth but due to complications of a difficult pregnancy. At that time the nearest doctor lived in Fort Laramie. He'd been in love with the babe from the moment he knew his wife conceived. The loss of his wife along with his unborn child devastated him. Annie was a reminder of his past he wished to keep buried.

Moisture filled his eyes, his thoughts turning inward to a pleasanter time. He didn't understand how, nonetheless when he kissed Annie, touched her, explored the lush curves of her body, he forgot Marla. Annie had this intriguing and fascinating way about her. With her back rigid, her eyes blazing, she marched head high through every difficulty placed in front of her. During their trip from Fort Laramie to the town, there had been several times he felt certain she would plead with him to turn around.

Annie never complained. Nor did she ask for that ticket back to Boston.

61

She wouldn't tell him if she was suffering. Annie would keep going despite his dire warnings or the pain she felt. Her dislike and fear of horses was evident until the last few days. Before they arrived in Denver City, she seemed to find a rhythm, a way of dealing with her mount. In his wildest dreams, he never expected her to recover from the first debilitating pain.

"Join the game?" Seth called out, lifting his drink as Deke walked up to the bar.

All he wanted now was a big glass of ale to wet the dryness in his throat. Not wishing to admit even to himself, he wanted to see Annie. The last week he'd chased one of the Jones gang into the deep forest. He lost the trail then he found the tracks again. After that, the trail went cold for a second time. One of Belt's men was rumored to be injured, a bullet through his arm. That fact was most likely the reason he got close.

Belt was a breed. Not that he had anything against breeds. He grew up in the mountains with the Cheyenne. Knew all the trails all the places to hide, places to lay over for a few days if hurt. If the man stayed with the tribe, he would never have found himself running from the law. The man was an outcast in every way. Once the two of them played together, hunted and fished together. They shared hopes and dreams. They were brothers in almost every way. Now…

One was sworn to uphold the law.

The other raided and killed. Deke knew exactly what changed Belt. He'd been away from the tribe for over two years when the man left under suspicious circumstances.

Sometime one of them would pay with his life. Deke didn't intend to be the one. With his back to the bar, he stared at the saloon doors. Wouldn't do for a lawman to have his back to impending trouble.

When he rode into town a few minutes ago, he saw her light in the window upstairs. His first instinct was to visit her. See how she was fairing. A week had passed. A softly rounded woman in his arms would be heaven. He'd tasted her, knew her scent, felt the weight of her breasts in his hands watched as her nipples hardened in anticipation of more. She set fire to his soul. They were all wrong for each other. He didn't intend to marry again. Leaving Annie alone was imperative.

Annie was the kind of woman a man married.

She would never approve of a dalliance with the local sheriff.

He finished his drink then walked into the night. Overhead stars twinkled in the velvet blackness. The moon was a sliver occasionally ghosted by drifting clouds. The weather was chilly for the second week in June. There had been snow in the higher passes. His heart pounded, wishing to be with her.

Leaning against the pole outside the saloon's swinging doors, he stared down the street to her place. She should be getting ready for bed, brushing her hair, undressing. Rolling down her stockings. She wasn't. He could see her silhouette flitting from one spot to another in the upstairs apartment. What the hell was she doing?

"You need a woman tonight?" Pauli stood beside him, her hand on his shoulder. He felt her breasts pushing against his back.

Pauli was a pretty woman. Her hair dark, her eyes a silver gray. He slept with her before, before Annie. Now, he didn't want any woman except the doctor. "Yes."

He sifted his hands through his hair his gaze still centered on Annie's upstairs bedroom, memories of her long legs filling his head. The way her backside felt cupped in his hands. He shouldn't have touched her so often or teased her with intimacies that could never be. He wondered what she was doing. A cup of coffee along with a bit of small talk with her would be nice. Wouldn't be enough though. He would want to seduce as well as claim her intimately. She would give anything he asked. He knew that from the few sexual encounters between them.

Pauli ran her nimble fingers down his chest to his waistband. "Not even a rise. You hurtin' bad, lawman. Go get the girl. If you want her that is. Seems to me you do."

Deke grunted. "Nah, just understand what I can't have. She's not going to be here long. This life is too rough for her. No one is going to go to her."

"She's a beautiful woman inside and out," Pauli said as she watched the window along with him. "I went to see her the other day. Asked her questions I've always wanted to ask a doc but never did because they are always men. She knows her business. If I ever need her,

I'm not going to hesitate going to see her."

With one brow arched he turned to her. "You were her first patient?" He was skeptical. The dance hall girl in the saloon wouldn't be able to pay her rent. Pauli did sell her favors but she was more particular than the girl who kept to the upstairs room at night.

"Don't know...probably. She's real nice though. Had nice things to say about you," Pauli suggested with a sly smile on her painted mouth. "Think she's in love with you, lawman. You feel the same about her." Her words were a statement rather than a question.

Love? Never. He thought about what she might have said about him, thought of all the things she called him during their trip. "Like bastard and ass..." Deke said dryly watching for a reaction from the woman.

"Yes, well...she did tell me you tried to dissuade her from setting up practice in Denver City. Still think she's sweet on you. You should go see her, kiss her again. Take her to that lonely bed of hers."

"Annie would slam the door in my face. She wasn't all that keen on the first kiss."

He remembered the taste of her, the way her breasts felt in the palm of his hand. His imagination ran wild.

"From my vantage point seemed she liked that kiss you gave her just fine. Watched you through the window. Should remember to pull the curtains so you don't give the town a show they'll want to talk about for days," Pauli said softly, her grin wide. "Go on or are you a coward?"

Hell, where Annie was concerned, he was afraid he'd get in over his head. Hell, he was afraid of his shadow. "Need to keep my distance from the woman."

"Now, what good would that do you? You're hankerin' for her. Go show her who the sheriff of this town is."

"Keep my sanity, that's what distance would do for me."

"You are a coward." She laughed tilting her head back. She looked to the window. "She's still up. Might be waitin' for you to put in an appearance. Don't want to disappoint."

Chuckling softly, he agreed with Pauli. "I'm shakin' in my boots, that's what I'm doing. You're damn right, I'm a coward. Besides, it's too damn late to go callin'." He understood the excuse for what it was.

"I'll walk you over. You could dream up some malady of some sort. You could tell her you had a headache. She could doctor you. Rub her fingers on your temples."

"A woman's ailment? I'd not stoop so low as to make up a reason to see her. I'm not courtin' the woman. Best you get that notion out of your head. Well, lookee there." Pauli pointed to a dark figure leaving the home slowly walking down the steps. "You should go see what your little lady is up to. She shouldn't be out alone this time of night. You and I both know that for a blessed fact."

His gut twisted while he watched.

Annie walked down the steps then headed to the outskirts of town. Deke pushed away from his leaning post swearing softly. Muttering beneath his breath, he agreed with Pauli. "What the hell does the fool woman think she's doing? Going into the forest by herself. Could be the death of her."

"Appears the Doc is going for a walk in the dark. You could go with her. Meet her in a dark place. Kiss her again. Find a soft bed of grass to lay down on while you explore all her secrets. See what she's really feelin' for you. A woman can tell by a kiss. Is it the same for a man?"

His breathing hitched as he worked himself up to make certain she got back home safely. "She's goin' to get herself in a pack of trouble this way. She is trouble. Told her as much."

She should stay in one place at night, keep her pretty little fanny safe. Nothing good would come of her wanderin' around at night. This wasn't Boston. There weren't street lights or signs to guide her. Hell, he'd bet she couldn't tell north from south.

"Better get a move on or you'll lose her in the dark. She looks like one determined woman," Pauli cackled before turning back into the saloon.

Long strides brought him down the middle of the street in the same direction Annie walked. He caught a whiff of roses on the wind. His gaze narrowed as he watched her navigate a trail that led deep into the woods. What did she think she was doing? A woman didn't just go for a walk at night...in the dark...in the woods. Even the saloon girls knew better than to do something so foolish.

Furtively, she glanced over her shoulder. He didn't believe she saw him though she lifted her skirts before picking up her pace. He lost track of her through the dense foliage. In his mind she was rushing head long into difficulty. A few more minutes, she'd find herself amongst the thick trees. She wouldn't be able to see anything. Probably wouldn't be able to follow the ragged trail.

His heart raced with panic. He didn't like the fear for her simmering inside. Her slim frame disappeared. He raced forward, bent on having a good hard talk with her, shake a bit of sense into her stubbornness. He slipped into the forest behind her. His strides lengthened. Something slammed into the back of his head. Swiveling to catch his assailant, he went down hitting hard, losing his breath. He strained for air.

Annie was in his arms sprawled across his chest. She pushed against him, pounded his chest with her fist. "What the hell!"

He held onto her struggling form for a few seconds while he tried to figure out what was happening. His hands on her shoulders, he shook her. "Annie!"

"Deke..." She pushed away from him, her hair a tangled mass around her face. "What are you doing here? It's night...and dark."

"That's my question."

His voice was gruff, impatient with her. He grinned though. She was in his arms exactly where he dreamed she would be practically every damn night after he deposited her in the doc's office what seemed like weeks ago. Tenderly, he stroked her back, held her waist savoring the moment for as long as she would allow. The warmth of her pushed against him, all her beautiful curves in his hands. He inhaled the delicate aroma of warm, willing woman coupled with roses. He was a fool for dreaming.

"I was going for a walk." She sounded indignant. "What are you doing?"

She was a terrible liar. There was more to this than she was willing to tell him. Before he left her tonight, he meant to discover the truth. "And...you suddenly decided to bolt?"

"I...well." When her small pink tongue passed across her lips, she left a dewy trail of moisture behind. She tempted. Aroused. Provoked.

Bringing his thumb to her lip, he tested the softness the wetness. Thanked the moonlight. He wanted to savor her before she decided she didn't like her position on top of him. He barely held her. She could escape any time. Her mouth was half open, enticing him. The breath he drug into his lungs helped clear his head. "Why did you bolt?"

"You shouldn't be touching me," she sighed when he ran his hands down her back, settling her snugly between his legs.

She held onto his shoulders. Slipped her hands through his hair while she was denying their contact.

She was right about what she told him. It was pure danger to hold her. Since she fell into his arms surprising him, he was willing to endure the hazard. He didn't entice or provoke this meeting. He persisted. Understood there would be more to the answer than he wanted to hear. "Why, Boston?"

One hand rested on her sweet, little butt. He swept his fingers along the curves, one side then the other. Instantly, his body reacted, hardened. Heat flared to his groin. All of him jumped to life at the sweetly hot sensations coursing through him when she wiggled against him. She stimulated, enticed, seduced. She did it all unknowingly.

Her lips were moistened again, soft breathy little puffs of air swept across his cheek. Open-mouthed he kissed her hard, touched inside swept his tongue along the contours of her mouth, touching tasting exploring every part of her he found. Her scent was of the sweetest roses, her taste of the red Bordeaux found deep in the sultry warmth of her mouth filled his senses. Someone, he heard, sent her a crate of Bordeaux as well as Chianti. He'd like to learn who her benefactor was.

He rolled. She was beneath him now without a word of protest. A soft broken sound came from her parted lips. Gaining his senses was a priority. "Why?" he asked again prodding her, shaking her just the tiniest bit. He couldn't afford to let this go without a reasonable answer. The feeling that she was doing something dangerous did not leave him even with the sweet temptation of her body beneath his.

"You won't like what I have to tell you." She placed her finger on his lips. "I don't want to hear you swearing or your lectures. I did what I did. I would do it again. I took an oath."

"Didn't think I would like it the moment I saw you racing toward the forest. Tell me, Boston. What trouble have you gotten yourself into now? What will I…?"

His voice turned harsh, bitter if he had to be honest with himself. She bedeviled him riled his senses. He raced to protect her even in her stupidity.

"Let me up. Walk me back to my home." Her voice was soft, seductive in nature. "Have a glass of wine with me then we can talk."

What ploy was she up to? She couldn't possibly be thinking of seducing him into forgetfulness. A glass of wine would never make him forget what might have happened here tonight. He stood. Extended a hand to help her. Silently they walked the distance back to her home. At the top of the steps, he looked to the saloon. Pauli stood outside. She raised a hand in approval to him.

He wasn't going to stay the night nor was he going to bed Annie. Even though she tempted all his senses, she wasn't for him. Grimly, he pushed the door to her living room open. With her back stiff, she walked inside then whirled on him.

"You had no right to kiss me!"

Her tiny hands were fisted pummeling his chest.

Unwilling to react, he rubbed his jaw recalling the slap in her apartment that sent his head reeling backward. She was strong for the tiny little thing that she was. He grinned. "Didn't hear you complaining at the time. Do you have more of that wine I tasted when you kissed me?" He purposefully goaded her. "You did ask."

She didn't answer right away. She poured him a generous glass. Stiffly, she held the glass out to him. "There. Satisfied?"

"Hardly. You've a lot of answers to give me. Who's your benefactor?" he asked as he sipped the fine drink. It was good.

"One of my uncles." This information she didn't give begrudgingly. "He owns vineyards, one in Bordeaux the other in Italy. Not at all sure exactly where it is. He raises olives too. Makes olive oil." She drank deeply of her own wine. "I'll also receive olive oil from him."

"He sends you crates of the stuff? Must be a rich man," he asked walking to the sofa to relax while he tugged the answers to his questions from the little hellion. Deke held up the glass, watching the red liquid twirl in the crystal. "This is much better than olive oil. What the hell do you do with olive oil?"

"Yes...he does...and is. I'm his favorite niece or so he tells me. But then, he tells all his nieces the same." She sat in a chair across from him, her hands clasped tightly between her knees. Her eyes huge blue saucers. She caught her bottom lip between her teeth.

Scratching his chin, he tried to make sense of her rapid flight into the woods then her more rapid return to civilization. While he didn't mind being bowled over by her or holding her in his arms again, he needed to understand the cause. What or who taunted her to leave safety. He stared hard at her hoping she would give him the information he requested. The information she told him would be forthcoming whenever it pleased her. So far, she remained mute.

"I'm waiting." Truly he tried for patience. She wasn't making this easy. "I'm not a man of tolerance. I've about reached my limit."

"For what?" she asked sweetly as if she thought he could forget. Her wine was half finished. She looked as if she felt trapped.

Beneath his breath he swore, cursed softly. Clenching his fists, he waited for her to talk to him. He understood she didn't intend to make this easy for him. He would have to use his wits. "Why were you in the forest? Why did you suddenly bolt?"

At this point he wasn't at all certain how he could wrest the tale from her sweetly provocative mouth. He wanted to shake her until her teeth rattled. She was sitting with lips thinned, soft lips that didn't appear to be opening to spout the words he wanted to hear.

When she tugged in a deep breath of air her bosom rose incitingly, tempting. With every female gesture she enchanted him. Now was not the time. She stood, walked to a desk behind him. His gaze followed her wondering what new game she was up to. This wasn't a game. He would have to make her understand. After she returned, she handed him a piece of paper. He looked at her, questioning.

"Read it."

Slowly Deke opened the missive. It didn't say much. Wasn't

signed.

Meet me in the woods near the copse of aspen at ten o'clock. A wounded who needs tending. Bring your medical bag. I can't risk coming to the office. Make sure you come alone. Don't tell the sheriff. If you do, you'll never see Denver City again.

A patient

Anger raced inside. He swallowed hard willing himself to exercise every bit of self-control he could manage. Resolutely he crumpled the paper into a ball tossing it into the fire. She was too foolish for words. The temptation to reach out and grab her, shake her, hold her, scream, yell pull her into his arms and kiss her, seemed so strong that it was like a current of lightning ripping through him. "You..." the rest of his sentence stuck deep in the back of his throat.

Thoughts of Belt swept his mind. She risked everything by going alone.

God, she was something, so vibrantly alive. Her eyes were like blue flames. He yearned to touch the contours of her face. There was so much passion in her words, so much grace in her most subtle movement. If he stepped closer, he could breathe in the scent of her flesh.

"Damn you, Deke! I know it was foolish. I have to help those in trouble. I took an oath!" She sat down across from him again. She was looking at her fingers as if she was terrified of looking at him. "If it's any consolation, I won't do it again. I was terrified the entire time I was out there."

"Damn straight!" His blood boiled, churned until the tempest heated to an inferno. "You little fool. You could have been killed, raped..."

"Kissed..." she added before he could finish talking.

Her arms were wrapped around her slender form. She was shaking.

A wave of heat rushed through him. "Yes, kissed by a man who has no business kissing you."

When she was close to him, he couldn't seem to help himself. When he touched her, he lost rational thought. She was a whirlwind in his soul. He couldn't keep his hands from her. Deke wanted to feel her kiss again. Wanted so much more.

He tamped down the raging currents of energy and fire ripping through him. "What do you think he wanted...the author of the letter?"

She poured them both more wine. With her glass in hand, she strolled around the room stopping at the window to peer into the blackness of the night. Annie was still trembling.

"Help? He needed you to fix a friend. Don't understand why he didn't show up. If he did, what were you going to do?"

Quickly, she looked away. When she turned her attention back to him, she lifted her delicate shoulders. She stiffened then, rich dark lashes falling over her ever so blue eyes. "I don't know. Help anyone who might have been hurt."

"The noble gesture. You didn't bring your bag. You didn't have anything with you to protect yourself. Next time something like that happens come to me before you set off on a fool's mission."

He understood she wouldn't. Annie Lundin was just too damn independent for her own good. She would forge out on her own never asking for assistance, find trouble. Something must have happened to Belt. The man would be in touch with her again. He needed to set his deputy watching her place. Belt was a wanted man.

"I didn't know you were back in town. You've been gone. I couldn't have gone to you. The message said not to."

She touched her lip with the tip of her tongue, once again her body shaking.

He knew damn well she didn't walk across the street to his office. "Did you try? As it turns out, I was at the saloon watching your window. I would have gone with you if you asked. The fact of the matter is that you didn't try to contact me or my deputy."

Annie winced at his harsh words. Her eyes widened. She used a moment to wrap a shawl around her shoulders as if the feeble gesture would stop her shivering or protect her. "Why? You didn't...watch."

"Yes, I did. By the way, you should close your curtains at night. Some of the patrons in Reilly's like what they see through your windows."

He hadn't seen anything. When she undressed for the night, did

71

she close the curtains? It wasn't something a gentleman should be wondering about. Hell, he was no gentleman, never laid claim to the ridiculous notion. If she stood in front of the window to disrobe, he'd watch then he'd go upstairs and shake sense into her.

"Did you? Like what you saw?"

Her breath stammered from her lungs when she challenged him. As if she couldn't remain standing, she fell onto the sofa.

"Immensely."

He couldn't help the grin, wouldn't hold the smile back. She had to understand she was a beautiful, desirable woman.

She drank down the wine as if it was water. "You've watched me before? Undressing...?"

No, but other people watched what was happening in her home. Pauli watched him kiss her. If he'd taken his desires farther, Pauli would have seen a whole lot more than she should as could any man. "Why did you bolt? After all, if you had the noble intention of giving aide to criminals, why did you suddenly run away?"

"A noise, I heard a noise and I," she touched her tongue to her top lip. "I was frightened, terrified I'd done something stupid. That was why I turned, ran as fast..."

Deke waved his hand in the air, dismissing her words. "Most likely you heard me. However, that is the first bright thing you've done in this scenario. All your other actions were stupid, foolish, reckless." He finished with impulsive. "You can't act like a man because you are not as strong as a man." He needed to rattle her enough so she would think before she reacted. Doing so he figured would be nearly impossible. "This isn't Boston. There are no streetlights on every corner. No street signs to tell you where to go where to turn. What would you do if you got lost? Turned around so you didn't know which way to walk?"

"Don't you think I understand that?" she paused pulling in a deep breath of air before she finished. "It's late. You should go."

He saw her ploy. He wasn't going to be dissuaded so easily. "Why? Because you have a busy day tomorrow? You need a good night's sleep for all the patients you are going to see?"

He was baiting her again. As far as he knew Pauli was her only patient. This unknown man would have been her second.

"Yes."

"Rearranging the bottles of medicine that aren't being used? Checking over all your supplies so you can order more of the ones you've used the most?" he asked politely. "Have you used any?"

"Yes!"

She turned from him, her shoulders shaking as she tugged the shawl tighter. Her fists clenched so tightly around the fabric he thought the material might tear.

The shawl wouldn't protect her from a man. At the moment he didn't like himself. He pushed her too far. For her sake, he should back off. He couldn't. Stiffening, he set himself back on the path he knew was right. "Go home to Boston, Annie. I'll take you to Fort Laramie tomorrow. Hell, if you're afraid, I'll even ride back to Boston with you."

"I'm not afraid of going home. I'm not afraid to live in Denver City or..."

He didn't want her to be afraid of him. His voice softened. She appeared so damn vulnerable he almost swept her into his arms. He prodded her mercilessly. Now there were tears clouding her beautiful eyes. "What are you afraid of, Annie?"

Despite the fact he didn't wish it to happen he tempered his voice. She was trying so damn hard to succeed here in Denver City. She didn't stand a chance in hell of that happening.

"You," she said softly tears slipping down her cheeks. "I'm afraid of what you make me feel. I'm afraid of caring too deeply."

Deke Sullivan stiffened at her unexpected reply. He wanted to fold her into his arms, keep her safe from the world, especially from him. Since the first time he saw her in the ballroom, he felt that same protective need surface. She made him feel things he didn't want to feel. Since his wife died, he swore off women, good women. Annie Lundin was better than good. He wasn't worthy of a woman such as Annie.

"You need to go home."

Once more his voice assumed a hard edge. He strode to the door reaching for his hat, needing to put distance between him and this woman who touched his heart like no other. Inside he still bled for Marla. When he kissed Annie, he forgot about the woman he once called wife. Hell, he forgot everything except how Annie felt in his arms. Guilt swept through him.

"I'm not leaving here...ever!" There was a wealth of determination lacing those few words.

He saw that resolve in her eyes as she wiped the unwanted moisture away with the backs of her hands. "You'll die here if you don't go home. When that happens, you'll still go home but your departure will be in a pine box. If you're not in a city, you've no idea how to behave. What to do when trouble threatens your very existence. How are you going to pay your rent when you have no patients?"

"I've money."

"Your father is wealthy."

"Yes, I'm also part owner of the shipyard in Baltimore. I would never go back to Boston. It's not my home nor would I go to Baltimore. Except for a few, the people don't like me. Behind my back they call me a whore."

He stopped short for a moment trying to assimilate her words. "You aren't going home?"
His Annie a whore? He needed to find out why. Not tonight though. This evening he meant to put some distance between them.

"No!"

~ * ~

With a sense of loss Annie watched Deke leave her home. Out in the woods she'd been terrified afraid of her shadow. She knew she was foolish to go. Nonetheless, Deke was a stubborn, pigheaded man. He was impossible to deal with. He didn't listen. She didn't know how to talk with a man who thought he was always right.

Deke Sullivan didn't know anything about her. She just told him more about herself than she intended. More than she told anyone except Tira, her stepmother.

She touched her fingertip to her lips. Allowing him to kiss her had been a huge mistake. After the first time she should have learned her lesson. If he was right about one thing, he was correct in the assumption they were all wrong for each other. Why then, did he kiss her creating heat and longing inside then push her away as if he couldn't stand to touch her? Deke Sullivan wasn't like any other man she'd ever met. He was tall, broad of shoulder, lean of hip. He cared. He was protective.

Leaning against the windowsill, her head against the cold windowpane, she watched Deke walk down the street to his office. He lived in his office, at least that is what it seemed. His deputy, Taylor Douglas was his name, met him at the door. They talked for a few minutes. Taylor left, walking to the saloon. She should have gone to the deputy. Next time, if there was a next time, she would seek help.

Annie looked at the clock. It was after eleven. She needed to go to bed. Sleep tonight would prove elusive. Patients were what she needed not sleep. She could sleep anytime. Deke was right. She had lived here for more than a month. One woman, Pauli, from the saloon across the street came to see her. That was all. Mrs. Webster, the woman who was expecting, didn't come for a check-up when she sent a note to her that she should do so.

The pounding on her door surprised her. Trembling anew, she turned from the window. A chill slipped down her spine as she thought about the man she was supposed to meet in the copse of trees deep in the forest. She wrapped her arms around her body to ward off the chill. One more look to the street below told her she wasn't going to get help from either the sheriff or his deputy.

She hoped the person outside pounding wasn't Henry Tubbs come back to attempt to seduce her or ply his form of sweet-talking. The man made her skin crawl. With great wariness, she walked slowly to the door. For a few seconds while she hesitated, her hand rested on the latch.

"Anyone in there!" A man called out. "I've got a sick..."

Holding back her fear, Annie opened the door. The man carried a small child in his arms. He stepped into the room. "Bring the boy downstairs." Just with one look, Annie knew what was wrong with the boy. He had measles. If she didn't act fast, there could be an epidemic in town. Even if she did, there could still be multiple cases before the week ended.

"Who else in your household is feeling poorly?" she asked while she quickly led the way down the stairs to her office.

She worked quickly, efficiently. Not waiting to hear more, "How is the fever? Is it high?" His face was flushed with heat.

"His ma's sick. What is it? What does he have?"

He sounded bone weary, his voice coming across exhausted from stress. He hovered over the table, waiting, worried, his hands tightening as he anticipated words from her.

"Set him on the table," she told him softly. The boy moaned. "I need to take a closer look at the boy before I diagnose."

She understood this man would distrust her. Previously, he had made his thoughts about her perfectly clear. He didn't trust a female to doctor his wife. Nonetheless, she was all he had.

When she touched the child's forehead, the boy was burning hot. The flat red spots at his hairline as well as his neck could be caused by irritation, a rash. It didn't have to be measles. There was no way for her to tell. No test to perform that would give her the answers she needed. When she opened his eyes, they were inflamed. He had conjunctivitis. He coughed, the sound dry and harsh.

Looking up at his father, she asked pertinent questions. "Does he have a persistent cough, runny nose or sore throat?" she asked as she fetched a basin of water along with a soft cloth.

She ran the cooling cloth along his forehead, cheeks then neck. From the back of his throat, he moaned softly.

"His ma does, all that you said. What's wrong with them?" he asked. "My boy has a cough too, just started this afternoon. He was feelin' fine, playin' with his older sister out in the field. After dinner, he went to bed. Said he was too tired to stay up. When his mother checked on him, he was burning up. She told me to bring him here, told me, too, that she was feelin' poorly."

"Believe it to be measles. You've got to stay quarantined with your family. Can't let this spread throughout the area. Have you seen anyone this last week? Your children?"

She would have to get a hold of the sheriff. He as well as his deputy needed to contact the people on this man's list.

"Haven't seen a single individual. We don't like visitors much. Ma schools the kids so they don't come into town. Sometimes..." He stopped talking seeming to think better of telling her anything.

"How many children do you have?"

She was thinking they must play with someone. Kids would find other kids to play with despite their parent's wishes. "There must be close neighbors or kin that you see. We will have to check on all of them."

"Five, well four, we're expecting the fifth in a few months." Mr. Webster rubbed the back of his neck, a small groan of what must be fatigue emanating from him.

Annie swallowed hard wishing she could tell him he should take precautions if he wanted his wife to survive into old age. While she never heard of birth defects affecting the fetus, there wasn't a lot of data about measles. What she did understand was there would be a very real possibility of premature birth for Mrs. Webster. She would need to see her to assess the situation. If Mr. Webster continued to refuse her, there was nothing she could do. She was becoming more resigned these good people of Denver City didn't want a female doctor. Agreeing with Deke about this came at great cost.

"You need to keep bathing your son with the cool water. Keeping the fever down is imperative. I'm going to walk across the street, see the sheriff. Tell him what is happening here. Your nearest neighbors need to be informed as does the rest of the town."

Mr. Webster gave her the list of neighbors. She picked up her shawl then headed to the jail where she last saw Deke. Well, she had a patient. What did he know? The patient came to her because the barber couldn't help.

Measles.

She had the disease when she was seven. Didn't believe she could contract measles again. She was safe. Annie walked quickly. Her breath held in her lungs for several seconds while she followed all the steps in her head that had to be accomplished to ward off a full-scale epidemic.

Opening the door without knocking she was surprised to see Deke stretched out, his feet on his desk, his hat covering his eyes. He snored. She smiled softly at the apparition in front of her. During the journey to

Denver City, she didn't recall him snoring. Perhaps this was a ruse he was performing for her benefit. To her Deke Sullivan was a soft spot. He got under her skin, tempted her with challenges. He was exactly the type of man her father warned her about. Peter was the kind that Jamie would have liked. Her father was so wrong about men.

He snorted softly then sat up quickly whipping his hat from his head. He blinked several times as if he tried to wake. "Annie? What the hell? Thought you were home tucked up into your bed. Good Lord, it's after midnight. You shouldn't be out by yourself."

"Measles," she said softly, her fears spiraling. "I've got a case of the measles in my office. We've a lot to do before morning. I know you're tired." She spoke to him keeping her distance, watching him closely, waiting, hoping after that a short prayer. "Have you had them?" Her gut tightened while she anticipated his answer.

He shrugged his smile bright. "Little darlin' you've nothin' to worry about where I'm concerned. Don't all kids get them some time or other?" he asked blandly standing to his full height. "Who's the—"

She cut him off with a wave of her hands. "One of the Webster boys as well as his mother. You're going to have to ride out there. Tell all his neighbors they have to stay put for the next fourteen days. Otherwise, we might have a full blown epidemic on our hands. This isn't going to be easy. The saloon has to be closed immediately. We'll set Riley's saloon up as a command center for the sick. All the other businesses will have to be closed as well. People need to stay indoors or at their homes until there are no more cases."

"She's pregnant." Deke was strapping on his gun belt. He slipped a knife into the sheathe on his calf. He grabbed his slicker from the stand behind his chair.

"The baby might come early. Mr. Webster will have to keep a close watch. Hopefully by then he will change his mind about a woman doctor."

Deke seemed more than willing to carry out her orders. She thought he'd protest when she mentioned closing the saloon as well as the entire town.

One of Deke's dark eyebrows arched upward in question, "The

man's got a problem with you doctorin' his wife? Thought for sure she'd be one of your first patients. Who would have thought?"

"So far Mr. Webster has refused to allow her to come for a checkup-up." She was biting her lip. Going over all she knew about cures, in her head sorting the foods and herbs that seemed to work. It didn't matter. The man was bigoted not to mention prejudice. "I'll go back to the office. Let me know when you tell everyone. Will Riley put up a stink about his place being closed?"

"Nah, Riley won't care. Webster's a damn fool, always has been. Taylor is at the saloon. I'll get him then we'll be on our way." He stood at the door seeming to wait for her. "First, I'm going to walk you home. You shouldn't be out alone on the dark streets at this late of an hour. Not after what happened tonight." Deke rubbed his chin, "Not any time for that matter."

"Thank you."

She smiled at him welcoming his presence. On her way to his office her breath caught at every shift of a shadow. She'd been terrified.

"Send Mr. Webster home then go to bed."

"The boy's fever...well, we need to get it down before I'll send them home. As soon as the boy—"

"Don't want you around the measles," he blurted out, his temper seeming riled at the thought of the town doctor attending patients even though tending sick people was her job. The town was paying her to do just that.

"Why, Mr. Sullivan, you're beginning to sound like my father." She grinned again unable to help herself, watching the play of his emotions cross his face. "He never wanted me to become a physician. Told me I might get sick. Did everything in his power to dissuade me. Though once I was accepted and enrolled in school, he lent me all his support. Father is proud of me now."

"Right at this moment the last thing I'm feeling for you is fatherly," he gritted out as if he didn't want to talk to her.

He stood by the open door while he allowed her to pass through. As they walked, she felt the heat of his body next to hers. Knew his strength his scent. He placed his hand at the small of her back guiding her to her home. Her breath caught at the slight contact. He could do that to her, make her dizzy with thoughts of kisses.

With a gentle kiss to her forehead, he stepped away from the door. Gently, he ran his knuckles along her cheek. "Be careful, don't take any unnecessary risks," he told her before he turned and walked away from her. "If you get any anonymous messages, come to me before you do anything foolish."

In her head she'd been going over suggestions for Mr. Webster to help treat the infectious agent in the blood. She stepped inside before unwrapping her shawl. Deke hugged her quickly then he vanished in the darkness of the night. He was headed out of town to spread the message. At the door she watched for several seconds.

Mr. Webster looked up after she entered the office. When he spoke his voice faltered, "His fever's down, Doc. What do we do now? He's goin' to be, okay? Right?"

"Good about the fever. You will have to keep this up as soon as you get him home. If your other children have no symptoms try to keep them as isolated as possible. Give the boy and Mrs. Webster eggs and green leafy vegetables if you have any. If you can mix garlic with honey, that will also help ease some of the discomfort. Most importantly you need to keep the fever down. If Mrs. Webster starts having contractions, come for me or bring her here."

"Don't want no woman doc delivering my child."

Annie felt as if he slapped her in the face. She couldn't do anything to combat the ignorance or the narrow-mindedness of ill-informed men. All she could do was her best. She stiffened her shoulders, praying for a calm voice. "I see, well...the offer will remain. I can help your wife if you allow me to do so. I've delivered..." she didn't know how many children during the course of her medical training she helped into the world, "...a lot. I wouldn't let anything happen to your wife." That was a bold statement since with childbirth there were no assurances. If early, the little tyke might not survive.

"Won't change my mind, ma'am." He bundled the little boy into the wagon. "Never even allowed a midwife to see to her. She made it through all the births with no trouble, no trouble a'tall."

With a heavy heart Annie watched them drive away. If something happened to his wife during delivery, he was ill equipped to help her. Up until now he had luck on his side. Measles could complicate the birth, especially if it was premature. She hoped and prayed Mr. Webster would change his mind. Stepping inside, she closed and locked the door. Upstairs, she went into the bathing room with a bucket of hot water. Before Mr. Webster's visit, she'd planned on a hot bath. After the visit, more than anything she needed to soak in the heat. She felt dirty. After a few hours' sleep, she would visit the saloon and Mr. Riley. She needed to inventory all the resources at the town's disposal.

Once the water was heated and, in the tub, she slipped into the soothing liquid. The glass of wine she poured earlier to help her sleep sat on a stool next to her bath. She closed her eyes. This was heaven. A hot soak was always wonderful.

Thoughts of Deke filled her, the infuriating controlling man. In such a short time, he was coming to mean a great deal to her. She needed to sleep. The next few weeks could be long as well as exhausting. For now, she didn't want to think about what could come with the dawn. She hoped this first visit from the Websters would stop the disease in its tracks.

She dozed.

She jerked awake, her lashes fluttering as she tried to bring herself back to reality. A breeze flowed into the room from an open door. She had locked the door. Urgently, she searched for a towel. The bath sheet was across the room near the fire so the fabric would be warm. The distance seemed miles away. Beneath her ribs her heart thundered. Sounds of footsteps rifled to her. She thought her heart would stop either that or race so fast the organ would burst from her chest. It seemed to be doing both intermittently.

When the tall lean body filled the doorway, she slithered farther into the soapy water. Wet streamers of her hair slid across her shoulders. He'd never seen her naked. No man save her father when she was a baby had seen her with no clothing.

"D-Deke…"

"You didn't lock your door. That was foolish, stupid. Did you forget when you lived in the city?" He stepped farther inside while he dusted his hat on his thigh. "Thought you'd be more careful now after we talked, after I warned you."

Blast him! She did lock the damn door. Right after Mr. Webster left, she locked her office. The upstairs door wasn't locked. She'd let the man in then raced downstairs with him following.

"Go away, Deke." Her voice became a breathy whisper of air as her heart pulsed haphazardly. "Don't want you in my bedroom. I've got nothing on me."

"I see that." He grinned. His eyes focused on her.

After picking up her glass of wine he sat down on the stool by the tub. He sipped appearing thoughtful. He continued as if she wasn't taking a bath, naked. "Everyone has been told about the measles. Riley will expect us in the morning. Have you had the measles?"

Annie covered her breasts with a washrag. He should have asked that a long time ago. "Can you sit over there?" She pointed a quivering finger to a spot on the other side of the room. "Or on the bed?" She inhaled deeply, closing her eyes while she tried to ignore the fact that he was watching her. "When I was seven."

He rubbed his jaw as if thinking of something to say. His gaze remained fixed on her, on all of her. "Kinda like the view from right here. Since you've had them, I don't have to act like your father."

"Ass..." she muttered, her voice low.

She felt embarrassed, humiliated, she needed to run. He'd see all of her if she ran for the towel.

"Been called that before." He grinned, a half-smile quirking on his lips, assessing her. Standing he set the wine where he found it. He walked away.

A long, slow breath of air slipped from her lungs. While she shook, she watched his broad shoulders as they narrowed to slim hips and tight buttocks. He picked up the towel hanging in front of the fire before returning to her. His eyes simmered, darkening to such a deep blue they almost seemed black.

He held the towel in front of him. He asked, "Is this what you need? Stand up, I'll wrap it around you. Get you warmed up. You're shivering."

"Drop it on the stool, or the floor. I don't care. You can leave," she amended when she realized the wine was on the stool.

"Don't be foolish."

"Deke…please."

"We need to talk, Boston. Get dressed. Meet me in the other room."

The towel he'd been holding pooled on the floor beside the tub.

She didn't know what they needed to talk about. Nonetheless, she was heartily pleased he left. Dear god, he looked at her naked. She tilted her chin. She wasn't different from any other woman. He'd seen more than his share of that fact she was certain. Still, this wasn't something she was used to.

Swiftly, flying though her clothing she dressed in a soft blue muslin gown. She didn't bother with corset or pantalets. After a brief look in the mirror, she headed to the parlor. When she stepped through the door, he handed her a cup of coffee.

"Thought I would get to sleep until dawn. What happened? This encounter could not be good."

Dread rippled through her. There was something terribly wrong.

"One of the families we visited, well…three of the children are sick. The parents both contracted measles when they were children. They've agreed to stay quarantined in their homes for the fourteen days you required of the Webster's. There's going to be more cases. This won't be finished in the fourteen days you allotted."

"If more in each family get sick, they will have to remain in quarantine longer. This could take forever."

"Do you think the man you went to meet might have had the measles too?" He queried thoughtfully.

"It's possible. We still don't know why he changed his mind about seeing me," Annie said wishing she had all the answers.

"Just as you heard me in the forest, so did Belt."

"The renegade you told me about earlier?" she asked, stunned by the revelation. He was too damn illusive. She needed to learn more. "Can we find him? Ask the man a few questions?"

"No," Deke was shaking his head. "His hideout has proven impossible for me to discover its whereabouts. God knows I've tried. When it comes to your safety, don't want you anywhere near that man. Want to keep you alive as well as in one piece."

She sipped the coffee he handed her earlier slowly sifting through his words. "You've brought food?"

"Yeah, brought fresh baked bread. Mr. Meade is cooking up a storm over at the saloon waiting for the sick to filter in. God knows I hope they don't. Pauli is setting the staff to cleaning up the upstairs rooms in case we've need of more space. As I said, don't see this bein' over any time soon."

Annie felt tired to the tips of her toes. This was what she wanted, patients. She never bargained for an epidemic. Once more she prayed the few cases they knew of were isolated cases. Deke told her the Webster's neighbors didn't spend much time in town. His kids didn't go to school. When morning came, all the families with school-aged children would have to be informed.

She ate the bread. The food was delicious. Her stomach rumbled. Hours might pass before she could eat again. When she finished, Deke stood, held out his hand.

"Come, Doc Lundin, you got patients to see. People will be stopping by the saloon just to see what's happening."

With a heartfelt sigh, she rose. Hand in hand they walked the short distance to the saloon. He was right. She wanted patients.

Pauli greeted them a grim look on her face. She was dressed in a somber gray gown that buttoned to her neck, a very different look for the vivacious middle-aged woman. "Come inside. Unfortunately, we have two more cases. Riley waylaid the man before he reached your office since you said you wanted everyone to come here. Taylor is going to stand lookout for more people who might need assistance."

"Yes," Annie said as she tried to see around her.

She brought all the herbs she had on hand. She needed to send Deke to the general store for garlic and honey, vegetables. She made up a list.

"Two children, I'm thinking they caught it at school. Today was

84

the last day before summer vacation."

"Could have waited a few more days," Deke muttered as he perused the list she handed him.

"Put them in one of the guest rooms upstairs. They are brother and sister. The mother is with them. Both mother and father have had the measles," Pauli said. "When their fevers are down, do you want them to go home?"

"Yes, we've got to make certain when the people leave here, they will live. We need to remember the infection treats adults more severely than the children."

Annie moved quickly, Deke at her side as more cases were brought to them. They sent the most severe to rooms on the second floor. The mild cases they sent home with instructions for when the fever increased. As the day progressed it became more apparent that this had indeed become an epidemic.

At the end of the day, Deke escorted Annie home. He carried a bowl of venison stew along with more freshly baked bread. They left Taylor in charge until the morning with Pauli on call for further assistance if the rooms became overloaded.

Once inside her apartment, she collapsed on the sofa thinking she didn't have the energy to eat. She didn't even have the strength to drag herself to her bed. Deke wasn't allowing anything of the sort. Before she could lean back and close her eyes, he hovered over her handing her the stew along with a huge piece of bread slathered with butter.

"When you finish with that, I'm giving you a glass of wine."

As if he had an abundance of energy, he set a couple of huge pots on the stove to heat water for a bath before he sat down to enjoy his meal.

"You don't have to wait on me. I can do for myself," she smiled at him, glad that he was doing that very thing.

He scooped up some of the gravy with his hunk of bread. "You're exhausted. Not used to so much work. Just want to help where I can."

"There you go again thinking I'm some delicate hothouse flower. I'm not. You have any idea how many hours I spent awake during medical school? Do you?" She wanted to poke him in the chest to make her point. Damn him for still thinking the worst of her. "What do I have to do to prove to you I can handle most anything?"

He grinned at her. "Go ahead and poke me. We both comprehend you are a delicate hothouse flower, fragile, too tiny, feminine to the tips of your pretty little toes. Though I'm proud of your efforts today. You did prove yourself a competent doctor."

She wiped the bowl clean with her leftover bread thinking she'd never done anything like that before. Since this morning she'd eaten nothing. She watched as Deke collected her bowl along with the spoon. He set all the dishes in the sink then went about preparing the water for her bath. Relaxing while he worked, she sipped the wine, her eyes closing. She jerked awake when he took the empty glass from her hand.

"Your bath is ready," he murmured softly. "Do you need help?"

There it was. His leering grin returned. "If you are asking if I need help undressing, the answer is no."

"Too bad," he said softly. "Always want to lend a helping hand."

"Where do you live?" she asked, wondering if he meant to sleep in his office again. Offering to share the bed wouldn't work at all.

"Don't worry about me."

"Deke..."

"I'm going to bed down at the saloon. Pauli keeps a room for me upstairs. Actually, the place is in the attic."

"You share with Pauli?"

Jealousy ripped through her. She didn't have any right to question Deke about his relationships.

"No, do you care?" His hand was extended. "You don't want your bath to get cold."

"It's time for you to leave."

He nodded seeming to understand. "I'll lock the door behind me."

She heard him whistle as he sauntered down the steps. While she waited to make certain he did leave she held the bath towel next to her chest. Swiftly, she dashed to the window. He did enter the saloon instead of his office. He was going to sleep there. Why did she feel as if she should have asked him to stay? Heat suffused her. She was being ridiculous. A man like Deke would never want her. He told her too many times she didn't belong. His kisses were just teasing, telling her how out of place she was here.

Wanting him was all-wrong. He was a gunslinger. She was the daughter of a whore. Her mother wasn't a whore though. She had been her father's mistress until she died in childbirth. Jamie Lundin never loved her mother though he was her only lover. He cared for her. Annie wanted a man who would love her unconditionally.

Escaping the title of whore was not possible. Deke deserved a woman who didn't come with that burden attached to her.

~ * ~

Nightmares ripped through her one after the other. Every time she closed her eyes and dozed, she found herself assaulted by the memories. Images along with recollections that were a part of her life since early childhood. Tira did as much as possible to shield her from the horrific memories. Once she became an adult there was nothing any one could do to stop the rumors or the gossip. Medical school had been good to her even when she met and fell in love with Peter Bentley. Peter was nothing like Deke. Peter was charming, courteous…a liar, dishonest.

Peter was suave as well as debonair. His smile lit up a room. The first time he grinned at her, her stomach flipped over. He understood women flocked to him. The man came from one of the wealthiest families in Boston. When he approached her the first time to dance, she nearly swooned from excitement rushing through her. In her entire life, she never thought a man such as Peter would want to waltz with her, hold her in his arms. She was always so very shy, never venturing beyond the background. While he wasn't overly tall, she reached the tip of his nose, she never cared. Compared to Deke, his chest wasn't a wall of muscle nor were his shoulders as broad or his thighs so well-formed. His dark brown eyes always seemed to be drenched in amusement.

Too much time passed until she understood his amusement was about her. He thought she was awkward. She was. Peter labeled her the daughter of a whore. So, of course, she was also a woman of lose morals. He believed he could have anything from her he asked for. Despite her achievements in medical school, he strove to set her up as his mistress.

He expected her to fall into his plans without blinking an eye. His arrogance was unbelievable.

Because her mother had been mistress to her father, he assumed the same for the daughter. Even when she told him no, he continued with his plans. He purchased a lavish townhouse, beautiful furniture as well as a fashionable wardrobe.

Damn the man, she didn't want anything to do with him. She told him no so many times. He never listened.

She left Baltimore with the stigma of her past attached to her never expecting to arrive in Boston with the same dishonor. Fighting the taunts along with the jeers all her life, she hoped to put all that behind her when she moved to Denver City. As to date she was successful. Deke didn't know anything about her mother. She didn't want to tell him. Having him look down his nose at her wasn't tenable.

How could she tell Deke she didn't deserve his kindness? When he heard who her mother was, he would never fall in love with her. He'd scorn her just like everyone else she met. If she were honest with herself, she fell in love with the man the moment he rubbed the liniment into her throbbing muscles. Possibly she fell in love with him when he rescued her from Peter in a back alley of Boston then acted as if he was her savior. Maybe it was when he bought her donuts and coffee.

She could never tell him her truths.

He deserved to know the facts.

The first time she met Peter, he gallantly kissed the back of her hand telling her that he was proud of her endeavors at medical school. After all, women needed women to doctor them, to help birth their children, discovering later he thought of her as a glorified midwife. Her first encounter with Deke was far different.

Annie never had a beau. At town dances she was well-known as the girl who would hold up the wall. Her only friends were her nearby cousins who she occasionally visited. They were all younger, well not that much younger. The Andrews along with the Lakelands were not truly relatives of hers. Once she thought herself half in love with Jess Andrews. He was wild, reckless, handsome as sin. He didn't return the sentiment. Thought of her as a sister, nothing more. She never wanted to be his sister.

Not as attractive as Deke Sullivan though. No one was as good looking as Deke. She wanted to give her heart to him to do with as he pleased.

Jess Andrews wanted to move out west, wanted to ranch. Perhaps that was part of the reasons she sent her application to Denver City when the notice appeared in the medical school newspaper. She held her breath for weeks while she waited to hear from the small western town.

Peter, the first time he pulled her into his arms for a waltz, he held her too close. His hands pressed against her waist, slipped lower when he danced her onto a secluded balcony. His open-mouth kiss shocked her, surprised her. She disliked the sensation when his tongue pushed between her lips. Her body jerked unsure how she should react. Annie didn't know how she should feel. What she did know was that she didn't care if he kissed her again.

Peter was the first man who ever kissed her. Deke was the second. The kisses were like night and day.

When they parted, he laughed, touched his finger to her wet lips. She didn't understand his pleasure came because he was thinking of the other parts of her he intended to sample. Peter was a smart man, however. He waited, bided his time until he thought he had her wrapped around his little finger willing to do anything he asked.

She spent her entire life fighting off the whims of men who labeled her a whore. Nonetheless, she was so thrilled that a man wanted her for herself, at least she believed that to be the truth. In this instant, she didn't listen to the sixth sense that always seemed to get her out of trouble.

Deke Sullivan was trouble. He was pure male danger; arrogant, domineering confident in all he did. If he wanted, he could have slept with her at any time on the journey here. Now, he taunted, teased, enchanted her every sense. His scent was evocative, manly, spicey. When she literally ran into him in the forest, when he kissed her, she knew instinctively she wanted him to explore her, to touch, caress and so much more.

Peter made certain he explained to her what he would do when they were alone in the privacy of the house he planned to keep her in. At first, she listened not understanding the man wasn't talking about marriage. She was glad to be away from him. Glad to never see him again.

Deke was nothing like Peter.

He would never lie to her. She owed him the truth about her life.

Chapter Four

The measles epidemic lasted a full month. Deke understood Annie was exhausted when the last case spent the required fourteen days in quarantine. She needed rest, time to heal her body. During the month a few of the residents decided she might just do as the town Doc. With Pauli's encouragement the women began to come see her about feminine issues. Now, Deke decided she needed a day off. He was going to shanghai her, take her swimming in the pond near his ranch house.

He wondered if she could swim. Teaching her would be a delight. She sure as hell couldn't ride worth a damn when she arrived in Fort Laramie. What kind of person traveled west when they couldn't ride a damn horse? She did live by the ocean. Her father owned a shipyard and built ships. His Annie was most likely a fine swimmer.

Meade was packing him a picnic lunch; fried chicken, potato salad with dill pickles along with a variety of berries. He was going to purchase a bottle of wine. Thought better of it when he remembered the wine she received in crates from one of her uncles. That was so damn strange.

The Bordeaux was the best wine he ever tasted. Perhaps they would take more than one bottle, one of each, Chianti as well as a Bordeaux. Spending the entire day well past the setting of the sun would be fine with him. He wanted to tell her about his childhood. If he was lucky, she might tell him something of herself. He wanted to know about the men who attacked her in the Boston alley. So far, she stayed quiet about that episode in her life.

On his way to her office, he whistled a cheerful tune. The sun was shining brightly on a day that would be hot. A few clouds dotted the late spring sky. He two stepped the stairs to her living quarters eager to see her again. Knocking on the door, he waited.

When she opened the door, her crystal-clear blue eyes were wide

91

in surprise. She tossed her head to remove a stray lock of hair. "Deke?"

"Good mornin', little darlin'. We're going for a picnic, you and me then swimming. Get your swimin' gear." He stepped by her apprising the room. "Two bottles of your wine, a Chianti as well as a Bordeaux. I've got all the food we'll need for the entire day."

She was wearing a light pink day dress with a scooped, gathered neckline. Didn't seem to have fasteners on the front or the back. Easy on, easy off, he grinned thinking perhaps he might get lucky this afternoon. Nah, he wasn't about to ruin the day by taking advantage of her. Though if she gave him reason, she might like something more than friendship...

Ah, but a man could dream.

"Deke..." Annie closed the door then followed him into the room. "What are you talking about? I can't go anywhere. Might have patients." She looked as well as sounded indignant.

He liked it when she got her dander up a bit. A woman should fight for what she believes in. His Annie did just that. "They can wait." Side stepping her, he strolled into her bedroom, sorting through her armoire. When he didn't find what he wanted, he turned to her grinning devilishly, "Do you have something to wear when you swim?"

A pretty picture she made standing in front of him, her tiny little hands fisted on her hips. "No, women's swimsuits are a threat to life and limb. My stepmother nearly died while she was trying to swim in one. Nearly sank to the bottom of the pond."

"What are you talking about?" He leaned against the wall; his arms crossed over his chest while he swept his gaze along her body. His smile grew broad as he thought on the possibilities. "Does that mean you swim buck naked?"

"No! Not that it's any concern of yours," she huffed clearly miffed at his not-so-subtle suggestion.

"What do you wear? Your chemise and pantalettes? That wouldn't hide your delicious little body from any man wanting to look."

Today he would look if given a chance. She must understand all her beautiful curves would be revealed if she did so.

"Yes, nonetheless, I don't swim with men or a man..."

Her face turned a beautiful shade of pink. Her fingers wound into and out of her dress leaving creases.

"Today you're going to swim with this man. Do you take an extra pair?"

He pulled out both a chemise along with matching pantalettes. Both had tiny pink ribbons. To his touch the fabric was soft, silken very feminine. He didn't have to close his eyes to imagine her wearing her underwear and nothing else.

Annie was feminine and silken from the top of her wheat blond hair to the tips of her delicate pink toes. Eventually, he would discover just how silken she was. "Should we put these in my saddlebags?"

She grabbed them from him, wadding them in front of her. "What are you doing, Mr. Sullivan? You can't have my underwear."

He held up his hands, laughing, "Now, don't be angry. I'll be more than happy to take these in my bags for you. If we don't bring your underwear with you, you won't be wearin' one stich of clothing when I toss you in the pond."

"I can't go swimming." She looked as if she wanted to go with him.

"Every good doc deserves a day off for good behavior. Have you been good, Boston? Actually, If I was to be honest with myself as well as you, I'd prefer a tiny bit naughty. Can you be naughty? Go swimming. Naughty girls are infinitely more fun than good girls."

She turned from him with an exasperated rush of air. Her back was stiff. She needed coaxing or this picnic lunch would be wasted. He stepped to her, his arms going around her waist, drawing her slight body next to his much bigger frame. Her tiny little rump was soft next to him. She rested her hands on his forearms, pushing now as if she thought her insignificant strength would remove them. He nipped at her neck, laved then teased again. Her taste was so sweet, enticing, delectable. He needed more. She shuddered readjusting her position. He grew hard. Hell, it was what he wanted, just not before they rode.

He flattened his hand on her belly slowly spreading his fingers. A small broken sound sifted from her saucy lips. She whispered her words holding no conviction, "I'm not going with you."

"Yes...you are." He turned her, bent down so his shoulder

93

captured her waist. In a swift economical move, he lifted her to his shoulders. Her sweet butt pointed skyward. "I'm abducting you."

She shrieked. Her fists pummeled his back. "Deke Sullivan! Put me down!"

"I'll put you on your mare. If I have to, I'll put you across my thighs then take you to my swimmin' hole. We're going swimmin', Little Darlin'. There ain't nothin' you can do to change that fact."

"Your swimming hole?"

She pushed upward using his back to get more height. Tried to turn her head so she could see him.

"Behind my house up in the hills. The water will be ice cold, take the heat of the day away, refreshing. Exhilarating. Thrilling. You never told me if you can swim." He was pleased. She no longer fought. "Wait, need to capture us two bottles of wine."

He whirled, carefully missing furniture. In the kitchen, he procured the bottles.

"You can put me down."

"Like you where you are." He settled his hand on her rounded bottom, enjoying the soft feeling beneath his hand. He would like to explore her legs then higher beneath her skirt.

She squeaked. Squirmed. Cursed. He laughed. When they reached the horses, he helped her mount. "You are an ass," she hissed.

"You love me anyway." He leapt on his horse. "You goin' to come along nice or are you goin' to play hard to get?"

"Suppose I don't have much of a choice, now do I?" She smiled sweetly at him sending him a spicy look. In the depth of her eyes, he saw secrets he'd like to uncover.

Sweet and spicy, just how he liked his woman, "Nope, you know I melt when you smile at me like that. Do you swim?"

"Like a fish," she told him.

"Good, so do I. Was 'fraid you swam like you rode a horse."

He could hear the indignation in every breath she inhaled. He enjoyed the feisty side of her, enjoyed the rigid back she showed him. Knew when he teased her, she would retaliate. Could hardly wait to see what she would do or say.

"What do you actually have in mind, Deke Sullivan?"

She nudged her horse so she road abreast of him. Her voice was syrupy.

He tipped his hat back, his eyes raking along her perfectly shaped form. "Rest and relaxation for the feisty doc of Denver City, a bit of a swim then food and wine. Tonight, we can stay to watch the stars twinklin' in the midnight black sky if you've a mind to ride back in the dark. However, there are other options."

"Is that all? Why do I have this feeling that your intentions aren't pure?" she asked as she seemed to search his face with concentration.

His bark of laughter gave her pretty little forehead creases. "Deke Sullivan, pure? Never. When I'm in my eighties if I make it that long, I sure as hell hope I'm never described as pure."

She guessed too much. Yes, he wanted her to relax and enjoy the beautiful day. He also had a bit of seducing in mind if she was amenable to the notion. A bit of kissing, a whole lot of caressing, his plans didn't go much farther than that. What happened after the strokes along with the kissing depended on Annie Lundin as well as how she reacted to his attention.

He pointed. A fawn along with its mother walked across their trail. A blue jay screeched while a squirl skittered up a tree. Far above them an eagle soared on the wind currents. Bees buzzed on the wildflowers adorning the sides of the trail. Deke brought into his lungs a deep breath of pine-scented fresh air. This country he held so dear to his heart wasn't for the weak.

"Have you changed your mind about me?" she asked, tipping her head a little, studying him. "I'd like to know."

He heard the wary tone in her words. Hoped she was good with this adventure he invented at the spur of the moment. Even though he didn't want her to leave, he had to tell her what he thought. His voice turned gruff. "No, still believe you would be happier in Boston. This country is harsh. You're not seeing the weather in the winter. Snow can pile up to the top of a roof."

"I'll never go back there, Deke. I hate the city along with the people who reside there. They are all prejudice bores." She leaned forward as if she tried to see him better. "I'll never be happy in Boston. Don't you see? I can't go back to a place that makes me unhappy. Won't ever go back to Baltimore either."

No, he didn't see anything yet there must be more to her story. It might be better for him to listen than to make judgments. He didn't understand why she would be unhappy in a city. Damnation, she grew up in Baltimore. "Tell me. Tell me what happened to you to make you loathe the place where you grew up."

When she tugged in a deep breath of air, her bosom rose and fell. The movement was beautiful just as she was. He wanted her to fit here in Denver City, to belong. Maybe he judged her too soon and too harshly. Just because she was a little bit of a gal, didn't mean she didn't possess inner strength. Giving her a chance might work for both of them. If she left, he'd miss her more than he wished to believe.

"Would you listen to me? Truly? You wouldn't play judge and jury? I've wanted to tell you things about my past. The reasons why I ventured to the west, to this small town in the middle of nowhere. Why that man attacked me. Why I'll never go back."

"You haven't." He wanted to learn all he could about her. "I'd be happy to listen up. What is it about your past that is so difficult for you that you run to more danger?"

"My past isn't something I speak easily about or to any stranger..." she paused for a moment tugging in a long breath of air. Her eyes were wide pools darkening as she appeared to recount a time she didn't want to remember.

"A stranger who kisses you?"

His query was honest and sincere. He kissed her more than once. Did she dislike his kisses? He didn't believe so. She was intelligent as well as beautiful. Annie embarked on a male oriented career.

"You've done more than kiss me," she told him her voice sweetly soft. "You've..."

"Not much."

No, he'd like to do a hell of a lot more than touch and kiss. He'd like to make love to her. She fit him perfectly even though...even though she didn't belong here in the wilds of the Rocky Mountains. Annie hated the city. She breathed a piece of sunshine into his life. Annie was a passionate woman. He'd like to tap into some of that raw desire. He'd like to learn all her secrets.

He heard the soft sound of her laughter. She cocked her head to one side. "Seems like a lot to me. No man…well that's what I should tell you. Where I grew up the children, well…they wouldn't play with me. When I grew older and my father and stepmother couldn't protect me, the boys called me a whore. They tried to take liberties I didn't want to bestow on any man. Just to feel safe, I couldn't go anywhere by myself."

Her words caught him by surprise. His brows creased together *Whore? What the hell?* "Why?" She mentioned something to that fact earlier.

He couldn't fathom a single reason why her friends would call her a name such as that. To Deke, she was everything sweet and innocent.

"My mother was my father's mistress. They never married. He never loved her. Nevertheless, he did care about her. He would have supported her for all of her life, me as well. My mother died in childbirth, my birth. When Tira came to Baltimore, she lived with my father for months before he finally married her." She sighed faintly. "I guess because of my mother as well as my stepmother, the good parents called them both whores. Naturally, I was cut from the same cloth. We did have a few friends who blamed my father on Tira's status. Told him he took wicked advantage of her innocence. She loved him though. Tira could never tell him no about anything."

That was too much for his poor male brain to digest all at once. No little girl should be subjected to name calling, labeled before she was a woman grown. No older lady should be either, especially not a lady so beautiful and sweet as Annie. His curiosity rose several notches. "What about the man in the back alley? Does he play a significant role in your decision?"

"He wanted me for his whore. Actually, he wanted to call me his mistress. It's a fancier more refined title. The name, mistress, sounded better among his peers than whore." There was no emotion in her voice or her expression when he looked her way. Her face appeared blank. For a moment her rigid posture vanished.

He thought she should be angrier. "You don't think?" He felt tongue tied at the moment, his thoughts a jumbled mess. He never thought of her in that light. Yes, he wanted her, wanted to make love to her, meant to do just that today if she didn't tell him no. He would have to change his mind. He wasn't about to treat her as Peter Bentley did. She was not someone to take advantage of.

"You aren't like Peter or the others. Deke, I've wanted to tell you my story so you would have a reason to stop…well you needed to know about me. Now that you do, you will…" She passed her tongue across her lips. "…you won't want me in the same way. Do you wish to take me home?"

"Hell, I'm no virgin," he bit out harshly watching her recoil from his insensitive tone. "I've slept around. You haven't. You're innocent to the very tips of your delicate toes. If anyone here is a whore, it's me."

She blanched, her face turning white as newly fallen snow. Instead of the rigid set to her shoulder he was growing used to, she trembled, her body shaking. "Something else you should know about me. Neither am I…a virgin."

Once again, Annie shocked him. She was always so shy. When he touched or kissed her, she seemed innocent. She certainly needed work with the kissing. He was certain she had no experience with men. "Hell!" The realization came to him with blinding clarity. Annie had been raped by this Bentley fellow, possibly his cronies too.

She seemed to recoil from his explicative. "I've never been with a man willingly…except you. I haven't totally been with you."

She seemed to want to get everything out. Her words rushed, she looked to him as if she needed confirmation of her very existence. There was moisture in her eyes.

His heart went out for her. God, no woman should be abused. "What ever happened is not your fault. You don't have to explain anything to me. I'm not your judge and jury."

He reached over to touch her hand. Her fingers were cold, frigid and icy to his touch. He wanted to right all the wrongs that had been done to her. He couldn't. All he could accomplish was to ease her burdens, help her understand she was a beautiful, loving woman. "I don't care if you're a virgin or not. I would kill any man who forced you."

Annie flinched as she shifted in her saddle. Her brows were creased together in fine lines across her forehead. She pulled in a breath of air. "Don't want you to kill anyone. I've taken a vow to help people not aid in ending lives."

"The man in the back alley?" He comprehended the truth before she could answer. He recalled the way she fought him, the other men who meant her harm. He'd known they were bad seed then. He knew more now.

"Peter Bentley. You've guessed right if you're thinking he raped me as did the others who were there. When you saw them in the alley, they wanted one more time with me beneath them before I left Boston. You stopped them. Thank you." Her words were spoken between clenched teeth. Clearly, she was in pain. "I was too terrified at the time, to understand why you helped me. Just thought you wanted to hurt me as everyone else did."

Deke was at a loss for words. What happened to her was a while back. It was in her past which she seemed to want to put behind her. She didn't appear to need consoling words. He was certain if there had been tears over her lost virginity, they long since dried.

"I'm not sure what to say."

He wanted to reach out to her. Sensed she didn't want empathy or sympathy. No pity either. His Annie would want to get on with her life, forget the past she could not change. All she could do now was look to her future.

"Do you still want to take me on this picnic. Am I a fallen woman in your eyes? A whore? A slut? A harlot? Whatever name you want to put on a woman who gives herself to any man?"

This time her words sounded bitter almost hostile. She was straightening her back, expecting the worst. "I'm stronger than you think. As I told you before, I'm no hothouse flower. No orchid like the ones my uncle grows. If you don't want to be seen with me, I understand."

Too dazed by her revelations to think straight, he wanted to take her into his arms, hold her, tell her any man worth his salt wouldn't care about her lack of virginity or what happened to her in the past. All that now mattered was the present along with the future. He wanted her in his future. Wouldn't care about gossip and rumors. She was so damn innocent, sweet, spicy too if one stopped to take a look. "I would like to wine and dine you until neither of us could eat or drink anything more. If you're asking me if I care about a piece of skin stretching across your vagina, the answer is no, a resounding no!"

"Vagina?" She quirked an eyebrow as if she was shocked by his word. "Thought you might have said something crude. I'm surprised by your use of the clinical. Although…"

"I just like to talk as if I'm a backwoodsman. I've been educated. Been to West Point, graduated top of my class."

Her eyes widened in what appeared to be surprise. "Is that how my father knows you?"

"Yes."

"Suppose you should tell me more about yourself. It's your turn." She stared pointedly at him for a few seconds then she broke out in a grin that swept his breath from his lungs. He discovered a tiny, kissable dimple by the side of her mouth. He hadn't noticed the small indentation before. Supposed she hadn't smiled all that much. His breath caught in the back of his throat.

He ran his hand along the length of his thigh to erase the moisture on his palm. "It is my turn only…" He pointed to the lake in front of them. "We are here. How about after we eat then swim, I'll tell you more about myself."

"We should swim before we eat."

"Should we?"

Lifting an eyebrow, he wondered why she would say that. Frankly, he was starved. Not for food but ravenous for Annie. He wanted to make love, eat then swim in that order.

"Yes." Once more, her grin did him in. "We'll enjoy the food more when we are hungrier."

While her voice was prim her smile was flirtatious. It appeared she put the telling of her story behind her.

Lust surged to his groin, swept through his body at an alarming rate. He was hungry for food as well as Annie. He wasn't going to treat her as if he expected her to give him her favors especially now that he understood part of her story. If she wished to do so, she could dictate the terms of this fledging relationship. Playing by her rules would put a different spin on his intentions. Still...

"Swim first," he told her thinking about her swim attire.

She would look adorable in her chemise and pantalettes with the miniscule pink bows the nipples of her breast very clear through the thin wet fabric. There would be nothing left for his imagination. He leapt from his horse in order to help her. Her hands on his shoulders she leaned into him when he picked her up. She was as light as a feather, fragile, delicate. She didn't belong here anymore than his wife had. The woman he once loved never thrived in this wild territory. They should have stayed in Fort Laramie where she didn't have to contend with the elements.

For as long as he dared, he held her against his length, felt the gentle curves he adored. He set her on her feet. With a quick slap to her bottom, he sent her to change into her swimwear. She sent him a ferocious look. "Over there, behind the trees."

He handed her the underwear anticipating her revealing. Ah, but he'd seen most of her in her bath the other night. "I'll be in the water waiting for you."

Her eyes widened. He wasn't certain if she was thinking about him waiting for her or if she was thinking about the other night when she was naked in her bath. Perhaps her thoughts were entirely different. When she stepped from behind the trees, she would be very nearly naked. By the time she was submerged, her skimpy clothing would cling to her as if they were a second skin.

Wearing his buckskins, he waded into the water. In other circumstances, he'd head for the water with nothing between him and the liquid. Once the cold glacier fed water reached his thighs, he dove. Coming up for air, he shook his head gasping for oxygen. Water droplets scattered around him. While he waited, he stroked across the pond then back, his body warming to the temperature as he got used to the cold. The water was refreshing. He knew he couldn't stay in the lake much longer. He floated.

"Don't look."

Her voice carried over the water. When he reacted to the command, she saw her peeking from behind a pine tree. She looked so damn cute, adorable in her shyness. Her little nose almost the only part of her she revealed.

"Why would I look?" he drawled his voice slow and whiskey smooth.

What a question? More than anything he wanted to watch her.

She hmphed. "Turn around." Her small hand created circles in the air.

He did. Waited, until he heard the splashing along with the gasp of air to accompany the dive into the cold water. Once he felt the ripples from her entrance across his body, he turned to see her. She stroked toward him. She pulled up about a foot away.

The water was crystal clear. He saw the rosy buds of her beautiful breasts tightly hardened. Tempted. She would have no idea. The nipples were firm, hard, the coldness creating the delicious image. If he didn't stare too long, she might not realize how much he witnessed of her.

"Invigorating, don't you think?" he asked unable to remove his gaze from the saucy woman who seemed to spike his desire.

So much time passed since he cared for a woman. He was no longer certain how to go about courting. Well, he'd already done more than courting. He'd passed the courting stage.

"Frigid," she retorted while she tread water in front of him. "Whose idea was this?"

Deke wished he didn't have different ideas from the ones she questioned. "You wanted to swim first, eat later. We can do whatever your heart desires."

He wished he dared pull her into his arms. The heat generated from their kisses would warm both of them.

She grimaced at him, splashed his face. He sputtered while he wiped the water droplets from his eyes. After his vision cleared, he saw her swimming away. She was fast. He would give her kudos where her water abilities were concerned. Leisurely, he pursued her. He wasn't in a hurry to catch her. Eventually, he would. Sometimes taking one's time in the pursuit generated more pleasure.

She stopped at a boulder jutting out on one side of the pond. He watched her delectable little butt as she shimmied up rocks to sun herself. If she had any idea how much of her he saw, she would blush crimson from the roots of her hair to the tips of her toes. When he reached the rock, he pulled himself up, sitting close to her.

"Beautiful scenery," he murmured without looking at her.

Even though he spoke about Annie, he gazed at the hills between the trees.

"Oh." Her sigh of seeming pleasure was long, heartfelt. "You're right. This is so much more beautiful than a person can see in the city. Thank you for bringing me here. I'll always remember today."

He would also remember today. "If you dry off in the sunshine, the water is going to feel cold again. Maybe we should swim back, sun ourselves while we are indulging in food."

"Want to stay here forever soaking up the sun." Though she spoke through chattering teeth. "Don't want to return to the water."

"There is a path around the lake. We could walk." Her feet were bare. The notion wasn't acceptable. He offered just to see what she would do.

"No..." She wrapped her arms around herself to stop the shaking.

Before he could react, she scurried down the embankment then dove into the pond. He followed wishing to play and warmup. Grabbing her ankle, he yanked her into his arms after that beneath the water. She came up for air, sputtering, appearing indignant. She was grinning though.

She reached for him, her hands on his shoulders, she pushed him under. He found himself eye level with the very curves he wanted to explore with his teeth and tongue. Not so innocently, he let his cheek rub against her nipple. Her body jerked. Besotted, he thought she wasn't immune to him.

When he surfaced, he grinned, staring into the crystal blue clarity of her eyes. She looked confused, wary perhaps, even trying to disassociate herself from her feelings. He waited for a reaction, a slap to his face was what he deserved for his audacity. Instead, she rose above him, her hands on his shoulder to push him under again. The action was a blatant invitation. She wanted to resume the sensual play between them.

His hands on her waist, he tugged her close. Her body aligned perfectly with his. This time when his mouth closed over the tight bud, he sucked her veiled crest into his mouth. She arched against him. Her belly pressed against his erection. He let one hand drift to her backside, caressed, letting his hand roam to uncharted territory. She was…enchanting, delicious, all his. She warmed every cold place inside. He wanted her forever, longer than forever perhaps into eternity. Briefly, he switched his attention to the other breast.

After he surfaced for air, he framed her face with his hands. His mouth closed over hers, hot, hard demanding she gave back to him, everything in return. Sweetly, Annie accepted the advance and retreat of his tongue playing with him, teasing as if she understood all he wanted. He kissed her before. Inside, she was hot and sultry, complex. Dark. Secretive. There was so much to his Annie girl, his Little Darlin'.

Deke pulled back to gaze into her feminine features. She was shaking from the cold. Her lips were slightly swollen from his kisses. He didn't want to leave. They had to warm themselves. "We need to get out of the water." With great tenderness, he pushed wet strands of her hair from her face. "Come on."

~ * ~

Annie understood the consequences of her action more than most innocents. She wasn't innocent. The way she felt when he caressed her was something she didn't understand. When Peter touched her, kissed her, she felt nothing except revulsion. She was shaking now. The trembling was not caused solely by the temperature of the water. No, it was caused by the sweet tempest he created inside her, the secret places he touched by his caresses.

Her body tensed with pleasure. Butterflies danced in her stomach. She was a doctor. Understood anatomy. She'd been taken brutally and thank God, there were no consequences that time. He kissed her again…teased with his tongue…sucked…laved. She pushed against him. He withdrew, touched her forehead with his. "Race you to the shore."

He didn't follow her right away. When she felt his body close to hers as she swam, she knew she would lose the contest. He gave her a head start and she still couldn't beat him. He was faster as well as stronger. By the time he could stand thigh deep, he held out his hand to her. When she let his big hand enfold hers, he tugged her upward, his strength incredible. She rose swiftly to him, the length of her smaller form pressed against his body. All her air rushed from her lungs when she gasped from the heat, the mercuric contact.

"We've got to get you dry."

He swept her into his arms, striding confidentially to the horses. After he set her on her feet, he rummaged in the saddlebag retrieving two towels. He dropped one on the grass. Briskly, he rubbed her shoulder then lower covering territory he caressed earlier. He dried her legs then handed her the towel. "I'm sure you can finish. You mustn't take a chill."

Bending over at her waist she wrung her hair out before wrapping the towel around the long strands. "What now?"

His lazy slow smile coiled inside, caused her body to ache with potent need. Nothing she encountered beforehand prepared her for what was happening to her now. After Peter, she never thought to crave a man's kiss...his touch...intimacy. She'd been afraid of men. Somehow Deke was different. She never feared him, even that first day when he was in her apartment, teasing her with sexual innuendos.

Annie watched while he rubbed the towel on his chest. His muscles rippled, his belly contracting. He disappeared for a moment. When she saw him again, he wore dry buckskins. His shirt was open in the front revealing the hard wall of his chest. The need to explore assailed her. Heat flushed her cheeks. Embarrassing thoughts beset her.

She sucked air. When compared with Peter's masculine form, there was no comparison. Deke Sullivan was pure male animal, dangerous yet also kind. Gentle yet hard. Peter didn't care about anyone except himself. Deke cared about her, cared about so much.

With no trouble she could lose herself in the depth of his glorious dark eyes. "I...she swept her mouth with her tongue, leaving moisture behind. "I should get dry clothing."

"You should." His grin told her he was watching her, studying her

105

every move. If he decided on a course of action, he wouldn't change his mind.

After looking down at herself heat suffused her cheeks, hotter and brighter than before. Her hands didn't know where to cover first. Two small hands could not keep him from seeing all the glorious parts of her. His eye gleamed...darkened... Annie couldn't get to her clothing fast enough. She didn't know...the tree. Sprinting she covered the short distance to dress. Her gown along with her petticoats were not where she left them.

"Deke..." She peaked around the corner. "What have you done with my..."

He sauntered to her, his eyes mischievous. "This what you want?" He was holding out her gown along with her second set of underclothing. "You have to come and get them."

She was taken aback by the humor she saw in his expression. He was enjoying her discomfort. "Ass..."

His bark of laughter sent her anger boiling higher. "Been called that more than once." He dangled her gown in front of him, the fabric swinging, tempting. So far away.

She wanted to reach out then grab them. She also knew it would be useless to do so. "You can see me."

"Seen all of you before. Got nothin' left to show me that I haven't seen...well...that's not entirely true. There are parts..." He left the rest unsaid.

She grabbed at her gown. He turned swinging the dry pantalettes and chemise over his shoulder. He taunted...teased... Annie snorted. He walked away from her, putting distance between them.

Deke grinned shamelessly.

Not wishing to get any closer, she found her private spot behind the trees. Swiftly, she stripped off her wet garments then pulled her gown over her head. She groaned when she saw the tips of her breasts pushing against the fabric. There was nothing between her naked flesh and the gown. She would be no more clothed than she'd been in the water.

Despite the lack of clothing, her back straight, Annie walked from her spot behind the tree. She tilted her chin. Her voice quivering, she proceeded to vent her opinion of his shenanigans. Shaking her finger at him, she began, "I suppose you're pleased. A gentleman would never act this way."

Ignoring her comments, Deke held out a piece of fried chicken for her. "Hungry? I'm starved. Have a seat." He patted a place next to him. "You should have learned long ago I've never pretended to be a gentleman."

"Where is my underwear?" She poured herself a large glass of wine, filling the cup to the brim, all the while staring pointedly at him. She wanted to stamp her foot, understood doing so would never change the facts.

Lifting his broad shoulders, he commented, a twinkle in his dark eyes, "In my saddlebag. Put them back since it appeared you didn't want them." He bit into his piece of chicken chewing slowly while his gaze was riveted on her. When he finished, "Meade's a damn good cook, don't you think?" He gestured for her to try her food.

Annie tried to forget about her state of dishabille. The feat proved to be impossible. She drank the wine. The Bordeaux was delicious…sweet…heady. Just as it always was. After she sat next to him, she accepted the chicken along with the plate of potato salad. He held out a berry to her. When she tried to take it from him, he shook his head.

"What do you want this time?" Deke seemed to play games with her, with her fluctuating senses. This time she had no idea what he was getting at.

His charming grin disarmed her, charmed every nerve within. Sensuously, he ran the berry across her lips. Now he held the fruit inches away. "Open up, Little Darlin'" his voice sounded rich and dark, haunting her, bedeviling her body, her will. He captivated her, intrigued. Enchanted. Thrilled. He understood exactly what to do.

She touched her tongue to her top lip in anticipation for the berry or whatever he planned next uncertain if she wanted the sweet juices of fruit or his lips on hers again. His touch was infinitely sweeter and hotter than the food he enticed with.

"Decide, Little Darlin'."

Opening her mouth before closing her eyes, she waited. Nothing happened. Her lashes flew open, questioning him. Confused further by his behavior, Annie no longer understood what exactly he wanted from her. He was such an enigma of changing standards.

"Want to see your eyes. If we are going to share kisses, don't close yourself off from me, Annie." He cleared his throat. "Open…"

Feeling like a fish waiting for the hook she opened her mouth. He chuckled, letting the berry settle on her lips. He followed the delicacy with a hard open-mouth kiss. She sucked air, gasped in surprise. He demanded and cajoled expecting the same type of response. When his tongue explored, nipped with his teeth and laved she fenced with him. She rubbed her tongue across his, felt the friction. The kiss seemed magical, enchanting. Only with Deke did she feel these wonderful sensations that swept an inferno throughout.

A broken sound.

Soft mewls of pleasure.

Shattered air inside her lungs.

Annie wound her fingers around his neck then into the silken strands of his hair. She sighed softly into his mouth. Deke inched his way lower. He found tender territory down her neck then across her collarbone. Kissing her along her shoulder, he nudged the fabric of her dress downward then lower still. Beneath the dress she wore nothing except her skin. He knew that. Had contrived the situation. This was no accident. Suddenly, she was terrified of what might follow. Never before had he been quite so bold. He dared what he wanted. She'd known another man like that.

The image of Peter flashed in her head. "No!" Annie pushed on his shoulders, frantic to put distance between them. Slowly, Deke withdrew, a frown of concern creasing his brow. Her nipple now hard, elongated and damp from his attention. She gasped at the image then stared hard at him.

With a quirked eyebrow, he looked at her then her breast. His voice soft, butter smooth. As if he read her mind, understood her deepest, darkest fears. He touched her gently, ran his knuckles along the outside of one breast. "I'm not Peter. You have to look at me. Know I'll never hurt you. I'm nothing like him. Know that I will always stop if you say the word."

Closing her eyes, she sipped air then one more time. On a wobbly breath of air, she spoke her true feelings. Annie wanted him to understand. "I..." she swallowed the lump of fear the image generated "know that. It's hard though. I'm not afraid of you. It's just the memories that flood my head."

His voice was harsh before he softened the tone. "You need to forget about that man. He's your past. I'm your future. Think only of me."

Once more, he coaxed with gentle kisses down her neck back to her mouth, nipping, savoring. The kiss was deep, long, intoxicating. He pulled away. "Can you do that? Think just of me."

Annie shivered, her body quivering deliciously with each new caress. Oh, how she wanted to forget all that was Peter, all that he did to her. She nodded yes to his question before she forgot everything except the way his touch felt. Her stomach flipped over, coiled with anticipation. He would pursue her further, urge her to give herself to him. She didn't know if she could do that.

Once again, he tugged on the fabric of her gown. The dress slipped below both her breasts. When his lips closed over a hardened pinnacle, she gasped. He sucked and laved with teeth and tongue. She arched to his exploration enjoying the pleasure sensations. The moment seemed to be filled with lightness as well as sunshine that would only grow hotter.

"You are so beautiful." His touch was light as he explored the bared skin to her navel.

"Bah...! I'm certain you tell that to every woman you want to bed," she whispered, dismayed to feel such depth of jealousy at the thought of Deke with another woman.

He was experienced. He didn't have to tell her he wasn't a virgin for her to comprehend the truth.

"I've never told that to a woman I've slept with and I've never brought a woman to my lake before. Never swam nearly naked with another woman, you may rest assured. You are the only one, unique in every way. Very special."

She closed her eyes, suddenly wishing she dare believe him. Dismayed and angered by the force of emotions she felt. She was as angry with herself as she was with him because she realized she wanted to be with him, wanted him to teach her what it would be like to have a man make love to her. She'd never known anything except force. Fear still encapsulated her, kept her from giving him all he deserved.

Unhurriedly, he pulled away from her touching her cheek tenderly with the back of his hand. After that she felt his mouth pressing against the pulse at her throat felt his hands stroking her breasts. She lay perfectly still, swallowing trying very hard not to want…

His lips teased, caressing her flesh. His hand rested on her belly. The muscles constricted. At the juncture of her thighs, she ached. She ran her hands along his chest, felt the crisp softness of his hair.

She didn't dare breathe. Her dress bunched at her hips. His hand roamed across her breasts moving slowly downward along her hips, across her thighs, behind her knees. She kept her eyes closed afraid if she opened them the man touching her would not be Deke. She stiffened when his hand rested at the juncture of her thighs.

Unexpectedly, he stopped. Her lashes flew open, confused. She'd wanted him to make love to her. No, she was afraid to succumb to him, to another man. He became motionless as if he suddenly realized she wasn't ready. She wanted him and yet…

After he sat up, he pulled her dress up from her ankles, adjusted the bodice. The darkness of his eyes unnerved as well as thrilled her. It pleased her to know he wanted her. He stopped though. Deke was not going to make love to her, at least not at this moment.

Her lashes fluttered against her cheeks for an instant before she opened them again. "I'm sorry," she spoke faintly, truly regretting she couldn't give him all that he wanted all that she wanted in return.

"Peter?" he queried the name sounding to her more as a demand than a question. "Forget him!"

Now his voice was harsh. He sounded angry. Instead, the next words were whispered to her so very soothing. "He's a ghost of your past who haunts you. If you let him, he'll rule your entire life. I'm nothing like that man. If you allow it to happen, you and I can create a future together."

Annie smoothed her skirts, knowing his words as the truth. Deke was right. He was nothing like Peter. "You stopped though? I didn't say no."

Annie knew she was accusing him when all he did was read her body.

"Your body told me no. I didn't want to stop touching you. Give me a reason and I'll make love with you, to you. Give you more pleasure than you could have ever imagined. I'll let you ravish me if you like. All of the above. You can have *carte blanche* with my man's body if you ask. Only if you forget Peter, though. Your eyes tell a tale all their own. Forget the loathsome man, Little Darlin'. He doesn't merit your thoughts."

He pulled her into his arms, her back against the wide expanse of his chest. His hands were splayed across her belly sending shock waves of explosive need through her. Even though he ceased his roaming fingers and mouth, Deke still toyed with her senses, her nerves stretching thin. He would continue the coaxing in a heartbeat if she gave him one indication that she would welcome the sweet-talking.

"It's too soon."

Her whisper troubled her. So very much she wanted to tell him she thought only of him when he touched her. That was the problem. She didn't have an issue when he kissed her. His kisses were nothing like Peter's kisses. The difficulties came when he did other things, when his hand roamed between her legs.

"True."

His hand rose to a spot beneath the curve of her breast. He toyed with the underside. "Your flesh feels like silk and satin. So soft...so very soft."

"We barely know each other."

Annie understood the excuse for what it was. She knew him better than any other man of her acquaintance. Before she allowed him inside her body, she should know him better than that.

"True."

One thumb enticed the tip to harden again. The sound of his voice rumbled against her back.

She squirmed. Her head fell back against his chest. "Deke..."
"Yes?"

Both his large hands once again splayed across her belly. His fingers reached across, touching her hip bones.

"Are you starting again? Do you still want to make love to me?"

Her voice paper-thin wobbled for a few seconds. She felt as if she skated on thin ice even though she understood above all else he wouldn't take what she wasn't willing to give.

"Yes…if you can forget the other man. I don't want you seeing Bentley when I'm deep inside you. Don't want you calling out his name when I give you pleasure."

"What if…?"

"You tell me no?" Once again, his fingers drew her skirt along her legs higher then higher still. "Are you going to?"

She felt the ripple of his long sigh across the top of her head. "I'm not ready."

If she could manage to convince herself of the opposite, she was though. Aroused, excited, she wanted him more than she'd wanted anything. Annie couldn't bring herself to tell him she wanted him. The words seemed wanton went against all she'd ever been taught.

"Tomorrow?"

"Maybe."

His voice softened. He spoke as if in pain as if by denying him, she tortured him. Perhaps she did because she felt pain. "Do you want to see my home. We will have to stay the night. I'm not going to take you back to town in the dark. If I take you to my home, I'll consider that an invitation for more love play. The gesture will mean you're agreeing to forget the bastard who hurt you and you will also be agreeing to sleep with me."

"My reputation?" she queried realizing it would no longer be pure and chaste.

Everyone would believe she slept with Deke whether she did or not. Life as she knew it in Boston would continue. For her there would be no escaping the gossip. Men would call her names. They would expect certain things from her.

"Pure as the driven snow. Told Taylor I was taking you to Aspen Falls. Seems they wanted another physician's opinion on a very important diagnosis. You were the obvious choice. Told him we would be back sometime in the next two days."

"You lied?"

He expected her to stay at his ranch for two days? She never agreed to that. She wanted to stay with him forever.

"Not entirely. I've named my ranch Aspen High. You see…I value your opinion about everything. I have an urgent matter that needs your tender care."

He caught her hand in his, settling the palm on his erection. "I might need your help before the night is finished, before the sun peeks its bright head over the Rockies."

She turned, one hand on his chest as she pulled her other hand from under his. "What is your game, Deke Sullivan. In my opinion, all men have a game they play. Though yours does appear rather obvious. Are there rules I've no idea about? If so, you need to tell me before I commit to something I might regret."

"The game is about you as well as me. It concerns our future if we are to have one. At this point in time there are no rules." He smiled, his hand now resting on her shoulder teasing the fabric of her dress lower once again. "My plan is to love you thoroughly. Given up on convincing you to go home. If you're going to stay here…" He lifted his broad shoulders a masculine gesture, his smile broad and so very charming. "Nothing more, nothing less. I'm not devious, Little Darlin'. You've guessed my intent. Haven't made what I want a secret. For tonight at least we belong together. As for the future, I don't have a crystal ball that I can see into."

Annie wasn't certain of her feelings. She wanted him to want her…to love her. Slowly, the fleeting images of Peter that were standing in her way grew dimmer. At thirty she didn't have a lot of qualms about saving herself for the right man. She passed that age a long time ago. Peter saw to the demise of her romantic dreams. It was possible letting him love her would be…would be wonderful, cathartic. He wasn't about to take anything she wasn't willing to give. Doing so would contradict a lifetime of teaching. Deke didn't believe she belonged here. Why did he pursue her this way? She had too many questions. At the moment, the answers didn't truly make a difference to her.

Tira, her stepmother, made a bargain with her father. They were together as a couple long before they wed. All her life she worked so hard for people to think of her as someone other than a whore's daughter. Now, she was about to put her future reputation in the hands of this man, this very special man. She wanted to stop the intense feelings his very essence created. Her body as well as her mind was in violent turmoil. She also wanted to understand the beauty of the right man making love to her. Was Deke the right man? At this moment she thought so. She would have to decide. He made that fact perfectly clear. Whatever happened was her decision.

A thin breath of air rippled into her lungs. Her body hummed with the sexual feelings he began to teach her. She ached for him. "You haven't made your thoughts concerning me a secret. The first weeks we spent together you told me in no uncertain terms that you believed I should flee back to the city. Said I didn't belong in the Rockies. Have you changed your mind?"

"The question is relevant." He stroked his jaw, his gaze focused on her eyes. "Did, didn't I? It's possible I've decided I was wrong. Guess one could say I have changed my mind, at least to some degree. Suppose I'm hoping I can keep you safe. I've discovered I want you. You're the most beautiful woman I've ever met."

She sat against him again. He handed her more wine. She tried to ease her breathing. The attempt wasn't working. "You don't care about my past."

How could any man want a tainted woman for anything more than his mistress? She wasn't going to become any man's mistress, not even Deke's.

His long fingers tightened around her waist. "If I cared about your past, I would expect you to care about mine. I lived with the Cheyenne. I did everything they did. Most whites think of the Cheyenne as savage. Do you believe I'm a savage?"

She laughed softly. He looked as if he never heard her laugh before. Perhaps she never laughed with him. "Sometimes. Sometimes you act very savage, a savage beast. No, I don't think you are a savage. Peter is and he has no ties to the Cheyenne."

Suddenly, he tickled her, pushing her onto her back. She laughed again, setting her hands against his chest as if she wanted him to leave her. She didn't. He kissed her hard and quick before pulling her back to sit in front of him.

"When am I ever a savage?" he asked mockingly his gaze roaming heatedly over her.

She discovered his warmth seared her to her toes.

"You suggested the label," she told him indignantly. "I just agreed. You were a bit ferocious just then."

"Harsh, angry at times, demanding because in this country one has only an instant to make decisions that could mean life or death. I know this country because of my upbringing. There is a lot I know because the Cheyenne taught me how to survive in this untamed land. When my uncle found me, my life changed. He sent me to school, insisted I learn to read and write to speak English fluently. The man also insisted I follow in his footsteps. Sent me to West Point. After I graduated, I was cavalry. Spent some time in the west. I was a liaison between the tribes for the army. Since I spoke several languages, I was important to the cause for both native as well as white."

She rested her head against his chest. Her thoughts probably as confused as his had been at the time. "Did you ever go to war against your tribe, your people? It seems you were straddling two very different worlds. Either side could have killed you."

"No, suppose luck was on my side. Mostly, I fought the Seminole in Florida. Once I served my time, I went home then resigned my commission. Couldn't live with the Cheyenne again. I changed too much. I was too white in thought as well as my skin color. Don't ever forget in many ways I still think like the People."

Annie concentrated on all he told her. She had so many questions she didn't know where to begin. She remembered the half-breed, Belt, he spoke of. Curiosity was something she sometimes had too much of. "Who is Belt? You're looking for him. Why?"

When he started to speak, she heard so much pain, anguish in his voice. She thought perhaps she pried too much. Against her, she felt his body stiffen, his muscles growing taut. After a long pause, he began,

115

"Once he was my blood brother along with another man. He cut himself off from the tribe when he murdered a woman. The People don't commit murder against their own."

"Murder?" Surprised by the revelation, she mulled that over in her mind for some time while she listened to the even cadence of his breathing. She knew the tribes warred with the settlers. They killed all the time, swept into homesteads and annihilated entire families. "Who did he murder?"

For several seconds, Deke looked away. His expression changed. Finally, he spoke. "My adoptive mother. One might say she was in the wrong place. Others believe she fought with him about me. You see, he no longer trusted me. Belt wanted me outlawed from the tribe. Seems since I entered the white world, he argued that I would betray them."

"Was the deed intentional?"

"I thought so. Belt denied the fact. Still, when the question was pursued, he fled the camp. By doing so, he sealed his fate pronouncing himself guilty. His actions condemned him in the eyes of the tribe. He was culpable." Absently, Deke ran his knuckles along her cheek then her neck.

She pushed against his chest seeking the warmth as well as security of his body. Perhaps they both needed healing. Annie didn't know if she possessed the means to help a person when there was so much lacking in herself. She wanted to be the one to give him more reasons to smile. She wanted to be the woman to give him a reason to love again. She sensed he ran from the possibility of love just as she did. Annie thought she loved Peter before he betrayed her.

"Now Belt continues on a lawless path. He's wanted dead or alive all over the west. I've reason to believe he's holed up in a camp near here. I also think he's the one who sent you the message. Why is beyond me. Unless there is something terribly wrong, he would never expose himself the way he did."

"So, you want to collect the reward? Bring the man in to stand trial?"

"Yes, to the trial. He has a great deal to account for. I want him to pay for some of his sins against mankind. No, to the reward." The following pause was long. "I don't like the fact he knows about you. Knows that I'm protective where you are concerned. He must have..." Deke stuffed his hands through his hair. "He must have seen us when I brought you from Fort Laramie to Denver City. He would know about us when I chased after you the night you were supposed to meet him. I'm certain he watched. Must have known when you turned away you were afraid."

When his fingers left her body, she felt cold, bereft. The thought seemed wrong yet he brought the fact up. "You think he might have seen you escorting me? Why would he care?"

"Belt knows you're the doctor at Denver City. I'm the sheriff. That makes you vulnerable. He can use you to get to me. It's what he wants. The man is seeking revenge for his dismissal from the tribe. In some ways, I was the cause of all his problems. Revenge is a powerful motive."

"Someone would do that? Use a woman to get to a man?"

Annie knew her words were true. Peter used her just because he could. He used her for his personal gain. Gave her to his friends the one and only time he had control just to stroke his ego. He enjoyed using women. He enjoyed seeing their pain. He enjoyed watching his friends take her.

"This situation is nothing like Boston. Belt is dangerous in a different way. He won't hesitate to kill if he's forced into a tight spot." His murmured words got her to rethink everything she knew and understood about men.

He was wrong in that thought. "Peter used me then he let his friends have free access to my body. Peter is a dangerous man. Because Peter allowed it to happen, I was just as vulnerable there in the city as I might be here. Did you think men were different if they lived in a well-populated area? If they are rich?" Her words were spoken with disdain. The bitterness in her voice was evident.

It appeared he made up his mind. Bluntly he spoke, his words unforgiving, "It's time to go. The ranch is a short distance from here. It won't take long." He stood extending his hand for her. "Once we get there, we can figure out what happens next between the two of us. I'm not at all positive either of us knows what we want."

She was going to his home. There was nothing he could do or say that would fix things if anyone discovered what she did, even if she chose not to sleep with him. He would never offer marriage, not that she wanted to wed any man. She would never vow to obey.

Blind loyalty or obedience was not for her.

~ * ~

Grinning, thinking of his plans now that the he received the information he sought, Peter rubbed his hands together, delighted with what he read in the letter he opened a few minutes ago. He would find Annie. When he did, he would teach her about devotion as well as allegiance to the man who was willing to set her up in luxury. He found he wanted her more than any woman he'd ever met. The woman was a fool, a gorgeous fool, smart as the dickens too. After he found her in Denver City, he would drag her back to Boston. She didn't belong in the wilderness. Didn't matter to him if she came kicking and screaming, she would come with him. She would be his mistress as he planned from the first moment she waltzed into his life. When he learned of her parentage, his idea was cemented in his mind. Annie would service whoever he told her to. Among his friends, he wasn't possessive. He liked giving female gifts to his buddies, enjoyed sharing. Always pleasing to watch.

To Peter, it seemed he wanted her from the first instant he saw her. In the arms of one of the professors at her medical school, she was whirling around the dance floor. When they stopped for punch, she flirted shamelessly with the young swains standing around the punch bowl. She was wild and untamed, beautiful, too damn beautiful. He needed her. Both her mother along with her stepmother were whores, willing to give themselves to a man without benefit of marriage. Jamie Lundin did eventually wed Tira. Nonetheless, with those women as role models what else could Annie be?

He hardened with lust watching her sway in time to the music. Her bosom was large, bountiful. She would overflow his hands. One of his friends nudged him, pointing to her as if he had the same idea. Usually, he was the man who procured the next woman for their use. Peter wondered just how long it would be until he grew bored with the luscious woman he was watching now. He rarely shared until he did grow tired of the woman. Perhaps with this little lady, it would be more fun to share at the same time he was having her. A threesome or even a foursome would be different, unique. Titillating. They could watch, cheer each other on, comment on technique.

Facing away from the room, he readjusted his trousers. After he felt more in control, he strode to her. She was tall. She came to his nose. That was something he would have to overlook. There were ways. When she lay on her back, her height wouldn't matter.

Surprising her, he picked up her hand, bent to gallantly kiss the back. Saw the gentle response in the darkening of her eyes along with the slight tremor of her form. She responded quickly to his polite advance. His pulse leapt. "I'm Peter Bentley."

He looked into her eyes then let his gaze settle on swell of her bosom. She tugged at her hand. Peter let it go. He waited for her answering response. When she didn't offer him her name, he asked, "Who are you?"

She flushed a becoming shade of pink. Turning her head for an instant she looked the other way. "Annie Lundin."

"Ah, Annie a fine name for a fine woman. Would you like to dance?" He wanted to hold her in his arms, test the ripeness of her curves against him, fondle then tug on the hardened tips of her breasts. He needed to taste all of her. If she allowed him to do so, he would waltz her into the alcoves to steal a kiss, the first of many.

She nodded, "that would be fine. You will have to watch your feet though. Seems I've two left ones when it comes to dancing."

He laughed softly, "I doubt that. Watched you dance with the older man. Never stepped on his feet once."

Pulling her into his arms, he expertly guided her around the room. The music changed to a livelier tune. He found the secluded spot he intended, guiding her into the private space. It was dark. The night air chill. Stars sparkled in the velvet blackness above. They were alone. The railing pressed against her back. Her hands rested on his shoulder, pushing as if she wanted to get away from him.

"Peter, what are you doing? Don't believe we should be outside alone."

"Oh, my dear girl we should be right here. Alone is best."

"Take me inside," she tried to move away from him.

His hands tightened around her waist holding her in place. She was flush against him. Her lush breasts pushed against his chest. "Annie," he murmured softly. His hand drifted along her spine, along the sides of her body. "You've kissable lips. May I kiss you?" He didn't wait for her to answer. His mouth pressed against hers. His hand slipped from her waist to her backside, tugging her against his stiff member.

"Peter..."

She struggled in his arms, pushing at him, wriggling against him, exciting him even more. Annie was a fine specimen of woman. She would be his soon.

A kiss first.

With his teeth and tongue, he pressed her lips open. He was inside her now, her heat boiling, sending him straight into the tempest he created within himself. She seemed eager now that he convinced her what was happening would feel good to her. He stopped to look at her. He wanted her to return the kiss. He would have to go lightly. "Let me kiss you, truly kiss you, Annie Lundin."

Peter was watching her eyes. She appeared dazed, a bit disoriented. Annie was perfect. She was obviously innocent. He would be her first lover. He did enjoy virgins. She had no idea how to kiss. He would teach her what he liked.

Her small hands rested on his shoulders, her fingers clinging to his jacket. He pushed her so she was bent over the railing, needing to hold on to him so she wouldn't fall. She no longer struggled. Her fingers tightened even more on his shoulders. "I-I don't know what you mean. Truly kiss?"

"That's obvious. I'm going to kiss you again. Open up for me, sweetheart. Open up those pleasantly kissable pink lips of yours. Let me explore you. Don't push me away. I won't like it if you do."

Peter tried to soothe knowing full well he would get more from her with sweet talk. Sometimes he didn't have the patience he needed to charm women who knew nothing of men. If he wanted Annie, he would have to control himself, bide his time until she gave herself to him. He couldn't frighten her.

"I don't think this is the right place or time," she murmured, her breath coming in short little pants that thrilled Peter. The pulse at the base of her neck beat hard and fast.

"What better time? We are alone. The moon along with the stars are very romantic. Do you want to kiss me as much as I do you?"

"Maybe," she sighed faintly, her tiny fingers wrapping around his neck, gliding against his flesh as if she wanted him.

He understood she wasn't immune to him as well as his advances. Gently, he brushed his lips against hers, nibbled softly in hopes of deepening the kiss then taking all that he wanted, not tonight but soon. If he wanted her, he would have to move with sensitive care and concern. She wasn't going to fall into his arms as he previously thought. Peter never gave up on a conquest. Come hell or high-water, Annie Lundin would be his, in his bed before the week ended. He would taste as well as sample all the scented charms she possessed. She would never refuse all he wanted to give her.

"Open, Annie, let me show you what a kiss can be all about."

He wheedled, cajoled until she gave into the pressure of seduction. Gradually, she opened for him.

He pressed his tongue inside her lips, explored the heat, the fire that was Annie. She moaned delicately. Passing his hand across her breast, he smiled with her gasp. He pulled away, knowing when he was ahead of the game. She needed him now. He would leave her wanting and expecting something more.

That was all for the night. He would make certain he saw her again the next day or the day after. He left her with a kiss to her nose. Her mouth was swollen from his ardent attention. His body hardened once he gained entrance to her sultry heat. This was torture for him. In the long run, his patience would pay off. His next step would be to touch her breasts, weigh them in his hands, taste and suckle then if she became more willing, he would take her home. After that, he would install her in a townhouse purchased for her use as well as his pleasure.

Hell, he didn't even care if she continued her study to become a doctor. In that respect, she could do as she pleased. Where he was concerned, all she needed to do was be at home in the evenings to see to his immediate pleasure and needs.

Chapter Five

"Deke, I can't see my hands, can't see the trees or anything else for that matter. There is no light. The moon isn't even shining from behind all these trees. How can you stay on the trail? A branch just slapped me in the face," Annie said sounding petulant as well as winey. "Are you certain you know where you are going? Thought you told me it was only five miles. Seems we've been riding for hours."

"A short distance, Little Darling. We're only about five minutes away from my ranch. I'll warm you up with hot coffee laced with a generous portion of whiskey when we get there. You just follow me." Suddenly, he had a different idea. He slowed his horse to ride beside her. He leaned close. "I've never heard you complain so much. Your crabbiness is rather endearing, a side of you I've never seen before. Gives me a chance to do this…"

In a swift move he was certain she didn't see coming, he reached for her, swept her from her mare onto his lap. She shrieked. Batted at his hands. She laughed for a moment before she pounded her small fists on his chest. "Deke! Stop this. You can't ride with me on your lap. I'll fall. You'll fall. The horse will stumble. We'll end up eating dirt. I weigh too much."

"I won't let anything happen to you." His laughter, he understood, might anger her. In his arms she stiffened, her back rigid against his chest. "Turn sideways. Rest your pretty little head on my chest. When you are in my arms, you won't be getting' any branches in your face or anywhere else on your precious fragrant body. Relax now, I know it's dark. We should have left the lake earlier. My fault that I got caught up in kissing your lovely soft lips. I'm not going to allow anything bad to happen to you."

He was thrilled when she did give over to his command and placed her head on his chest. He ran his hands along her arms, understanding the night was growing chill. She didn't have appropriate clothing. In that he didn't prepare ahead of time. They did not plan for a ride in the evening. High in the mountains the nights could become frigid even if the day was hot enough to swim. He was a fool. Her teeth were chattering. When the sun dipped behind the mountains, the temperature always plummeted.

Even if he didn't have ulterior motives, his home was closer to the pond than the town of Denver City. He knew before they left, they wouldn't have the time to return to town. While he wasn't bothered riding in the darkness, he didn't want her to fear the nights. Evenings in the woods were precious. All manner of life came out that one didn't see during the day. A hoot of an owl, the swoop of a falcon after his prey. Cougars roamed the countryside in the darkness. The rustle of rabbits along with mice as they scurried for protective shelter could be heard. While the nights could be peaceful, they could also be dangerous.

"Somehow, I know you won't. I trust you," she murmured as she held onto one of his arms.

Annie pressed closer to him seeming to snuggle against him seeking the warmth his body offered. Next to him she felt cold, too cold. She was shivering her teeth chattering, constantly.

He wrapped his arm around her, pulling her close while he guided his horse with his knees. Her mare followed behind as if she understood where her next meal and warm stall would come from. At the moment, the only sounds were hoofbeats along with each of her breaths. Well, he heard the rattling of her teeth too.

Her simple words of confidence filtered through him, pleasing him. It had been a long time since he felt so deeply and intensely for another human being, especially a woman. His first wife died a long time ago, eons it seemed. He'd been alone in the world ever since. Deke liked his life that way after the woman he loved passed on. Now, when he looked at Annie, he barely remembered his wife. When he stared into Annie's eyes, he wanted to forge a new life with this woman. Unfortunately, they both came with baggage, his dangerous in nature. If she committed her life to him, she wouldn't understand what she was getting into.

Could he ask another woman to marry him, to share his life in this wilderness, to risk her life? Anything could happen. Chills swept through him. This existence already was the death of one woman he loved. Did he love her or just want her? At the moment he didn't know the difference between lust and love.

Was there a difference?

Maybe the two sentiments shared some characteristics.

"We are going to be at the ranch soon. You will accept what I tell my people about our relationship? No one will spread gossip about our private lives."

He wondered what she would think when she saw all the people who worked for him. They were all friends of the People. None spoke English. They would tell no tales. Still, they would witness the fact he slept with her. At least he hoped she would agree to share his bed. When they were at the lake, she'd agreed.

Women changed their minds.

He wouldn't force the issue. Knowing her history he understood she would need time to adjust to a new and very different relationship. Deke realized he wanted more than one or two nights with Annie. A lifetime would not be long enough. If she conceded to all he asked, he would quit his job, concentrate on ranching. For the longest time, ranching had been his dream. The dream died with his first wife.

"Good, even with your body heat I'm freezing."

Her teeth chattered. She reached her hand to him, touched his chin.

He jerked from the glacial contact. His concern for her raced to his head. They had not been riding that long. He felt her hands. She was right, they were icy. "Why didn't you tell me?"

Her feet as well as the rest of her must be just as cold. She didn't wear clothing suitable for travel at night. Her shoes were delicate slippers not sturdy riding boots. She wore nothing under her dress, not even underwear, because he'd withheld the extra clothing. At the time he believed it to be a good idea. He enjoyed thinking of her naked beneath the gown. He was a damn bastard.

"I just did," she spoke softly.

He didn't like the thoughts shooting to his brain. She should have told him a hell of a lot sooner. Deke nudged his horse to a trot, hoping to reach the ranch house before she froze to death. She would need to get warm. First thing would be to order a hot bath along with the hot coffee and whiskey he thought of earlier.

Annie wrapped her arms around him. Her head nestled against his chest. When the stable boy came out to greet him, he spoke in Cheyenne. Told the lad to take care of the horses. With Annie still in his arms he dismounted, strode quickly to the main house.

He was greeted. He ordered the necessary items sent to his room. Taking the stairs two at a time, he reached the master chamber. He set her on a chair in front of the fire. Flames glowed and danced in the grate sending shimmers of golden light in the room across her face. The warmth settled around him. He hoped the heat encompassed her as well. He couldn't believe he'd been so shortsighted.

Hurriedly, he hunkered down in front of her. After slipping her shoes from her feet, he held each one in his hands until they warmed. The tub was brought into the room to be set near the fire. Towels were hung near the flames to heat. She looked nervous. "I'm not going to disrobe and ravish you." He almost laughed, the look in her beautiful blue eyes endearing.

"What are we doing?" Her entire body shook with cold or fear. He wasn't at all certain. When she held out her hand, it quivered. She was still too cold.

"You are taking a bath to warm you up." He brought her hands to his lips, blew warm air on her fingers. "You are like an icicle."

"I did tell you." She retorted as if she wanted to defend her actions. "I can't help the fact I get cold so easily."

"Yes."

He didn't know quite what to say at that revelation. Annie told him after she was nearly frozen to death. She would have to do better in the future. The minute she felt the chill, she should have spoken to him.

"Yes?" She hit him on the shoulder. "You cad!"

"Is that better than ass?" he queried with a snort.

He wanted to laugh. Didn't dare until he understood exactly what she was feeling.

"No, yes, cad is better than ass. Just by a tiny hair."

He composed himself, thinking of the gravity of the situation. "I should have known sooner." He didn't understand how to teach her all the new things she would have to learn if she stayed. In this country, she wasn't self-sufficient. No one was. Just as he would have to lean on her for some things, she would have to rely on his skills and expertise on other matters. "You were freezing to death and I had no idea." His voice held an accusing note that was necessary. "Yes, you told me but not soon enough."

Her teeth were still chattering, her lips blue. Even the tips of her fingers were blue. Marie entered with steaming water filling the tub. The bath appeared heavenly. He'd love to share the heat with her. That would be for another time.

"Are you going to stay here?" Annie asked as she looked from his housekeeper to him. "I..." she caught her lip between her teeth. "Would it...?"

He somewhat understood her reservations. Could read her mind on this issue. As much as he would like to stay and enjoy watching her, he wouldn't. Not on this occasion. Deke understood she needed time to adjust to the newness of this situation. "No, you'll have privacy. I'm going downstairs to see what my cook can rustle up for us to eat. Are you hungry?" he asked softly. "You didn't eat much earlier."

She did laugh, her eyes twinkling as if she knew some joke, he didn't. "I don't eat much, Deke. You're going to have to get used to my miniscule appetite. Nonetheless, I am hungry."

"You are small. Guess you don't have much need for a lot of food."

"If I ate as much as you, well, then you'd probably be able to roll me down hills."

He would still love her. That thought jerked his mind in a new direction. She stood with her hands clasped in front of her when he walked backward from the room. "I'll be back in about ten minutes. You get warmed up. If there is anything you need or want, pull the bell cord. Maria will come see what it is you need."

He whistled as he walked down the steps thinking he must be in heaven. He didn't know what would happen tonight. Though he was optimistic. At the lake her response to him was hesitant yet packed with raw passion as well as laced with sexual curiosity. He reached the kitchen.

Bella was cooking something spicy, a Mexican dish that contained ground beef along with onions and jalapenos. He saw the tortillas freshly made sitting on the counter. His stomach rumbled in anticipation. Bella was wonderful, a magnificent cook. At times the food was a bit too spicy. Slowly over time, his pallet became used to the heat.

"That smells mouthwatering." He dipped a fork into the mixture, tasted. "If possible, better than mouthwatering. Not too spicy either. Don't think Annie is ready for your usual fare."

Bella swatted at his hand. In a different language she told him he needed to wait for dinner commenting on the fact she left out some of the heat because of his beautiful woman. Bella was as round as Annie thought she would be if she ate too much. He didn't care if she grew large, the more of her to touch and explore the better.

His cook's hair was turning white around the edges. She wore a black dress along with a white apron. Her eyes were dark, a very dark brown, her smile contagious. She turned her attention to the rice simmering on the stove.

"Be back in a few minutes," he told her.

Bella nodded seeming to understand what he was saying. "We will eat upstairs in the bedroom tonight." He winked understanding Bella would comprehend why he wanted the privacy.

When he passed the stairs, he looked up. Thoughts of Annie naked in the tub flitted through his ever-masculine brain. If he had his way, he'd race up, perhaps join her in the heated water. They could heat the liquid even more. Ah, but that wasn't their reality, at least not yet.

He told her he would give her privacy. He meant to do just that. Rushing her was not part of his plans for their burgeoning relationship. He wanted to move at a pace she was comfortable with. Tonight, after dinner he had plans. All his employees would be in bed, retired for the night. At the crack of dawn, they would return to work.

Outside, he leaned against the porch railing staring off into the night sky. The wind changed from earlier this afternoon. They would be in for snow soon, not uncommon for the middle of June. One of his old friends, a stable hand, came to stand beside him. They talked for a while, spoke of the weather. Talked about him coming to stay at the ranch permanently.

A lad followed. The boy, Angel, came from his village. He was going to be twelve in two months. His father died in a raid against the crow. His mother gave birth to a child two years ago. The crow were the natural enemies of the Sioux and the Cheyenne. Angel jumped at the chance to come with him to his ranch. The boy wanted to see more of the world. Everyone understood more settlers would come west. The natives would be pushed away from the plains ever higher into the Rocky Mountains. Deke knew the government would continue to go back on their word concerning the treaties they signed. First hand, he'd seen this particular scenario happen too many times.

Angel wanted to be like him, a law man not a rancher. The thing was Deke didn't want to be the sheriff forever. Angel wanted him to teach him how to shoot and draw fast. He wasn't about to teach him how to become a fast gun. In his opinion, that wasn't a profession any young man should want to excel at. At the ranch, Deke took Angel under his wing, guiding him, teaching him English. The boy would learn quickly. He was bright, astute at so many things.

Deke looked to the summer sky. The branches from the trees covered most of the sky. A few stars twinkled above. He would teach Annie to find her way by the stars, the big and little dipper, the north star. She should understand how to save herself if she got lost in the woods if for some reason, he wasn't with her. The stars would be her street signs. She would learn what she could forage from the earth along with what she couldn't. She would survive.

If Belt had taken her, the half breed would not have allowed her to live, not if she saw the camp. Deke didn't think he would murder her. No, he would put her somewhere in the forest. Annie wouldn't have any idea how to find her way home. There were no road maps in the forest unless one knew where to look. Annie did not.

The unexpected premonition of danger terrified him spitless.

Chills slithered down his spine as he thought on her fear if something like that happened. Suddenly, the hair on the back of his neck stood on end. Someone watched. He turned quickly.

Nothing.

No one.

Annie…?

He wanted to see her, to touch her make certain no harm came to her.

Belt!

His heart thundered. What if the man found his way into the house? Deke raced inside then up the steps. Barging into the room, the door banged against the wall. He sucked in a hard rough breath of air as he searched the place, every nook and cranny.

He stopped short when he caught sight of her. God, she was beautiful. She stole his breath. Caused his heart to cease beating.

Annie sat on the hearth, brushing her hair, wrapped in a towel. The ivory of her shoulders glowed where the light from the fire touched upon her. When the door hit the wall, she jumped then gasped in surprise. Her eyes were wide, pools of blue. Shadows of red and orange from the fireplace shimmered around her casting her creamy white flesh in vibrant colors.

He leaned against the wall, watching her, feeling contrite as well as apologetic. Terrifying her had been the last thing on his mind. "I'm sorry I frightened you. That wasn't my intent when I flew into the room."

He couldn't tell her of the strange sensation that assailed him. Belt could still be out there watching waiting for a vulnerable moment. He wasn't afraid for himself only for Annie.

"You did…frighten me. That wasn't well done of you." With one hand she clung to the towel. Her lips were no longer blue, just pink, rosy begging for kisses. "You shouldn't be here. I'm not wearing anything…" She hesitated then for several seconds while they stared at each other. "Why did you rush in here?"

A wide grin spread across his face. "Seems you have a towel to cover you." He imagined her beneath the meager covering. He'd seen her breasts, touched them. While he had not seen her wearing nothing at all, he would soon. Her cheeks were flushed with heat, an endearing shade of rose. He wanted to see if the tops of her breasts were also colored in that bewitching shade. Thankfully, she was no longer blue anywhere.

"Could..." She swiped her tongue across her lips leaving a trail of moisture behind. "Could you retrieve my pantalettes along with my chemise? I could get dressed. Believe they are still in your saddlebags."

"I could. Why would I want to do so? You're a delightful picture just as you are now. I've a robe you could wear while we eat. I promise it will cover all of you."

Looking at her Deke had trouble sipping air. His body sprang to life wanting her desperately. Heat flooded him, burned. Unknowingly, she tortured him. Thoughts of her wearing his clothing in addition her bear flesh touching the robe left his body steal hard with need.

"I don't have any other clothing. If we don't go back tomorrow, what am I going to do?" She lifted her shoulders, the towel slipping slightly with the gentle movement. She tugged the cloth back into place.

This was perfect for his plans. He winked at her. She shot him a scowl as if she read his mind. Most likely she did. "I could keep you in bed for the duration. You wouldn't need anything to wear."

She turned from him. He wondered what exactly she was thinking. Was the proposition to preposterous? Distasteful. He didn't think so. She would disagree. Seconds ticked by while she seemed to consider different phrasing to his suggestions.

Swirling to meet his gaze, her cheeks pinker from embarrassment he assumed. "Do any of the people who work for you have anything I could wear? Could that be a possibility? Don't want to remain naked or nearly so."

"No, I'll fetch your underwear. It won't take but a moment."

He ran his hands though his hair wondering if he dared mention his wife. If they were to stay at the ranch for any length of time, he would have to do so. He cleared his throat understanding she already knew of her existence. How she would feel about wearing her clothing was something else entirely. "My wife...my well, she was about your size. Possibly you are taller. The skirts will be above your ankles. Since I left the ranch as soon as she was buried, I didn't get rid of her clothing. Do you mind too much?"

Even to his ears he sounded hesitant and uncertain. Why would anyone want to wear a dead woman's clothing?

She smiled at him. The gesture reassured. "That would be nice. No, I wouldn't mind at all. A dress would be preferable to nothing at all." She clutched at the towel. Her eyes focused on him. "Or your robe although the offer was kind."

Deke reached for the bell cord. "Maria will be happy to bring you something. I'll wait for you downstairs."

He fled the scene. If he didn't know himself better, he'd chastise himself for the lost opportunity. At heart he was a coward. This situation wasn't at all what he expected when he decided to take Annie swimming this afternoon.

What had he expected? She would fall into his arms as well as his bed? She never thought she would be coming to his ranch. Neither did he. Her presence here was just as much a surprise to him as it was to her.

Once again, he turned on his heel, leaving her to dress. He passed Maria on the way down the stairs. He stopped to tell her what Annie needed. Maria grinned wide then nodded. She seemed pleased that the misses would be staying for a few days. Maria would take care of Annie. She would see that she was clothed properly.

In the parlor, he poured himself a brandy. He sat down on a chair looking into the fire, actually staring at the flames. He was in a fog, dazed by the rapid change of events. This was what he wanted, what he orchestrated. Would she wish to give up her career to come live with him? She worked hard to become a doctor. He realized at that moment marriage was part of his plans. Perhaps that was expecting too much of her. Until he asked, he had no way of knowing. It was too soon to propose a life together.

Deke finished the first brandy then went on to pour himself more. Tempted to race up the stairs so he could see her, he held himself still, sipping the amber liquid, twirling it within the crystal glass warming the liquid between his hands. The forced patience grated on his nerves.

Maria stopped by to tell him she found a few things for the sweetheart he brought here, his *novia* she assumed. Told him it was about time for him to move on to find someone else to share his life. He needed to fill his home with children and their laughter. She wanted him to stop risking his life by chasing Belt, the low-down polecat.

Waking up each morning with Annie by his side would be a dream come true. What made him think a sophisticated lady such as Annie Lundin would want anything to do with him? It wasn't too long ago he tried to convince her to return to Boston.

The slight sound from the doorway caught his attention. Startled, he looked up. Surprised too that he allowed his brooding to hinder his usual alert self. It was rare that man or beast could sneak up on him.

The tentative smile she graced him with sent a shaft of lust to his groin. She plucked at her skirts, staring at the hem. His gaze found purchase on the bodice of the gown. If the corsage was any smaller, she would overflow. He thought his robe might better protect her from his lecherous notions than this dress which clearly didn't fit her. His wife was smaller everywhere even though Annie was willow thin, there were places…

Deke tried valiantly not to laugh. He managed to subdue his humor with the barest suggestion of a half grin. Her face turned a gorgeous shade of crimson when she caught him staring at her breasts. When she tugged in a deep breath of air, he thought she would spill out, the sight delicious.

Maria strode in talking nonstop at Annie. Obviously, she was trying to reassure her. Annie didn't understand a word she spoke.

"Maria says you look fine. She also is telling you that she's going to fix a few gowns for you if we stay here longer. The dress you wore to my ranch is in the laundry along with your underclothing which she retrieved from my saddlebags."

Maria retrieved all the underclothing. That could mean only one thing. Annie was naked beneath the dress. Another delightful thought to fill his brain.

"T-tell her thank you."

Maria nodded appearing to understand the words. She smiled at her before she swept from the room.

"Maria has always been with me. She's been after me to quit my

133

job in town, settle down." Deke shrugged lifting his shoulders in a half-hearted gesture. "Until now, I haven't been ready to settle. Bella, my cook, has created an amazing dinner for us. She'll serve the tortillas and meat sauce in my bedroom in a half hour. What would you like to do until then?"

Annie sat, clearly made uncomfortable by the low cut of the dress. "Do we have to eat in the bedroom?"

"Yes."

He wanted privacy to talk or to seduce, whatever came to mind. They couldn't have the privacy or intimate conversations he wanted in the dining room. Both Maria along with Bella would hover, making certain they would have all the food and wine they needed. They would be in and out constantly.

"That's it? Yes?" She looked as if she would like to throw something his way. "No discussion on the matter?"

"Sherry? Whiskey?" He tried for politeness.

Soon her miff would have to be dealt with though he enjoyed the bits of anger she directed his way. She would learn once his mind was made up, he usually could not be swayed into taking a different direction.

"Whiskey."

She sat down in a chair next to his. Her hands were folded in her lap, her toes tapping. Maria did not bring her shoes. He'd like to see her toes closer. At this distance they looked adorable. At least no part of her was blue.

He poured her a hefty glass thinking she appeared ready to down the entire bottle. The drink would somewhat cool her temper unless he managed to rile her again. For the longest time, she didn't look at him.

Getting straight to her thoughts was important. So he could read her mood, he asked, "What are you thinking?"

"I need to go back first thing in the morning," she blurted her eyes widening with the statement. "The patients…"

"No!"

With the huge breath of air she inhaled, for a moment he thought he would get the delight of seeing the tender pink tips of her breasts move from behind the fabric. Swiftly, she tugged her gown up.

"No? You can't keep me here against my will."

"In this case, I can. You agreed to this outing. Have you changed your mind?"

He dearly hoped she was just feeling a bit out of her element. The dress was simply too revealing. She was too uncomfortable. If she thought about this afternoon, the thoughts would also discomfit her. He needed to ease her feelings of embarrassment. If he didn't, this evening could end in a disaster.

"I need to see my patients," she repeated more determinedly.

"An excuse that doesn't hold promise of becoming true. You have no patients to speak of, Annie." He leaned forward, his forearms resting on his thighs, his expression assuming a serious edge. "It's going to snow. I won't risk your life in a snowstorm. I'm not dictating to you. The weather will make traveling dangerous."

"It's summer. The storm can't be more than a few flakes. How do you know?"

The disbelief in her tone startled him. He wasn't used to being questioned.

Teaching an innocent to the ways of the mountain in this short of a time would be nearly impossible. "The wind changed. Snowfall might be light, might not be, we won't know until midmorning or later in the afternoon. Can't start the trek into town when travel might be detrimental to your health…and mine. You were nearly frozen to death on the short ride from the lake. You've nothing to wear including sturdy boots to keep your feet warm."

"Oh…"

Her dark lashes fell against her cheeks for a moment.

"More whiskey?" he asked when he noticed her glass was nearly empty. He wanted her relaxed then wondered just how relaxed he wanted her to become. He wanted all her faculties in place. Wanted to know when he made love to her, she was agreeing.

"No, I…"

"You?" he queried wondering once more her thoughts.

~ * ~

Annie didn't want to go home. Her wish was to be in his arms. She didn't understand why she was being so obnoxious or why she was making this scenario difficult for him. She was so out of her element she didn't know if she was coming or going. They both understood she would melt in his arms. At the lake she'd already done so. Tugging at her bodice seemed to make everything worse. When she gained a quarter inch, if she let go of the fabric, she lost a half an inch.

Deke didn't seem to be able to look anywhere else save her outrageously exposed breasts. A man shouldn't have to undergo such torture. She tugged a pillow from behind her before holding the softness against her chest. He lifted one of his elegantly arched brows when she did so. His slow easy smile told her he understood her ploy.

"That works," he said unable to stop the chuckle from disconcerting her more. "Can't see a thing of interest."

"You're staring at me."

She was going to ask why. She knew why. He told her several times how much he liked her breasts. How much he liked to taste them, kiss them. Honesty, she liked that too.

"Yes," he spoke softly a hint of laughter in his word. "What gave me away?"

"What is it with your short answers?"

Her annoyance with herself grew. She was acting like a shrew. It didn't seem she knew how to stop herself. In this situation, she was annoyed with herself as well as terribly uncomfortable.

Bella entered, a smile forming on her plump lips. Her hands planted on her waist, she too stared at her. Once more, Annie tugged at the bodice, wishing it higher. Moisture filled her eyes. This wasn't the way she saw this evening enfolding. Deke didn't seem to care. From everything he said, he would just as soon see her wearing nothing at all. Maybe she should just oblige him.

He lifted his broad shoulders, his jacket tightening across his shoulders. "More words don't seem necessary. You are right of course. The tops of your breasts are lovely."

"You're wearing more than I am," she announced with a hard

edge to her words.

His crack of laughter wasn't appreciated at all. "I will remove anything you like," he told her, his voice easy-going, his masculine smile all-knowing. "I'm sorry the dress does not fit to your liking. That is not my fault. Maria has offered to remake a few things for you. The offer is generous. Unfortunately, the sewing will take time. It cannot be accomplished this evening."

She scowled at him, her lips thinning. "You're enjoying this."

"I would never take pleasure in your discomfort. I forgot..." He tapped his fingers on his thigh, once more seeming to assess her attire. "When I offered the clothing..."

"That your wife was petite. Everything I am not."

Annie was not a virgin. She regretted that fact. She was tall for a woman as well as too thin. She always felt self-conscious around tiny females. If she could take that one horrific night back, she would do so. If she never met Peter Bentley again, she would swear to never think bad thoughts.

Before she could gasp a breath of air, he hunkered down in front of her. His dark eyes tender. He placed her hands in his. "Annie, you are beautiful. Don't ever forget that fact. I like you just the way you are. You're intelligent. From what you've told me, I understand you've not had everything easy as I would have expected. I don't care who your mother was or that your stepmother fell so in love with your father that she broke societal rules in order to be with him. I would that I..."

"You're just being nice," she murmured wishing she could accept the compliments as given.

She'd never been good at anything like that. Where relationships, man or woman were concerned, she was so self-conscience. This dress didn't help matters.

"Have I ever lied to you?" With the advent of the sudden question his voice was harsh, demanding. He pulled her to her feet. His hands around her waist. The breath she tried to inhale stuck in her throat. "I'm not lying to you now, either. You need to have more confidence in yourself."

Astonished, Annie found herself flush against the length of his body. He was hard everywhere she was soft. Peter had not been that way. She remembered the way Deke kissed her, the raw heat generated by his hands and mouth. For a moment, she lowered her eyes unable to meet the power of his gaze.

"No, at least I don't believe so." She looked down, studied her feet until she could speak. After she looked up, "Have you lied?"

"No and I'm not going to begin now. You are lovely. Your breasts are amazing, beautiful, not as beautiful as you are inside. You know how much I want to touch and caress you, every part of you? I also want to get to know what makes Annie who she truly is. At this very moment, I can barely wait until after dinner. I pray you'll be agreeable. I've been attempting to move slowly so as not to frighten you. Don't ever forget I want you."

With a finger under her chin, he tilted her head. Slowly, he inched closer. The hint of whiskey whispered across her cheek. His lips brushed gently on hers, erotic, slow, enticing.

Nothing more.

Bella stood in the doorway, clearing her throat several times to get their attention. Annie didn't know how long she stood framed by the door. She'd hungered for that kiss since he startled her when she was wearing nothing but her towel.

"We've company," she murmured as she turned her head toward the door.

Annie found she was shaking.

The woman was grinning, smiling happily as if she wanted them to continue kissing. Her eyes were alight with happiness.

"Bella!" Deke roared when he took the time to look up.

"Mr. Sullivan."

The woman spoke to him, rapidly all the while gesturing with her hands. Annie couldn't understand anything that was being said between them. After the woman left, he smiled at her, brushed his thumb across her moist lips. "We'll have to curtail this for another time. It seems dinner is served. We wouldn't want the meal to grow cold."

"No, don't suppose we would."

She started to walk, heading for the stairs, her mind focused on his words.

"Deke!"

He swept her into his arms, holding her close as he stepped toward the bedroom. She would have to decide what she wanted soon. It seemed at least for the moment; he took all decision-making capabilities away from her.

After he pushed the door to his bedroom closed with his foot, he kissed her on the forehead then her nose. He chuckled softly at her look of chagrin. He set her senses all a kilter, her stomach fluttering wildly. She didn't understand what she felt. One moment he was serious, the next playful. This decision hovering on the horizon wasn't something that would be easy for her.

"Hmm…" He sighed brokenly as if he was enjoying the meal just by the wonderful way the food smelled.

They both sniffed the air. Whatever Bella cooked up, the scent was delicious. "What is this?" she nodded her head in the direction of the table.

He didn't intend to answer. Slowly he set her on her feet. This time the kiss was far from chaste. The contact heated, creating shivers of raw passion as his open mouth descended on her lips. Fire erupted. He tasted of the whiskey he drank in the parlor. He used his tongue to demand she respond completely to him. His teeth tugged on her lower lip when she tried to resist the smoothly calculated advance. She didn't understand why she resisted, why she held back the raw passion that raced through her bloodstream. His kiss burned. This was what she wanted. Still, he kissed her, seemed to keep kissing her until neither could swallow air.

A broken sound slipped from her mouth. He laughed. She gave up all pretense of denying her reaction to him. In his arms beneath his tender assault on her senses, her body melted. His tongue swept inside played, fueled more passion, ignited the tempest. Her hips arched against him begging for something more something that only he could give. Without effort he generated a raging whirlwind of wanting, of passion. Her desire for him flared, spread throughout.

Slowly, seemingly reluctantly, he set her aside. His arms remained around her. Bending, he touched her forehead with his. His breathing was as ragged as hers. She was amazed her kiss could do that to him.

Bella cleared her throat again chattering nonstop seeming to scold. She took her by the arm before guiding her to the table she along with Maria must have set. Their dishes were covered. The scent heavenly. Her stomach rumbled, or was it his she heard. Bella even pulled out the chair for her.

The cook and his maid stood at attention while Deke finished seating her. Hesitantly, she looked from one woman to the other then toward Deke. "They aren't going to stay there, watching us, are they?"

He grinned at her seemingly amused by her question. "Only until you tell Bella how delicious the meal is. You must taste the food. She is waiting for a compliment."

"She won't know what I'm saying…will she?" Annie was certain this was all amazing.

"I'll translate. Bella just wants to know if the enchilada is too spicy. She toned the recipe down just for you. Whatever you do at least until they leave, don't cough then guzzle water. Take a small bite just in case."

Stunned a little by Deke's words, she nodded, wondering if the food would be eatable. Just in case? Whatever did he mean by that? After Deke took his place across from her, he gestured with his fork for her to eat. She drank in a long deep breath of air worried now after what he told her.

Doing as he advised, she tasted a minute portion. Chewing thoughtfully, she smiled moving her head as if she liked the food. Deke turned telling them what she conveyed. Only a few seconds later the women left. The enchilada was delicious. Not to spicy. She sipped the red wine Deke poured in her glass.

"Not too hot?" he asked while he lifted his fork to eat. "I hope you can eat more than you did at lunch."

"The food is fine. I'll reserve judgment until I have a larger portion."

She ate. Found that she was hungrier than she thought. At the noon time meal, she ate little because she was nervous. Now she was too. Nonetheless, she managed to eat half that was dished out to her before she had to put down her fork.

"Glad you like it? Bella likes her food spicy. Know though that it's quite alright if one adds more jalapenos to their own." Deke pointed to the bowl of hot green peppers sitting by his plate. "No, not tonight." It seemed he read her mind.

After he finished with his meal, he poured more wine, leaning back in the chair to watch her. His eyes darkened sweetly. Once more his gaze rested on her bosom. For some reason, she wasn't as embarrassed as she'd been earlier even though she felt some heat flood her face. Perhaps she was getting used to his blatant perusal of her. Either that or it was the wine.

Deke lifted his glass in salute to her. "Would you like to move to the couch by the fire? We could get more comfortable."

Annie wasn't positive what he meant by get more comfortable. Nonetheless, she had ideas. She supposed she wanted to see what would come next. Tonight, she didn't want to pull away from him or have second thoughts as she did this afternoon. This untried relationship was far too important to her. She wanted to know what could come of it.

Deke touched a chord in her, one she fancied him to resume playing. She never felt anything like this before. She remembered the way Tira used to look at her father. They both looked as if they wanted to close off the world so they could be alone. At the lake she felt something like that when he strummed her body so expertly. His touch was mercuric, magical. Enchanted by him was how she felt.

"Yes," she whispered softly barely able to speak. Her thoughts pummeled around in her brain making her witless.

Deke stood beside her, his glass along with the remains of the wine bottle in one hand. "Wait."

Swiftly, he strode to a side table to set wine and glass down. He returned for her. She held her glass in one hand.

"Hold on." He swept her into his arms.

She laughed delightedly, loving the moments when she was in his arms. She would never trade them. "I can walk," despite her feelings she protested.

"Of course you can." He touched the tip of her nose with his lips.

"Would be a bit disappointed if you couldn't. In the end I wouldn't care.

When they reached the sofa, he set her glass next to his. Before she could blink, she sat on his lap. She turned to smile at him. His eyes were alight with amusement as well as desire. The room was lit with a few candles along with the light from the fire. His knuckles gently swept along her neck, stopping at the base.

"I wany you to make love to me tonight. Even if it seems I'm holding back, I'm not. It's just that I don't know what to do. I'm so very uncertain. Not about you but about me."

"Positive?" One of his eyebrows was lifted high in speculation. "I have to be certain this is what you want."

"Yes," she breathed out softly.

"If you tell me to stop, I will. Won't like it. Nonetheless, this is about you. About your pleasure, not mine. What happens here tonight has to be right for you." He ran his thumb along her bottom lip. "Do you remember how to kiss me?" he chuckled softly as he nipped lightly on her lips tugging at them to open for him.

This time she understood what he wanted. This time she thought to tease as well, pretend she still didn't understand what he asked her for. She touched his teeth with her tongue then withdrew, keeping her mouth closed to him. When he turned his attention to the lobe of her ear, she sucked in a draught of air. He pulled back to look at her, his grin devilish in the extreme.

"Little tease. I like you like that. You can tease this man all you want. Just be careful how you torment. It could come back to bite you." He tongued, laved, enticed with his mouth down her neck to the base to return to her ear with delicate nips.

When he returned to her mouth, he covered it hotly with his, running his tongue between her lips, tweaking with his teeth until she opened for him. Her fingers rose from his chest to his shoulders then higher, kneading his skin. While he kissed her deeper and harder, she wound her fingers through the silken strands of his hair.

A tiny broken sound came from her lips. She moaned softly enjoying the heated kiss, the desire he brought to her with the storm he brewed within her. Her fingers roamed down his back. She wished he didn't wear so many layers of clothing.

As if he sensed her thoughts he rose above her, ridding himself of the buckskin jacket he wore. Unfastened his shirt so the fabric hung open. Now that she could almost touch his flesh, she felt more heat. She played with the ties holding his shirt together in front. Again, reading her thoughts, he tugged the shirt over his head then tossed the clothing aside. Slowly, he unfastened the back of her dress taking his time, touching, caressing, stroking while he seemed to enjoy the heated shivers coursing through her, drowning her with need. His fingers traveled the length of her spine then back. The bodice gaped open. If he wished he could see her, all of her breasts. He called them adorable.

"What do you want me to do?" Her words quivered, trembled, while she waited for his answer. She wanted to make this right for him as she somehow understood he would give her the sweetest pleasure.

"Be yourself, Boston. Just be yourself."

"I don't know…"

"You can touch me anywhere you like." His lips found purchase at the base of her throat, kissed and nibbled, sucked until she arched against him. Continued until she moaned softly the sounds coming in gentle fragmented ribbons from the back of her mouth.

Annie followed suit, running her hands along his back, touching each vertebra. When he moved to look at her, she swept her hands across his chest, brushing his tiny nipples. His groan rumbled up from his chest.

"I want to pleasure you too," she murmured wishing she knew what he would like her to do to make this good for him also. He told her she could touch him anywhere. She explored lower with her fingertips, feeling the contracting of his stomach muscles when her nails passed across the hardness of his belly. She moved back to his nipples wondering if he felt the same sensations as she did when he touched her breasts, the hardened peaks.

"Just by being you, you give me enjoyment." He groaned again when her fingers dipped beneath the band of his pants. His hand found hers, brought it back to his chest. "Little Darlin', that's too much delight for the moment for this man to endure. Don't want to embarrass myself our first time out."

With his chin, he pushed at her bodice. The fabric lowered, the tops of her breasts exposed. After he looked at her again, he grinned. He returned his attention to lowering her dress. When there was nothing between his gaze and the hardened tips, he touched each pinnacle with his tongue then his teeth.

Returning to her lips, he kissed her again, then again. A few minutes later he returned his attention to her breasts, sucking, laving, biting gently until she was beside herself with the need he created. He pushed her dress lower, following the fabric with his mouth. His tongue wound into her navel then lower until he kissed her belly. Her body jerked, quivered. She ran her hands along his sides then his back again. He kissed her lower.

"Lift your hips."

She did so. Her dress joined his shirt on the floor. He brought her to the fur in front of the fire. Laid her down. He showered his attention to her legs the inside of her thighs, lower to the backs of her knees then lower still until he reached her toes. Almost reverently, he kissed each one. "Just as I remembered, tiny as well as delicately pink just like the rest of you."

"You know I'm not tiny," she gasped out when he was between her thighs, pushing her legs apart with his knees.

His hand cupped her mound, his finger sliding through her folds, massaging, teasing her until her hips bucked. He looked at her, watching her intensely. "You are to me. Have you ever really looked at me? You are tiny."

"N-no…I'd like too though."

She wanted to see him with nothing on. She pushed at his pants wishing he would take them off so she could see all of him.

He stopped her with the same reply as he gave her earlier. Rising above her, he kissed her again, his fingers still wreaking havoc on her senses. She moaned as her body began to climb higher and higher. She felt this strange stirring of her senses. Pulses swept through her as her body thrummed to life under his expert tutorial. She felt as if he unraveled her one tiny thread at a time.

She closed her eyes, felt his touch with each leap and crackle of the flames near them. His long fingers stroked her intimately, within as well as without. She clung to his shoulders, threaded her fingers through his hair, then fell back…he was with her, running his hand up and down her body, his palm just slightly rough, touching, stroking.

Again, he played, toyed. Never in one spot. Always roaming. Her body danced to the rhythm he orchestrated. Slowly, deliberately. His fingers traced patterns around her breasts, her aureole, the pinnacle. His lips followed where his fingers strayed. Once more he settled over her, his weight above her, hovering, she opened her eyes, seeing his face again, half in shadows, half in the light. She felt the sweet ecstasy of release, her body captivated by the sensations generated so easily by his hands, his lips, teeth and tongue. He was a master directing the scene.

She found that he took off his buckskins. His erection, his penis, pushed against her entrance. The pain would come in a moment. She held her breath, stiffening, waiting for the part of this that would cause the agony she remembered. His body would rip into hers. He seemed to understand her emotions.

Deke pushed her sweat-damp hair from her face. His eyes tender with concern, "Hush, Little Darlin', I'm not going to hurt you. You're ready for me. Tell me no if you like. Nevertheless, I want you to understand. I won't hurt you."

Annie could not do so. She would never tell him to stop after the exquisite pleasure he just gave her a few seconds ago. He would do his man's thing. She would endure whatever was to come. Believing this would not hurt for her was impossible.

In a flash, he was inside her, holding very, very still until she sighed softly in her ecstasy. It seemed he held his breath waiting for her reaction. She liked the way he felt deep inside, his weight above her, pressing, giving her feelings of security, safety. She didn't realize this could be so nice. When he began to move within her she gasped with the erotic sensations produced by the slow tempo.

"Deke!"

Her eyes were open while she studied the lines and creases in his expression. She touched her hand to the side of his face. "It's all fine. I want you, you know."

She bit her lip still waiting, feeling his body move in then out with measured exquisite precision. While she expected the agony she'd known before, now she felt only the sweetest pleasure he promised. He didn't hurt her. Annie's body began to soar, feel the magic, the enchantment the burning desire. He inflamed her.

The feel of his flesh was slick and hot, vibrant, powerful. His every touch spread hot molten fire throughout her body. She would always remember the tenderness, the gentleness of the night, the fire of the flames as her body once more exploded in sweet hot sensations that rivaled the earlier mating.

This was sweet, sweet heaven, nirvana to her soul she thought as she slowly drifted back to the reality of the night. Deke. Deke gave her so much. He gave her a reason to forget her past as well as perhaps a reason to think about her future. Measured in slow moving moments, he was becoming her reality. He wanted her. She needed to understand what that meant.

For the longest time he held her, stroked her back, soothed the ragged breathing that was all she could do. She pulled in a long sweet breath of air.

"Annie?" he asked the sound of his voice hesitant, uncertain. "Are you alright?"

"Thank you," she murmured softly feeling as if he single-handedly changed her life. "Thank you for…" She wasn't at all certain how to finish the sentence.

She wanted to know how he felt about what happened. He might have thought she didn't like the sex. She did.

"No. Thank you, Annie." He ran his hand across the tips of her breasts down to her navel then back. He smiled when she gasped aloud, "You are so very sweet. This time with you was everything I ever dreamt of experiencing."

She laughed softly feeling a weight lifted from her. She had no previous knowledge. She was new to lovemaking. This was her first time. She wanted to do it right. "I've never thought of myself as sweet. Other women are sweet, they fawn over babies, they take the time to care about everyone. They say all the right things at the right time." She lifted her shoulders smiling at the strange look in his eyes, the simmering darkness that seemed to tell her that he still wanted her. "I don't do that. I'm a nice person but I'm not sweet."

He pulled her closer so her head nestled in the hollow of his shoulder. Squeezing her shoulders, he spoke softly, "Hush, I think you're sweet. That's all that counts."

His words gave her confidence, made her smile. More than anything she wanted to look at his masculine body, peruse the differences between them, touch him as intimately as he did her. She pushed against him rising over his big form, the tips of her breasts touching his chest. She looked at him allowing her gaze to travel the length of him. As she ran her hand down the center of his chest, across his belly, he slowly began to grow. She froze. Her gaze shot to Deke's face.

He laughed, his eyes so dark they were very nearly black. He ran his hand along her back stopping to cup her bottom. "If you keep that up, we'll have to make love again."

"Would that be so bad?"

She smiled softly at him, thinking she could do this all night if he was willing or they fell asleep. Whichever came first. She'd never stayed awake the entire night.

"You liked it that much?"

He laughed, his hand cupping her bottom, fingers trailing along the backs of her legs, once more enticing, seducing her to his will. She imagined it was her will as well.

She closed her hand around his length. He groaned, flipping her onto her back. His mouth closed over hers, hot, hard, demanding she returned all the passion he asked for. They made love once more then again. The night was indeed long and filled with love.

~ * ~

Belt paced the confines of the small shack high in the Rockies. He needed the doc. Well, no, his woman, Miss Ivy, needed the doc. When he sent Doc Lundin the message earlier in the week, he believed she would come alone. Instead, Deke was there trailing after her. His nemesis followed her into the forest. He couldn't show himself. Couldn't risk another encounter with the sheriff. He was a wanted man. If something happened to him, his woman would not fare well. She would most likely die in this cabin so far away from civilization. He'd meant to keep the doc at the cabin until Ivy gave birth. It would happen anytime now.

He was going to go after her again, find the doc then drag her up here to the hideout. Problem was he couldn't risk discovery. He didn't want to kill her. As far as he could see his choices as they stacked up, he didn't have a choice. It was either the doc's life or his woman's. He didn't know what to do. All he understood now was that he was afraid for Ivy's life along with that of their unborn child's.

Belt paced, finding no answers in all his thoughts. Questions, damn questions, that's all he had. He could bring his woman to the doc. That was a very real possibility. The snow would keep him from doing so even though he believed Deke would keep the doc at his home until the snow melted. If he left Ivy in the doc's office, she would be safe. When Deke returned with the doc, he would leave.

Damn, he was terrified.

What Deke didn't know was that he didn't murder his mother. He knew who did. Couldn't prove the fact. All the evidence pointed to him. After he ran, his guilt was etched in everyone's mind. The only person who could clear him of the crime was Deke's mother. For Belt, there was no going back. He'd done too many things he was ashamed of.

Belt tried to save her. That was why he'd been at the scene when she was discovered. No one believed him. They all wanted to see him punished, exiled. He left the camp, banishing himself from his friends and family. After that, he got caught up with men who were on the shady side of the law. Fell into their plans with little persuasion needed. At the time he didn't care. He lost everyone he loved. As far as he was concerned, he had nothing to live for. In truth, if his woman died, he didn't want to live.

Now, he was a loner along with his woman. He wanted to marry Ivy. Unfortunately, he had nothing to give or offer, no life. Because of him, she labored to bring his child into the world. He ran his sweating palms down his legs before stuffing his hands through his hair. She was going to die if left here by herself. He needed to put her in the wagon, take her to the doc even if it meant his capture. Ivy's life for his might be the only noble thing he ever accomplished. The good Lord understood over the last few years he thought only of himself. At least he did until he met Ivy.

Miss Ivy's life was worth far more than his. His decision made, he lifted her into his arms. When he stepped outside, snow fell in wild flourishes. The night was thick with the flakes. He wouldn't be able to take the wagon. He would have to carry her on his horse to the doc. He couldn't wait there. Perhaps he could leave her on the front porch.

"No, Belt." She reached up, touched his arm. "No, you can't give yourself up for me. I'd never forgive myself. I don't need a doctor as long as you're with me. Don't go." It seemed to take a concentrated effort on her part to say so many words. "I'd die without you by my side. I love you."

"You do need a doc and I can go."

In her eyes, he clearly saw her suffering. He didn't dare leave her. His body shook with fear for her. A sixth sense told him she wouldn't survive if he didn't get help.

"I've not had a contraction in hours. Give me more time. When the snow stops, you can go for the doctor. Promise me you won't do anything to put your life in danger." Tears slipped from her eyes.

He never believed anyone would care for him as Ivy did. He was a man blessed. What he couldn't do was allow her to pass from this earth. He had to do everything he could for her. She rested her head against his chest. She was right in too many ways to count. If he risked his life, who would protect her? He couldn't do so, not from a jail cell or a grave. He gave into her pleading heading back inside.

"Thank you," she sighed softly when he set her on the bed they shared.

"Truly." He looked at her hard. He could always tell if she lied by her eyes. "You've not had any contractions for a while?"

"Truly."

She sat against the wall, smiling shyly at him. Even the fact she carried his child, she had this innocent timid air about her. He wasn't going to let her leave him. Didn't want his baby to die either.

As soon as the snow stopped, he'd hightail his rear to town. He'd bring the doc up the mountain to tend to his woman. To save her, he would make a bargain with the devil.

Belt sat on the bed next to her, held her hand in his. She was small. The pregnancy had been difficult for her. He didn't want to leave for the day and a half it would take him to get to Denver City then return.

He couldn't leave her alone.

For him there was no choice.

God, if she had the baby and she was here by herself. Shivers rippled through him. She wouldn't survive.

The decision made again, he stood. "I'm leaving now." *The sooner the better.*

"It's dark."

"I know the way. You understand I won't get lost. I'm half Cheyenne, a half breed."

He puttered around the small cabin, setting things out for her she might need.

After he finished, he bent over to give her a quick kiss.

"Don't take any chances," she told him her voice soft, sweet as sugar.

He stoked the fire leaving plenty of wood for the time he'd be gone. "You know me."

This time he would have to be very careful. Her life along with his unborn child's life would depend on the care he took.

"I do know you."

She had more tears in her eyes.

"I'll be back with Doc Lundin. I promise."

Belt never broke a promise to her. He wasn't about to do so now.

Chapter Six

Slowly, Deke opened his eyes. Annie was spooned up next to him. His hand rested on her soft belly. Needing to feel the satin skin again, he stroked her hip then her stomach up to her breast, his palm grazing her nipple. After he brushed his palm against the tip, the pinnacle hardened. A tiny mewl of pleasures slipped from her lips. He grinned. She was still asleep. He could tell by the soft cadence of her breathing. Seducing her would be child's play.

For a few seconds, he toyed with her rose-colored nipples; tugging, twisting, flicking with his fingernail. Then his questing fingers moved lower to stroke between her legs to find the sweet honey he created as well as the tender jewel nestled there. Pleasure sounds. Mewls. Moans. When he ventured between her legs again, she was hot, slick with need.

He kissed the back of her neck, nipped the lobe of her ear. She moved against him. Her body's response was fast. Her passion overflowed.

Slow precision, enticing her, he pushed his erection into her. Withdrew. Pressed again. Moved farther. He touched her womb, withdrew. The slow steady cadence generated more miniature sounds of pleasure produced and received. She pushed back, her delectable little bottom touching his belly. He kissed the base of her neck, bit gently.

"Deke…" she sighed into the pillow. Her hands touched upon his. She dug her fingernails into his wrists. "Deke!"

"Yes, Little Darlin'. You said my name. What is it you would like?" He held her, once again pushed inside her velvet tight core until he touched her womb. "You are just as sweet by the mornin' light as you were last evening."

She climaxed. Her tight sheath kissing the length of him with the throbbing of her release. With a guttural sound he climaxed within her,

151

spilling his seed again. He held her, soothing the tremors ripping through her body. She was sweat slick as was he. Maria would come with bath water soon. He would leave her to bathe in peace while he took his bath downstairs in one of the extra rooms.

The clock ticked away seconds, he held her in silence, his cheek resting against the softness of her hair. Morning gray light slanted through the window. The snow he thought to see materialized in full force. Through the curtains he watched snow fall. He was rarely wrong about the weather. His instincts served him well. The deluge of white stuff would not stop anytime soon. Hours would pass before the trails were clear enough for safe travel. When they were, he would take her back to Denver City despite the fact he wanted her here.

Tossing back the covers he stared at her lovely white body. He would never get enough of looking at her, tasting her. Just the sight of her aroused him again. She tried to hang onto the quilt. He wouldn't allow her to do so. Her long hair was a mess, curling around her back as well as her breasts, hiding parts, other parts playing peekaboo with each movement of her body.

Playfully, he swatted her on her rump. She cried out indignant at his gesture. "Deke! Stop that. You're a monster."

"I've been called worse. Rise and shine, it's time to get up. The morning is almost gone. This is a working ranch. We've chores to do."

Naked, he strode to the bell cord, pulled. Turned to see what she was up to. He lied to her. If any chores needed doing, he employed hired hands to keep the ranch running.

Annie sat up, pushing her hair away from her face, exposing her front to him. He grinned watching her nipples harden in the chill of the morning. She pulled once more on the quilt. "Why did you hit me?"

Shrugging, he gazed at her. He wanted to touch her again. He supposed he should think twice about hitting her, even playfully. As large as he was, he could hurt her. His breath breaking, he was concerned. "Did I hurt you?"

"No," she told him indignantly, her lips thinning while she scowled at him. "That isn't the point though. Why?" she repeated, once again holding the covers over her.

The problem he was encountering was that he didn't entirely know why. He supposed he just wanted to touch her. If he'd caressed her softly, he would be inside her. While there was nothing wrong with that, he wanted to see what the day would bring. "Maria will be up with hot water for a bath if you like." He tugged on the discarded buckskins from the night before then his shirt. Grabbing a jacket, he swung it over his shoulder.

"What are you going to do?" she queried softly watching his every move. "What are we going to do?"

"Take a bath downstairs. Check on the weather. If the snow stops falling, we can start out first thing or wait until after lunch. I'd like to stay here another day or two if you're amenable. Give the notion some thought. Staying here would be a nice change of scenery for both of us. Would also give us a chance to pursue our feelings for each other."

He paused studying her face for some indication of what she might like. She didn't reply. He felt obligated to give her a chance to make the decision. "The choice is up to you. Think about it."

Before he left, he sat down on the bed. Once again, she was in his arms. An urgent need to stay assailed him. He kissed her hard, tasting her one more time before he left. She was just as fine now as she'd been last night as well as a few minutes ago. Letting her go, he stood, hands on his hips, gazing at her perfect features.

"I…"

Annie began then seemed to back off, for some reason unwilling to finish her statement or thoughts.

He watched her saucy pink tongue leave a trail of moisture along her lips. She seemed hesitant to tell him. One eyebrow lifted while he watched her scowl.

"I?" he questioned her.

He didn't like the idea of having to drag her feelings from her. He wished she could tell him whatever came to mind. It was obvious she wasn't used to sharing her feelings, especially with a man.

She heaved in a deep breath of air before she began to speak again. "You know I want to get back to town. My reputation will be shattered into tiny pieces if we continue to play at your ranch. Someone will find out. When that happens, all will know what we've been doing. You promised anonymity. I don't quite believe we can have that. I'll be the same outcast here as I was in Boston as well as Baltimore. Don't think I can bear that. A pariah again, or more specifically, whore is not a name I would appreciate."

They'd been over this more times than he wanted to recount. Except for a word or two no one here spoke English. No one would be able to spread gossip about their relationship, not that anyone he employed would do so. Reminding her would probably result in waste of breath. If she was adamant they leave, he would have to kowtow to her wishes. After all was said and done, he wanted her to be happy.

Tugging in a deep breath of air, he grinned wickedly. The rest of their stay here, he meant to make perfect for her. "Maria left another dress on the chair near the tub. Hopefully, the gown will suit better than the one from last night. Although I did appreciate the view the ill-fitting dress provided."

"You would."

She tossed a pillow at him, her smile picking up his spirits.

He held it for a few seconds, bringing it to his nose, appreciating the soft scent of Annie that lingered there. His voice husky, he spoke softly. "Consider that a challenge I won't forget. I will retaliate when you least expect."

"A challenge?" For a moment, she looked bewildered then it appeared she began to understand the tenor of his wicked thoughts. "Seems since you swatted my backside we're even. No retaliation needed."

At that moment, Maria arrived with the entourage carrying the hot water. The housekeeper's grin spread from one side of her face to the other. She asked about the gown. He told her Annie had not the time yet to try it on. Deke reassured his housekeeper that he was certain the dress would be perfect. Told her they slept late enjoying each other's company. Maria's grin widened at his words. The women in his employee had been after him for years to find another woman. While they all mourned Marla, they told him that he needed affection, children to brighten his day. Until he met Annie, he didn't want another woman.

If Annie knew what he was saying along with Maria's responses, she would blush from the roots of her hairs to the tips of her delightful toes, the ones he tasted last night. He realized he liked to see her blush. The sight was always delightful. Her temper was delicious too.

"Is my bath ready?" he asked just before he kissed Maria on both cheeks. "I'm also famished."

He sent a cheeky grin to Annie. She grew from a soft pink to a brilliant red. He was a man well pleased.

"*Si*," Maria told him, nodding her head, her gray curls bobbing with the movement.

She told him the water was steaming. Best he hurry so breakfast wouldn't get cold. If he was late, Bella wouldn't be pleased.

Maria also told him he should be enjoying this bath with his *novia*. There should be no reason to draw two baths when they would have so much fun sharing the suds along with the washcloth. It was only right. Deke chuckled thinking the same. This morning he wanted to give her privacy. He also wanted time to think about what would come next between them. He had ideas. Rushing her would most likely backfire.

Annie didn't seem to think about the consequences of their love making. He did. If she did become pregnant, they would have to deal with the repercussions. Marriage would be the only way he would proceed. If she refused, he wouldn't give her a choice. No way in hell would a son or daughter of his find themself labeled a bastard as she had been. She could be pregnant now. At that thought he felt a swelling in his heart. He could ask her a few pertinent questions that would give him possible answers. She was a doctor. She shouldn't be embarrassed.

He hoped she carried his child now though the odds weren't that great.

One night.

Before he left, he collected clean clothing from the armoire. While he strode down the steps to his bath, he whistled feeling absolutely wonderful. For the longest time he'd never thought to marry again, never thought to have children. Something about Annie Lundin stirred that part of him that had been dead and buried since his wife died. He certainly had not spent the time since her death celibate. Nonetheless, his encounters with the female gender never amounted to anything remotely romantic. What happened was sex, nothing more. What could be romantic about saloon girls and ladies of the evening? Oh, but there was a widow who pleased him immensely. He would not be back to the widow anytime soon.

Shucking off his shirt and pants, he walked into the bathing room meant for him. A cup of coffee along with freshly baked bread covered in butter and honey sat on a bench near the tub. The coffee contained a touch of milk and no sugar, just as he liked the heady brew. He picked up the newest edition of the paper from back east. As he began to read, he swore softly beneath his breath.

"Damn..." he whistled softly, thinking about all the repercussions.

The United States was still at war with Mexico. He prayed it would be over sooner. Damn. He'd been involved with so much in Denver City he didn't know anything about what was happening in the rest of the world. The papers always arrived late, after the fact. There could be peace now. Reflecting on the matter, he set the paper on the bench exchanging it for his cup of coffee. He drank, mulling over the facts he read. This war didn't have a hell of a lot to do with him or Annie. They would continue in the same vein. Nothing in this part of the world would change. The government could not call him back to service. They tried over a year ago or was it two? He'd done his time.

Returning the cup to the stool, he absently washed. The hot water soothed his body. When he finished, he leaned his head on the rim of the tub, closing his eyes, thinking about Annie, planning his life. What was happening in Annie's head was more important to him at the moment than a war he didn't want anything to do with. He resigned his commission a long time ago. Still, he understood the army might keep trying. He would refuse. His life was here in Denver City.

It was too soon to approach her about marriage. Once again, he reminded himself, he shouldn't rush her. She would have to decide that her practice was not as important as a husband along with a family. She worked damn hard for her diploma had hopes and dreams. Would a woman of that caliber give up something she coveted since she was a little girl? Her father tried to dissuade her, finally coming to grips with the fact he couldn't change her mind.

Not easily.

How could a night in his arms serve to change her mind?

If she was pregnant…that fact would change everything. He didn't want her to resent him because of conception of a child. She might. There wasn't anything he could do to change what happened between them. They both made their choices. She agreed. She must know what they did…

Deke stayed in the water until the liquid turned tepid. He dressed He sighed softly, wondering if Annie was downstairs yet. If she'd smell of the jasmine soap, he knew Maria would bring to her bath. Well, she would have washed her hair. If she did so, she wouldn't be down until the silken strands dried thoroughly. Her hair was so thick and long it would take time to dry. Perhaps he should pay her a visit. He was good at combing wet hair along with other things. It was the other things that would stop them from having breakfast in a timely manner. The bed would be far too close to ignore.

Bella would be displeased if they missed breakfast.

Walking into his office, he sat behind the desk ruffling through some of the old wanted posters. Concentration did not come easily as his mind continued to drift to Annie coupled with the big bed in his room. Finding these men was far more important than a war. They were all dangerous to society. All of them committed crimes they needed to be prosecuted for. They were men who threatened society.

He found Belt's picture.

WANTED DEAD OR ALIVE.

Deke wondered what went so wrong in Belt's head that he could join with a ruthless, savage gang. The Jones gang was known through the west, south past the Rio Grande for their brutality. At first, he didn't believe Belt was capable of murder let alone killing his mother. Damn, he wanted to believe his friend. Wished there was some way to discover the truth. The only people who could do so were unavailable to him to question.

Belt ran, reinforcing his guilt. He fled the possibility of judgement as well as punishment by the tribe. He was a coward. As closest kin, the punishment would have been up to him. The facts would have made a difference. Now, all he wanted was to capture the man alive. Death was not part of his feelings or intentions. He wanted to sit Belt down then listen to his explanation of events. The truth was more important to him than anything.

Frustrated at the scenarios here, he sat back for a moment, rubbed the bridge of his nose as if the simple gesture would ease the tension he felt. In this lifetime, he didn't believe he would ever learn the truth.

On his desk, there were other pictures of wanted men. They didn't tug at his heartstrings as the picture of Belt did. What if the man was innocent as he once claimed? In all the years when they were growing up, Deke never knew Belt to lie. People changed. He closed his eyes, thinking of his mother, wishing she could tell him what he wanted so very desperately to learn. Would welcome a chance to speak to her again even as a ghost. He knew people who believed in the afterlife. He would believe if his mother would come to him. Shaking his head, he wondered if he hadn't gone a bit daft in the head.

His adoptive mother was gone. Had been for years. If she didn't appear to him when she passed to the other world, what made him think she might show herself now? He tugged in a huge breath of air letting the oxygen simmer deep in his lungs until he could hold the air no longer.

"There you are. What are you doing?" she asked, watching him, her head tilted slightly to one side, her bottom lip caught between her teeth. He wanted to do the same to her lip.

Annie stood framed in the doorway to his office. Her cheeks were pink, turned that color he assumed by the heat from the bath. Her hair curled beguilingly in wheat-colored locks down her back. She didn't bother to pin it up. Her blue eyes sparkled as if she wished to share some amusing anecdote with him. She was a sight for sore eyes bringing light to the very center of his office. She always brought sunshine with her.

Deke held up the wanted poster, tapped the picture of Belt he'd been staring at, reminiscing. The drawing of Belt featured, in the center the words that said anyone could bring him in dead or alive and receive the bounty on his head. "Looking over unfinished business. This has been bothering me more and more since the message was sent to you. Since you wandered off by yourself in the dead of night."

She sat down on the chair across from him. Her hand reaching out to him, covering the top of one, comforting. Hers was warm, soft. "Do you have to do that? Seems by the look on your face reminiscing is not bringing good memories. Can't you just forget about the man? Let some other law man or bounty hunter bring him in to justice?"

"In some ways looking at him does. Helps me recall the man I thought he was before all this happened. The boys we were together so long ago…a life time."

He leaned forward, his forearms on the desk taking her hand into both of his. It seemed he looked for affirmation that his thoughts of Belt's innocence weren't unfounded. Annie had no way of giving him that reassurance. He wished she could do just that.

"What if he's innocent? He told me he didn't kill my mother. He's been on the run skirting danger for so many years. An innocent man shouldn't have to live like that."

"Was he ever known to lie?" she spoke gently as if she understood the turmoil rumbling through his body.

"That's the point, Boston." He saw her grimace at his use of his pet name for her. He supposed he shouldn't remind her that once he thought she didn't belong here. That was no longer the case. "No. Not until this incident. I should have listened to him, been a better friend. Hell, at the time not one person sat down to listen to his story. Everyone assumed he was guilty."

"That can always change," she pointed out. "If you want you can…well, you'll have to find him first. Don't believe the man wants to be found. Could be detrimental to his health."

Deke let out a long slow breath of air. Slowly, shaking his head, "I don't think so. Nothing can change what he did after he fled. I wish it wasn't true. Wish there was a way to go back in time, to rewrite history."

"You could stop your vendetta against him if you actually believe he might have told you the truth of what happened that day. At least the truth as he knew it to be. Did he ever say he knew who actually murdered your mother?" Her question was relative.

Perhaps he did know. Maybe the man was threatening him. "After what he's done, riding with the Jones gang, Belt will always be a fugitive. What he did or not do to my adoptive mother will never change that fact. Bounty hunters will continue to search for him. Eventually, one will get lucky."

Drumming his fingers on the table, he wished with all his heart life turned out different for Belt. Once so very long ago, he was blood brother to him. In this time, he searched for the man wishing to confine him for the rest of his life. Now, he just wasn't at all certain what should be done about the man who was once his friend.

"What if you ceased to search for your once friend. Would that change anything?" she queried, standing to walk around the room, stopping at the window.

She would see the snow was about a foot or more deep, not suitable for travel. It started snowing in the middle of the night. Hadn't stopped since. When would she mention the fact?

Her question was good as well as logical. "If he stayed wherever the hell he is now, no one would find him until he made a mistake."

"A mistake?"

It seemed to Deke her curiosity was peaked. "He needed you for a medical reason. At least I believe it was Belt who sought you out. If it had been any other man running after you that night in the forest, he probably would have taken you, asked questions later. It was me who tailed you. He couldn't risk recognition."

All those words were true. Belt wanted to confront him about as much as he wanted to confront Belt.

She was playing with the fabric of her dress, shaking the fabric. Before this, he barely looked at the gown. Maria or the young woman helping her managed to conceal Annie's bosom from him. He liked the other dress better. He liked the alteration to their conversation too. Until he could decide on a plan where Belt was concerned, he'd rather think about her, about what was beneath her gown or better yet, what wasn't. He wanted to pull her into his arms, kiss her senseless.

When she looked at him her eyes were shining with a strange light. Something he didn't like. Perhaps it was too soon to pursue other fantasies. While she appeared to be thinking she rubbed her lips together. "What if he comes for me again? What if he has good reason to seek me? What do I do? I'm a doctor. There was an oath I agreed to uphold."

"You don't go!"

His voice boomed harshly. His fisted hand hit his desk hard. He wished the sound along with the tone would convince her to obey.

"I'm a doctor," she repeated, he assumed for his benefit. The strength of her gaze met with his, clashed. If he didn't miss his guess, she was furious. "I've taken an oath to save people," she argued with him. "I wouldn't have a choice."

Deke didn't like arguments, especially with a woman. He needed to yell at her there was always an alternative plan. His way of thinking was the right one. "You come for me. He will have to understand I'm part of the package. We go together or you don't go at all."

"You might not be in town," she pointed out her voice soft as if she tried a new tactic.

She would understand she couldn't out yell him.

His Annie even lowered her lashes. He was beginning to dislike conversations with her when she lowered her voice another octave. He understood she would always present a sound defense for her behavior. This time as well as most times, her reasoning was complete from her view, not from his. "You wait for me to return," he gritted out thoroughly frustrated with the line of conversation.

He wanted to think as well as talk about more enjoyable pursuits.

Annie grimaced with his harsh words. Delicately, she spoke to him, her words well chosen. "Sometimes life as well as death doesn't wait for the sheriff. At times a person has to act first."

Understanding that fact as truth then accepting the notion when it came to Annie's welfare were two different topics. In his humble opinion, Annie was far too willing to risk her life. He sucked in air thinking perhaps a change of subject for the next few minutes might be nice as well as prudent. He didn't have one doubt she would resume this topic at some time in the near future. Once she was on a role, she was like a dog with a bone, she didn't let go until she worried the damn thing to death. Nor did he have any doubts if any man or woman came to her needing her expertise would she deny them or tell them they had to wait for Sheriff Sullivan to ride into town. He well knew there were times he was gone for more than a week. His deputy would have to take on the role of Annie's protector.

Deke looked up, staring hard at her, trying to make his point with the harshness of his voice. Immediately, he regretted the tone. "You can get Taylor. In any case, he's going to be the next sheriff of Denver City. He knows what he is doing as well as any man. You're not to go anywhere out of town alone."

He wondered how many times he would have to repeat the order for the terms to sink into her lovely head. She was just too damn independent. Stubborn. Tenacious.

She would never agree with his ideas. Annie would do as she pleased. Would tell him his wishes were archaic as well as coming from a male dominated mindset, meant for a different century.

She nodded seeming to accept that assumption he uttered. Once more she smoothed the fabric of her new gown. Her smile disarming, resigned. "Very well, if you are gone, I will get Taylor to go with me. Though that will leave Denver City without law enforcement."

His hoot of laughter sent creases to her forehead. He was relieved that was the only argument she could reiterate. "It's a sleepy little town." He paused, his thoughts roaming. "Not much for a sheriff to do unless someone gets too drunk over at Reilly's. Are we agreed?"

He wanted to get on to the topic of snow. Playing with her in the drifts, seemed to be on his mind. She would get cold. He would warm her up. He had something else planned he hoped would delight her.

Her smile stole his heart along with his breath. Somehow Annie always created a song to sing in his heart. He almost had a change of mind. Frolicking in bed would be more fun than playing in the snow. Ah, but the cavorting in his bed would come after the snow romping. A tryst in the hayloft would add a new dimension to their loving.

"When are we going to return to Denver City?"

She got right to the point he was expecting to hear about sooner. She progressed in a huff. "I've a business to run. You know that."

The breath of air he'd been holding while he was thinking of delicate carnal pursuits sifted slowly from his lungs. Yes, she did have a business, a business with no patrons. She could keep insisting. "Perhaps tomorrow. Depends on the weather." He waited for the backlash to his announcement understanding full well the essence of her thoughts on that topic.

"I have my practice to see to."

Her rigid back sent her bosom forward. Her anger sizzled brightly setting his body on fire. Her passion raged, he only had to tap into the flames to reap the benefit.

Without answering, he stood, extending his hand. He slanted her a slow, lazy smile, feral in nature. She looked at him, her eyes an icy blue, not understanding the sexual hint in his eyes. Obviously, she comprehended he was changing the topic, which didn't seem to make a difference. This very second, he wanted to toss her in the highest snow drift so he could make his point. After that, joining her there came to his mind. He grinned, thinking about the warming up of their bodies later.

Taking her time, she placed her hand in his. She rose of her own accord. Before they left the front door, he wrapped a warm cloak around her shoulders then donned his heavy winter coat along with a pair of leather gloves. His hand at her waist, he guided her outside to the front porch. His intentions too many to count.

Snow rose to the top of the steps, glistening in the bright sunlight. The pathway leading from the house was buried in the soft white flakes. He gestured with an arm, encompassing the snowy scene. His lips quirking, he said nothing. Sometimes a man didn't need words. Sometimes facts were facts. They spoke for themselves.

"You've made your point," she murmured as she leaned into him, her head resting snugly on his chest. "It's beautiful. In Boston when it snowed, the carriages would make the snow dirty almost as soon as the flakes fell. That doesn't happen here, does it?"

"In the towns, yes. Here at my ranch, no. Your safety is my first concern, my responsibility. We will have to stay until all this white stuff melts. After that, the trail will be muddy. We should give it a day to dry out." He felt her stiffen next to him. Heard the soft sigh of disappointment.

"My responsibility. My safety is up to me," she bristled. "I can take care of myself."

Asking her which direction the town lay was on the tip of his tongue. Out here she couldn't find her way. He didn't need to belabor his point. Left to her devices, she would be lost. This was not the course he wanted the rest of the afternoon to continue. "Do you recall the challenge?"

He spied the six-foot drift about ten yards from the front door. The soft mound looked perfect for what he planned, a short dalliance. He'd never made love in a snow bank. This was a challenge to him also.

With confusion in her expression, she shook her head. Suddenly, it seemed to dawn on her. She shrieked, then rushed down the slippery steps. Her foot slid out from under her. She began to fall, her hands whirling in wide circles. Nonetheless, she was able to break the fall by landing on her precious little backside, her saucy expression turning to one of astonishment. He didn't think she would be bruised. If she was, he would tend to her. In almost the same instant, while he was observing her mouth gaping open, she formed a snow ball. With amazing accuracy, she let it fly. The weapon hit him squarely in the jaw. Stunned for a few moments, he could do nothing except gape. Regaining his equilibrium, he hooted with laughter, renewed determination filling him with ideas.

"Seems that I do recall your challenge."

She grinned mischievously, scrambling to her feet, slipping, bracing her body with both her hands. She took off, putting distance between them, laughing, seeming to enjoy the confrontation. Seemed his Annie could give as good as she got. Every second, he was learning more about this adorable woman.

"Wherever you run I'll catch you."

His male arrogance shone through. Single mindedly, he stalked her path, eating up the distance between them. She shot another snowball his way. He ducked.

"I'll…" she was laughing hard, bent over at the waist as if she was also winded.

What he didn't understand in that feminine ploy he witnessed, would come back to haunt. The trick was not to gain air, but to make more snowballs. She had five made by the time his leisurely strides brought him close enough for him to be an easy mark.

He found he couldn't dodge all the missiles. Two hit him in the face, a third on his chest. By the time he reached her, his face dripped with melting snow. He was also laughing while he hefted her into his arms then tossed her over his shoulder. "You will not win this contest, Little Darlin'."

She pounded on his back with her tiny fists. "Put me down!" she cried out laughing. "Where are you going? Deke? I'm warning you. Don't you dare!" She cried out as if she guessed his intent.

She squirmed and arched, seemed to be pulling every trick she could think of to dislodge herself. His Annie wasn't going anywhere except into the soft snow.

He had every intention of putting her down. However, not in the manner she intended. Not wishing to rush this scenario, he ran his cold hand along her warm, naked leg to find purchase on her rear. She gulped, air sputtering and shrieking her outrage.

"How naughty, you've nothing on beneath your dress. I would have never guessed. Is this an invitation."

"Not to what you have in mind. I didn't have any underwear to put on. Maria, well, she didn't..." she gasped continuing in her efforts to pry herself from his hold.

"The challenge," he reminded her with a bark of laughter. "Didn't you know the man always wins. I'll have to tell Maria how delightful her *faux pas* was. No pantalets, my, my…"

"You're wrong, Deke Sullivan. I'll get back at you when you are least expecting me to do so. Just you wait and see. This contest is mine to win."

Again, to no avail, she squirmed, twisting, and turning her body in an attempt to dislodge herself.

"We'll see about that."

Standing in front of the soft bank of snow, Deke paused for a few seconds. He tossed her into the drift before following her down into the soft blanket of snow. "Hmm…you look delightful to me. How will you get back at me? I can hardly wait to discover your ruse, after that employ

165

offensive measures. Tit for tat won't put you on top of the game we play."

His hands framed her face. He kissed her open mouth. He was pleased her lips parted for him. Inside she was spicy and sultry. She was still laughing while she tugged his shirt from his pants. When she fashioned snowballs, he had not. Her hands were icicles to the touch. He nearly jumped from his skin when she caressed his back, in the process warming her hands.

"The challenge," she whispered as her hands heated at his expense. He appreciated the way she played the game.

She wouldn't win.

~ * ~

Deke was a fine one to speak of challenges, contests to be won or lost. She could meet him on every level then raise him one. Maybe he was bigger and stronger but she could always use feminine charm along with ingenuity to beat him at the diversions he wanted to play with her. If he didn't warm his hands on her, she would be surprised.

Annie was ready for anything he shot her way.

His mouth found hers again, tongue dipping then sliding against hers. When he pulled away, his whispered word endeared him to her. He spoke softly, warmly, his voice thick and rich. "Witch," he murmured.

"Neanderthal," she said.

He closed her smile with his. Kissed her hard before pulling away to look into her smiling eyes.

"Don't ever forget the fact," she told him saucily feeling smug as well as competent to play her game.

What he didn't know was that he was going to dance to the tune she initiated. For the first time, she felt an equal with him even though he was stronger. Over the course of the last twenty-four hours, she discovered ways to manipulate him, delighting her senses. He wanted to please her. However, he would never do anything that would jeopardize her. Annie supposed she should appreciate that fact. If she wanted to be close to Deke, she would have to learn to live with the overprotective bear. That part of him would never change.

Her smugness didn't last long. She no longer possessed the winning hand. She found she didn't care. Before she knew what was happening, his nimble fingers unfastened her gown. Was reminded she wore no underclothing. The ice of his hands curled around her breasts. His nimble fingers flicked the tight buds before he warmed her with his mouth along with his tongue. His teeth nipped tender flesh, until she moaned her pleasure.

"Deke!" she cried out at the first contact, understanding even before he completed the act he would do so.

He pulled away. Immediately she regretted that. Apparently, he had no intention of leaving the snow drift. She shivered then whimpered softly when his mouth closed over her nipple again. Sucked. Laved. Nipped. "We can't do this here. People will see!" She pounded on the solid muscle of his broad back. "Deke, please…"

He changed his attentions to her other breast before rising above her to kiss her again, to ravage her mouth with the sultry heat of his. He was unbearably hot, sweet. His scent was potent, dangerous. Her nails dug into his shoulders. He trailed kisses down her neck, back to her breasts. Her fingers wound into his hair.

"Where should we do this? If not here?" he asked looking at her with a half-smile. "I can't think of a better place. No one would dare interrupt us."

"Somewhere private," she told him wondering if he cared if his staff watched them making love. She certainly cared.

"No one can see us here. The snow bank makes this private. We could go into the barn. The hayloft would be nice and private, a bit warmer too. Actually, we could make use of the snowdrift then the barn. The environment is a new adventure to me. Suppose it is to you also."

He laughed softly then kissed her again, gentle then hard. Tender. Overwhelming. Heated.

A river of flame flew through her body, burned her. His touch mercuric, enchanting, she squirmed as he continued his leisurely assault on her senses. Where he was concerned, she had no recourse, no way to resist the tempest and fire he so easily aroused within. Somehow her dress was completely unfastened. He kissed her naval then lower. She had a mole just below her belly button. He didn't notice that last night. Now he touched the mark with his tongue. "You don't know that," she panted, her breath seeming to desert her while her heart shouted.

He stopped then looked around. He rose on his elbows leaving her nearly naked body to feel the brunt of the cold air sweeping across her. When he looked down on her he grinned. "There is absolutely no one here. We are alone."

Annie hit him on the shoulder. His grin was too wicked. She understood he would do as he pleased. If it pleased him to make love to her here, he would. "I mean it! Not here, Deke Sullivan. I'll never forgive you. You just like to embarrass me. I will be mortified to the tips of my toes." She paused straining for air, while he continued his gentle assault on her body. "Not in the hayloft either," her voice whispered.

She heard the resolute sigh. He settled his forehead on hers, his long fingers still toying with a hardened peak, still arousing, stirring, unraveling. "Some year you will not be quite so shy. I want you this instant not a moment later, Annie. Don't want to wait to get you to the bedroom. I'm going to make love to you here and now. In the snow."

"I'll never forgive you," she repeated earnestly though she understood her words were a lie.

They held no conviction. He would most likely know it too. Eventually, she would forgive him anything. Right now, making love where anyone could stumble upon them...well, she didn't... couldn't imagine. He sounded positive no one would blunder upon them. Still...

"You will," his slow lazy words sent tiny shivers rippling throughout. He seduced and charmed. His sweet-talking enchanted her. Bewitched. "I guarantee that. No one here would dare." His lips framed hers, the groan of desire rumbling from his chest made her forget her fears of discovery.

She slid her nails across the naked flesh of his back. He tugged on her skirt. The material slipped from beneath her hips. She wished now she wore pantalets. She had none this morning to put on. Not for one second did she think he would do something this outrageous. Deke would constantly surprise her. He would laugh at her embarrassment then charm her out of it.

Tiny mewls of pleasure. A broken sound. Fragments of breath. She gasped when he unexpectedly thrust inside her. She didn't know when he unfastened his buckskins. The mating was fast and hard. Annie cried out her pleasure, climaxing almost as soon as he entered her. The guttural sound she heard above her signaled his pleasure. His seed flowed inside her; hot, liquid heat filling her. Annie closed her eyes soaking in the ecstasy. This pleasure was not something she ever thought to feel at the hands of a man.

She wanted to stay in the snow bank with Deke inside her forever. Needed to feel the weight of his body on top of her pressing against her. Her hands cupped the hard muscles of his buttocks. His body contracted when she did so. "Little Annie, if you don't want to do this a second time, you should stop playing with fire," his voice was a low husky growl as he spoke to her. He nipped the lobe of her ear.

She jerked in response.

"Mayhap you should stop playing with me. Where is my dress?" she questioned while she moved her hand along the snow in hopes of finding the gown. "If it's all wet..."

"What?" His chuckle was soft, low, arousing in its sensual way.

"I'll get back at you somehow. The challenge." Putting on a damp gown would be unwelcomed a well as uncomfortable. "You're an animal, Mr. Sullivan."

"You love me anyway."

His lecherous grin coupled with the waggling of his dark, perfectly sculpted eyebrows sent heat strait to her core. She wanted to get out of here as quickly as possible. His words chilled her. Did she love him? Did he mean what he said? What if he was only teasing. If she did love the brute, showing him would never be prudent.

A few seconds later they were both dressed. She looked back at the space in the snow they just occupied then to the barn. He saw where she stared.

"On to the hayloft?" he queried while he twirled a lose piece of her hair around his finger. "The barn will be warmer. I can guarantee that fact."

Her mouth gaped open for a moment. Quickly, she snapped her

mouth shut. Perhaps she should play his game differently. Thought better of it. "Another time," she murmured smiling at him, tilting her head flirtatiously to look at him. "I'm not in the mood."

She realized the challenge in her words. He would not let that statement change his mind. He would make certain she would be in the mood sooner than later.

For the second time, she found herself slung over his broad shoulder. "No time like the present. What else have we got to do? We can't go back to town yet."

Again, he ran his hand along her legs, playing, toying with her oversensitive flesh. "Animal..." she muttered with a gasp as his fingers delved more intimately between soft folds of skin. Her body jerked with the pleasure he meted out. Even though they just made love, she was aroused again, stimulated to the point she could never tell him to stop. This arousal business couldn't happen so quickly as well as this often. Could it? What was it about this man who had her panting with need every second she was with him? Even when she was not.

"Compliments, my love. Have you forgiven me yet?"

Inside the barn light filtered through the window up above. The air was redolent with the scent of hay and horses, the oil used to shine the leather saddles.

"That wasn't a compliment," she told him sweetly, as least she tried for that tone.

Doing so was devilishly hard when he continued to arouse every feminine inch of her. His hands traveled up and down her legs, touching, teasing, provoking a response. Annie was certain if he chose to enter her now, she would climax immediately. She was nearly there.

"It's most likely better than ass or bastard. Hang on." He started up the ladder.

She gripped him around his narrow waist doing exactly what he commanded. When they reached the top, he walked a few feet. Deliberately, he allowed her to slide down his hard male length. She felt all of him, including his steel-hard erection straining against the fabric of his pants. He was just as stimulated, aroused, needy as she was.

After a few seconds passed, he was chuckling, turning her by the shoulders so she could see the bale of hay, the wine, the food along with the blankets. He was giving her a picnic in the hayloft where he was going to ravish her. She smiled. This was wonderful.

"Wine?" she asked him trying for a pleasant voice.

At this point she wanted him to finish what he started between the snow bank and the hayloft, drink wine later.

Deke didn't answer. Instead, he sent her a lecherous grin, one that sent the inferno he began earlier sweeping through her. He poured them each a full glass. "It's all I can do to stop myself from tossing your skirts this very instant."

He drank long and deep, watching her as the wine tumbled down his throat.

Unhurriedly, she sipped wishing to keep her senses under control. Doing so was devilishly hard when he looked at her the way he was doing. She felt as if he stripped her bare, as if he saw her without clothing. He would not have to do much imagining.

"When did you plan this?" she asked trying to divert her thoughts from the way he looked with very little on his large masculine frame.

"Bella thought we could use more privacy. She helped me. You know that she likes you. Adores you."

He dished up plates of ham accompanied by boiled potatoes. There were strawberries on the side, some spring peas along with tiny onions. He brought a quilt up to cover them, to keep them warm.

Annie discovered she was hungrier than she thought she would be. Neither ate much at breakfast. Slowly, she was finding a way to put her past behind her at least the parts she didn't wish to remember. "You're incorrigible," she murmured thinking that was a trait she admired as well as enjoyed.

"Seems I can't get enough of you." He told her, lightly using a finger to trace a path down her neck, stopping at the pulse that beat so very hard. "I want to see you naked all the time. If I thought for a moment you would cater to my wishes, we would both be naked now. Though we will be soon."

Her over stimulated body clenched, tightened at the thought of watching him eating when he didn't wear a stitch of clothing. "Can we not talk about that? I'd like to eat if you don't mind. When I'm around you butterflies inhabit my stomach, dancing as well as playing as if they belonged there. When that happens, there doesn't seem to be room for food." Her breath along with her words wobbled from the back of her throat.

"I like to watch your eyes cross when I say something I know will embarrass or shock you." He spoke softly, his wine scented breath so close to her cheek she felt the whisper of air flow across her.

"Does that mean you want me to starve?" she asked as she managed a bite of potatoes, chewing as well as swallowing.

His brows creased together. "I will make certain you eat. Even give you a second or two to digest the food."

He sat back, crossing his long legs in front of him while he leaned against the stack of hay. He placed a berry in his mouth chewing slowly while he stared at her. He wasn't gazing at her face. She felt heat rise as he stripped her of her clothing with the way he contemplated her. She turned from him a curse on her breath.

His yelp of laughter followed.

"You have no shame," she countered unable to look at him until she tugged her sensual thoughts and images into the back of her mind.

"Not where you are concerned. No shame, no shame at all." He did back off though eating another berry.

Annie managed to clean her plate before he began the seduction once more. She sipped her wine studying him wondering when he would challenge her again. The sweet tang of the liquid slid down her throat. She drank more, feeling a bit dizzy when she finished the glass as she was unused to more than one glass of wine in an evening.

"Enough," he told her taking the glass from her before setting it on a nearby stool. "I want you to feel as well as remember all that we do here…in the hayloft. We might not ever find time for a tryst in the hay another time."

Oh, god he was going to make love to her again. She wanted him to do so. Needed to feel him deep inside her, completing her filling her with his heat along with his seed. Setting her on fire. When had she given herself so completely over to this man? She didn't know. What would happen to her plans for her life? Again, she didn't know. She had a practice that was far from thriving. Goals, too, had always been part of her life.

Before she could protest her gown was on the floor of the loft. She didn't ever intend to protest his ardent attention. He was also naked. Their clothing scattered. He barely moved from his position. As he pulled her up to straddle him, he crooned tenderly in her ear. "Ride me, my love."

My love?

She eyed his erect member, then looked to his grinning face. For an instant she didn't understand what he wanted. His fingers caressed and stroked intimately. He captured a nipple between his teeth, bit gently as she arched against him. The ensuing pulsing of her body grew. She felt the tremors escalate to a fever pitch. Felt his arousal brush against her feminine softness.

His hands around her waist, he lifted her until she felt the hot tip of his penis at her entrance. Leisurely, he settled her on top of him.

"You're in control."

His voice so husky and whiskey smooth, stimulated, aroused further kindling the tempest.

In control? When had she ever been in control?

She gasped when he thrust inside her. He was hard and long, a steal rod inside her. The friction of his movement sent her ever higher to that pinnacle of release she knew and was coming to cherish.

Her fingers wound into the softness of his hair. His fingers played with her nipples then the most sensitive part of her.

"Deke!"

Her body took over. He was wrong, she was not in charge, didn't think she'd ever been. He composed everything they did. Planned every silken move.

"Annie," his guttural voice called out her name when she felt his seed spend itself into her.

Sated she fell against him, her head resting on his chest, his penis still deep inside her.

His sperm entered her.

With a strange sense of foreboding, the thought hit home. Her stomach curled; butterflies danced. She didn't know how she felt. For the first time, realization as to the consequences of her actions hit her fully. She could be pregnant. They took no precautions. Tightly she closed her eyes, fighting off the unwanted images fluttering dangerously in her muddled brain. They weren't wed. If she was pregnant, the child would be a bastard. All the horrific rumors would start again. This time her child would suffer. She put a fist in her mouth to stifle the strangled sob threatening to erupt.

What had she done?

He seemed to notice her sudden withdrawal from their playtime. He pushed her damp hair from her face as he slipped from inside her. His brows arched as he studied her. When she saw his member damp from her as well as his seed, she whimpered.

"What's wrong?" he asked his voice soft but still husky as he pulled the quilt around them. "I thought you enjoyed the new..." he cut himself off, clearly worried about her tangled thoughts, the strain it would be impossible for him to miss.

Annie tried to stop the tears from forming in her eyes. Truly she tried. He caught a drop with a fingertip brought the liquid to his lips. "It's all wrong! This..." She waved her hand around the hayloft.

"What is?" He clearly appeared baffled by her sudden statement, his dark blue eyes turning black with emotions she wasn't certain she understood.

She didn't want him to be angry.

A doctor, she was a doctor and she should know better. The consequences. She was so immersed in the experience all she thought of was her pleasure the ecstasy that soared inside her when they were together. Unable to help herself she was shaking her head, denying everything, denying the nature of their intimacy, the logic that she should have realized sooner. If he hadn't thought of her possible pregnancy, she wasn't about to say anything.

A man deserved to know he would probably be a father sooner than he expected. Oh, no...oh...God, no she couldn't tell him. What would he think of her? He would believe she tried to trap him. Deke would think of her as the whore everyone else did. She would be forever dammed in his eyes. Moisture clouded her eyes.

A doctor should know the consequences of what they did. Should understand the biology of mating. A good doctor would put the needs of the child first. She should have told him unequivocally no. There should have been no sweet talking.

Should know better than to do something like she did without thinking of the results. Not once, not one time did her mind travel farther than the pleasure the two of them shared.

She drew in a deep breath of air. Held the oxygen inside until she thought she would die. "I can't talk to you when we're both naked," she blurted before she could evaluate the comment for what it was, an excuse to put off the inevitable. She didn't want to tell him what she just now realized.

His little half grin, the one that always sent heated shivers to the tips of her toes, did so again. "I'm not dressing until we've finished the bottle of wine and eaten all the food Bella packed. Can't risk my cook's wrath. We don't have to talk. There are other pleasant pursuits we can indulge in."

She let out a strangled sound before looking away. She pushed against him, "No, Deke, I can't eat. My stomach is churning. I'm…" She licked her lips. "…terrified!"

He rubbed his hand on the back of his neck, his body tensing. "Terrified of me?" His hand under her chin, he urged her to look at him, his eyes narrowing. "Why?" His voice assumed a different tone.

Annie shook her head. "Not of you. Of, of…" she couldn't speak the words that would make the thought of a possible pregnancy more real. Having a baby was a huge responsibility. She didn't know what to do.

"Of?" he queried appearing unwilling to give up on this conversation. "You must tell me more. If I'm doing something or if I could do more to help. Did I do something to hurt you?"

"Believe you've done enough." Her strident voice caused more concern to build on his face.

"Annie, you got to spit it out, whatever this terror is."

When she pulled her gown off the hay, to cover her breasts, he allowed it. She was trembling, shaking and she couldn't seem to stop. He pulled her into his arms. She felt his warmth, his confidence flood into her.

"I don't want..."

She did want to tell him. It was just that she didn't want to have a baby. She'd never thought a baby would be for her. Never expected to have a little being dependent on her. It wasn't as if she didn't want a baby. She never thought to marry. She didn't have to look at a calendar or count the days between. She was always on time. There wasn't a better day for her to conceive than these last few.

"What don't you want?" His voice was patient, encouraging. His large hand ran up and down her back soothing her. He calmed her. She just couldn't say the words that would condemn her in his eyes.

She buried her face in his chest fought the aphrodisiac that was his scent, the taste of him. If she picked a father of her child, Deke would be first in line. He possessed all the characteristics she would look for. What if he didn't want children? Even one?

She tried to fill her mind with courage to spit the words out as he suggested. Her throat was clogged with fear, parched dry as a desert. This was something she never thought to do. The last days were burdened with firsts. Some good some bad. She spent the last twenty-four hours selfishly thinking of herself.

Heaving in a huge breath of air she blurted on a soft sob of despair. "A baby!"

Once more he tilted her chin so she was looking at him. "I would love you to have my baby. What makes you think you might have conceived." He spoke tenderly, sincerely as he continued soothing strokes.

She believed him. Some of the pressure she was feeling eased slightly. "Y-you do?"

He dried the tears slipping from her eyes with his thumb. "I do. Do you think it's true...that you're pregnant?"

He didn't mince words, shot straight to the point. "Yes."

"Why?"

Gulping, sobs erupting that she couldn't tamp down no matter how hard she tried. "This is the perfect timing." She closed her eyes to ward off the searing of his eyes upon her.

"Why don't you want a baby?" he asked sounding patient even though she heard a hard edge to his voice. For some reason she didn't understand, he was angry.

"We..." She gripped her gown wishing he would give her enough distance so she could dress. Blurting out the obvious, she spoke again, "We aren't married."

When she looked at him this time, he was grinning, his smile wide. "That particular problem can be fixed. Are you asking or just suggesting? I would expect some one of your background to be on one knee with the proposal."

She wanted to hit the arrogant man. "I...I don't want to be married either. Don't want my baby to be born a bastard."

"Our baby."

"Yes, I imagine so," she sniffed. "There has never...well..."

He ignored her statement as if her opinion didn't count for anything. "We can see the minister in Denver City as soon as we are able to return. The problem will be remedied."

He kissed her on the forehead then her nose. Laughing softly, he ran a finger down her neck to stop at the pulse point. He acted as if he was more than pleased. Deke was making arrangements. They barely discussed this.

"You aren't listening to me."

"I won't have a bastard," he said calmly, way too calmly. "Marrying you would be a pleasure not a hardship. There is no reason to wait."

That was the tone of voice that meant he would have his way no matter what she said or wanted. What anyone else thought didn't count. Well, she didn't want her child to be a bastard as she was. Her father always loved her. Nonetheless, at this point in time, her father could do nothing about the fact he never married her mother. She didn't want to shackle herself to a man just because of a baby.

She had to do so.

Because she didn't want her child to carry the stigma of being a bastard for his or her entire life.

"That's not a reason to take part in a wedding."

Perhaps that was the best reason of all. A child was a perfect motive. If he didn't want to live with her, he didn't have to do so.

"Good enough for me," he murmured softly.

He was placating, humoring her. "Y-you don't love me," she accused understanding that she'd fallen in love with Deke Sullivan. She expected him to counter the indictment.

"Annie," he still spoke softly only the hard edge to his voice returned. "We need to think of the child first. You know that for the truth. This is no longer about just the two of us along with our pleasure. I don't intend to stop making love to you. So, a pregnancy would have happened eventually."

Everything he mentioned was true. She might not be pregnant. She was. She'd not thought of consequences only of herself. Two people shouldn't have to pay a lifetime for a mistake. Making love to him had not been a mistake. They could have taken precautions. Arguing with herself wouldn't change their misdeeds.

"I know…but Deke, It's not fair to you." She placed her hand on his chest. He was shaking. She didn't know why, probably from anger. "You will be stuck with me for the rest of your life." Moisture clogged her throat. She didn't want to cry again. "I don't want you to hate me."

"Need I remind you that you will also be stuck with me. Would that be so bad? Hmm…I don't have a lot of bad habits."

No, if there was anyone she wanted to find herself stuck with, the man would be Deke. "No," she told him honestly. "No, no it wouldn't."

"When we are back in Denver City, we'll get hitched. Let's go tell Bella and Maria. They will be glad to know."

"We can't tell them I'm pregnant." Her voice trembled, panic lacing the words as he brought her to her feet. In one deft move he slipped the gown over her head and fastened it.

In the next instant he was dressed. "No, we are not positive that you are increasing. We will tell them our love story."

"Love story?" With the back of her hand, she stifled a bitter laugh. She would never have a love story.

"Deke!" The call came from below. "Deke, you up there?"

"Levi? What is it?" Deke turned his attention to her. "Let me help you down. If this isn't something serious, they wouldn't interrupt. Got a horrible feeling simmering deep in my gut."

On the ground floor, he held her, one arm wrapped around her shoulders. She leaned into him wishing…what was it she wished for? She couldn't be certain. No, she knew exactly what she wished for. She wished for Deke to love her.

"We've found tracks around the house then leading into the woods. Should we follow them?"

"Belt?" she whispered, a slip of panic ebbing through her.

"Possibly," Deke said hugging her close, a protective gesture she realized. Deke spoke again, "I'll go with you. I'm going to take Annie to the house."

On the front porch he kissed her tenderly. "Don't leave the house. If you stay inside, you'll be safe. Promise me."

"Yes."

From the doorway, she watched Deke ride off with two of his men. She didn't want to go inside by herself. Didn't want to end the conversation they were having about the possible baby the way they did. The ending was so abrupt. He was so determined. Deke would have his way. Soon after they reached Denver City, she'd be a married woman.

Would that be so bad?

The men disappeared. For several minutes she stayed on the porch leaning on the wrap around railing watching the nothingness.

"Finally, I have you alone." The deep masculine voice coming from behind her startled her.

She jumped, her heart in her throat. "Belt?"

With the hit to her jaw, she crumbled to the floor. For a moment, she saw the man. After that, darkness.

~ * ~

Belt didn't like hitting Deke's woman. After what he witnessed in the snow drift, he had no doubt about that fact. He didn't see any other way to get her to come along with him peacefully. Deke would be furious with him. Never forgive him. He waited while the two of them played in the snow then in the barn somewhere. The time it took to lead the men astray was child's play.

Now, he needed to hightail it out of here before Deke caught on to the subterfuge. Deke would return looking for blood. He would guess what happened. His woman was beautiful, almost as beautiful as Ivy. There were times he wished he could go back in time, to the old ways. He crossed too many bridges to do that. He had to deal with his present the best he could. All he had control over was his future. At least he hoped he still had some input.

At this moment his only concern was for Ivy. He draped Annie Lundin over his thighs, her head dangling. When she woke, she'd be disoriented as well as damn uncomfortable. Her head would pound. He wished he had time to look for her doctor's bag.

He did not.

An hour later, after covering his tracks, he rode up to the small cabin situated high above Denver City. The place where he called home. Having Ivy run out to greet him would have been nice. Carefully, he dismounted, keeping Annie in his arms. Pushing the door to the shack open with his foot, he entered.

Unmoving, Ivy lay on the bed. Swiftly he put Annie on a chair before racing to Ivy. Her pulse still beat. Her breath was labored, barely there. She was alive. A small moan slipped from her. With glazed over eyes, she stared at him. Ivy reached up, trying to touch him. Her arm fell back to the bed. She was so very weak.

"You came back."

"What is it?" Belt asked as he pushed sweat dampened hair from her face.

"I'm going to die. Aren't I?" she whispered, her voice weak.

"No, no, you aren't. I'm not going to let anything like that happen," Desperately, he tried to reassure. "I brought the doc from town. She's going to make everything right. You'll hold our baby in no time. Both of you will be fine."

She cried out as a cramp seized her seeming to wrap around her body. Ivy squeezed his hand hard. "The baby won't come. I've been in labor for hours. Right after you left last night the pains started." The words seemed to take all her energy. She closed her eyes. She looked exhausted.

Belt didn't know when Annie woke. She stood beside him before nudging him aside. "Let me see. I'm going have to examine her. You should have told me the truth. I would have come to help. You didn't have to knock me out."

"Without telling Deke?" he asked, not believing she would do such a thing.

When he set out to retrieve Doc Lundin, he never intended to risk either woman, especially not Ivy.

"Yes. Without saying anything to him. I'm a doctor. He can't dictate to me when it comes to my patients."

Helplessly Belt watched as Annie touched then felt along her abdomen, looked at her, never commenting. "How is she?"

"The baby is turned the wrong way," Annie spoke gravely as she busied herself with preparations for the delivery. "This is serious. I don't know if I can save her or the baby. I'll do my best though. Get me water and soap."

Not save them?

Do my best?

Belt's mouth went dry. Moisture clogged his throat. Ivy had become his life. He would die if he lost her. Without conscious thought he did everything the doc asked of him. Throughout the next few hours, he followed every order. Mesmerized, he watched as Annie scrubbed her hands with the soap then bade him to do the same. Blindly, he moved through the shack, shaking his head, doing just as he was told. His heart was in his throat, his nerves strained so narrow he thought they might crack.

"She will scream. This will hurt her. I don't like this but I have to turn the baby so the child can be born head first. Trust me. I'm going to have to put my hand inside her. You have to hold her still, make certain she doesn't move." Annie kept her words soft.

"I understand. It's the same with a horse." Desperation for his woman caused his throat to clog. He did understand. The birth wasn't normal, far from it. He could lose this woman he loved with all his heart. After he met her, she slowly changed him, taught him how to feel again, how to believe in himself. The task wasn't easy. He was not a willing pupil. She coerced as well as manipulated him until he bowed to her wishes.

Hours seemed to tick by while Ivy screamed in pain. The cramps came so close together it didn't seem there was time for her to recover between them. Once the baby was turned it was only a few minutes before he could see the head. A few pushes and the baby would enter the world. Ivy was weak though. When the time came to push, she was barely able to do so.

With the back of her arm, Annie wiped sweat from her brow. "You have to help her, give encouragement. Make her mad. Give her a reason to believe she can do this. The head is cresting. Only a few more pushes and your child will howl at the world. Sit behind her, support her. Push on her belly when there is a cramp. This has become as much your job as it is Ivy's."

They worked hard. Belt told her things that made Ivy's eyes widen with shock. She swore at him, cursed him in the language Belt taught her. He smiled at Annie as the baby slipped from Ivy into her hands. She collapsed against him, her body trembling from fatigue. The greatest joy enveloped him.

"You have a son," Annie said in seeming awe while she held the newborn. Her eyes misted over.

"You've done it. The baby is here." Belt told Ivy as he listened to the first cries of his son.

Ivy opened her eyes to look at the baby before closing them again. She was exhausted. Belt decided he wasn't going to put her through this ever again. He couldn't risk losing her.

Annie handed the baby to Ivy. "Open your eyes. Your sweet baby needs you. You can rest after you've fed him. You've a baby boy."

Ivy's eyes blinked a few times. Slowly, she lifted her arms to hold the squalling child. Annie set him on the bare flesh of her stomach. "Hold him tight. He wants to get to know you better," she whispered.

Renewed energy seemed to sweep into Ivy. When she looked up

and spoke, her eyes were shining. "He's beautiful. He looks just like you, Belt."

Belt wasn't going to contradict her. At the moment the boy was wrinkled and bloody. His arms along with his legs were thin sticks. He had the loudest voice. Maybe that part was just like him. The boy would have a fine war cry. He would teach him everything he needed to know to survive in this angry world. He would teach him so much he would never end up as his father did, hunted by the law.

"He certainly is the most beautiful baby boy I've ever seen," Annie murmured, smiling at them. "Now, if you'll hand the child over, I'll wash him then wrap him up in a warm blanket. After that you can feed him."

Ivy did so. She rested her head on the pillow Belt plumped for her. "Do you think he is beautiful too?"

Belt swallowed the lump in his throat. "Very."

His voice cracked with the blatant lie he told. He watched his woman smile then her eyes close. He had so very much to be grateful for. Annie saved his love. He would forever be in her debt. While he waited, he would have to pray to all his gods that Deke would forgive him the transgression of stealing his woman. He would return her in one piece. For Belt, there had been no other choice. Without Annie, Ivy along with his boy would have died. Tears welled in his eyes. He didn't care who saw the moisture.

Annie taught Ivy how to feed the child. When they were finished, Belt set the boy in the crib he'd made.

After she turned toward him, Annie set her hands on her hips. The look in her eyes told Belt he wasn't going to like what she was about to say. "Both child and mother are doing well. She didn't bleed too much. It's time for you to take me home."

"It's dark." He prevaricated. Leaving Ivy was not an option until morning, until he was positive she wouldn't need the doc again.

Her hand shaking, she pointed outside the window. "Belt," she began heatedly, her voice stern, "that can't possibly make a difference to you. The black night would not stop Deke. Both of you know these mountains with your eyes closed. You have to take me home. Ivy will be able to reach over to the crib if the baby wakes. You don't need to be here. She is strong. Has the baby to live for. Nothing will happen to her while we are gone. I promise."

As much as he regretted his words they had to be said. "I can't do that, take you to Denver City or back to Deke's ranch. It's too dangerous for me. Nevertheless, I'll take you to a safe place, a spot where Deke will find you. I'll leave tracks any greenhorn can follow. Deke is no greenhorn."

"As you wish."

This time when he mounted, he pulled her up in front of him securing a blindfold. He couldn't risk her telling Deke where to find him. Even though he didn't believe she would. Throughout the night, they rode in silence. Belt finally pulled up in front of a lean-to.

"You will recognize the place, yes?" he asked eagerly, hoping she would be too afraid, praying too that Deke would be here soon to sooth whatever fears she had. "You will be safe here. Would you like me to build you a fire?" That was the least he could do.

"Yes," she nodded, searching the area. "Yes, to both questions."

He dismounted helping her down. Before he left her, he built up the fire. He gave her a worn blanket to wrap around her.

"He will find you here. Stay safe, Deke's woman. I will pray for you always."

"Take care of your family. Go somewhere you can keep them safe. Deke no longer holds you accountable for his mother's death."

Her words couldn't be true. He fled after he was questioned. Every member of their tribe held him accountable. Belt stopped before turning down the trail to his cabin. He would have to backtrack before heading home.

Deke appeared not too long after Belt left. Now he stood at the lean-to, Annie in his arms. Deke held a hand high in the air. For a moment, Belt thought his boyhood friend would come after him. After all, he was a wanted man. Deke was a sheriff. To his surprise, Deke shook his head then waved as if he understood why he'd done what he had to do.

Belt whirled his horse then set off for the shack high in the mountains. He would move higher into the Rocky Mountains as soon as his woman was strong enough. He would build Ivy and his son a log home, one that would keep them warm in the winter and cool in the summer.

Life would be good to them.

Chapter Seven

Deke's emotions were torn, ragged at the seam. When he discovered the false tracks left by Belt, he raced to the ranch, his heart beating savagely while fear for her life stretched his nerves to a point beyond repair. All the time, he told himself she was fine. If she remained in the house, nothing would happen to her. Levi consoled him. Also apologized for falling for the trickery perpetrated by Belt. The tracks were so obvious.

None of that mattered to Deke. Placing blame would not alter the situation. They could apologize all they wanted. Unless or until he retrieved Annie, there would be no forgiveness coming from his heart or his mouth.

Belt's trail was not easy to follow. When he discovered the tracks, they led to the last place he and Annie camped before descending on Denver City. The reality was that when he made camp for that last night with her, he could have reached the town before dark. Truth of the matter, he wanted one more night alone with her.

He was a selfish bastard then, still was now. After she told him about the impending baby, he lost all ability to reason. Elation was the only way to describe his feelings coupled with fear something might happen to her or the child. Two pieces of information that served to deflate the wind from his lungs was that neither did she wish to marry him or have the child. Changing her mind was imperative. How to do so…he had no idea.

The announcement of the news she carried his child so soon surprised him at first. After he thought for a few seconds, a woman doctor would understand feminine cycles. Would know what happened when a man was with a woman intimately. Chuckling softly to himself, he realized it took her a long time, almost an entire day, to come to the conclusion she was pregnant. She must have never thought about the consequences of making love. Until that one moment in the loft when she drew away from him.

Deke wanted to see her. Needed to hold her in his arms then sooth her fears about the upcoming marriage as well as her pregnancy. He didn't have one doubt she was pregnant, not after what she told him. Strangely, she wasn't even embarrassed talking to him about her monthly.

When he pulled up in front of the lean-to, he thought to see Annie. She wasn't there despite the lateness of the hour. He circled back to make certain he read the tracks right. Scratching his head, at the soft hoof prints, they were laid out clear and true. In this case there were no false leads to follow.

The hour was growing late. Darkness descended coupled with the chill of the evening high in the mountains gave him cause to search the hills surrounding him. He worried he missed her or misread the tracks. Breath held tight he waited in a secluded spot. Belt would bring Annie here. He was certain. If it was Belt who abducted her.

As the minutes changed to an hour, he grew restless. When he heard the soft tread of hooves, he stiffened, drawing his rifle. While he honestly didn't believe Belt would harm her, he wanted to prepare himself if his instincts were wrong.

His first sight of her sent his heart pounding. Deke tore a breath of pine scented air into his lungs. Annie rode in front of Belt. Her eyes were covered. Perhaps that was for the best. Since she didn't know where Belt took her, she wouldn't be able to lead him to the home.

Deke didn't want to be the man to bring in his friend, especially not now while he did no harm to Annie. Instead of riding to greet them, he remained hidden. Once Belt finished with the fire then mounted to leave, he slowly rode toward the camp, revealing himself.

While Belt held up his hand in salute, Deke did the same hoping this would be the last time he saw his one-time friend. Belt could never return. For the moment, they parted as friends. After he listened to Annie's story, he would decide on the direction of his thoughts where Belt was concerned.

Annie stood in front of the fire, the blanket wrapped around her watching the enfolding scene. She didn't run to him as he wished. She didn't move at all. When he walked closer, glimmering tears slipped down her cheeks. Thinking the man hurt her, he almost mounted to ride after Belt.

She held out her hand to him, shaking her head. Her eyes filled with tears, dark circles surrounding them. "No, the tears are for Belt, his life…" she sounded so choaked up he needed to hear the story.

At the moment, all he wanted was to hold her in his arms, rock her to sleep. She had to be exhausted. The day for both of them had been exhilarating then trying. He dismounted seeing to Pye before walking to her. He wasn't at all certain what he should say to her.

When he reached her, she still stood in front of the fire. A smile lit up her face. She held out her arms to him.

He folded her in his warm embrace. "Ah, Annie, what happened? You didn't listen to me. Did you?" He never meant the first words from his lips to be accusatory. "I told you…"

She placed a cold fingertip to his lips, "Hush, I did listen. It's just that, he was waiting for me on the porch. All I did was watch you go. I meant to return to the house as soon as I could no longer see you."

"If you'd gone right inside then shut the damn door, he would not have been able to capture you."

His mind was on one idea, her safety especially now since she carried his child. In this environment she would have to learn to obey.

Once more she was shaking her head, smiling at him. "What I did would not have mattered. Belt was there, waiting. Besides, I'm glad he took me. If he'd told me why he needed me, I wouldn't have this blazing headache." Gingerly, she rubbed her temples. Quickly, she changed her tune when she witnessed the scowl crossing Deke's face. "It's going away. Will be gone as soon as you hold me a few more minutes."

His frown deepened. "How did he hurt you?"

She lifted her thin shoulders that shouldn't be carrying the burden that she did. He wanted to know everything that happened when she was away from him. In time, he would ask the questions. Turning her, he massaged her shoulders while he waited, feeling the tension gradually ease.

"His wife, I'm not so certain she was his wife, was having trouble giving birth. The baby's head didn't drop. I had to turn the little boy around in order for him to be born." She was breathing heavily, fatigue etched in the corners of her beautiful eyes by deep lines.

"The child lived?" he asked feeling relief when he saw the tender smile form on Annie's lips.

If anything happened to Annie, he'd never forgive himself the pleasure he sought in her stunningly fragile body.

"He did, a little boy. I'm happy the birth was successful. When I got there and examined Ivy, I didn't know if I could save one let alone both of them." She pressed her body against his, her head tucked neatly into the hollow of his shoulder. "I think Belt helped a lot. He encouraged her when it seemed she gave up. She was so tired she couldn't expel the baby even though its head crested."

There was so much to talk about, to discuss. For now, he meant to see to her needs, not his. Any conversation that needed to be shared between them could wait. Annie looked as if she was ready to drop. "Are you hungry?" Before they slept tonight, he meant to teach her how to find her way in the forest or anywhere besides a town with city streets.

"He was the most beautiful little boy I've ever seen," she sighed softly. For a moment her mind appeared to drift to another place and time. "The baby looked just like Belt except he had his mother's baby blue eyes."

Deke was positive if they had a baby boy theirs would be more beautiful. All the babies he'd seen before when they were newborns were wrinkled as well as red. The thought gave him pause.

A beautiful newborn? Did they exist? He would never tell Annie his thoughts.

Moving in front of her, he held her by her thin shoulders as if he meant to shake her. She still didn't answer his question. If she didn't, he would force her to eat. She must be starving. "Are you hungry? Did Belt feed you?"

Her eyes widened as her body jerked in surprise. She looked at him as if he was crazy. "I'm not the least bit hungry. Though there wasn't time for me or anyone to eat. Once the child was taken care of and I knew the mother was doing fine, I insisted he bring me home."

"You haven't eaten since we were in the loft," he reminded her, his voice gentling.

"Neither have you."

"You're not home," he chuckled, pleased that Belt brought her here.

He would have her all to himself. After he returned to the ranch, Bella brought him a bag of food for when he found her. It was just ham sandwiches she told him. He'd been grateful for the consideration. Now it was either time to eat or get on with the needed instruction. Belt could have left her anywhere. She might have gotten lost walking in circles. Deke didn't know if she could find her way from this place to Denver City.

"No, he told me he couldn't do that. Wouldn't be safe for him. Said he would bring me where you would find me. Guess he was right. I didn't want anything to happen to him. If something bad happened, who would take care of Ivy and the baby? They wouldn't live."

"Come with me since you don't want to eat. You've a valuable lesson to learn." He positioned her in a clearing, looking above at the twinkling stars. "Can you find the north pole?" he asked uncertain if she would have any idea what he spoke of.

She grinned at him as if the question was stupid. "My father taught me to sail. Of course, I can find the North Pole. I know stars just as well as I know how to tie knots. Well," she paused, "I'm not very good at tying them or untying them."

"Show me," he spoke softly hoping she would understand all this then apply the knowledge to the forest rather than the ocean. The environments were all different. His hands rested on her shoulders as she stared at the night sky.

"It's up there, the brightest star at the tip of the little dipper. On the ocean it's much easier to see unless it's a cloudy night, though the stars are bright here too. The trees tend to get in the way. If you can't find the little dipper one can use the big dipper. The two stars in the cup point to Polaris."

He found that he was both impressed as well as surprised. "Ah, so what way is north?" he asked while unable to resist the satin finish of her bare skin, he traced his fingertips along her neck.

Beneath his hands she stiffened. Over her shoulder she stared at him, "I don't know. Is that important?"

"Seems your father taught you very little. Knowing the names of the stars will not help you find the direction you need to travel."

He shook his head at the thought he would leave her sailing blind.

"Never learned how to tie the knots he tried to teach me either. Doubt if my lack of knowledge is his fault," she mumbled seemingly disconcerted by the fact she didn't recall something so important.

"What is the point of locating the North Star if one doesn't understand how to use the information?" he asked, touching the tip of her nose with his fingertip uncertain whether to laugh at her chagrin or cry.

Under his fingers he felt her lift her slender shoulders.

"Well, I do hope you listen better to me than your father. Annie, if you are looking at the North Star, which you've shown me you can find with ease then everything you see is north of you. All you need remember is that the tips of your beautiful breasts will always be pointing north. If that's the direction you wish to travel all you need do is follow your saucy little titties."

She gasped when he ran his hand across her nipples. "That's crude!"

"You'll remember. Won't you? On the opposite side, your delectable fanny will always be pointing south." He squeezed her delicious butt. "Where is your right arm pointing?" His teeth nipped at the back of her neck.

Squirming then sighing softly, she spoke, "East..."

"Your left?"

"West..."

"Good, if you know Pine flats is northeast of here what are you going to follow?" He chuckled softly while he helped her with her answer, running his palms along the tips of her breasts, enticing a response.

She spit out a breath of air, "I'm not answering any more questions after this. I'll follow my nose and my right arm."

His hoot of laughter gained him a glower. He was pleased she understood. "You won't forget now, will you?" He prayed she'd never find herself stranded by herself in the forest or on the ocean. He didn't intend to lose track of her ever again. Plans had a way of going awry.

It was time to get on with the business at hand. His thoughts drifted back to what she told him about Belt and Ivy. If he could find them, he would take care of the two people most precious to Belt. The man didn't know that though. Tenderly, he led Annie to the lean-to, motioning for her to stay. There he brought bedding along with the bag of food Bella gave him. After he had everything the way he wanted, he tugged her hand, motioning for her to sit.

"We're going to eat first. Then…" His mind pondered a myriad of scenarios. She would have to agree to them.

"I'm not making love with you again," she told him, her tone holding no conviction, her gaze wandering over him, looking pointedly at his crotch. She was contradicting her desires.

What difference did it make now that she was pregnant? Women had strange ways of thinking. Remaining celibate until the birth would not stop the fact that she was pregnant now.

"We'll see. However, I didn't have that in mind."

He handed her one of the sandwiches Bella packed for them before tipping the bag of wine to his lips. After he drank, he handed it to Annie, watching her.

She drank the wine then she ate the sandwich. He was afraid he would have to argue with her about eating. He smiled at her, pleased with the news of impending fatherhood. "Good job, you're eating for two now."

Her dumfounded look sent a bark of laughter from his lips. She creased her eyes together, pointing one of her slender fingers at him before fervently poking him in the chest. Annie was clearly annoyed. He wasn't at all certain as to why.

"I am not." She told him looking more indignant than he ever saw her before. Her gaze skimmed her body. She pressed the fabric of her gown to mold her slender figure. "I'm not any bigger than I was two days ago. Much more time will pass before anyone save you can tell about the transformations within me. You are so wrong in your assumption...the ridiculousness...steals my breath."

"You are carrying my child," he spoke gruffly.

Now he felt indignant as well as put upon. He didn't mean anything untoward about her eating habits except she didn't eat enough with or without a baby in her womb. Eventually, she would be delightfully rounded. Her breasts would grow tender as well as enlarge. She would be charming.

Eventually.

Deke grimaced when he realized his mistake. He spoke without thinking past the end of his nose. Apologizing was out of the question. She still needed to eat. Needed to keep up her strength even more so since she would want to continue to work.

Not that she had any clients.

"True." She grinned at him as if she understood what he realized an instant before. "You wouldn't know I conceived except for the fact I told you. Your careless words were presumptuous."

"If not for two, you will have to eat for more than one before you know it." He defended himself as he didn't want to give over on his declaration. Needed to protect his stupidity with more foolhardiness. It appeared by the rigid set to her jaw she was about to call him out on the ludicrously of his thoughts. Holding his breath, he waited for what would come next.

"Have you ever seen a newborn? Or fed a small child? Ever noticed what they ate?" she queried with sugary sweetness.

Her eyes filled with amusement at his expense. He wasn't certain where she was going with this. Needless to say, he was going to regret something else before she finished with him.

He nodded, "Possibly fifty or so during my life with the Cheyenne."

Now, he understood exactly what she was about to point out. He had no recourse except to surrender. He held up his hands She'd done him in quite handedly. "I would wave a white flag if I had one."

"Did any of them appear to be my size?"

Didn't seem to him she would cut him any slack. Swallowing his pride would be the next step. "No."

He didn't have the luxury of explaining. When a woman was right, what else was there to say.

"Point made," Once again, she smiled sweetly at him before taking the bag of wine to drink. She suddenly set the wine aside. Looking concerned. "Don't believe this is good for the child. Do you have water?"

His sigh was long and strained. He wasn't going to argue with her tonight about anything. At least an argument had not been his intention. As far as he could tell they agreed about the marriage, *for the child's sake*. He needed to change her notion to something that had more to do with her feelings for him. The marriage needed to also be about them. More than anything he wanted her for his wife, needed to spend the rest of his life with her.

Deke held no hopes that she was in love with him or even beginning to feel more serious thoughts about him. So far what was between them was lust. Nothing more. He prayed that with time, their lust for each other would become love.

Though…he was falling in love with her. Allowing any sentiment other than love into the equation was not possible. If she didn't love him now, he would do everything possible to change her mind. Tugging her against his chest, he held her, his hands splayed across her abdomen. A child rested beneath his fingers at least he prayed it was so. She would tell him the baby was not even as big as the head on top of a pin. He didn't' care. Savoring every moment of this time was his intention.

"Tomorrow we will ride into Denver City. By the end of the day, we will be a happily married couple," he told her his voice softening with emotions when he spoke.

Deke understood he was rushing her. Wanting this so damn bad he could barely sneak in a breath of air.

She tried to turn in his arms. All she managed to move was her head. "I'd like a few days to get ready, a wedding dress perhaps would be nice. Would that be too much to ask? Why does the marriage have to take place tomorrow?"

Because he was in a hurry to call her his wife.

"A wedding dress?" he queried baffled by the request for a few

seconds. He scratched his head, thinking about the best way to answer. Nothing came to mind. Staring at the top of her head, his fingers drifted upward until they touched the underside of her breasts. Ah, her breasts would grow even larger than they were now. Without any effort he could appreciate that. It seemed now she waited to answer him. He wasn't at all positive his query needed an answer. Of course, she would want a wedding dress. What woman wouldn't? He wasn't an ogre. She should have whatever she wished for.

"Yes." She settled back against him pressing her delectable butt against his arousal. "I want a wedding dress, not white, but perhaps eggshell blue."

Eggshell blue? "Hell and damnation woman! Why not white?"

He felt angry with her, knowing the answer before she could utter the words. She shouldn't put herself down or announce to the world she wasn't a virgin. In requesting a blue dress, it was exactly what she was doing. He wasn't going to allow anything like that. Her feelings were important. So were his. If he had any say in the matter, she was going to wear white.

Her arms and shoulders lifted slightly; he felt the movement against his chest. She didn't try to turn in his arms this time. The words that followed were uttered slowly. He heard the pain in her voice. "Because I'm not a virgin. I would be lying to those who witness the ceremony. I wouldn't do so."

No, she wasn't. Neither was he. If he wished to wear white, he would god damn whatever criticism might ensue, wear white. "Do you want to broadcast to all the people in town that you don't deserve to wear white? Thought you wanted people to have a good opinion of you, of us. Don't want to begin our marriage with gossip or rumors that might need explaining. You will have a white dress made for the day. I'm not going to entertain any other misguided notions!" He didn't even care if she had a special dress except for the fact she wanted one.

Needing to put the discussion aside and concentrate on more pleasant pursuits. Deke brushed a few strands of hair from the back of her neck, nibbled slightly. She squirmed against him, pushing herself back as if she wanted to be closer. Earlier she told him she didn't want sex with him tonight. Well, that was just too damn bad. If he could seduce her to change her mind, he meant to do so.

"Yes."

Her sigh of pleasure echoed in the tiny space they occupied. Her body reacted to strokes of his hands and lips.

He nibbled and laved in erotic places. Ones he'd come to understand made her melt. Making love to her now would be far more prudent as well as enjoyable than discussing the color of wedding dresses. Anything within reason would be hers. He wanted to make her forget she told him she wouldn't make love to him again. Doing so would not be a chore. She wore the same gown with nothing beneath as she had this morning. If Belt did pluck her off the porch, she would have nothing on beneath her skirts. He sure as hell meant to find out. Her bare skin would be easy to explore as well as entice her to his way of thinking.

Without hesitating, her gown was open to him. Her bared breasts were held by his hands, her nipples cradled by his questing thumbs. Before she could voice a protest, the dress was over her head her shoes off. His clothing followed.

"I do wish to make love to you tonight. If there are no more objections or queries about our upcoming wedding, I mean to give you all the pleasure you deserve." They were under the blankets, pressed bare skin to bare skin. Nothing stood between them.

Annie was slick and warm when he touched her between her thighs. She rained her nectar on his hands. He played with her, toyed, explored to his heart's content. His mouth closed over hers ravishing, over and over again. In seconds he was inside her moving slowly in then out as she gave every indication she would climax soon.

He loved to hear her throaty little sounds of ecstasy. While he was still deep inside, she explored him, raked her nails across his back. Her core kissed the length of him as he guided her toward the climax that was inevitable.

When she cried out his name, he let his seed explode inside her. If she wasn't pregnant before, he would do everything in his power to make certain she would be soon. He trusted her words though.

Whispering softly close to her ear, wishing he had the time to make love to her one more time, "We need to get up at the break of dawn." He turned her so her back was flat against his chest. "Go to sleep, Little Darlin'. You need your rest."

"Yes," she sighed softly snuggling close to him, her delectable little fanny now snug against his groin "So soon?" She was breathing deeply, her exhaustion so very evident. He needed to think of her well-being first.

"Are you warm enough?" He could get used to this, Annie in his arms, her body pressed against his.

She was asleep. For the next hour, he was left with his thoughts. Thoughts now that centered around what he would do about Belt. Annie delivered his child tonight. She formed a bond with the man along with his woman. While he'd been flirting with the idea of giving up his vendetta to allow Belt to live in peace, he'd not yet reached a conclusion. Annie might be angry with him if he chose to continue searching for him.

He would have to decide.

The dawn came too soon. The sun was brilliant, no clouds to speak of in the sky. Animals chattered all around them welcoming the morning. Her soft breathing filled him with wonder along with the fact that she was about to become his. She carried his child.

This man couldn't be happier.

How the hell long would it take to have a dress made? Maybe they could purchase a white dress from the mercantile. He was pretty certain she wouldn't agree to a store-bought wedding dress.

She turned in his arms, the softness of her breasts pushing against his chest. A quick dalliance would prove to be delightful before they returned to Denver City. Once in town, he wasn't at all certain how much time he would have with her. She would be making wedding plans. He would have to steal the privacy they needed to have together. Perhaps he could sneak up her back steps without being seen by anyone. He'd have to remember to pull the shades in her bedroom.

He wasn't going to sleep without her before or after they were wed. Ah, hell Bella and Maria along with the rest of his ranch hands would never forgive him if they weren't part of this wedding. By having a wedding dress commissioned, he just signaled to one and all this was an event. There would be a real ceremony along with a true celebration afterward. People would be invited.

Waking her would be difficult. Unable to stop himself, his hands curled around her breasts. He liked the fact they slept naked. She was used to him after only two nights along with a day of lovemaking. She was the most passionate woman he'd ever been with. He stroked her thighs. She opened for him. His hand curled around her woman's mound, pressing into intimate petals of skin, slickly-hot, wet folds welcoming him.

Slowly, from behind he pushed inside her. She moaned softly, moving back against him, inviting him deeper, deeper still. After parting the silken strands of her hair, he kissed the back of her neck. Her little mewls of pleasure delighted him. A broken sound escaped her slightly parted lips. She purred.

The moment she woke, he knew. Her breath sifted into her lungs in a startled gasp. Within her core, he moved faster, harder. She cried out his name when she reached her climax. This was heaven. He didn't want to leave here. To spend another night in the privacy of the lean-to would be bliss-filled.

"Deke..." Shakily she collected air into her lungs. "Thought we had to leave at the crack of dawn."

The time wasn't much passed the first rays of the sun braking above the mountains. "Waste an opportunity to make love to my soon to be wife? Nah, a few minutes after that exalted time will do just as well."

He rolled over, his forearm across his eyes. Once they reached town, there would be a million things to do. There would be little alone time with her.

Deke sat up gazing down at her. In all her glorious disarray she was beautiful. Affectionately, he pushed long strands of hair from her face. Lightly kissing her cheek, he removed his covers resigned to the fact they had to leave. Someone had to get up first. He supposed he could put the coffee on the fire to boil.

Swatting her bare backside, he chuckled remembering that was how he prodded her to leave the bed yesterday. He did enjoy the contact as well as the look on her face when she turned to glower, her eyes narrowed in mock anger.

She rolled over, questioning, her forehead creased. "Another challenge, Deke Sullivan? You didn't win the last one. Is this a new attempt to settle the score?" she queried turning over, exposing her breasts to him. "Where is my dress?"

The challenge could come later when she was least expecting it. He meant to surprise her. "You understand, Little Darlin' if you want a wedding gown that single fact changes all the dynamics of our wedding. Bella, Maria along with everyone else who works for me are going to be outraged if we don't have the wedding or at least the reception at the ranch. They will never forgive either of us."

When she stirred to a sitting position, she held the covers in front of her. She seemed to be mulling over her comment about the gown. "I never thought of that. Does my wanting a wedding dress change all that?"

Perplexed, she appeared even more beautiful. "Do you still want to have a special gown?" He was definitely hoping the answer would be a resounding no. A marriage as soon as they rode into Denver City was his preference as well as the most expedient. If they wed sooner than later, he wouldn't have to sneak around to figure out how to sleep with her without the town believing she was compromised.

Annie smiled sweetly at him. He was beginning to understand that particular look. The answer didn't bode well for a speedy wedding coupled with a wedding night in the near future. With every passing second it seemed their marriage along with his wedding night was going to be farther in the distance than he wished.

Women had a way of changing a man's plans.

"Yes, Deke, I would like to have a special gown. It's something I've actually thought about since Tira married my father. I was six then." Her whispered words sent his heart skittering. "You don't mean to deny my one request, do you?"

Hell no! "If we do this, you must know that the wedding will take on a more formal tenor. My cook along with my maid will want to help with the meal plans. There will be flowers along with food for the celebrations afterward. All sorts of people will be invited. A cake that will feed everyone in Denver City."

"A wedding cake? Flowers? Your friends?" Her smile widening as he added to the list of items that would stand in their way of a hasty wedding.

"Yes, a cake. Bella will make the confection at least three tiers." As the list grew Deke was beginning to feel put upon. Inwardly, he groaned even while he wished to give Annie everything she wished for.

Nothing he could do or wanted to do would stand in her way of the day she probably thought about since she was a little girl. She just admitted as much about the dress. When the wedding cake presented itself and he saw her wistful smile, the way her beautiful eyes lit up, he knew he was doomed to a real wedding.

"Does that mean the wedding will be at the ranch?" she asked looking hopeful.

He gave up. Nothing was going according to his plans. "Wherever you want. We could marry in the church then drive to the ranch for a celebration. If you like, we could do both at the ranch. I'm certain the minister would be conducive to whatever you would plan. If he's not, we'll give him something extra to make it worth his while."

"Let's have the wedding at the ranch. How long do you think it will take to get everything ready?" She beamed. There was no other word to describe the expressions flitting across her lovely face.

"You're the bride. You make all the final decisions."

"We could do it in a week."

~ * ~

Annie never thought in her wildest dreams she'd be getting married. Neither had she thought about a wedding, at least not since she'd been a little girl. By the time she entered medical school, she'd come to the conclusion there would be no suitors for her. Peter changed her thinking only to discover he wanted her as a mistress not his wife. All she would wish for now was that her father along with Tira would be there for her. Asking Deke to wait until her parents could travel from Baltimore to Denver City, she understood that request would be asking too much from him. The travel would take too much time. Even her need for a wedding dress confounded him. She supposed all he wanted was to get the wedding done and over with. She imagined it was a man's way. Once a male of the species made up his mind to marry a woman, he wanted the deed done so he could take her to his bed. That problem didn't seem to stop Deke.

First thing after she cleaned up, she would write to them. Tell them about the impending nuptials. The message might reach them sooner. They still would never reach Denver City in time for the ceremony. If possible, it would be nice if Tira and her father could be here for the birth of the baby. That plan seemed more reasonable.

In some ways this day reminded her of her first descent into Denver City with Deke. Just as this morning, she held so many hopes close to her heart. The first time she thought she would at last be able to practice medicine. The epidemic was the closest she'd come to presenting herself as a competent doctor. Last night, she felt useful as a physician. To her delight, she saved both the mother along with the child.

This day she made the trek to begin a new life with the man she was falling head over heels in love with. She told him she didn't want to marry. That was a lie as was the fact she told him she didn't want the baby. More than anything she wished for both. Now, she didn't even care if she never practiced her desired career. After all this time, she recognized the fact that men would never trust women to see to their health needs. All she would ever be was a glorified midwife. If that were the case, she would do her best in that scope.

Deke was willing to wait a week to be married so she could have a gown fashioned. That fact in her mind set him above most men. She understood he was postponing the wedding just for her. Except for her father, a man never put her needs in front of his. Her heart swelled with the tender feelings for this man who was sweeping through her at a frightening pace.

"We should see the minister first thing, before we do anything else," Deke told her when he helped her down. "We can apprise him of the date as well as inform the man where the wedding will be."

She'd been sitting in front of him for the two-hour journey home. His hands played with her body the entire time, teasing, sweet-talking.

Her body pulsed with the pleasure he charmed her with, tempted her with. He knew she was thoroughly aroused when they rode into town. She was an easy mark for this man who seemed to enjoy keeping her burning with her need for him. So far, he didn't speak of this evening. She supposed he would spend the night as the sheriff catching up on information. For her, spending the evening alone in her bed didn't warm her.

"After that I'm going to the dressmakers," Annie told him thinking the sooner she commissioned the gown the better chance she would have of getting the dress in time for the wedding.

"You will purchase a white gown. Don't want my bride wearing eggshell blue or any other color. It's my only request. Do anything else that you like," he grumbled while he set his hand on her waist to guide her up the steps to her apartment above her office. "Promise me."

Deke opened the door for her. Annie stepped inside. Her heart lodged in her throat when she looked at the two people sitting in her living area, sipping coffee, grinning besotted as if this wasn't the biggest surprise of her entire life. It might well be.

"Father!" She ran to him, her arms open wide, ecstatic to see him. It seemed to her he read her mind. They would both be here for her wedding just as she wished. She didn't even have to write to them. This was a dream come true.

Jamie wrapped her in his arms. Until Deke, he was the only man who could give comfort to her. Tira stood beside him, beaming, "Surprise you, did we?" She laughed watching the pair seeming to wait for her hug. Tira admonished her with an underlying tone of disquiet. Tira would see through all her attempts to keep what they had between them private, "Where have you been? When you weren't home, we started getting worried about you. Mr. Taylor at the sheriff's office tried to convince us you were fine. You went to help someone in another small town? Is that right?"

"We...yes, that's right." Annie looked at Deke as if he had an explanation then back to Tira. By the look on his face, he meant to leave all the answers to her. She didn't have one clue as to what to tell them. So ashamed of all she'd done, she wanted to vanish into the walls. She didn't know how to tell her doting parents she'd been with this man, in his bed.

On a brighter note, she could tell them about saving Ivy's child. If she did that, she would have to explain how she was kidnapped. "When did you arrive?"

"Two days ago. Someone said you and the sheriff rode up to Aspen...something, couldn't remember the rest of it," Jamie suggested his voice filled with curiosity. Annie understood he was after the truth.

"I'll leave the three of you to your reunion."

Deke started to back from the door, clearly uneasy with the sudden change of events. She was certain Deke didn't like the ensuing confrontation any more than she did. He pinched the bridge of his nose as he seemed to study her. "I'm certain the three of you have quite a lot to talk about. Wouldn't want to interrupt."

He was a coward. She wasn't about to allow him to abandon her. "No, you don't." Annie grabbed his arm, guiding him into the room. She kept her fingers wrapped around his arm. "Father, this is Deke Sullivan. Of course, you know that."

She looked at Tira. "Tira, my stepmother. Yes, we went to Aspen Flats. A patient needed tending, a baby...needed to be turned around. If I didn't go, both might have perished." Guilt swept through her at the blatant lie. She never lied, especially to her parents. She should just tell them the truth about what she did last night. The truth wouldn't come back to haunt her. Ah, but Deke said he named his ranch Aspen Heights so it wasn't a complete falsehood. The Aspen part was true.

"Yes, we know each other. A pleased to meet you is no longer appropriate. In case you forgot, I hired Deke to watch over you. Didn't he tell you? I see you went with Annie to keep her safe. Thank you." Jamie held out his hand to Deke.

The two shook hands to reacquaint. They observed each other as if trying to see into each other's soul. They reminded her of two bulls dancing around each other seeking supremacy. For Annie she was left with an uneasy feeling that her father knew what she'd been doing with Deke.

I'm thirty. My father has no say over what I do or don't do.

"I'm Tira. Just who are you to our Annie?"

Leave it to Tira to cut to the chase then see through all the seething and underlying feelings sweeping between them. Her stepmother was always blunt. Tira would understand that her father was thinking the same. They were her parents. The two of them would have answers. They would see the way she looked at Deke…love in her eyes. There was no getting around the fact she cared deeply for the man.

Annie thought she might have heard Deke groan then it seemed he stiffened. He pushed back on the brim of his hat revealing the cold shimmering of his eyes. His hands settled on his hips as he watched seeming to take in the scenario in front of him. He wasn't a man to be bullied. She didn't think that was her father's intent though if Jamie guessed Deke bedded her, there would be words exchanged. It would make no difference how much respect he had for the man before.

After a long pause while everyone stared at him, Deke cleared his throat. He seemed to relax, "I'm the groom. Your daughter is marrying me in a week." The words were blurted quickly as if he couldn't think of anything else to say. "Now, I'll let the three of you have some privacy to talk over whatever you like. I'll go by myself to see the minister. You can go with your stepmother to the dress makers." Again, he started to back from the room.

Faces fell in confusion. Annie felt heat rise to her cheeks before sending the heated picture of her embarrassment to the rest of her body. He didn't have to be so blunt, calculating. He could have tempered his words, been more discriminating. The information would come as a total shock to her parents. She was certain they would protest the hasty marriage. She would have to figure out how to become a buffer in this situation.

"You don't say?" Jamie said rubbing his chin while he searched his daughter's eyes for confirmation of the truth. All he would see was the heat on her cheeks. He would understand why she was so red. "Thought it was customary for the groom to ask the intended's father for her hand. Perhaps you forgot that step, son." Jamie's hands were clasped behind his back, his jaw clenched so tight the muscle ticked in agitation.

Annie cringed wishing the two would take their discussion to another room. Spending a bit of alone time with Tira would have been nice.

"Didn't know you would show up a week before the wedding," Deke spoke blandly, his arms crossed over his chest, as he seemed to study her parents, his eyes narrowing in apparent contemplation.

He wasn't backing down. Was he? Somewhere before starting for the door and reaching the portal, he abruptly stopped. To Annie, he still appeared as if the foremost of his thoughts was to bolt.

Her father continued to rock on the balls of his feet, clearly meaning to defend his cub. "Could have sent a message, son. Since the nuptials are in seven days, you probably have had a while to let us know. Keeping us from knowing wasn't well done of you." Jamie continued in that same vein, pushing Deke for a suitable answer, one he would like.

Deke didn't have a response that her father would appreciate let alone accept.

Tira seemed to be calculating in her head. Her eyes widened as if she understood something Annie wanted to keep secret. She tapped a slender finger on her forehead, "You've only known each other two months or so. Well, you were also together on the train west along with the stagecoach. Must have been love at first sight."

Deke grinned. "Hardly, ma'am." He tipped the rim of his hat.

At least for Deke, his words were too true.

Annie grew hotter. She felt an instant need to slap him silly. After that she wanted to vanish into the woodwork. He had no right to put her on the spot that way even though his words were accurate. She cleared her throat, hoping to clarify some of what he spouted. "Actually, Deke spent the first few weeks trying to convince me I didn't belong in the west, especially the Rocky Mountains. During that time, we got to know each other better. He's taught me a few things."

She supposed that was an understatement as to what went on between the two of them as she recalled his lesson about Polaris.

"Sounds like a real love story," Jamie muttered, clearly displeased by the events. "The groom doesn't think the bride belongs in this territory. Not a great beginning for the newlyweds. What brought you to the point you're considering marriage?"

Tira clasped her hands together bringing them beneath her chin. Annie knew the gesture quite well. It was her thoughtful position. "A relationship a bit like ours don't you think, Jamie? I fell in love with you the first time I saw you at Ella's wedding. I knew then we needed to get to know each other better. That's why I sailed to Baltimore. Why, I tried to convince you to teach me how to build ships. You wanted nothing to do with me. At least that's what you led me to believe. It wasn't the truth though, was it?"

"Our love story was nothing like this," Jamie said in his defense, projecting his hand around the room so they would understand. "We loved each other only we didn't want to say the words to each other. You knocked my socks off when I found you scurrying up the mast of one of my clippers barefoot and..." instead of finishing the statement he swallowed hard.

Annie could finish that statement for her father. Tira had unbound her breasts. Her father saw her pretty much as if she wasn't wearing anything. In any case the thin shirt Tira wore left nothing to his imagination.

"Father," Annie cut in, waving her hands in front of his face so he would pay attention to her. "We are getting married in a week. With or without your blessing, best you come to terms with that fact. We just decided...yesterday. I was going to send a message this afternoon. What I want to know is what are the two of you doing here? You also didn't write. It's not your usual way to surprise me."

"What's the hur…?" Jamie asked then suddenly realized what the hurry might be about. His brows drew together as he looked from Deke to Annie then back again as if he was examining their motives. When he set his gaze on her belly, she knew he was guessing she was with child.

Tira grabbed his arm, her smile wide. She started to tug him from the room even while he seemed to resist. "We should leave the happy couple for a while. I'm certain they have a great deal of planning if the ceremony is going to take place in a week. Dinner?" Tira asked. "Here or at the hotel? I would help you cook. Your father and I will shop. What would you like?"

"Here would be fine. Can you come back around six? We should have most everything taken care of by then." Annie asked wishing there was a hole she could drop into.

Her father understood exactly why the hasty wedding. He wouldn't approve. However, unless he wanted her to give birth to a bastard, he could say nothing in the negative. Bottom line, he could not object. She could throw the facts in his face. Tira had been pregnant when they wed. In fact, her baby brother was born before they married. Jamie had no grounds to judge any man.

"I'll be here at five sharp to help you with the meal. Can I do some shopping? What would the two of you like? The men can discuss their feelings over a brandy."

Tira repeated her earlier offer as she led Jamie from the room, their footsteps echoing down the stairs while she held her breath.

Annie fell back on one of the chairs. Mortified, she closed her eyes, her head resting in her hands. "They know I'm pregnant." Her voice was soft, whisper thin, cracking as she spoke the last word. She looked to him for encouragement. "I...this would have been so much easier if they weren't here. Writing to them would have been less confrontational. I don't know what to do."

"Does it matter?"

Deke stood in front of her before pulling her into his arms. He was strength to her, protective power. While she understood he couldn't fix all their problems, he was holding her. She leaned into him soaking up the warmth he offered. His big hand soothed as he ran the palm up then down her back. "We will wed no matter what they think or guess. Unless you say something, no one will know you carry my child. You won't show for months. You won't give birth early. I don't see a problem."

"Y-yes...it matters. H-he's my father. I don't want him to think I would do this with just anyone." She couldn't tell him why it made such a difference to her. Her father would have to understand. All her life, she never intended to be pregnant before the wedding. If she were anyone else, she might not know about the conception. She might have her plan intact. That wasn't the case. She did know the truth.

"The two of them never had sex before their first child?" He lifted an eyebrow to the ceiling clearly speculating. "Tell me true."

"Tira was pregnant before they wed," she blurted. "Actually, had the baby before they were married. She fled the town hoping he'd love her enough to come after her. That was the first of my bad ideas. Father always left on trips. When he returned, he always told me how much he missed me. With my encouragement, Tira left for London the day before father was going to ask her to marry him," she spoke softly tears filling her eyes, her body shaking against his. "Doesn't mean I'm not embarrassed to admit I gave into your charming ways. I'm also ashamed that we could not wait, we couldn't do things in the proper order. I understand I'm too impulsive. I just go and whatever happens, happens."

"They will both understand when the child arrives in nine months. You've nothing to be ashamed of. If we don't tell them, they'll never know the truth. After all, you can't truly be certain you carry my child." He stroked her back. His soothing hands helped her raw nerves.

"Mother and father loved each other," she announced while she tried desperately not to cry. Moisture filled her eyes, tears slipped down her cheeks. "Father did go after her. She gave birth on board the ship. My little brother..."

She loved the boy so very much. Always and in some ways thought of the tiny baby as hers. He wasn't. He was almost twenty and a holy terror. Her brother would brake hearts.

"Ah, so love makes the difference. Perhaps they grew to love each other over time. Maybe as in our case the initial attraction was pure lust. Have you thought of that? We have nothing to defend about our relationship. Obviously, your father never told Tira he loved her. If he did, she would never have run."

"Was lust the only reason you seduced me?"

More than anything she wanted him to love her. She did love him. Couldn't say the words when she was so very uncertain of his feelings.

"Part but not all," he murmured as his big hand once more stroked down her back resting provocatively on her fanny.

"What's the rest of it?" she asked wanting to know what was in his head that he didn't seem willing to tell her.

"How about you, Little Darlin'? Was it just lust that sent you to my bed two nights ago?" he asked effectively stopping her questions and turning the tables. "Was the emotion only lust? Raw Passion? Or...could the feeling be grounded in something else?"

"No," she said softly, her words forming as she thought on his questions, "but the feeling was powerful. When you kissed me, touched me in ways I've never been touched before, I couldn't say no. Didn't want to in any case." She didn't know. Her attraction for him materialized the first night she met him, when he stayed in her apartment to protect her. After that the feelings grew with a speed that stole her breath from her lungs. From the beginning she had a relentless need to prove him wrong about where she belonged. There had always been a challenge between them, spoken as well as unspoken.

She proved her worth as well as where she belonged.

Pushing away from him, she felt a bit better. She touched his chin while she watched his eyes darken with what she was coming to understand was desire. "I want a bath before we go see the minister," she spoke looking directly at him. "I feel as if my entire body is covered with Rocky Mountain dirt. When we speak to the man...of God..." she wanted to feel clean, needed to wash away the shame of her behavior.

"I'll go to the boarding house and get a bath. Be back in thirty minutes. You be ready." Quickly, he kissed her then strode from her place. She poured a cup of coffee before setting out to heat the water for her bath.

Her parents were in Denver City. They would be in attendance for her wedding. She was certainly pleased her siblings did not travel with them. Her brother would tease mercilessly. She sipped the coffee. By the time she finished with the bath and the coffee she felt a bolt of energy surge inside her. Her confidence grew a bit. She told herself she had nothing to be ashamed of. The pregnancy was between Deke and herself. Her parents could guess all they wanted. She wouldn't tell them.

"Annie..." It was Deke striding though the door. She heard his footsteps. Caught his scent. Felt a surge of love center in her belly. "Are you ready?" He stepped into the bathing room, in time to see to the fastening of her dress. He kissed the nape of her neck, nibbled. His big hand cupped one breast as he flicked his thumb across the rapidly hardening tip. A little mewl of delight passed through her lips. She heard a masculine groan rumble from deep in his belly.

Lust was good.

Shivers rippled through her body from the top of her head to the tips of her toes. "Behave yourself. This is no time for a challenge. We've a minister to see. A gown to commission as well as a dinner to prepare. We don't have time for you to tumble me to the bed."

No, there was no time. Her parents could show up again at any moment.

"You're wearing far too many clothes," he murmured turning her in his arms, his mouth descended to capture hers for a quick hard kiss. "It would take far too long to get you the way I want you."

"You'll just have to work harder to get what you're after," she laughed softly as she waltzed away from him.

He let her go, otherwise he would have made love to her. She didn't have one doubt.

"The shivers and little trembling of your body I so adore will be more than enough to keep me sated until we can find the privacy we need to finish this," he whispered, his voice whiskey smooth and husky. He held out his hand to her. "I can kiss every new spot I uncover until you are naked. Come, let's go take care of the necessities so we won't have to hide our passion from the world as well as your parents."

He crooked his arm so she could place her hand on his elbow. "What do you think of my parents?" she asked after they reached the bottom of the steps eager for an answer.

Waiting, her heart pounded. She wanted him to like them. Damnation, she recalled her father hired the man to escort her. Jamie knew him inside as well as out or he would never have trusted Deke with her life.

"That we shouldn't lie to them," he spoke softly turning her head so she stared into his eyes. "Don't believe for an instant they will judge you or me. We fell into bed together. So what? We are two consenting adults who wanted each other. We're expecting a child so we are doing the right thing."

Annie needed to mull his words over for a little while. Consenting adults, yes. Expecting a child, yes, that too. Wouldn't be pleased to present the grandparents with a bastard. Again, the right answer was yes. She wanted more, longed for a loving relationship. If he could tell her he loved her, this would be perfect.

"Dinner will not be pleasant if we tell them the truth," she told him wishing there was another way. "Father will ask more questions. He might even ask about the baby. Do you have all the answers? I don't. For more reasons than I care to enumerate, I don't want them to know that I'm pregnant. That's one lie I'm going to perpetrate."

Deke ran a finger around his collar seemingly thinking over the situation. "Don't believe we should mention the child growing in your womb either. While you are positive and I trust your knowledge, it's far too soon to make an announcement of that sort. The impending wedding is probably the only shock we should give them for the time being. I don't want them to come to the conclusion we are only wedding for the sake of the child. We are not."

He was right. She didn't want to say anything about the child even though she was certain both her parents guessed they slept together. Even if she slept with him when she first met him, if they were any other couple, they might not realize she was increasing.

"You're right. No one should tell significant members of their families about a pregnancy before three months has passed," she said as if by rote.

It was something dictated to her by other women she saw who were awaiting the impending birth of their children. Too many babies were miscarried. Most happened within the first three months.

One of his perfectly sculpted eyebrows rose in speculation. "Why is that? Three months is a magic number?" He didn't appear to understand.

"Of sorts," she murmured softly. "Less chance of miscarriage. The farther along a woman is the more likely the child will survive." The very thought of losing her child sent moisture to her eyes. "If I lose the baby, do you still want me for your wife?" Her knees shook, terrified of his possible answer.

Gently he squeezed her hand. "More than anything. While the child's conception is incentive for a hasty wedding, I had every intention of asking you to marry me. You brought up the possibility of this child if you recall. I did not expect anything of the sort. I challenged you, made love to you in the snow, in the hayloft with every intention of posing the question."

"True again. I never expected you to ask me to marry you. I always thought I would marry for love."

She couldn't help the ensuing sigh. Her hopes and dreams now centered around this man who felt only lust for her. She supposed her love for him would have to be enough to last a lifetime.

"Not expediency?" he queried sounding a little bit angry with her.

Annie didn't understand his bubbling annoyance with her statement. What she said was true. "The way you say that makes what occurred between us sound sordid. I never thought. You seduced me," she accused feeling as if the conversation got out of hand too quickly. She didn't want to argue any more than it seemed he did.

"We are here. What do we tell Reverend Hays? That we are madly in love?" he asked, his sarcasm showing dreadfully, his eyes cold.

She braced herself for the ordeal to come. Seems all she did anymore was tell falsehoods as well as annoy him, "Whatever we have to tell the reverend, the wedding has to go on in one week. He can't say no because he doesn't believe we love each other. If we want to marry, what does it matter what the reverend believes?" Annie was quick to ask.

"We love each other then. Our feelings go beyond lust," he said searching her for meaningful answers. "That's what we tell him. Don't want the man to turn us down. He can you know. We'd have to go to Fort Laramie if that were to happen. That would take another week of our time along with more questions from your mother and father."

"Yes, we love each other," her voice floated out on a whisper thin thread.

She was trembling because she did love this man. For her, the words weren't a lie. She could never let him know the truth. Didn't want to find herself vulnerable if he didn't return the sentiment.

"That's good. Love is good. The good reverend will be pleased with the fact. We love each other then. Are we agreed?"

She nodded. For her, love for him wasn't a lie.

They stepped into the cool interior of the church. Walked until they reached the door to his office. Annie held her breath while she listened to the silence surrounding her. If the church was so cool why was her forehead beaded with sweat, armpits too? She swallowed the lump of air that was caught in the back of her throat.

He seemed to sense her fear. Seemed to want to help the best he could. "Easy, my love. This will all be over before you know it. Sip a breath of air. You need the oxygen."

Slowly, he turned the handle. Deke grinned at her as if to give encouragement. The door slowly swung open. Reverend Hays stood in front of them, a smile on his face. "Welcome."

Without pause, she turned to look at Deke, a million questions in her mind. The most prevalent one was that Reverend Hays knew why they were coming to talk with him. He waited for them. How?

Deke grinned at her, his smile broad, "Stopped by on my way to take a bath and change my clothes. Told him we would be over in about thirty minutes. Believe it was closer to forty." He squeezed her hand. Looking to the reverend, "Sorry about our tardiness."

"Your man did stop. I'm pleased to marry the two of you. I've always respected Deke. He's a good man. Fine sheriff. Sit down. You are such a charming couple, the doctor and the sheriff. A good combination," He gestured to the chairs in front of his desk. "All I need are a few details."

"Not to be the sheriff much longer, Reverend. Going to start ranching again now that I've a wife."

"Good, glad to hear that. A woman shouldn't have to worry about her man coming home for dinner."

Deke cleared his throat after he saw to her comfort. Annie decided she best keep her mouth closed during the interview, if that was what this was going to be. Often times she did her best when she didn't say anything at all.

Deke began as he slipped her hand into his. Tenderly, he rubbed tiny circles on her wrist. "One week from today we would like you to marry us. It will be a small ceremony with only a few friends accompanied by Annie's parents who arrived here while we were gone. Their arrival was a pleasant surprise."

Reverend Hays nodded his head. "I'll be pleased. The pair of you

213

look...well...when you look at each other I can see the love shining in your eyes. This is a wedding blessed in heaven. A man and a woman in love, God couldn't ask for more."

Once again, she wished she could fade into the woodwork. Instead, she smiled sweetly at the reverend.

"Yes, I'm very much in love with Annie."

For a few seconds he gazed at her, his eyes shimmering not with love but the heat of lust. Annie recognized that look. Had seen the same blaze in his eyes every time he made love to her.

Lust not love.

Oh, god, oh...god, she was going to have to lie again. She would go to hell sure as shootin'. "Yes, I do love Deke. He's been my rock ever since I met him in Boston almost three months ago." That wasn't a lie. Maybe she wouldn't go to hell. It was Deke who told the lies. She did love this man.

"You never told me that before, sweetheart. Your rock? Well, a man's got to be proud of something like that."

Annie didn't lie about him being her rock or the fact she loved him. She didn't want him to know or see the truth in her eyes when she spoke the words. "I would have never been able to reach here without his help. I would have had to hire someone in Fort Laramie, someone I didn't trust. I might have been lost going over the mountain when I didn't have enough air to breathe."

At that point, she clamped her mouth shut. She didn't want to stick her foot any deeper into her mouth. Deke and the reverend talked for what seemed like hours before they finally stood. She'd never been so relieved in her entire life. Extending his hand, Deke shook the reverend's. She supposed they figured out all the little details during his first visit. She was half tuned into the conversation and half tuned out.

Once they stood in the bright light of the afternoon sun, Deke spoke softly, "To the dressmakers? We will have a gown commissioned that you will love."

Unable to put one coherent thought in front of the other, Annie nodded. Deke took her hand into his. She understood the gown would have to be simple if the dress were to be finished in a week. In any case, she didn't like a lot of flounces and ribbons. Some lace she appreciated. Tira would want to be there with her. Why did they walk away? If Tira stayed a moment longer, she would have invited her to accompany her.

"Are you coming inside?" She knew her eyes were wide when she asked. Her throat was parched. "I..." she ran her tongue across her bottom lip. "Don't actually want to do this by myself. Your input would be appreciated."

"Only long enough to make certain your gown isn't eggshell blue. Otherwise, I trust your judgment. I will see if I can find Tira. I'm certain she is much better suited to give opinions about your wedding dress."

~ * ~

Tira looked over the meat Jamie picked out. The steak looked as if it would appeal to the rugged sheriff who seemed to capture their daughter's heart. First impressions to fall back on, she liked the man. When he looked at Annie, she saw desire and yes, love. With every gesture, he treated her tenderly.

"What do you think is actually going on here?" Jamie asked, his sarcasm coupled with a slow burn of anger more than apparent to Tira. "This is not all what it seems. The pair of them are keeping secrets. He seduced her. I know it!" His fists clenched.

"Two people in love who want to be married, nothing more. If there is something going on, the knowledge is not our business. If they have secrets, they both know them. Besides, don't believe I'd want to know any more details than I do now. Hmm...what else should we pick up for dinner?"

She flounced away from her husband clearly displeased with his thoughts. To her, it was apparent the couple was very much in love. It also seemed obvious neither shared their sentiment with each other.

"They are hiding something." His voice overly gruff for the situation seemingly unwilling to acknowledge Tira's words of advice.

Tira turned on him, poking him in the chest with her finger. "As I said before, whatever is going on between them is not our concern. You promise me, you'll stay out of this. The two are in love. That's all we need to understand." She hated the words as soon as they left her lips. Annie was special to her, had always been very special. She was a unique woman, brilliant as well as intuitive. She wished she had the time to sit down, talk to her as they used to do before she left for medical school. Tira agreed with her husband, there were things the two were hiding.

"They've been intimate," he blurted out as if that should make wit of difference in how they felt about the marriage.

"As were we before we wed. If you care to recall, I actually gave birth before we were married. Don't go so high and mighty on her or him. There's to be no judging where our daughter is concerned. She is a beautiful woman who deserves our love no matter what has happened between them."

Tira picked up an onion along with a few potatoes. She found snow peas that might make a good side dish. Placing two loaves of bread in her bag, she continued perusing the produce.

"Look who is come to help with dinner?" Jamie said softly for only Tira to hear. "Wonder what the hell he wants. Has this look on his face."

"Hello," Deke said while he tipped his hat back on his head moving from one foot to the other. "Don't mean to bother you, however..."

"However?" Tira asked sweetly. She loved seeing the insecure look on his handsome face. If she didn't miss her guess, the man was totally out of his element with them. "What is it you want?"

"Well..." Deke looked down the street before shifting his gaze back to her. He ran a finger inside his collar. Seeming nervous he tipped his hat away from the dark steel blue of his eyes.

Tira wasn't certain why he was stumbling over his words. All she could do to keep her laughter from bubbling out, she quickly said, "I won't bite."

He laughed, the tension seeming to ease. "Didn't think you would, ma'am."

Nonetheless, he looked pointedly at Jamie.

"My husband won't either."

"Speak for yourself," Jamie said softly while he studied Deke.

"The man has a lot to answer for. I hired him, trusted the man with my daughter."

Deke cleared his throat before he blurted through gritted teeth, "Annie would like to see you. She didn't say exactly those words. I believe she'd like help with her wedding dress. She wanted me..." His words trailed off with a lift to his shoulders that was all masculine in Tira's mind. "All I wanted was to make certain she didn't pick out eggshell blue fabric. She promised me she wouldn't do so."

"What on earth? Eggshell blue for a wedding gown?"

When Tira looked back to Deke the expression on his face confirmed her guesses. By everything Annie and Deke said she expected they'd been together intimately. The color of the dress cemented that notion. Tira placed the items she was carrying into Jamie's hands. "You and Deke get to know each other better than you thought you knew each other when he hired you. Finish picking out the food for our dinner. I've a daughter to help. Thank you." She backed up watching the two men. "Don't do anything you'll regret, Jamie. He's going to be our son-in-law. You respected him before. Respect him now. In a week, he's going to be part of our family."

When Tira entered the dressmaker's she saw her daughter, face pale, sorting aimlessly through fashion plates. Annie never possessed fashion sense. Her mind was always someplace other than the latest styles. Deke was right. She would need help.

"Would you like a second opinion?" Tira asked stepping beside Annie, her hand placed on her shoulder. "I see you've picked out white satin. Good choice to start."

"I'm hopeless. Though you know that for a fact." Annie let a long rush of air from her lungs, moisture simmering in her expressive eyes. "None of this means anything to me. How can I pick out such a special gown when I don't have a clue as to what I'm doing?"

"Let's see what we can do with this situation to change it around. I know from the past you don't want flounces or ruffles, nothing elaborate, simple is the best for you. Your tastes have always run to unassuming. Am I right?" Tira eliminated several possibilities. They were down to about five choices. "Now, what would you like, lace? Pearls?

Perhaps something to show off your amazing figure?"

Annie shot her a grimace.

So, she didn't think her figure was amazing. Deke must like her curves. He definitely seemed to appreciate Annie.

"No pearls...a bit of lace around the top of the corsage would be nice. Something that would hang nicely from my bust, I think." Annie graced her with a half-smile. "Maybe...is that all wrong?"

"This day, along with the dress are about you. If you like what you are choosing, the choice isn't wrong." Tira set several more selections aside. They were left with two prospects. "Would either of these two styles suit you? Don't believe you could go wrong with either dress," Tira asked, her heart going out to Annie.

The little one was getting married. Tira recalled so many adventures they had together. Would never forget the time Annie tied her to the bed while she was practicing knots. Her cheeks flamed. Jamie found her spread eagled on his large bed in the captain's cabin of his ship. That was the evening they set sail after she promised to give him whatever he wanted. Damnation, the man should never judge Deke. Deke was a pussycat compared to Jamie. Jamie deliberately set out to seduce her.

Annie's eyes welled up with tears while she nodded then pointed to one. Tira wanted to pull her into her arms to discover why exactly she cried while she was picking out a wedding gown for what should be one of the best days of her life. She should be brimming with happiness, chattering about how wonderful Deke was. Again, she reminded herself this was not her business. Still, this would not be a small worry if Annie's father witnessed the tears. She needed to get to the bottom of this before dinner. If she didn't, there might very well be a reckoning Annie didn't want to happen. When it came to his first born, Jamie was overly protective. Well, no, he was overly protective with all his children. It was just that none of his other children were called bastard or whore.

Right now, Jamie might be grilling Deke about why the hasty marriage. In her mind there could be only one reason.

A pregnancy.

The two had not known each other long enough to suspect that Annie was increasing. Her Annie was a doctor. She would know about her body. Certainly, so much information, she'd not had when she was in Annie's position. Jamie had to tell her she was with child.

Quickly, the pair finished with the dressmaker gaining reassurances since the pattern was so simple, it would be easy to finish in a week. Annie was to visit again in two days for a fitting.

"Shall we go for a walk?" Tira asked, looping her arm in her daughter's. "The men will have to see to dinner. Do you think they will be able to create something edible?"

Tira laughed understanding Jamie's best dishes were pancakes and bacon. On the side, he was fairly nimble with scrambled eggs and fried potatoes.

"Will father fry the potatoes? I think that's the only way he knows how to cook them. Don't know if Deke can cook on a stove. He does do well with beans over an open campfire. The coffee he makes is always divine. At six in the morning all coffee would be heavenly," Annie mused as if thinking about some event in her past.

"Do you have any of Uncle Logan's Bordeaux or Chianti in the apartment?" Tira asked as they walked along the wooden planks in front of the stores.

"I have lots of the wine. You should know since you've always kept me supplied. Deke likes the Bordeaux."

"In that case we won't starve. Tell me why choosing a wedding gown has you in tears."

Tira got straight to the point. She didn't have time to waste being hesitant.

"We lied to you and father. Lied to the good reverend too. I'm not a liar. Today, I think I told more lies than in my entire life."

Tira mulled those words over in her head. "Were the lies because your father and I showed up?"

Annie was shaking as well as nodding. "It's lust. He doesn't love me. That's not the worst. He only wants to marry me because of the baby." She gasped seeming to suddenly realize what she blurted. Annie turned, her hands on Tira's arm. "You can't tell father. Please…please don't tell him. He'll murder Deke. I do love him."

Tira nodded that she wouldn't tell Jamie. "No, your father doesn't

219

need for me to say the words. He wants to hear what he's already guessed from you. If you're unwilling to say anything, don't."

"He's guessed?"

"Yes, you know the only reason for a hasty marriage is a bun in the oven. Deke strikes me as being an honorable man. What I don't understand is how you know so soon?"

"I..." Annie paused, her body tensing with the realization Tira might not believe her. "We...we made love two nights ago for the first time. It only takes one time."

"True." Tira spoke cautiously wondering at the rest of the information Annie was withholding. "That's not why you know though, is it?"

"The timing was perfect for a child," Annie admitted.

"You've only made love that one time?"

Annie was shaking her head, a tear slipping down her cheek. "No, two more times, more. I don't want to tell him to stop. He's..."

"You do love him?" Tira didn't wait for an answer before she continued. "Deke loves you too. It's obvious in the way his eyes shimmer when he looks at you. The two of you should tell each other exactly how you feel. This marriage he's proposed is not because of the baby...or lust. Although that might be part of the reason. It might also be the reason that gave him the courage to act. There should be no lies between the two of you. Jamie and I had too many lies to count that kept us apart for far too long. Don't let that happen."

Chapter Eight

Deke swore softly as he watched Jamie butcher the potatoes. He was certain Annie would not have wanted them fried. He was also pretty sure that the snow peas were going to find themselves over cooked, mush to be exact. For a few seconds, he thought that if Jamie wouldn't be too offended, he should walk over to Riley's saloon and order dinner for four.

Sitting back, his legs crossed in front of him, he sipped brandy. He wondered when the questions would begin flying. By the look in his eyes, he had a wealth of concerns. Jamie continued to look furtively at him, deep scowls on his forehead. Deke didn't think Jamie's thoughts were worth a penny. In any case, if he grilled him about Annie's possible pregnancy, he would have to decline giving information. Annie's delicate condition was none of her father's business.

Hell, Deke wasn't even certain he believed Annie knew. It was far too soon to jump to conclusions.

Jamie tossed the steak into the pan to fry. After that he stared at him hard, his eyes narrowing. "Why can't you wait for the wedding? Hell, a year! Why the hurry? Seems the two of you barely know each other."

Those were fair questions. None of them Jamie Lundin's business. He rolled the glass between his hands, watching the amber contents swirl. "If I had my way, we would have married today. Wanted to do just that."

"Suppose Tira's and my arrival stopped that," he growled, his voice menacing his eyes shimmering with fire.

"No."

Deke didn't want to give the man easy information. As far as he was concerned, Jamie Lundin would have to pry words from his lips. He decided he might very well enjoy a verbal scuffle with the man as long as Annie wasn't around to hear.

"No?" One of Jamie's eyebrows shot up. He turned the potatoes over. "No? Is that all you've got to say for yourself?"

He sipped more of the fine brandy. If he could drown himself in the liquor and forget this encounter, he would be a man pleased. He counted Jamie as a friend until today. Well, he had a lot to say. He just didn't want to gift this man with the information despite his respect for him. Leaning forward he set the glass on the table before putting his hands on his thighs. He supposed there was no way for him to avoid a confrontation.

Sarcasm coating his words, Deke drawled, his gaze riveted on Jamie's. "If I had my way, we'd be married now. Want Annie as my wife…the sooner the better. Your arrival had nothing to do with anything. We decide to wait before we knew you stopped by, treating us to a surprise visit."

Jamie turned the steaks. The fire sizzled, flames from the lard in the pan shooting toward the ceiling. Deke hoped the man wasn't about to set the little apartment on fire while admitting he couldn't have done better. Thought about Bella, wished his cook was doing the cooking. They might have some spicey steak enchiladas to enjoy instead of burnt steak along with soft snow peas.

"What did cause the two of you to postpone the wedding bells?"

Deke understood his reluctance in answering the questions was only prolonging the inevitable. Jamie would learn the answers or die trying. Telling his wife would be ever so much easier. Jamie didn't like him at this moment for good reason. The man thought he seduced his little girl. He did.

"The wedding gown."

"Ah…" Jamie's head bobbed up and down as if he understood completely.

"I'd do anything for your daughter. A wedding gown was not a lot to ask. If it would make her happy, the wish was hers."

He did realize he would do anything for Annie. Pleasing her pleased him.

That time his answers gained a smile from Jamie. "I feel the same about my wife as well as my children. Annie's has always known she has a place in my heart. I'm glad you want to make her happy at the expense of your plans."

"Your little gal stole my heart back in Boston."

Damn, he didn't mean to tell the man anything so private. Needless to say, he received another grin. Perhaps silence wasn't the way to proceed with Annie's father. "Do you think that steak is going to be edible?"

This time the scowl coming from Jamie was not directed at him. Jamie stared at the sizzling meat. "The steak maybe, the potatoes a resounding yes, the snow peas no. You've any ideas? Tira won't be happy if there is no dinner."

Deke hooted his laughter, changing to a low rumble as he surveyed the mess Jamie created on the stove. "We order from Riley's, the saloon across the street or we fill up on wine. Guess those are our only choices."

"How much time do you think we have before the ladies get back from the dressmaker?" Jamie asked while he looked out the window toward the saloon.

"Darned if I know. Don't have any clue as to how much time is needed to pick out a wedding gown. Seems like a pretty big job to me. Probably have another hour. What do you think?" He could run over, make a quick trip then be back.

Jamie dumped everything in the garbage. "Let's go. Even if they get back before we do, they'll be pleased when we bring them something that will taste good." He carried the bag downstairs before getting rid of it in the trash.

At Riley's they ordered a dinner exactly like the one they were supposed to prepare. "Think they'll guess?" Deke asked as they made their way back to the upstairs apartment, his stomach now rumbling. He and Jamie were now linked together in a small crime. If no one suspected, they wouldn't tell.

"Of course, neither are stupid. The nice thing is that we will feed them a decent dinner," Jamie said with a snicker. "Even though we didn't cook. My wife is much more pleasant to be around when she is not hungry. I know Annie is too. When she was growing up…still do for that matter…bought most of our food from the boarding house across the street."

When they stepped inside the apartment the women were sipping wine, smiling 'I knew it all along smiles' graced their serene expressions. Tira set her glass on the table as she strode to collect the sack of food from her husband and kissed his cheek. She didn't say anything. Neither did Annie. Annie set the table. Tira arranged the meal on the table along with utensils to dish up.

Jamie looked at Deke, grinned. Deke didn't know what to think of this silent exchange between husband and wife, daughter, too, if he looked closely. The women didn't say anything but acted as if nothing untoward happened, as if they didn't toss in the garbage what should have been a perfectly good meal. Annie would most likely realize he didn't know how to cook except over an open campfire. Jamie had done an admirable job with the potatoes. The rest of the meal…well…the rest of the meal deserved to end up as it did, in the garbage. How did a cook ruin a steak? Seemed to Deke the act took a great deal of effort.

Someone had to say something sometime.

That person sure as hell wasn't going to be him.

The plates were filled, wine poured. Deke never encountered a situation as awkward as this. As much as he determined not to speak, he did so now. Cutting through the eerie silence was a necessity in his mind.

Clearing his throat, he looked up from the perfectly cooked steak to speak his mind. He had to get Annie's parents out of town so he could be with her for the rest of the week. Taking an extra moment to think before speaking, "The two of you should ride out to my ranch tomorrow morning. I'd like you to stay there while you're visiting." He pointedly looked at Tira, "You can help Bella plan the menu for the reception. Maria will be happy to take directions as to the flowers and whatever else you want for decorations."

"Where will I be?" Annie asked sweetly, her fork resting on her plate, her glass of wine almost to her lips, while her pretty eyes shot spears of fire his way.

He didn't want to tell her she'd be in his bed or perhaps more truthfully that he'd be in hers.

Deke grinned. Held up his glass of wine in silent salute. He did enjoy her when she confronted and challenged him. "Wherever you would like to be. I thought you would prefer to continue your practice here in town. What if someone needs a doctor? We don't want to leave the town shorthanded," he told her smiling at her as if they both overlooked the fact she had no patients, no clientele. "I have to make a smooth transition with my deputy. At the moment, I plan to stay here."

He didn't want to give too much away. By here, he meant in Annie's apartment, not the boarding house. Nonetheless, he hoped the small ploy about her practice would sooth any objections to Annie staying in town. After all, she was the doctor here in Denver City.

"You're right," Annie agreed as if finally understanding his ploy. "I wasn't thinking. We could ride out to the ranch in three days after my fitting or even the day of the fitting if that's more suitable."

Tira leaned forward, patting Annie's hand. "That's a splendid idea, dear. Don't you agree, Jamie?" She turned back to Annie, "Why don't you give me a list of suggestions for the celebratory feast? I'd like you to have everything you like."

Jamie leered at Deke, who understood exactly what Annie's father was thinking. Deke planned the scenario well. He would be able to see Annie anytime it suited both of them. He didn't plan on sleeping alone for the next week. Until her parents showed up unannounced, there weren't any obstacles to his plans. Now, with Tira's help the situation was easily manipulated.

The smile he shot Jamie was brilliant as well as smug. If he were to start counting, he won this round hands down.

"We should stay in town," Jamie said, his voice harsh while he drummed his fingers on the table. "Wouldn't want Annie to miss out on time with her mother."

Tira jumped into the conversation proceeding as if she agreed with Deke not her husband. "No...I want to see the ranch. The place where Annie will be living. Besides, Annie and Deke need time alone to sort out some of the prewedding jitters both seem to be feeling. Do believe there is a lot unsaid between them. Don't you agree? We can help plan the menu for the feast." She smiled demurely at her husband before she winked at Deke.

"That's my poi…" Jamie abruptly cut his statement off as it seemed he saw his wife's glare of displeasure a change from a few seconds previous.

"Annie must work for a living. These two need to decide how they will proceed once they are a couple. They will have to decide if Annie wants to continue with her practice, also where they choose to live. Perhaps they want to divide their time between here and the ranch."

Deke's soon to be wife jumped into the conversation. "While you know all my favorite foods, Bella likes spicey. She will temper her recipes for our unaccustomed pallet. I'll be happy with anything the two of you decide."

"Spicey?" Jamie asked, a perfectly sculpted eyebrow shooting toward the ceiling.

"Even though her name is Bella, my cook comes from a solid Mexican household. She is wonderful, her cooking delicious. I'm certain the two of you will find the cuisine delectable, much better than what we might have served tonight."

He was delighted to see Annie confirming his sentiments. She was nodding her head, clearly trying to convince her parents to stay at the ranch. Maybe she wanted to sleep with him as much as he did her. "We'll come out after the fitting as well as the day before the wedding. As you say, Deke and I have a lot of logistics to figure out. At the moment," she confessed, "I don't have a lot of patients."

"I'm not going to remain the sheriff. Taylor knows that he will take over the sheriff position in a week, sooner if possible. I'm focusing my attention on my bride as well as the work at the ranch."

"Your ranch makes enough money to maintain a wife along with a family?" Jamie asked, his tone sour. It seemed he still looked for some means to discredit him.

"It will."

Deke wasn't about to tell anyone, especially not Jamie Lundin that he was independently wealthy. He didn't need to work. Did so simply to stay away from boredom, certain now that with Annie in his life he would never be bored again. He tapped his fingers on the table before sipping the wonderful Bordeaux. "Do appreciate this wine." He lifted his glass in salute.

"I'm certain the ranch will be more comfortable than the hotel," Tira said as she flashed Jamie a smile that Deke felt certain would get her anything she wanted.

"There are horses. You can ride if you wish. Unless you might get lost," he added while he thought about Annie's beautiful tight nipples always pointing north when she located Polaris.

He thought it strange she knew all about finding the north star but not how to use the point to direct her feet. She told him she never listened to everything her father told her. He prayed she would never have to use the directions he gave her. Nonetheless if she did, he also prayed she listened to him.

Jamie's eyes narrowed, the tone of his voice hardened again. Next, when he spoke, he sounded indignant. "I don't get lost."

"This area is different than the ocean," Tira reminded him. "You did get lost that one time…" She stopped talking seeming to see the fire in her husband's eyes. She brushed lose curls from her face. "Well, that was a different time as well as a different situation entirely. I'm certain you won't have problems navigating a forest. You are so adept." Tira slanted her gaze at Jamie's lips.

Jamie visibly gritted his teeth. It seemed Jamie brushed off the sarcasm they all heard in the tone of Tira's voice. "If it is what Tira wants, we'll stay at the ranch. We do expect to see the two of you more than once between now and the wedding," Jamie said as he picked up Tira's hand to hold it within his.

Deke nodded, pleased that so far he was getting what he wanted, albeit the pleasure came because Tira seemed to be on his side. If she wasn't, he didn't harbor one doubt that the parents of Annie would be remaining in town for the week. What he couldn't figure out was exactly how he was going to go about sleeping with his bride tonight. Her parents were still residing in Denver City. A bit of sneaking might come in handy.

Tira and Annie removed themselves from the table to sit near the fire. He topped off the glasses of wine. "Shall we?" he asked Jamie as he headed toward the sink with a handful of dirty dishes. Deke had no idea if the man would follow. Most men didn't do dishes.

The man seemed to understand what he spoke of. "The dishes? By all means."

"We made the mess," Deke shrugged as he began to clear more of the plates. "Suppose if we didn't have to buy dinner, the ladies might have done the chore."

"You've come up a notch in my mind," Jamie said as he filled the sink.

Yes, well, if washing a few dishes caused Annie's father to think better of him, he'd wash dishes every night. At home he had servants to do the chores. Actually, he enjoyed this particular task. Gave him time to think about the day's events along with planning for the next day.

They finished then joined the women with another glass of wine. Deke stared at the clock, wishing Tira and Jamie would take their leave. He understood they would not. If the evening was to progress the way he hoped, he would have to leave first. At the saloon, he could watch her apartment. Would know when her parents left to find their beds at the hotel.

Later, he rose slowly, sifting his hands through his hair, hiding a huge yawn. After that, he stuffed a bunch of air into his lungs while he gazed wistfully at Annie. She lifted her delicate shoulders in acceptance of the situation. She understood. He wanted to tell her to leave her door unlocked. Hoped she could read the message in his eyes.

Annie walked to the door with him, her hand tucked snugly into his. He hugged her. With her parents looking on, he wasn't going to stir flames that were already heated by kissing her in front of them. Annie walked down the steps with him, apparently with other ideas about what she wanted. At the bottom of the steps, he pulled her into his arms. His roving hands traveled the length of her body, stopping at delicately erotic spots he loved to caress.

"Leave the door open for me," he whispered softly next to her ear delighting in the fierce shiver whipping through her.

He nipped at the tender lobe. He loved the way she responded so swiftly to his sweet-talking. She was raw and passionate, a lover he would never grow tired of bedding.

"My parents…" she whispered in a thin voice.

"Won't stay here for the night. After they go to the hotel, I'll come check on you. Don't intend to spend the evening in a cold bed when I know what lies across the street."

Her expressive eyes crossed as she seemed to think about his intentions. "I…do you think it's wise? If my father finds out he might…"

"If not for the creation of your gown, we would be man and wife right now. The wedding is planned. No need for your father to threaten me with a shotgun. Your father is beginning to come around. Tira seems to want what is best for you. At the moment, she thinks I might fit the bill."

"Annie…!" Jamie's voice roared into the stillness of the night.

"It's my father," she sounded as if she were still a little girl.

Deke supposed a lot of young women would sound the same way under a similar condition. She no longer needed to answer to his beck and call. "She'll be right up."

Deke chuckled when he heard the snort of derision coming from the second floor. Unless Jamie intended to interrupt this intimacy, he would stay put.

Framing her face with his hands, his lips closed over hers, savoring the warmth he found. She swept her tongue along the inside of his mouth. He opened wider for her, sucking, tasting enjoying the short embrace knowing full well there would be more of that to come. In anticipation, his heart thundered beneath his ribs.

Reluctantly, he pulled away, sipped a quick kiss across her dampened lips before tracing the line of her jaw with his thumb. Before he spoke, he kissed the tip of her nose, then her forehead, "Tonight. As soon as they leave, I'll be here. We'll finish this."

He left whistling as he walked toward his office. The night was warm. The day had been downright hot. Summer was about to descend furiously in the mountains. Even so they had snow two days ago. Here in the Rockies the weather could change with the snap of one's fingers.

"Taylor," he called out as he stepped into the jail.

"Deke!" Startled, the young man stood, knocking his chair over in the process. He ran his hands down the length of his trousers before stuffing them in his pockets. "You going to stay the night here?"

"Don't plan on doing so, not unless something happens to change my mind. Time for you to take over the command. I'm going to be a rancher in a week. Getting married. You're going to be the new sheriff in Denver City. Won't take no for an answer. Got plans."

The young man cleared his throat, for a moment seeming to have no idea what to say. "Well, congratulations are in order." Taylor lifted his coffee cup before taking a long drink. "I'm going to be hard pressed to live up to your shoes."

"This promotion shouldn't come as too big a surprise. Told you for almost a year I've wanted to move back to the ranch. I've sent the proper paperwork to Fort Laramie. The marshal should arrive by the end of the week to swear you in. Until then, you're in charge. I'm going to be in then out of town. The bride's parents are going to be staying at Aspen Heights."

"Take care," Taylor said while he remained standing.

With that said Deke left for the saloon so he could watch Annie's upstairs window as well as the path to the hotel that Tira and Jamie would be taking before bed. Slowly, he sifted in small amounts of air. Held the oxygen deep in his lungs before letting it go in a whoosh. He was afraid Jamie might decide one of them should remain with Annie. He also didn't think Annie would protest. If that happened, he'd be sleeping in a cold bed tonight.

Inside Riley's, he ordered a beer then strode outside to keep an eye toward her apartment. Standing outside the saloon, beer in hand, he watched. The lights shone bright in the living room. Her bedroom was still dark. He wondered what her parents were telling her. A sliver of fear slipped down his spine. Sweat beaded on his forehead. He didn't think her parents would be able to change her mind about the wedding, hasty or otherwise. That was always a possibility. How certain was Annie about marrying him? How convinced was she about her pregnancy?

They weren't going to wait to tie the knot. One week was too damn long in the first place. Once he decided, the choice was final as far as he was concerned. If he could spend the nights with her, the wait time would be easier. Sneaking around was just not something he was used to doing. A man grown shouldn't have to sneak to sleep with his woman.

Parents.

They weren't supposed to show up unexpectedly.

She was thirty. Had been on her own for a few years. Should be able to do anything she damn well pleased, including taking anyone she wanted to her bed, especially her future husband.

Beer in hand, he leaned against the post in front of the saloon. A warm breeze seemed to float around him. Smells of tobacco smoke along with warm beer and stale whiskey floated on drafts of air from the inside.

Pauli stood beside him. her hand on his shoulder. "Heard you was gettin' hitched soon." Her gaze followed the same path as his. "To the lady doc, the one I watched you kiss a few weeks back. By what I witnessed, that was one pretty good kiss. Always wanted to know what your kisses would feel like."

Deke couldn't answer that statement nor did he want too. Pauli was sweet but she never appealed to him in that way. Though he did sleep with her once. Knew after that it was wrong. "One week from today," he took a long drink of the beer. "One week." The time between then and now seemed an eternity.

"She's a looker, pretty as a juicy peach in the middle of August. Didn't think you'd ever tie the ol' knot. Now you found this smart as can be lady from back east. Think she'll belong here?" Pauli asked a bit of concern in her tone. "She could get lost between the ranch and the outhouse."

"Don't have an outhouse. Besides, she can find the north star."

He laughed to himself while he thought about the sweet and very spicy tips of her pretty breasts guiding her north. Even better the deliciously adorable fanny of hers taking her south. He didn't care about east or west or points in between. No, her fanny along with her sweet tits would keep her in the right direction, at least when she dealt with him.

"Still..." Pauli began sporting a wicked smile. She seemed to have more to say. "Am I going to have to go way out to your place to get my doctorin'?"

Deke cut her off, tired of the notion his little lady couldn't survive in the mountains. "She belongs. I'll make certain nothing happens to her." She will learn all the ways to survive in the wilderness. If nothing else, she would learn to sit her delicious little backside on the forest floor if she didn't know where to go.

"You look like a boy courting his first girl. Parent trouble? Who would have thought Deke Sullivan would be dancing around a mommy along with a daddy?" Pauli was laughing. "Got to be a first here. Wait 'til I tell the boys about this."

He wasn't in the mood to laugh or have gossip spread. What he did understand was the more he protested the more likely there would be rumors. Deke couldn't help but think about the last two nights. She was indignant when he made love to her in the snowbank, passionate, too, once he kissed her long enough for her to forget anyone could come along and see them. When he took her to the hayloft, well, that was pure heaven. His little Annie gave all of herself...to him.

"Don't like dancing around or fast footin' it to keep from confrontations. Didn't expect to have her parents show up asking questions."

Deke believed it would just be the two of them to do as they pleased. Oh, he knew the parents would visit sometime. He didn't think they would arrive this soon before they were married.

"She pregnant?" Pauli cut to the chase, her eyes questioning. "If she is, you know you don't have to wed her. There are other ways."

The stiffening of his shoulders would give away too much. He tried to temper the emotions rising in his voice. "Not that I know of."

"Just wondering why the all fired hurry. You never seemed like the marryin' kind before. You don't do anything in a hurry," Pauli said her attention focused on the doc's apartment.

"Wasn't 'til I met Annie. She's got backbone. One might call it grit. She's beautiful along with smart. Everything I've ever wanted in a woman."

He grinned thinking about the way she would stiffen when he did something she didn't approve of or was uncertain about. Just this week her backbone stiffened beautifully when he challenged her.

"Don't you go makin' up stories. It's those two lovely charms in front of her she has that call to you. Saw you starin' at her bosom more than once. A man's preference is always noticeable. You love her breasts more than anything," she continued to taunt, her grin giving her away. "Can't taste them enough to satisfy your base needs."

"Pauli!" he warned.

"Getting' to you big guy?" she chortled, the sound coming from the back of her throat.

"Her parents are leaving." He pushed away from the post before handing his glass of beer to her. "Take this inside for me. "He meant to walk behind the saloon then into the woods, coming at the steps to her apartment from the back way.

Arm in arm, her parents strode to the hotel before disappearing inside. If he could, he'd like to know what they discussed in his absence. In Annie's arms, she might tell him how they truly felt about him. Stuffing his hands in his pockets, he circumvented the building. Just as he planned, no one would see him approach Annie's stairs.

Quietly, he walked to her door, tapped lightly to let her know he was here. He pushed open the door, "Annie…it's me," he whispered. "Where are you?"

Suddenly, she was in his arms. He backed up a step to brace himself. "I didn't know if you'd be able to come." She was breathless, her hands winding around his back. "Thought they would never leave."

Swiftly taking all the possible precautions as not to be interrupted he locked the door. "I told you I would be here as soon as they left. Not spending the night alone now that you've been with me."

Kissing her, he backed her into the bedroom. When he reached the bed, he slowly lowered her to the mattress. Not too many minutes later their clothes were scattered across the bedroom floor. A broken sound rumbled from her lips when he entered her. Her fingernails dug into his shoulders. His teeth grazed her breasts, her belly then found their way back to her mouth. Her scent was of passionate woman, her taste evocative and heady. He didn't think he would ever get enough of his Annie.

Annie Lundin, soon to be Annie Sullivan filled every waking as well as sleeping dream.

She was his for all time.

Her nails marked the length of his back before digging once more into his shoulders. Tiny mewls of pleasure buffeted from her lips as she arched then coiled against him. He wrapped her legs around his hips, pushing deeper into her then deeper still. Her taste. Her scent. Everything about his Annie created magical enchantment. He groaned low in the back of his throat as he thrust harder and faster within the silken fabric of her core.

He collected his name in his mouth when she cried out in her climax. After he filled her, he rolled to his side. She rested her head on the hollow of his shoulder.

~ * ~

Annie played with the crisply curling dark hairs on his chest, ran her fingernails past his bellybutton to his groin. He clasped her hand, stopping the heady exploration bringing her hand to the middle of his chest. She sighed softly. Against the hardened wall of his chest, her lashes fluttered against his skin.

"I've created an exquisite little sex monster, hmm…" He held her hand in his, flatted her palm against his chest just above his heart. She could do him in if he let her. He needed another challenge. Would think on the next one.

"You don't want to make love again?" she asked pushing against him to see into his eyes. If he did desire more pleasure, the color of his eyes would darken until nearly black. "I would have thought…" She flicked a nail across one nipple in a fevered attempt to entice. She wanted him again. He taught her that he also liked to make love more than once.

He groaned as he attempted to still her hands once more. "Your parents could be knocking on the door at dawn," he tossed out the horrid notion while his fingers slid through the length of her hair.

"It's not dawn," she murmured pushing the tips of her breasts against his chest.

While she did want to make love one more time before the night ended, she understood the very real possibility of an early morning intrusion. She was always an early riser. Her parents would expect her up almost at the crack of dawn, but would they invade her privacy? "Father could end up in my kitchen cooking breakfast. That is a meal he can do. Mother prefers to sleep later." She watched his mouth, touched the bottom lip with her finger, teasing. We will have to rise before there is any chance of an interruption."

"The door is locked. We've no reason to be afraid either one of your parents will intrude this evening. If the need arises, I can always escape downstairs through your office door," he told her as he flipped her over, his explorations following the line of her spine to end up at her buttocks while he nipped and enticed all of her until she was moaning and writhing once more.

She didn't like the fact she couldn't touch him. When she tried to turn over, he stopped her. Wanted to run her fingers through his hair then down his back. Needed to feel his weight covering her.

"You have the cutest damn fanny," he murmured as he listed her hips then thrust inside.

He held her by her waist. Her butt was in the air while he was deep inside. Her forearms rested on the sheets in front of her. She cried out as she felt him empty himself inside her.

They snuggled together. She was cocooned in his strong arms. "You're right. We do need to sleep so you won't be dangling from the window if father comes early to make breakfast."

"Don't like heights," he muttered while he stroked her hair. "I'll make certain I'm up at the crack of dawn, perhaps even before. Don't even think Jamie Lundin will try to wake you up before then. He will understand this isn't his home. If he doesn't, his wife will make certain he remains at the hotel."

"They are probably tired from the trip from Fort Laramie," she sighed softly closing her eyes, enjoying the strength and power of Deke.

She remembered how exhausted she'd been when they reached Denver City.

When the knock on the door roused her the next morning, Deke as well as all traces of Deke had vanished from her bedroom. She smiled as she rolled over, rubbing her hand across the spot where he slept last night. The sheets were cold. Annie rolled over pulling his pillow to her chest, inhaling the wonderful scent of him. She would have to toss a robe on since she was naked. Her father was planning on cooking breakfast. Who else would pound on her door this early in the morning? She doubted if it could be a client.

"Annie, darling?" Tira's voice filtered in through the shut door. "Time for you to get up, don't you think?"

"We're here to cook breakfast," Jamie's voice boomed. "Promise I'll do better with the pancakes and bacon. They are my specialty."

She smiled, couldn't help herself. Fond memories of her childhood filled her. Recollections before Tira joined them came to mind. She remembered the first time Tira knocked on their door. She wanted a job at the shipyard building ships. Jamie was naked from the waist up. Annie asked him why Tira stared at his chest.

Jamie blustered. Never did give her an answer. Heat rose to her face. She stared at Deke's chest too, at his mouth, at his crotch...oh, my. Fascinated by every part of him.

With her robe tucked neatly around her and buttoned to her chin, she opened the door to her parents, welcoming them with a hug along with a quick kiss to each cheek.

"Good morning," she murmured as she pushed wild strands of tickling hair from her eyes. "Don't you think it's a bit early? I wasn't even up yet." She found that she was heartily glad Deke escaped before they appeared. Annie didn't know how nor did she wish to explain Deke's presence in her bed.

Heat rushed to her face.

Tira waltzed past her into the room, her gaze searching as if she half expected to find her groom where he shouldn't be. "We wanted to get an early start. Just this morning, Deke told us, he'd take us to his ranch. Did you want to come along too? We'll make a day out of it. Meade, from the saloon, told Deke he'd pack us a picnic basket. We can take a couple of bottles of Logan's wonderful wine."

A ploy, this had to be some means to make her go to the ranch then stay there until the fitting. Doing so did not fit her agenda for the week. She backed up shaking her head, her hands clasped beneath her chin. Deke would be able to accompany them. Without arguments, he would be able to return to Denver City in the evening. If she allowed herself to find herself talked into this fiasco…

"I can't. Have work here."

She did have to sort through her inventory of supplies. Her remaining as the doctor here might create a fight between them. Confrontations were so uncomfortable. She liked to avoid them at all cost. Deke never told her she couldn't continue as the doctor in Denver City.

"Nothing that can't wait, I'm sure." Jamie poured the flour into a bowl he retrieved from her cupboard. Found the eggs and milk. Finished with the other ingredients. He slid a pad of butter from a knife onto the hot skillet before setting strips of bacon into a frying pan. "We would truly enjoy your company. We're only going to be here for a short time.

"You know they can't be going back and forth from the ranch to Denver City. Why, Deke told us just this morning that the marshal won't be here until the end of the week to swear in Taylor," Tira said while she made the coffee. "Our beautiful, intelligent daughter needs to be available to the town. They both have responsibilities that cannot be avoided."

"I should change my clothes."

Annie slipped into her bedroom feeling overwhelmed. So much was changing so quickly. Closing the door she leaned against it, setting her head on the wood before closing her eyes. She reminded herself she was an adult. Her parents could not make her do what they wished. Could not make her feel guilty. Inhale. Exhale.

They saw Deke this morning. Talked to him. Several more times she flooded her lungs with air. Did they know he spent the night with her? No, they couldn't possibly. If they did, their demeanor would not be cheerful. Her father would make a point of giving his opinion. She shouldn't have to remind herself that she was no longer a little girl.

In haste, she sponged herself off. Didn't seem she had the time to heat water for a bath. Deke would be here soon to have breakfast with them. After that her parents would leave for the ranch. She would be alone with her thoughts. A few minutes later, her hand on the doorknob, she stepped into the living room.

Delicious aromas of frying bacon along with pancakes greeted her. Her stomach rumbled softly. While dinner last night was good, she'd been too nervous to eat very much. She inhaled a deep breath of the bacon scented air. This was heaven, having her father cook breakfast for her again. Her stomach rumbled its approval. For a few seconds, she felt giddy. She found herself enveloped in wonderful past memories.

When Deke joined them, he was greeted with smiles from her father. The early morning meeting must have changed her father's opinion of the man. The chatter during breakfast revolved around the trail to his ranch as well as what they would do over the next week. Deke arranged for their belongings to follow them in a wagon. Both wished to ride.

Annie felt a huge weight lifted from her shoulders. She'd been so afraid that Jamie would ask her if Deke shared her bed last night. So, when the knock on the door surprised them, her immediate thoughts went to the possibility of a client. She didn't have patients.

"I'll get that." Deke strode to the door.

She held her breath when she saw the man standing in the opening. He touched the rim of his hat before nodding. "The new doctor at Denver City will be here in a week," Seth Masters informed them. "Thought it was my duty to inform you that you will have to vacate the premises. All your things need to be gone from here before the new doc arrives."

Dazed, she thought she might faint. Her breath hitched in her lungs. In the chair she swayed. This was a blow she never saw coming. She closed her eyes, clenching her fists that rested on her lap. Deke stood behind her, his strong, reassuring hands on her shoulders.

When she thought her emotions were under control, she began, "Why? I don't understand. I haven't done anything wrong."

No, she had not. That fact didn't matter. The townspeople didn't like her because of her gender.

Why was she startled?

"The townspeople thought you did a credible job during the measles epidemic. The issue remains, the town doesn't want a female for a doctor. We advertised at least a month ago for someone to take your place. The man will arrive and will expect to have a place to stay. Now that you're gettin' hitched, it won't be so bad for you to give up the practice. You won't have to go back to Boston with your tail between your legs. You should have never deceived us, made us think you were a man. We'd a never hired you if we'd known."

"I didn't deceive anyone. You all knew, or should have known, I'm a woman. No one must have actually read the application." She was beside herself, mortified as well as indignant, all this in front of her parents. Her fists clenched at her sides, both overwhelmed as well as humiliated, she burst out, "I never lied!"

Deep inside anger simmered. Deke's hands still on her shoulders, he squeezed. Jamie appeared tongue tied which in and of itself was quite unusual. She was shocked her parents didn't immediately jump to her defense.

A very rare occurrence.

"I'm sorry. You can do that? Dismiss with no provocation?"

She started to stand. Pressure from Deke's hands kept her sitting. Tired of being subjected to displays such as this, she wanted to fight with all she could. Male domination could go to the very devil.

"Yes, the town can do whatever the people see fit. No one here wants a female to doctor us." Seth said, looking around the room as if he just began to see the people there. "Now that you know, think I'll take my leave though the scent of the meal certainly does fill a man's nostrils with good feelings."

If he was begging for an invitation to breakfast, he wasn't going to get one. "Wait," Annie rose walking toward him now that Deke removed his hands. "How? Who?" She had so many questions. Seth didn't appear eager to answer even one.

"The town decided they wanted a different doctor, one who is male. We advertised for him back east, same place we got you. The man answered. His name is Adair Crawford. As I said, Doctor Crawford is in route as we speak from Fort Laramie. He is accompanied by his assistant. The man accompanying the doc is a financial assistant, not a doctor of any sort."

"I see," she murmured attentively.

She thought she would have time to convince these people she was competent. Apparently, she did not. They judged her the first day they saw her then never changed their minds.

"It's good to learn that you understand what's going to happen here in the next few days," Seth said as he slowly backed toward the door.

"I don't understand anything at all. Is the town also ready to give me financial compensation? This was the most underhanded dealing I've ever encountered."

Annie swayed on her feet, her mind filling with anger buoyed with frustration. She was annoyed with the man, irritated with his antiquated notions about females. Would a woman ever be allowed to rise in a man's world? This entire situation was outrageous. Especially since she wasn't even certain she wanted to continue with the position. She didn't know what Deke expected.

"You best compensate her. I believe she holds a contract for a year. That leaves ten months. We won't allow the town to wiggle their way out of that contract."

Jamie turned his attention to her expecting her to retrieve the contract. Her father finally came to her defense even though his actions were late.

Annie understood exactly what he wished. He wanted her to bring him the agreement between her and the town, the contract that was signed. She rushed down the steps to her office. A few minutes later she returned with the document in hand. After her father read the paper, he looked at her nodding his head a smile on his handsome features.

He looked to Seth. His countenance was one that would harbor no argument. "You owe her wages for an entire year. Including what would be rent on the office along with the apartment. Can this town afford two doctors?" Jamie asked, a grim smile on his face. "Best your board figures out if that's possible."

Even though she was hurt, wishing she could crawl into a hole, Annie didn't want to make a big deal of this situation. Neither did she wish to be paid for work she wasn't doing. She wanted to focus on Deke along with the child she carried. She didn't care about the financial restitution. Though she also realized she needed to stand firm. Men should never be able to get away with this type of gender inequality.

"N-no one…not one person will come see her. Not even the women will come to her office!" Seth yelled clearly agitated at the position the town put him in. His face turned beet red. "We shouldn't have to pay a body for something they are not doing." Once he calmed enough to stop yelling, the man seemed to be gritting his teeth.

"Only because their husbands won't allow the women to see me. Pauli will come to me as will Betsy," Annie said softly even though she intended to stand firm. "I do want what is mine. What is owed to me. The new doctor can have the office along with the apartment if he wishes. I'll be living at Deke's ranch. Since the marshal will arrive at the same time, he can help smooth all the wrinkles. You will compensate me for what was stipulated in the contract."

"Pauli and Betsy are whores!" he yelled as if their profession somehow made them less human. "They don't count!"

Deke's big hand snaked around her waist. He drew her close. For a moment, Annie rested her head against his arm. The warmth of his big body next to hers warmed her. Annie suspected all along her time as a physician here in Denver City would end before it began. If anything, she was realistic.

Once Seth left, everyone seemed to start talking at once. Finally, Deke held up his hands silencing them. "Annie will have to choose what she wants to do."

He turned to her, touched his knuckles gently to her cheek. He looked into her eyes seeming to be able to read her emotions. "You don't have to give up the office. You were hired first. You can stand your ground, fight for women's rights. If that is what you choose to do, I'll stand beside you."

She noticed the smallest hint of amusement as Deke said those words to her. She doubted if he ever thought about women's rights before he met her. "I know. It's just that I was planning on living with you. Perhaps this is best for our plans together."

She held the tears back understanding her dream of becoming a practicing doctor didn't last very long. Two months, she'd had a little over two months to dream and hope. Without the epidemic, she didn't have one patient except Pauli from the saloon. It had never been in her nature to give up. Nonetheless, that was how she now felt. Perhaps it wasn't giving up. Maybe, just maybe, it was forging a new life for herself with new hopes and dreams.

"Ride with us to the ranch today. I promise I won't try to coerce the two of you to stay the night," Tira said tenderly seeming to understand they needed to be together. "…and I won't allow your father to do so either. It will be good for the two of you to leave the town behind for a few hours."

To stop the tears, Annie laughed. Tira looked so determined. Jamie appeared just as single-minded to do the opposite. She realized; she would do as she pleased despite what might be parental objections. They would sleep together before the wedding even if her parents objected.

"I no longer have a good reason to remain behind. Sorting through the new doctor's inventory and rearranging the items would be counterproductive when the man might want everything in a different order."

She wanted to chuckle when she noticed Deke shaking his head. Staring into Deke's vibrant blue eyes, she said just for his benefit. "We will return today, before it gets dark."

"Promise?" Deke's voice was husky, filled with passion. By the look in his eyes, she didn't think he believed she would be strong enough to go against her parent's wishes. "I will hold you to your word."

Annie knew Jamie understood the tone of Deke's voice by the scowl on his forehead. "Promise," Annie said, "When do you want to start?"

The ensuing week passed pleasantly. Tira along with Bella and Marie planned the feast for after the ceremony. Annie delighted in hearing the news whenever Deke brought messages. Her fitting for the gown went smoothly. She was pleased. Nothing except the impending arrival of the new doctor gave her reason for regrets. Oh, she didn't actually miss her loss of a job. What she regretted was the fact she had no patients.

On the evening before the wedding, Jamie and Tira arrived back in Denver City, with all the bluster possible. Tira made up a bed in the living room of her boarding house room. Jamie saw that Deke didn't go up to her second-floor apartment after the meal in the small restaurant in town. Jamie hauled him to the boarding house where he'd been staying before Annie arrived in Denver City.

"Everything has changed so much for you," Tira said softly between sips of the Chianti she poured, "Are you all right with giving up on your dream? I'm certain there will be a child coming soon. When that blessed event occurs, you will have a great deal to keep you busy."

Tira picked at the plate of cheeses Annie cut. It seemed there was something else Tira wanted to speak to her about.

"If you haven't guessed, I love Deke with all my heart. Is that what has you frowning so obviously? He's never told me he loves me. I do believe he cares though." One hand rested on her belly. It was still flat. So far there had been no changes in her body. Only a little more than a week had passed since they first made love. She supposed it would take longer than that to see and feel differences.

"That is good to hear since you've committed to the man. If you couldn't say those words, I would seriously lecture you about coming home with us. Without Deke in your life, there is nothing here for you."

Annie laughed at the supposition Tira made. Although what she said was true. If not for Deke in her life, Denver City offered nothing she would wish to stay to enjoy. "If I left without Deke, he would follow me." She set the glass she was drinking from on a nearby table. "Don't worry about me. He will make a wonderful husband and father when the time comes. I will continue to hope that at least the women will come to me for their ailments. In time, I might have a small clientele even if I'm only a glorified midwife. I'm confident once these good people come to trust me, I'll have babies to deliver."

"Indulgent, like Jamie?" Tira grinned shamelessly. "Willing to give his children everything they ask for? As well as his wife. Our children lacked nothing monetary or emotionally. Jamie is a wonderfully giving man."

"Yes, especially all the love. The two of you gave your children love as well as security." Wistfully, Annie looked out the window. She would miss him in her bed tonight. She was used to his warmth, his strong arms around her. She liked to snuggle against his chest, listen to the slow, steady beat of his heart.

"You'll have the wedding night," Tira whispered seeming to understand Deke spent the entire week in her bed. "I do suppose if you weren't pregnant when we arrived here you would be now. Your father and I both know he's spent the nights with you."

Annie gasped, surprised by Tira's comment then not so very surprised. "You know?" Annie tried to cover her grin with the back of her hand.

"Your father was beside himself. Every night he paced and swore. Blamed me for urging him out of town. It is exactly the way he acted with me. Told him he was the last man to be judgmental. We slept together long before we were married. As I've mentioned before, I even gave birth to our first child before we wed."

"You did."

Of course, she knew they were intimate before the wedding day.

"Absolutely! Now it's time for bed. Your wedding day will come all too soon. We don't want you to have dark circles under your eyes in the morning. Bella along with Maria will arrive by nine o'clock to help you get ready. I'm happy to know you have friends here. Those two women adore you."

That night Annie took her time settling into bed. For the longest time, she stood at the window, her forehead pressed against the windowpane in her bedroom staring at the saloon. At one point she was certain she saw her father and Deke as well as Levi go into the building. Taylor entered about five minutes later. Pauli stuck her head out the door then waved as if she confirmed her guesses. The woman would also be at the wedding.

Man's night out before the wedding.

Tonight, the bed would be cold.

Tomorrow night, she would be married to Deke Sullivan.

So much had happened since she met the rugged lawman, sheriff of Denver City, a sleepy little community high in the Rocky Mountains. She fell in love. At one point in her life, she didn't believe she was meant to have a husband or a child.

Well, she was never someone to dwell on the past or things that might or might not happen. This was her life now minus the practice. She would make him happy. No matter what, she would. She'd become the best wife possible.

~ * ~

The next morning arrived before she wanted to see the sun peeking through her window. She pulled the pillow over her head in a last ditch stand to garner a few more minutes of sleep. Hearing voices in the living room, she sat up knuckling her eyes to help erase the sleep from them. A few deep breaths later, she rose from the bed. She looked out the window to the street below. The dusty road as well as the boardwalk appeared just as it had the day before. Nothing was changed.

This was her wedding day. There were no regrets on her end. She prayed Deke was not having second thoughts. Bella and Maria were there helping.

Tira knocked on the door. She opened it. Buckets of hot water were brought in to fill the tub. Scent of roses filled the air when oil was poured into the steaming water. Tira brought her a glass of wine. Towels were warmed by the fire. Once the hot liquid spilled over her, she closed her eyes soaking up the heat.

The wedding was quick. The vows said. The bride kissed. Handfuls of rice were tossed their way while they ran to the wagon that would take them up the mountain. Deke swept her into his arms to set her on the seat of the wagon that would carry them to the ranch. Pye was tied behind. He leapt up beside her.

"Are you happy, Mrs. Sullivan. Have I told you how very beautiful you are today?" Deke leaned over to kiss her softly on the cheek.

"Very happy and thank you. You are the handsomest man in town," she told him while she leaned into his hard body.

She rested next to him, his embrace warming her. Closing her eyes briefly she thought about the future. Her hand rested for a moment on her belly. The child grew there. They would have a few months to get to know each other better.

This time when she opened her eyes, her breath caught in the back of her throat. Her heart forgot it was supposed to beat. She swallowed hard before she said his name. "Peter…" the hated name whispered from her lips in a thin stream. She didn't remember what she told Deke about the man. Nonetheless, he was here in Denver City sauntering down the boardwalk as if he owned the town just as he acted in Boston.

That was a possibility. Annie didn't forget the man was rich as Midas. She found that her body was shaking. No coherent thoughts entered her befuddled brain. It couldn't be Peter.

"What's wrong," Deke asked turning to her, lifting her chin with his hand. "Peter? What are you talking about?"

She felt certain she had told Deke something about him. Positive she told him he was the man who accosted her in the alley the night they met. Perhaps not. The only reason the horrible man could be here would be to cause trouble for her. At the medical school, her practice here had never been kept a secret. He could easily discover where she went if he wanted to pursue her.

"Why?" she asked wondering what she should tell him.

"I'll make sure he doesn't bother you. Peter..." He let the name hang in midair as if he was searching his brain.

"Peter is..." she moistened her parched lips. Deke's strong arm pulled her closer. She blurted the hated words remembering the time he took her, gave her to his friends, "...Peter is the reason I wasn't a virgin."

"The man in the alley?" he questioned her, his voice harsh seeming to understand everything yet nothing at all. "I'll kill him. He hurt you."

Her shaky laugh didn't leave her more confident. "Y-you can't. You're the sheriff. What reason would you give?"

"Not as of two hours ago. Taylor was sworn in before the wedding."

"We don't know why he is here. His presence in Denver City might not have anything to do with me." She tried to caution Deke, tried to make him see reason. If her father knew, he wouldn't see reason either. It would be far too easy to take the man into the forest then leave him to find his way out. Peter would never survive in that situation. "I don't want you to do anything rash."

Her skin crawled at the sight of the man who abused her, hurt her then offered her to his friends. In Boston, before she left, he wanted her as his mistress. Could he still want the same?

Doctor Crawford, the new physician in Denver City? Was he one of the men who forced her?

Her world began to implode.

~ * ~

"Miss Lundin, fancy meeting you here. You are a sight for sore eyes. I never expected to meet you in this small town nestled so far in the wilderness."

Peter stepped up to the wagon as if they were old friends. For her benefit, he was lying through his teeth. He hoped to make it seem his presence here was an accident.

"Mrs. Sullivan, to you. Best you get along with your business," Deke said, his voice gruff, instantly threatening.

"Ah, the little whore caught herself another rich man. She tried to marry me too. Discovered what she wanted, my money. That's why I had to let her go."

Her startled gasp at the mention of Deke's wealth didn't go unnoticed by either man. So, Deke never told her or allowed her to believe he was rich. Didn't have to work at being a sheriff or anything else. Didn't have to live in this out of the way place. Peter wondered if there was some deep dark secret of Deke's that kept him in the wilderness. It would be fun to uncover something so delicious.

He thought it was a touching gesture when Deke's hand closed over hers, a protective action. Well, Peter didn't travel all this distance to go home without Miss Annie Lundin. He came to Denver City to bring Annie back to Boston. He wasn't going home empty handed. The townhouse he bought for them waited. Adair Crawford didn't intend to stay in the rustic little town longer than he needed to help him bring Annie home where she belonged. The doctor held a vested interest in Annie. That night in the alley, he promised Adair he would have her.

Another touching gesture, when Deke turned to Annie, his knuckles under her chin, "We'll talk about my financial status later."

Then he glared down at him, his dark eyes cobalt, angry. The horses started moving.

Peter stepped back a moment as if he'd been punched in the gut. He knew from the night of the dance when he cornered Annie in the alley this man was formidable. He should have researched him better. When he discovered the man's fortune, he stopped. Believed he didn't need to know anything else. He rubbed his jaw remembering how easily the lawman decked him.

He would have to think on his plans. They might need a bit of revising. At this moment though, nothing mattered. He was going to enjoy a hot bath in the hotel along with a good dinner in the saloon. Adair would apprise him of the whereabouts of the ranch. Where they were headed. In the next day or two he would check out the surrounding area. The woman, if left to her own devices, would be an easy mark.

All he needed was a moment alone with Annie. Find a means to lure her husband from the property. She would not be difficult to abduct. She was such a tiny little thing. They would have to make their way back to Fort Laramie. The guide who brought him here was ready. Trifling things to a man with his aptitude. He felt certain he could follow the trail by himself. Still there were unknowns in the forest they would have to be aware of.

Peter chortled, realizing the wedding night might not be all that it should be. The little tidbit about Mr. Sullivan's wealth might put a damper on the lovemaking. He hoped so.

"Our little Annie's married to the sheriff," Adair said as he walked up beside Peter, a broad smile on his face. He let his insulting gaze rest on her bosom. "Still want to go through with your plans?" The new doctor turned to Peter as they watched the Sullivan wagon lumber away.

"Absolutely. I want Annie. Don't ever forget that fact."

Peter didn't. She'd become an obsession, one he couldn't live without tasting again. He didn't know how long he would keep her, just that he would bring her to the Boston townhouse to live until he found a new woman to take her place. He would share her with all his friends. Might even enjoy having her with other men looking on or even participating. He wondered if she would enjoy an audience.

"How?" Adair asked while the two men watched the wagons disappear from sight. "How do you plan to take her?"

"Bide my time. While I am in a hurry to get back to civilization, I'm not a reckless man. It wouldn't do to rush this job. I've a man in mind to help with the particulars." Thoughtfully, he rubbed his jaw while he mulled over different scenarios.

"Sullivan is a dangerous man. We can formulate a plan over dinner," Adair said chortling and tapping his finger on his chin as if he possessed a strategy. "At least we don't have to stay at the hotel."

"Dinner, ah, I've discovered the fair at Riley's saloon is quite pleasant. Little Pauli will offer her favors without a blink of an eye. If not Pauli, Betsy will do. We could share her tonight if you've a mind to do so. You suppose Sullivan slept with Pauli too? That's an interesting thought. Don't you think?"

"Something we can hold over Sullivan?" Adair asked as the two men turned to enter the saloon. "Doubt if he was honest with little Annie about his affairs."

Chapter Nine

One day turned into another then into a week. Deke was blissfully happy with Annie. She was everything he ever wanted in a woman. He told her about the inheritance that made him a rich man. He also explained that there was nothing the money could buy that would keep him from the mountains. He loved the Rockies and felt no need in building a larger fortune. She would have to be happy with what they had. Annie hugged him, told him she'd never been happier.

They made love in the loft again. Experiencing the snowbank one more time would have been wonderful. Unfortunately, the snow melted. Though come next winter they might be able to duplicate that experience. He took her to the lake where they swam naked, felt the slim layer of water between them when he held her in his arms, when he experienced the satin sheathe of her core. She was passionate as well as warm hearted. Her father turned out to be quite the handy fisherman and hunter. Tira seemed to love baiting her husband, teasing him with his sailing skills, only the boat they fished from was a row boat.

Looking backward the celebratory feast the night of the wedding was magnificent, the treats to entice the pallet never ending. Bella out did herself by fixing enchiladas as well as tortillas, beef and chicken. There were several spicy soups with a tomato base along with two types of rice and beans. The handmade salsa one blinding hot the other mild was a treat to his senses. The cakes were deliciously delectable the wedding cake standing three tiers high.

When Deke lay in bed with his new wife, he was replete, content. Annie wasn't. She was worried about Peter. No matter how hard he tried, he didn't seem to be able to chase away her worries even though he agreed with her the man's purpose here was all about her. If she didn't stray from the property, she wasn't in danger. Annie couldn't keep from remembering how easy it was for Belt to abduct her. One minute she was standing on the porch, the next she was slung over the half breed's horse. Deke told her the man would need help if his plan was to kidnap her. Neither understood his purpose in coming here. She was, after all, a married woman.

"You don't think Peter means to cause problems?" she asked while toying with the hair on his chest. His Annie loved to explore his man's body. "There is no earthly reason for him to be here in Denver City. It's not as if the town is a common destination for the rich. There is nothing here that would appeal to a man used to the diversions a city could offer."

"Except you," Deke spoke softly reaching out to caress her cheek. "You are why he traveled west."

Deke didn't want to tell her what he actually thought. The only reason the man showed up in Denver City was for Annie. Yes, Peter was here to cause trouble for her. What he didn't understand was Adair's role in the events even after Annie explained to him that Adair was one of the men who violated her that night also one in the alley. Adair must have signed a yearlong contract with the town. The thought the man meant to abandon the townspeople left Deke angrier. This was all a ruse.

He drank in a long breath of air as he tried to form the words that would not leave her more worried. Honestly, there were none. Annie needed to understand the truth, as it seemed to be playing out. "You have to be careful. Until both Adair and Peter are gone, you're not to go anywhere alone. Right now, you have your father to keep you company as well as Levi. Angel is not old enough to help out in a threatening situation. Tira is not strong enough. You can't be reckless or foolish. You can't pretend to be safe when in all possible scenarios, you might not be."

"Peter makes my skin crawl, the hair on the back of my neck stand on end. He is a detestable human. Why can't he leave me alone? I never encouraged the man." She touched her lips to his chin, trailed kisses along his jaw. Her lush breasts danced across his chest, seducing him. They could make love again. If they did, they would still have to figure out how to keep Annie safe. Deke didn't trust her to follow his directions.

"You've little to worry about as long as Jamie and Tira remain here as guests."

He understood that would not be for much longer.

"They are leaving in four days."

While Deke understood Annie would miss them, he would be heartily glad to have the peace and quiet he craved. He wanted Annie all to himself. Didn't like sharing her with anyone. On the other hand, her parent's served as a buffer between her and whatever Peter planned. Now a little over two weeks since he first held her, knew her intimately, she was more certain than ever that she carried his child.

So far, they made no official announcements about the baby. Jamie and Tira understood they were to remain quiet since nothing was for certain.

"Will you miss them?" he asked hoping the answer would be that she was just as eager for them to leave as he was.

"It would be nice if they decided to move out here. They won't." She laughed softly her breath ruffling across his chest. "Father has his business though they no longer solely build clippers. Everything is changing. Ships don't rely exclusively on wind. Tira is a big help with that. She's a genius when it comes to ship designs."

The four days passed all too quickly. Suddenly, it was time for their departure. Deke along with Annie accompanied her parents as far as that last lean-to Deke built the night before they reached Fort Laramie. The pair spent an extra night reminiscing after Jamie and Tira moved farther east. They lay beneath the stars counting each one, attempting to find more constellations. He showed her Cassiopeia along with Taurus the bull, others too.

His senses on high alert he listened to the silence surrounding the small area. The campfire crackling beside them seemed to be the only noise where there should be a multitude. He rose, agitated by the lack of forest sounds. Nothing seemed natural. At times, he thought what he didn't hear was his imagination caused by worry, the ever-present anxiety where Annie was concerned. His senses always kicked in to forewarn him of danger.

"We should go higher into the mountains," Annie said while Deke fed the small campfire he built for the night. She sat cross legged, sipping a cup of coffee appearing to watch the flames. "It's summer. The weather is beautiful. What else do we have to do? I want to see the mountains, enjoy all that you find so beautiful you don't wish to leave."

"Snow can still fall in the higher elevations this time of year. It's still early," he told her thinking he needed caution when dealing with his wife. Her curiosity could put her in peril. He would have to take heed. "If Peter and Adair were gone…" He paused in thought, still feeling the eerie calling of the wind, the restless movement of the night animals, the rustling of the aspen leaves, "…I might consider a summer camping trip. Next year this time we'll have a child to worry over. Do you remember your north and south." He was thinking another lesson might prove interesting. Although he didn't need a ploy to caress his Annie.

"I haven't forgotten anything."

She looked at his hands, left a dewy trail of moisture across her lips in silent invitation. She seemed to be thinking the same.

"Witch," he murmured while his body turned to steel.

He wanted to kiss her, the invitation from her apparent. She wouldn't refuse.

Repeating the gesture, she spoke softly, continuing the conversation. "I wonder what happened to Belt. Do you think he found a place far enough away that he can outdistance the law along with the bounty hunters with Ivy and the baby? He deserves a new start on his life." Annie asked sipping the coffee Deke poured, leaning toward him, into his broad chest.

He growled thinking the conversation should be about them rather than the man who was wanted by the law. He was no longer the law. His hatred for Belt disappeared the night he brought Annie home unharmed. The night he discovered why the man was desperate. "Belt will do just fine. He will take care of his family. He understands the forest. Since we haven't heard anything else about him, I assume if he doesn't have to come down from his mountaintop, he will live in relative peace."

He wasn't going to tell her he took the wanted poster of Belt when he left the sheriff's office. The poster was ashes in his fireplace.

"We could try to find him. They might need something."

"No!" He held out his arms, encouraging Annie to come to him.

If they tried to find Belt, they might lead the law to his front porch. "Stop talking about others, make love to me, Mrs. Sullivan. You've certainly provoked me the last few minutes with your not-so-subtle invitations," he murmured, his breath brushing across her cheek.

He nipped her ear then traveled downward to send shivers across her body.

Her little mewl of pleasure pleased him. The fragmented sound after he caressed her more intimately stirred with lightning speed. She leaned into him giving herself over to each caress of his hands.

Their clothing ended up in the back of the lean-to. Her white flesh against the darkness of his hands enticed mouthwatering swiftness. Teasing, he traced the aureole with his fingertip teasing until another broken sound slipped from her sweet, kissable lips.

The night passed. They woke with the dawn to start back to the ranch. Deke felt another ripple of fear spiral down the length of his backbone, certain they were being watched. After he reached the ranch, he gave orders to Levi to double the watch. Deke understood now that Annie's parents were gone, they were more vulnerable. Peter was a city slicker. Adair was the same. Who did the men have working for them? What lies did they deliver to the man? Whoever it was could move silently in the forest. He knew the land. Was one with the countryside.

"I'm riding into Denver City," he told her, his voice harsh his concern for her overwhelming. Deke didn't mean to frighten her. By the look on her pretty face, he did that very thing. Her eyes were wide luminous pools of terror. "Nothing to worry about," he quickly said. "Just some unfinished business."

Her eyes crossed when she looked at him. After that she tilted her head in question, "To see if Peter and Adair are still there?"

He could see Annie was trying to be brave. She was not succeeding all that well.

"Yes."

He gave Pye water then feed. Didn't want to frighten her. Adair should be the town doc. Shouldn't be leaving anytime soon. He didn't think that mattered to either man. "I'll return before dark."

"Why would Adair take employment then leave?"

Annie was leaning against the side of the barn. She appeared pensive, no longer frightened. She was trying to figure out what exactly the two men were up to. "Doesn't make any sense. Not really."

He stuffed his hands through his hair, frustration along with annoyance eating at him. "They came for you, Little Darlin'. I have to make certain they don't find a means to get you down the mountain then on a train back to Boston. While I'm gone, stay inside the house. Don't watch me ride away except from behind a window." Damn, he remembered another time when she was taken off the porch. "I don't want anything to happen to you. Don't believe any messages that say I'm in trouble or that I need you. Promise."

If the men abducted her, he would follow them all the way to the city if need be. Jamie would come to help. All that needed would be for him to send a message.

By leaving, he made her more vulnerable.

He didn't want to live in fear, without knowledge. Discovering exactly what the men were planning was imperative, the sooner the better.

He walked her to the porch then inside. Lifting her chin, he tenderly brushed his lips across hers. She opened her mouth, inviting him inside, toying with his tongue as he explored the tender inner recesses of her mouth. He groaned low in the back of his throat. "Promise me," he murmured his voice turning whiskey smooth. "Promise me you'll stay in the house."

"I'll stay inside the house while you are gone. The thought of Peter putting his hands on me is too horrible for words. If Bella will let me, I'll help out in the kitchen or get under Maria's feet while she is trying to tidy the house. I'm very adept at getting in the way of housekeepers. I will keep busy, won't get bored."

"Good girl." He didn't want to sound placating. Nonetheless, that was how he felt and sounded. "Stay inside. Take a hot bath to wash the trail dust off. Be ready for me when I return. As I said, I'll be back before it's dark. Want you in my bed tonight."

"You be careful too."

She pressed kisses along his neck then back to his mouth. Once again, she opened her lips for him. The act was gentle. He touched, tasted every sweet inch of her. He wanted to take her upstairs, make love to her the rest of the afternoon, then night. Bella would keep them fed. Marie would keep them stocked with wine. He would have the first night of a much-needed honeymoon. He would have Annie all to himself.

While Jamie and Tira were here another shipment of wine arrived from her Uncle Logan. They had enough to last for weeks perhaps months. They didn't drink that much. Another party might be in order. The house seemed quiet without their guests. She wrapped her fingers around his neck, pulling him closer. Leaving was going to be terribly hard when he wanted her so damn much.

"Annie..."

"Fine," she pouted prettily enticing him further. "I should be going with you though. You should take me with you."

"I ride faster without your company."

He placed a quick kiss to her nose. With that said and done, he slipped from the house. Pye waited for him at the porch. He mounted. The forest was still, eerily quiet. No one followed him. Whoever was out there, watched the house.

Less than two hours later he rode into the small town. He tied Pye at the saloon. Pauli would be pleased to tell him what was going on as would Seth along with the other men who plotted to get rid of their woman doctor. They were all a bunch of gossips, worse than any woman's sewing circle.

When he entered Henry, Seth as well as Art sat around a table, cards in hand. Sometimes he wondered why they didn't have anything better to do. Deke turned a chair at the table, straddled the seat. "How's the new doc? He any good? Lots of patients?" he asked as he motioned Pauli to the table. "Like a beer," he said as he watched the three men react to the question. All scowled.

"He's a real quack and sleaze ball," Pauli said before any of the men could answer. "His office hours are nonexistent. Sure am glad he wasn't here when the measles hit town. We'd all be dead. That little gal of yours nipped the measles before they had a chance to infect many people. Doc Annie knew exactly what she was doing. Nothing like that Adair fellow."

She sashayed off, her fanny moving provocatively. Deke grinned at the sight. She was always a little flirt. After that first time, he respected her too much to sleep with her. Didn't like sharing his women.

He'd have to tell Annie just in case rumors started to fly. She should know everything that might come around to hurt her. His past relationship with Pauli might be one. Someone might lie or spread a rumor that wasn't true.

Deke lifted one brow as he studied the men in front of them. The men all suddenly found a great deal of interest in the cards they held in their hands. "Any comments from you fellas or is Pauli the only one in town who feels that way?"

Seth shook his head, his face turning beet red. Sitting back in his chair, he cleared his throat. "Takes more interest in the town whore than he does practicing medicine," he finally blurted. "Wants to know all about your Annie."

"He and that friend of his, Peter Bentley, they…" Art turned his cards face down. "There's been complaints. Taylor has been rousted from bed to help out here in the saloon. Seems they leave damage wherever they've been. The gals working upstairs don't like them much. Those two are rough with the women."

Deke tipped his hat from his eyes, staring hard at the men. "You three thinking you might have made a mistake in hiring him?"

That's what it sounded like to him. After seeing those two in the alley with Annie, what Seth and Art had to say didn't surprise him. Those two men felt entitled. They took whatever they wanted. They were dangerous to anyone foolish enough to get in their way.

To his dismay, Annie stepped in Peter's path.

"Yeah, we made a mistake," Tubbs said gruffly as he glanced from one man to the other. "Doesn't change the fact no man in these parts is willing to take his long johns down for a woman even if she's a certified doctor. Don't want to be showin' my manly parts to a female other than my wife. Even then we just do it, you know. She doesn't see much."

"So, what you're telling me is that…"

"Those two are no good," Seth spoke quickly. "No woman wants to go to Adair either. 'Fraid they might find themselves forced to do something they don't want to do. The man ain't trustworthy. He's already poked himself into a woman who wasn't wantin' his attentions."

"I see…" Deke said softly. What was said didn't surprise him. "This situation isn't to anyone's liking. Neither was Annie. Nonetheless, what all of you know is that she's a damn fine doctor. Her loss is the community's loss."

His heart fell. In some aspect he hoped they would beg for Annie's return. On the other hand, he didn't want to spend half his time in town while she tried to catch-up with her clientele. He had a working ranch now. He had a wife he didn't want to share. He had a baby on the way.

Life was good for him. He didn't want to change one damn thing.

"Think it's only a matter of time before this guy leaves. We will have to find a new doctor," Art said tapping his cards on the table. When he looked up to meet his gaze, he spoke quietly. "You need to guard your woman. Heard tell that man Adair is with is after her."

Deke sat forward, intent now to learn as much as he could. He wanted to shake the man until all the truths were out in the open. "What have you heard? Tell me now."

His voice was calm even though he wanted to slam his fist on the table. Would if he believed the act would jar words from his mouth.

Pauli set his beer on the table before pulling up a chair. She looked to the upstairs rooms then back to him. "Heard there's a townhouse in Boston with her name on the front door. Of course, she won't hold the title. Didn't have to be a fly on the wall to know those two city slickers like to share their women. Your Annie is at the head of the list. Seems they didn't get enough of her when she was in Boston." Pauli held her hands in the air as if to silence him. "I won't' be telling anyone about that. Also heard she refused Bentley's offer to become his mistress. I'd watch her closely. You shouldn't be here in town unless Annie's by your side."

The warning pierced through Deke's heart. His fears for her safety rising at a record pace.

Pauli was right. He thought the same thing, ignored the warning in his head. Nonetheless, if the two men were both here, he didn't need to worry today. His mind returned to the third man, the one he was certain watched them, followed them when they escorted her parents' part of the way to the stage coach.

"They haven't forgotten about her then," he said softly, unaware for a second he spoke his thoughts out loud.

"Men like that don't forget women as beautiful as your Annie. That's why they are here in Denver City. I'd bet on that fact. Doc Adair's not going to stay in town. Well, hell, he hasn't even unpacked. The office is exactly how Annie left it the day you two were wed."

Deke absorbed all that he heard. The words worried and niggled in his brain. Perhaps he heard enough. The time had come to return home to see to Annie, to taste her again. Dear Lord, he could never get enough of her.

The scream from one of the upstairs rooms sent his heart pounding. He stood pushing the chair. His gaze riveted on the rooms up the steps. He turned to Art. "Go get Taylor," he hollered to the men just before he raced up the steps, Pauli behind him.

More footsteps thundered as he reached the top. A crowd began to gather behind him.

"It's Lila. She's entertaining Adair in her room. Maybe Peter too. Sometimes they go in together. If the woman says no, one will go in later once the other one has her pinned on the bed, naked. Lila won't give up the money for any reason," Pauli said nearly breathless from the quick race. "I know they've hurt her."

After trying the door knob to find it locked, Deke kicked the door open swearing softly. Lila was on the bed face down. Naked. Her face buried in the pillows. She couldn't scream now if she wanted to.

Adair straddled her, his hands squeezing tender flesh. Deke pulled Adair off her. Sobs wracked Lila's body.

Peter stood at the window, leaning against the frame, grinning while he watched. He didn't seem at all concerned.

"You shouldn't interfere," Peter said softly pushing away from the wall. "We paid our money. The woman's a whore. What does she expect? She's not hurt. The scream you heard was one of a woman's pleasure."

"A few bits of coin don't give a man the right to hurt a woman."

Deke looked up when Taylor walked through the door, his hand resting on his gun. "We'll see what she has to say. If she's hurt…"

"She's not," Adair said stepping back fastening his trousers. "She just got a bit exuberant. That's all."

"You going to press charges, Lila?" Deke asked through gritted teeth knowing the woman wouldn't. In a court of law, a whore's word was worth less than nothing. "This isn't the first time."

Lila turned over, holding the sheet to her bare breasts. Blood trickled from her mouth as well as her nose where one of them hit her. There was a bruise under one eye. Her cheek was swollen and red. Tears slipped from her eyes. Shaking, she pushed the moisture away with the back of her hand.

"Son of a bitch!" Deke roared; his hands fisted tight.

He drank in a rapid breath of cologne scented air. He thought about Annie, what she must have endured that one-time Peter forced her then gave her to his friends. Adair's unfastened shirt was now fisted in his hand. He held him close, nose to nose for a second. He wanted to hit the smug grin off the man's face. Instead, he pushed the man away, watched as he stumbled backward.

Lila glanced at the coin on her bedside table then to Peter, his face stretched tight, his lips thin. The grin vanished. "No…" she said softly her voice wavering. "There are no charges. Nothing happened. I'm not hurt badly. It's just a bruise that will go away in a day or two. Anyway, it was my fault. I slipped and fell."

"What did you say?" Taylor bent over to hear better.

"You heard her," Peter said, shoving through the onlookers. "She's just a no-account whore. She says she's not going to press charges. Haven't gotten my money's worth. Why don't all of you leave now. It's still Adair's turn at her. I'm next."

"Doesn't give you the right to hurt her. If she's not going to press charges, there is nothing I can do," Taylor murmured turning away from the scene. "If Lila wants to keep you here, that's up to her. Otherwise, you can take the coin back." Taylor began to urge the bystanders from Lila's room.

Peter and Adair remained in the room.

Deke was furious there was nothing that could be done for the girl.

"Go finish that beer, Deke," Pauli said taking his arm to lead him from the room. "Nothing you can do here. As long as women have to sell themselves, there's going to be vermin coming to see them. As I said before, Lila needs the coin. It isn't anything that hasn't happened before and won't happen again."

Deke inhaled a long shaking breath, fuming over the horrific situation he could do nothing to change. His body quivered with the raging anger simmering deep inside. He didn't want to see anyone hurt for any reason. A woman didn't whore for pleasure. Only reasons beyond her control sent her into that profession. For the longest time he sipped the beer, studying the three men playing cards.

It was time for him to return to the ranch. He needed a cleansing breath of pine scented fresh air, needed to hold Annie in his arms just to reassure himself she was safe. Needed her sweet scent to fill him, to warm him. He needed to find some means to get rid of Peter as well as the new doctor. Sitting and waiting was not something he was good at.

Suddenly, the feeling that something was terribly wrong hit him in the gut. He searched the interior of the saloon. Annie! It couldn't be Annie. Both men were here. They wouldn't...hell they would do anything.

She told him there had been two others who forced her that day. What had he done? He left her alone, ripe to be taken advantage of. She would not have left the house. Firsthand, Annie understood how easy it would be to kidnap her.

She was far too trusting, too impulsive. His breath wavered. He swallowed hard. Standing quickly, he knocked over the chair.

He didn't take the time to say goodbye to anyone. Sprinting from the saloon, he understood he couldn't get to his house soon enough. He remembered the leering grin on Peter's face. It was the expression of man who just got everything he wanted.

No! He played into their hands.

Pye raced through the forest trails. When he reached the ranch, he hollered for Angel, dismounted before Pye stopped running. Two stepping the porch stairs, he barged inside. The solid wood door banged against the wall sending vibrations throughout. At the entrance he stood still, searching the rooms he could see, praying Annie would appear with a bright smile on her lovely face, wondering why he acted the ass.

His heart in his throat, he cried out. "Annie!" He searched the downstairs rooms racing from one to another, yelling for her. No one answered his calls. He was met by silence. "Annie! Where the hell are you? Stop hiding from me..." She wouldn't hide. She would come running to him her arms outstretched ready for a hug.

Maria stepped from his office duster in hand. "Well, the devil, what's got you yellin' at the top of your lungs. She's in the kitchen driving Bella nuts. She's got her hands in the bread dough. There is flour spread over the floor from one end of the kitchen to the other. A real mess, she's made. Just glad it's Bella who has to clean all that flour not me," Maria said in a huff then a puff of air shooting skyward to send a wayward lock of graying hair into the air. "Don't you run off and leave her again, not with the order she has to stay inside. The house will never be the same."

"Thank you." Grinning now, relief swamping him he strode through the house to the kitchen his heart beating hard.

He still hadn't seen her. Needed to do so before he could breathe easy. The tempest inside still raged wishing to see his wife before the winds would calm. "Annie?" he stepped inside. Maria was right. The kitchen took a beating that was for certain sure. Bella was bent over. Her ample hips high in the air while she cleaned something on the floor. Slowly, she straitened to focus her attention on him.

"Annie went to fetch some water," Bella said as she slowly stood, her hand pressed to the small of her back. "She's made a horrible mess. Told her she has to find some other form of amusement next time you decide to quarantine her to the house. I ain't getting any younger. This mess ain't cleaning itself."

"Why didn't she use the pump?" Deke asked confused. He wanted to see her, touch her, smell her reassure himself nothing happened.

"Didn't know how to prime it. Water spewing everywhere until there was no more," Bella shrugged, her impressive bosom rising and falling. "There she is," Bella pointed out the window. "She's got a bucket of water."

Deke saw the moment a man grabbed her from behind. The pail

along with the water flew into the air. The man's hand slanted across her mouth, stifling the scream. Belly down, she was swept onto his horse. Then they vanished down the forested trail.

"Annie! No! Annie!" His heart forgot to breathe. Two minutes sooner this would never have happened.

Deke raced out the door to the barn. "Angel! Saddle Briar. Levi, get your horse. We're going after her. Bentley is not going to get her. He'll rue this day. Angel, ride into town. Bring sheriff Taylor out to the ranch. Tell him someone's got Annie. We need a posse if possible."

He didn't trust himself not to kill this man when he caught up to him. He would if necessary. Nonetheless, he meant to bring him in alive.

God damn, Pye was too winded to take. Deke rode him hard from town. He should have never left her. Told her not to go outside for any reason. He'd shake her silly once he caught up to her. After that he'd kiss her breathless.

The trail wasn't cold. He should catch up to her before dark. Hell, it was almost dark now.

~ * ~

Annie had been bored to tears all day long. She knew she was pestering Deke's servants, especially Maria and Bella. Once she started for the barn so she could give treats to the horses, she remembered Deke's warning. She stopped herself. When she volunteered to fetch more water, she thought the grounds surrounding the house were safe. There had been no one anywhere near all day. Levi reported to her at least every fifteen minutes. Angel came in the interim of each visit to tell her all was quiet. While she understood she needed to proceed with caution, she couldn't ask Bella to fetch the water when the mess, all of it, was her fault.

Angel didn't see a single solitary soul all afternoon. She hummed a tune as she walked to the well. Nothing was going to happen. Deke said he'd be home before dark. There were only a few more hours to wait. She started back to the kitchen.

Before she realized what was happening, she was knocked off her feet then thrown over a horse. At the sudden hard contact all her air rushed from her lungs. A hand settled on her rear to hold her in place. She squirmed. The man cursed then yelled at her to hold still or she might find herself on the ground trampled. She heard Deke calling her name. Stupidity should have been her first name, foolish the second. She should have listened to his dire warnings. Bella would have forgiven her. She could have called for Angel.

Her head bounced as the man sent his horse racing through the forest, avoiding the trails leading from the ranch. Branches tore at her. The ground passed in a blur making her dizzy. Bile rose to her throat. She clung to his leg afraid she would topple from her precarious perch. Night would fall soon. Here in the deep woods, she could barely see the ground beneath her as the earth flew past.

They rode for hours and hours. Now the trail the man took traversed boulders. The air grew thinner as they rode higher. Air barely penetrating her lungs, she felt light headed. Dizzy, she closed her eyes, trying to will the aches in her body to vanish. Suddenly, they stopped. The man dumped her from the horse. On hands and knees, she sprawled on the ground, her hair falling over her face.

Quickly, she turned over, her hands behind her supporting her body. "Who are you? You've no right to take me from my home."

She needed to flee. To run until she could run no longer move her legs. He would catch her. If she ran blindly, she wouldn't know where she was or where she was going. She looked overhead to find Polaris. Sighting the star would do her no good. She didn't know where the ranch was; north, south, east or west.

Deke would be close behind her. She should wait, bide her time. This man sat on his haunches eyeing her cautiously. He handed her a flask of water. "Drink. Don't see what the fuss is about you. You look just like any other woman to me. Why did this Bentley guy want you so bad? He said he would pay me in solid gold to fetch you for him."

She did drink. The liquid was delicious. It was ice-cold. She wanted to know what he was talking about. "Where are we going?"

He led the horse to the trickle of water descending from somewhere above them. The man stood on a rock seeming to survey the land below them. She could scramble away now that he wasn't watching her. Where would she go?

"I wouldn't do that if I were you," his deep voice rumbled from his chest. "You wouldn't get very far. Would just be waste of energy, yours and mine both."

Did the man have eyes in the back of his head? She supposed this wasn't his first abduction. She didn't recognize the man. She'd seen no wanted posters in Deke's office with his likeness. He was tall, broad of shoulder, his hips narrow, lean and wiry. His red beard was scraggly, nothing a competent barber couldn't fix. He wasn't as tall as Deke or as broad. Few men were. When he turned to look at her, his eyes were a deep brown. His lips were barely discernable from behind the beard. He wasn't going to allow her any freedom.

"I'll pay you more if you take me home. I know the sheriff. We won't prosecute."

"Get up." He strode toward her. His eyes narrowed on her assessing. "We're not stopping here. If you promise to behave yourself, you can sit in front of me. If not..." He lifted his shoulders, grinning at her.

"Instead of dangling head down." Annie couldn't stop the sarcasm from coating her voice. She'd been in that position once before. Didn't appreciate the blinding headache following. "Such a wonderous position. I'll promise."

The grin was unmistakable. "Instead of dangling," he agreed with a soft chortle. "Don't mean you harm girl. Just being paid to do a job. Need to get you to the train station then they'll pay me. I'm a bounty hunter. Let's just say, you're the bounty."

"I can pay you more to take me home, back to the ranch." She sought every avenue of escape she could think of. "Don't want to go back to Peter Bentley. He's an evil man." She played her last card. "He and that fake doctor, Adair, raped me." Nothing she said seemed to make a difference.

He scratched his stomach as if he was thinking. "We shook hands," the man said as he hefted her onto the horse before mounting behind her. "A man's hand shake is his bond. Don't want my reputation ruined by a tiny slip of a female, even if she's appealing."

Well, it was just her luck...a hand shake and she couldn't negotiate her way out of this. How did Peter find an honorable man among his wicked associates? He wasn't so honorable. He abducted her for a price. Perhaps she could find another way. Put the fear of her husband into his head. Somehow, she didn't think this man feared anyone.

Her luck.

"Deke will find you. He knows these mountains like the back of his hand." Annie tossed the statement out understanding the fact wouldn't frighten this man. She was bent on trying everything possible. "If you let me go, I won't tell anyone. You'll go free."

"Hope your man doesn't find me. Won't get paid if he does. Got to deliver you to the train to collect my money. Train's a long way from here." He nudged the horse forward. "Can't let you go free."

"He's the sheriff in town, the law. You could be in serious trouble. You will be on wanted posters, wanted dead or alive."

She tried another tactic understanding it probably wouldn't work either. Her mind was scrambling.

"Used to be. Know firsthand your man gave up his badge."

The man tightened his hold around her waist.

He did have to be knowledgeable. Curse him.

The fast reckless pace of the last few hours changed. To Annie it seemed he must have thought the danger of Deke following him was passed. He proceeded at a slow walk, carefully picking his way through the boulders. A brisk wind rose from the north. Wrapping her arms around herself, she shivered. The breeze chilled her to the bone. She tried to locate Polaris. Found that she couldn't see the star. Determined they must be riding south. The thought didn't do her much good. If she did manage to escape this man, she didn't know what direction the ranch was situated. He'd climbed high into the mountains. Now he descended. He wound, travelling one way then the other.

Deke was right, up here the night was cold. The stars she saw were brilliant against the black velvet backdrop they nestled on top of. Again, she shivered wrapping her arms around herself. They were once more moving higher. She thought they should be traveling toward Fort Laramie. Perhaps he meant to take her to some other place somewhere there was a train station.

"Your man won't be able to trail me in the dark. He'll have to stop for the night. We don't. Best you get the notion he's to going find you out of that pretty little head of yours. If you're smart, you'll use this time to rest, sleep. You'll need your strength if anything you've told me is the truth."

"Why are you telling me this?"

Not that his words made any difference to her. She knew Deke would continue to follow the trail as long as he could see. Understood he would never give up on her or his child. Her hands rested on her stomach.

"Don't want you to get your hopes up. He's not going to find you," the man reassured her, his tone dark, unfriendly came to mind. "I've covered my tracks. Up here on the rocks there is nothing for him to see. No way to track you no matter how good he is."

"He'll follow me to Boston if he has to. Deke won't stop looking for me. The Cheyenne raised him. He can track anyone anywhere. Even on rocks," she said as much to reassure herself as to enlighten him.

They were newlyweds. He wouldn't give up on her. He didn't want to lose her. She was carrying his baby. Over then over again she reminded herself of the pertinent facts.

Behind her, she felt the man shrug his broad shoulders. He brought her close to his chest as if he meant to keep her warm. Nothing would warm her. Annie felt certain she would be cold into eternity. "That won't make a difference to me. Not going that far. Once I hand you over to the man paying my salary, I'll be done with you. What happens after that isn't my business. If he catches up to you in Boston, good for your husband. I'll applaud his efforts."

"I see…"

She did too. He was going to take her only so far. Get his money. Leave her with Bentley along with his friend. She needed to figure out how to escape. At the moment, it didn't seem possible. She sagged against his chest. Her eyes closed. Exhausted, she slept. When next she woke, the sun was beginning to rise above the tree tops. It signaled the launch of another day.

They were still riding. He handed her the canteen of water. She drank. The day was going to be a hot one. Where was Deke?

"How are you feeling?" he asked her his voice deep and strong.

She felt horrible. Nevertheless, she wasn't about to tell the man anything. "Don't you ever sleep?" she queried wondering about his stamina and if he'd be so tired, she could get away from him.

"Not when I've got an ex-lawman on my heels," he murmured before handing her a piece of jerky. "Learned a long time ago to sleep while I ride. Some situations a man gets himself into can be too dangerous to stop."

Ah, he did take into consideration Deke's past job. Chewing the meat, she leaned against the man once more. His strong arm was wrapped around her waist keeping her from falling off. She was shivering from the cold. There was nothing he could do about that. He did though. A few seconds later, his coat surrounded her shoulders, the warmth not enough for her body to stop shaking.

A few hours later they turned, their direction taking them in a circuitous route. She closed her eyes again, needing sleep more than she needed to see what was happening or where he was taking her. The direction didn't mean anything to her. She could see no landmarks that stood out. Deke was right. There were no street signs here to guide her. When she opened lashes again, she found she felt a bit refreshed. The sun was descending now. They traveled east away from the setting sun. She'd been gone over twenty-four hours. Where was he? Where were they going?

Toward Fort Laramie? She didn't know. Didn't think she cared either.

Fort Laramie was the first place Deke would look for her. If he couldn't find this man's trail, he would head for the fort. She wanted to yell at the man, to rant and rave that she would pay him more if he would deliver her to Deke's ranch. Knew ranting would do her no good.

He shook hands with Peter.

A man's word was his bond.

Damn and blast, if he didn't sleep, she could never find a means to get away from him. She had this horrible feeling that even if she managed to escape him, he would find her. If that happened, he would not be so gentle. He'd probably hang her upside down again. Her head still pounded dreadfully from those first few hours when she did ride the horse in such an ungodly manner. It was not well done of him to threaten her again.

Where was Deke? He'd told her he was the best tracker around. That if anything happened to her, he would find her.

Something happened.

Where was he? What he didn't tell her was how long it would take him to catch up to her.

When the man picked up the pace, Annie didn't think anything of it. When he stopped then dismounted to study the terrain, she decided perhaps Deke was closer than she thought. He mounted again. This time they headed downward, the line of trees far in the distance. After they entered the forest, they would be more difficult to see. She swallowed hard, wishing and praying.

The war cry caught her by surprise. The yell came from above them. It wasn't Deke. The man was knocked off the horse when the other man hit him from behind. She clung to the saddle, biting her lip as she desperately tried to keep her balance. Her heart pounded as she gasped for each tiny splinter of air that didn't seem to want to cooperate.

Her rescuer was not Deke or was the man here to aide her escape? She squinted into the slowly darkening landscape. Shadows were all she could see. The two men rolled. Neither seemed to gain an advantage. Annie found she was holding her breath as well as clasping her hands tightly together while she watched them grapple with each other. She should spur the horse forward. Run. She didn't know where to run. Didn't know where she was. What good did locating Polaris do when she had no idea where she was or where she was going? The prospect of finding herself alone in the mountains terrified her.

She should do something to help. Good god, there were wolves out there as well as bears.

What? She heard the men talking. Recognized the voice. It couldn't be.

"Don't want to kill you. Agree to let the woman go…" A solid punch to her savior's jaw stopped the conversation.

The punch was returned full force. His head jerked back, hitting the solid rock behind him. He groaned. Closed his eyes for a second. The man who came to her aide seemed to gain the advantage. He pummeled his face, over then over again, until the man was unmoving on the rocks. His body didn't move. She hoped he wasn't dead. Her rescuer looked at her.

"Come…" The man stood, his hand extended. "We won't have much time. He will wake up then follow us. We have to hurry."

"Belt?"

Annie slipped from the horse then ran to him, wrapped her arms around him. She never thought she would be glad to see this man. She stepped back, staring at him, hesitating to do his bidding. He could mean harm to Deke. "What are you doing here?" She was breathless. She was stunned to see a person she'd never thought to see again. "You didn't know the man abducted me. You couldn't know."

"What I want to know is where is your husband. He's grown careless. A man shouldn't lose his woman. To my surprise I was out hunting and there you were. I followed to find out how willing you were to be with this man. Listening for a few minutes gave me a good deal of information." He lifted his shoulders a hair. "You needed rescuing. I decided to do the deed since you saved my wife as well as my child."

"Not willing at all," she muttered as she dusted her hands off on her ragged dress. The branches had torn at her, ripping patches in the gown. Her hair tumbled around her shoulders. She felt both bedraggled as well as exhausted.

"I'll take you back home, as far as I dare go. Tell me what happened to you? Why are you with this man?"

"It was my fault," she told him while he led her to his horse.

What she told him was true. She failed to obey. She didn't stay inside the house. After all, she was only going to the well. Guilt swamped her again, nestled inside her until she wanted to scream. She'd made such a mess.

"Your fault, you say? How is that so?"

He lifted her before mounting his horse. A small grin formed on his chiseled features. "As it was your fault when I kidnapped you?"

Annie found that once again, she sat in front of a man. She was admitting things she wasn't used to confessing. She should have listened. "Yes. I didn't follow directions. He warned me to take care."

"Seems to be a habit of yours. Deke should beat some sense into his woman before she gets into more trouble than she can get herself out of." He nudged his horse forward to a brisk pace. "I can take you to a trail. You will have to follow it home. Can't take you all the way. I'm still a fugitive. My face is still on wanted posters. Have Ivy along with my baby to think of."

"A wanted man."

Annie needed to tell him Deke burned the wanted poster. That likeness of this man was not the only one in the territory. He would never be able to walk among people without fear. "How are Ivy and the baby?"

She understood Belt could only do so much for her. The rest she would have to accomplish by herself as she recalled her lessons in navigation.

"She is fine. Yes, I'm wanted. Do you still remember how to find your way?" Behind her, Belt chuckled softly as if he knew something.

Annie's cheeks burned from embarrassment, suddenly realizing he watched the lesson. Must have seen Deke touching her, caressing her body to imprint the message in her mind. She squirmed uneasy with the knowledge. "Yes…" she hesitated wondering what he was thinking. "If someone tells me the direction to head, I can do so."

They entered the forest. Darkness surrounded them. Belt followed a trail for several miles. This was not the same trail her abductor took. She didn't know where she was. She couldn't find her way.

"How far are you going to take me?"

Her voice quivered with the fear she felt. She didn't want to be left alone on the mountain. All the night sounds seemed to escalate. Thoughts of wild animals accosting her entered her brain.

More than anything she feared, she didn't want to be left alone.

Belt let out a slow breath of air. His heart beating hard behind her. He was doing something that put his life in danger, that as well as his family's. He was doing so for her. "I owe you my wife along with my child. If not for you, I would have neither."

"I…"

The warmth his words gave her were impossible to explain or describe. Saving human lives was what she trained for, what she'd wanted to do since she could remember. The fact he acknowledged her as a doctor created a deep-seated need to continue in her chosen profession.

"My path will take you close enough for you to walk to the ranch in less than an hour. I don't know where your man is. I hope he is close. Don't like the idea of leaving you alone in the darkness, in a forest where you are not at ease. I will go back and look for him. If I find him, I'll tell him to go home."

"How did you find me?" Curiosity was getting the best of her.

"The gringo was careless," Belt chuckled softly. "He didn't expect you to have more than one man who would give his life to rescue you…." Belt paused in thought, "…and your voice carried. I recognized the sound when you spoke to him. Recognized the fact you didn't want to be with him."

"I've been gone for more than a day. How can you…?" She wasn't certain what she meant to ask. Belt grew up with the Cheyenne. He had amazing tracking skills. "How can you find Deke?"

"The trail the man took was not a direct one. At the moment, you are very close to the ranch. I'm going to help you down in a few minutes. I will point you in the right direction. You are not far away."

Annie clung to the coat, feeling a moment's guilt. She cast off the guilt as she reminded herself the man stole her from her home. He meant to give her to Bentley for his entertainment without ever asking why. He was not an honorable man. He deserved whatever fate dished up to him.

"This is as far as I dare go," he told her, lifting her from the mount to land softly on the ground. "You understand that if I could, I would take you right up to your front door. Don't wander off the trail. You will be fine. I will remain here for a while. If something happens, holler. I'll come for you."

"It's dark," she murmured searching the velvet blackness for any sign of light.

Annie felt as if she suddenly hated the dark. Wanted to have a candle to hold in front of her. Needed to see the light burning in a window at the ranch. Her legs shook, knees threatening to buckle.

He motioned upward. "The moon is nearly full. There is light for you. If you weren't such a lucky woman, clouds might ghost the moon as well as the stars. Can you find the north star from here?" he chuckled as she turned in a circle, searching.

"My father taught me on board one of his ships when I was about ten. He wasn't quite as graphic as my husband. He also never told me how to find directions from the sightings. Suppose the first lesson was wasted."

"Not the second," Belt said as if he hoped she remembered all that Deke taught her. "I hope you listened well to your husband. Taught my Ivy some of the same lessons."

She did. Annie smiled at the memory, loving the way his caresses felt when he emphasized what parts of her body she was supposed to follow.

When she nodded, she looked back to Belt. With a helpless lift to her shoulders, she said, "I don't know where the ranch is from here. You seemed to have set me down where there are trails meeting trails. I would get lost if I took the wrong path. My husband also told me that if I didn't know which way to go to sit down and wait for him."

She didn't want to wait. Didn't want to sit anywhere in the blackness of the night. The night was cold, frigid. She wanted a hot bath along with her bed. She wanted a hot meal. More than any of those things she wanted to feel Deke's arms around her.

He laughed again, the sound a deep, rich throaty noise, "The path you want goes to the north. If I see Deke, I will tell him to go home to his woman. That is where you will be. I will also ride back the way we came to check on your abductor. Don't wish to be wanted for murder. The man needs to live."

"I would testify on your behalf."

She would even though the other crimes he committed she could not get him out of with her testimony.

Wrapping her arms around herself, she found that she was shivering again. Annie didn't want Belt to leave her alone. Understood she couldn't beg him to stay with her all the way home. He put his life in jeopardy bringing her this far. She would have to walk. Drinking in a breath of air, she looked to him.

The courage she sought so desperately didn't seem to want to appear. "Thank you. Take care. If you ever need anything…"

"I would not risk your life by coming to you. If Ivy ever needs a doctor though…only then would I seek you out. I'm certain in time she will be with child again. She wants another baby though I'm scared to death for her. I cannot resist her sweet charms. You told me not all births are the same. I'm praying what happened with Ivy the first time will not happen again."

"Sometimes one can be enough. Though," Annie paused thinking to reassure the man, "there is no reason to believe she would have the same outcome with a second pregnancy. Everything could be normal. When she needs a doctor, I will be there for her."

"There are no guarantees that she won't. I love her. Would rather have her around me to love than another child."

Annie put her hand on his leg. She started a promise to him to reaffirm her earlier statement. "If you need me, come for me. Deke will not turn you in."

"I know. Of this I'm certain. I only wish…" He turned his horse unable to finish the words.

She watched him disappear in the darkness. There was nothing left to do except go home. She turned to the north, thinking of Deke's hands caressing the hardened tips of her breasts. How he so easily brought her nipples to hard peaks. She smiled softly, wishing he were here beside her.

In the darkness, she stumbled on a rock. She caught herself before she fell. She looked once more for the north star. Continued north. One step after another slowly brought her down the mountain. When the path gave way to an open field, she saw lights burning in the ranch house. She gave a startled little cry. Belt brought her much closer than he told her, than he should have done. She'd only been walking about ten minutes. Well, so afraid she might fall, she was shuffling not walking.

Running, she made it up the steps to the kitchen. She swung open the door hoping to see someone. "Bella!" she called out. "Maria! Anyone here?"

"Child?" Bella stood by the open door wiping her hands on her apron. She'd been in the pantry. "You're back. Where is Mr. Sullivan?"

"I don't know," she moaned softly, sinking down into a chair. "I...a friend of his found me and brought me home. Deke is still out there somewhere looking for me. There is nothing we can do save wait for him to return."

"You must be famished." Bella hustled around the kitchen. She found a loaf of bread along with smoked ham. Searching farther, she brought out cheese and sliced it for her. She poured her a glass of wine. "Anything else?"

"I'm starving. Thank you. Can I have tea instead of the wine."

Annie didn't think she should be drinking the wine. She was pregnant. Didn't want to do anything that might hurt the babe. It was just a guess. She didn't know.

"By all means, child. Whatever you want." Bella set the tea kettle on the stove for water to boil.

"Where are Levi and Angel?"

Annie picked at the food, savoring each bite. She didn't want to eat too fast. She'd been without sustenance for so long, she knew the food would not sit well in her stomach if she ate too quickly. One bite at a time, chew then swallow, she told herself to keep herself from inhaling the delicious food.

"Levi is with Deke. They left together to follow you. Angel went to town to tell Taylor to form up a posse."

Annie broke off a slice of bread. She lifted her hands into the air. "Here I am safe and sound. I no longer need finding."

The posse might find Belt. She cringed at the notion the man risked so much for her only to be caught.

She prayed they would not.

He was going to go back to the man who captured her. Belt could be in a wealth of trouble.

There was nothing she could do for him except worry...and pray.

~ * ~

Belt saw the posse before he reached the man who kidnaped Annie. Without being seen, he veered into the woods to avoid the men who would never hesitate to take him prisoner or kill him. The posters said Dead or Alive. There were only five men along with Taylor Douglas. He'd hoped to see Deke so he could inform him that Annie should be safely home now.

From a high vantage point, he watched. His horse was hidden from view. Now, he lay flat on his belly observing as the men approached the man who kidnapped Annie. Taylor called a halt, his hand in the air, signaling for everyone to stop. Belt couldn't hear what was being said.

He needed to leave.

The man sat up. Belt felt the first stirrings of relief. He'd not wanted to kill the man. The fight had been fair. Nonetheless, he would have been charged with murder if anyone could connect him to this man. He left no evidence. Only Annie knew. Somehow, they formed a bond, an alliance of sorts. She would never tell. This man who kidnapped her would have no idea who he was unless he saw a wanted poster. Air flew into his lungs as he once again realized the enormity of his bad choices.

They would have to let this man go. Except for Deke and Annie, no one knew what he did. Perhaps they wouldn't be so stupid. He could only hope and pray. After all, the posse was sent to capture the man as well as bring Annie back to Deke.

Taylor handcuffed his captive then set him on his horse. They took him down the mountain. Perhaps, the drama would end here. He watched them disappear into the trees. This man would have told the posse about him. Fear sprinted through him. He needed to go home to Ivy.

Belt felt his presence before he saw him. His body tensed ready to react. His fists tightened.

"What are you doing here?" The voice was strong, hard-edged.

Belt whirled to a crouched position, his hand on his gun. He stared at the dark shadow a few feet above him. This could be his demise. He understood the hazards in coming back here. He was looking for Deke. Now, all he risked could be put to the test.

Hands away from his sides, he straightened, willing to meet this new adversary head-on. "I wanted to see what the posse would do with the man who kidnapped Annie."

He didn't know who confronted him or what he should say.

"Where is Annie?"

Finally recognizing the voice, "Deke," he cried out softly, a surprised whisper. Sounds carried out here, carried too far. He couldn't risk a return of the posse. "She is fine. I took her home. Why aren't you with the posse?" he asked.

"Levi is. We split up a few miles back. Wanted to go in a different direction, cover more ground. The man who kidnapped her rode in circles. Wonder if he knew where he was going. Doesn't appear he headed for Denver City. You're responsible for that man's condition?" Deke asked as he mounted his horse.

"Yes," Belt said, his back stiffening. This would be his first and he hoped only explanation. "Had to render him prone before I could get to Annie. You best get back down the mountain. She's cold and tired. I left her close to the house. Probably got too close. Didn't know if you'd turn me in for the bounty. She told me you wouldn't." He shrugged, staring wishing he could see Deke's eyes. "One never knows. Ivy needs me. She would die if I don't return. She is only beginning to learn a few skills so she can survive the mountains."

"Burned the wanted poster. As far as I'm concerned when you brought Annie home safe and sound the other day, you earned your freedom. Nonetheless, the posters are still out there. Anyone with a mind to try and find you could collect the reward. You need to keep all of your senses alert."

"You're right, there are more posters where that one came from as well as more men wanting the money," Belt said eyeing Deke warily. "I will never be free."

"Yes, however, if you don't do anything in these parts…" Deke shrugged staring at the line of trees toward his home. "There won't be anyone looking for you in this area of the country. Your trail here must be cold. Your name won't be bandied about as a constant reminder about the bounty on your head. There will be others who will take your place. With luck, eventually you will be forgotten."

"Go to your wife. She has promised to come to me if I need a doctor," he laughed as he, too, looked at the retreating posse. "I won't. However, if Ivy ever needs one, I'll be on your doorstep."

Chapter Ten

When Deke walked into his home, he was met by Maria and Bella both chattering nonstop about Annie. They fed her. Maria told him she was now in a steaming bath in need of some tender loving care. After grabbing a slice of bread along with a piece of ham, he raced his way to the master chamber eager to see his wife, anticipating her recounting of the events.

He thought on his life without her. Recalled how he'd reacted about going to Boston to bring her to Denver City. He knew then his life would change forever when he met her. That uncanny sixth sense of his kicked in to tempt him. The first time he looked at her, he felt the inexorable draw. It was the best damn thing he'd ever done.

He wanted her.

Knew he would have her. She was his fate, his kismet.

Stepping inside the bathing room, he saw her naked, vulnerable to his whims. His breath caught in his throat. Every time he saw her naked, his body reacted with lightning speed. This time his reaction was no different. Her head rested on the lip of the tub. Damp tendrils of her silken hair hung on either side. The rosy tips of her breasts peaked enticingly above the waterline of soapy bubbles. Her eyes were closed. He watched the deep even breaths she inhaled. His body sprang to attention. He adjusted his buckskins.

Deke found that he wanted to join her. So far, they never shared a bath. There was no time like the present for new adventures. Stepping toward her, he unbuckled his gun letting the belt slip to the floor.

She heard. "Deke…! What are you doing?"

Annie sat up, her beautifully rounded globes he loved to suckle swaying against the top of the waterline. She touched her bottom lip with a fingertip. He wanted to hold her close to feel her heart beat against his chest. Powder blue eyes shimmered brilliantly.

"Enjoying the view." His voice dropped an octave.

"Oh…"

"Belt told me you found Polaris and that you knew which way was north." He stripped his shirt from his body staring at the hardened tips of her breasts. "You didn't need rescuing today. Well, at least not after he set you on the ground near the ranch. I thanked him. Says he owes you. Was glad he was able to help."

Her cheeks flushed a beautiful shade of pink. Settling back into the water, a washrag against her chest, she murmured softly, "I remembered what you told me." She flashed him the grin he loved. "I followed my nose."

"Ah, Little Darlin' it was not your nose you were supposed to follow. It was your beautifully hard nipples. They did the job I instructed. The tight rosy tips got you home."

He unfastened his trousers, hopped on one foot then the other while he removed his boots. His clothes littered the floor around them. He stood next to the tub, naked, his arousal blatantly obvious. He was hard steel needing her softness.

"W-what are you doing?" she asked sinking farther into the tub, her eyes wide crystal spheres of heavenly blue. "I don't…"

"Joining you. Can't think of anything I'd rather do than join my beautiful wife in the tub of steaming hot water. We've never shared a bath before. There's no time like the present."

Stark naked he strode forward, his smile wide. He anticipated the heat of the water along with the inferno of his wife, yearned to hold the heat of Annie against him, feel all her sweet curves.

"There isn't enough room for two," she sputtered pushing back against the tub. "I…Deke…you can't!" He was beside the tub looking down at her.

This was what all his dreams were made from; his Annie, naked, waiting for him. "We will make room."

He picked her up then sat with her in front of him, her back to the hard wall of his chest. He wanted to touch her everywhere, explore every soft exquisite curve that was Annie. His fingers moved her hair to the side, leaving room for his lips to touch, lave, caress. She was his magic. His hands were on her waist, then roamed higher along her ribs to slide his palms across the tight hard crests of her breasts that pointed north with the sighting of the north star.

Her breath caught. For a moment she held onto his wrists. Her head fell against his chest. Her fingers ran along his thighs. He heard the rapid beating of her heart, laved the pulse point at the base of her neck that seemed to thunder out of control.

His hands traveled across her shoulders to slowly glide down her arms. He removed the rag from the water, soaped it. Brought the soapy cloth across her legs, parting them, caressing the tender feminine folds he found between them, the places that would leave her breathless when he touched her. Found the tiny treasure that brought her exquisitely to that point where she always cried out his name.

She arched begging for more.

His hands roamed upward, the cloth touching upon her breasts, his palm massaging over the hard peaks until she squirmed beneath the tender erotic assault. He wanted her so desperately. She wanted him.

He knew what she longed for, and where. Her response to this seduction was rapid, potent as well. He did come to seduce though she whispered that he should leave her to bathe alone. Ah, but she truly didn't want him to leave her. Not now, not when she was so close to ecstasy. In his arms, he allowed her to turn. He touched her anew, his stroke upon her upper thighs, his kiss suddenly searingly hot against her breasts until she did cry out. Still, he caressed her, his lips found tender sensitive flesh.

With her in his arms he rose from the water. Dripping, he set her upon the furs in front of the fire. The flames colored red, gold, blue as well. His mouth worked its way upward along her body until the bulk of his weight settled enchantingly between her thighs, and the hard pulse of his sex teased damp heated tender zones on her woman's body so different from his, so very unique, the sweetest of places begging for his entry.

She reached for him, meeting the powder blue of her eyes before closing his for a moment only. He needed to watch her. Wanted to see the pleasure he created in the shimmering of her eyes. His tongue curled around a hardened tip of one breast, sucked then bit gently. She made a purring sound. Finally, he thrust into her, deeply, slow, measured so he felt her pulses against his sex. He held his body above hers as he pressed harder and harder and deep, deep within. Mercuric magic possessed him.

Annie buried her face into his neck and shoulder. Ragged puffs of her breaths tantalized him. Her nails gripped him harder, clinging to him, sending heated flares of raw passion deep into him. Now there was nothing gentle, subtle, or slow in his movement. The loving was ruled by a reckless fury and passion along with near-blinding speed. She clung to him desperate for release as her teeth bit into the skin of his shoulder. Her fingers once more dug into the knotted muscles of his arms then back.

He reveled in the soft gasping cries ripping from her lips. He was achingly aware of the tender sweet curves of her body pressed so tightly against him. She was satin and silk. He moved, held nothing back as he felt the pulsing of her body, the waves of ecstasy begin to mount and draw him farther into the silken heat of her womb. She arched against him, seeking, searching, writhing as he filled her.

She was magical enchantment, pleasure so sharp the sensation stole his breath.

Finally, wave after pulsing wave of shattering ecstasy ripped along his sex. She pressed her face hard against him again, seeming to brace herself as the shudders tore through her then into him. He felt the soft smoothness of her against him with a sudden gentleness then sweet filling warmth. She gasped, still clinging to him.

Moments later, he eased himself to her side.

He didn't touch her. She realized he lay beside her on an elbow, studying her, grinning besotted. She caught her bottom lip between her teeth, turning to meet his gaze. Her eyes were dazed in passion.

He wanted her again.

Deke couldn't stop watching her. He posed the question he needed answers to. If she was going to survive in the mountains, she needed to learn to obey his orders. "Care to tell me what happened? Why you defied my order to stay put?"

His voice was harsher than he intended. Under the circumstances, he couldn't help himself. She risked her life for a pail of water.

Deliberately, she closed her eyes to him. He watched the slow even movements of her breaths as she sipped in air. When she opened them again, she looked away for a moment, seemingly unwilling to speak.

She didn't want to look at him. "I was wrong," she spoke in a soft whisper. "I'm sorry. The day was so…"

"That is not what I asked. I'm not expecting an apology although the words are nice to hear," he told her trying for patience in this matter.

Where Annie's life was involved, he had none. This was the second time she'd found herself kidnapped from her home. It wasn't going to happen a third time. "Let's take this one question at a time. What happened that made you leave the safety of the ranch house? You promised me. Life or death," he mused. "I thought you understood the danger. The reason you left was life or death?"

For a moment she scowled at him, her expression sour. "I'm certain you know the answer to that. You were there. I heard you cry out my name," she blurted, once again turning her head from him.

Moving with patience, he ran a hand across her still flat belly then upward. With his fingers holding her chin, he turned her to look at him. "I want to learn your version. Need to understand why you put our baby at risk. You understood what could happen. Peter wanted you. Adair was going to share you with him. Was intending to bring you back to Boston where he had a townhouse for you to live in then service him along with his friends. By your actions, you walked into his tender loving hands."

She pushed him away, sitting up to reach for a wrapper. She didn't catch hold of the fabric before he jerked her back to him, angry she was avoiding his questions. All he wanted were answers he could understand.

"It was my fault!" she bit out, furious as well as annoyed with him. "I didn't see anyone. Levi as well as Angel reported all afternoon that there was no one around. There was no reason to make more work for Bella when I was capable of bringing water from the well so we could prime the pump. So we could get water."

"You defied me. If you told them about your promise, Maria along with Bella would have understood."

Deke didn't know what else to say. His fury simmered. In this world, she needed to heed his advice, in this case a direct order. He needed

283

to trust her. As the facts stood now, he couldn't count on her word.

She blatantly defied him. Annie had no idea what men would do to gain what they wanted. She didn't understand how beautiful she was. To any man breathing, she was a prize worth possessing. While most wouldn't go as far as Peter Bentley to have what wasn't there right to possess, she needed to understand why he feared for her safety.

She was his wife. No one else would have her.

"Yes, wouldn't exactly call what I did defiance though," she continued to argue. "I understood there was no risk..." She let that sentence hang in the air. "I guess there was."

His eyes bore into her hoping she would understand better what he was about to say. Holding her by her shoulders, giving her a tiny shake, "What the hell would you call what you did? There was no risk?" He couldn't fathom why she was arguing so intensely. Everything she did that afternoon put her life in jeopardy. "I was so afraid for you."

Not so subtly she lowered her lashes. When she looked at him again, she arched her perfectly shaped eyebrows at him, "A miscalculation in judgment?" she questioned seeming to think he would agree.

When pigs fly!

His hoot of laughter seemed to surprise her. Her lips thinned. She pushed away from him. "Not so fast, Little Darlin'. At last look, Peter is still in Denver City, his crony Adair along with him. If the man who abducted you explains who hired him, I'm certain Peter aligned with the doc will hightail it back to Boston as fast as their little feet will carry them. Without me along coupled with my ignored dictates, in other words, you are still in danger."

She sighed softly. Her mint scented breath rippled across him. He wanted to make love to her again. Didn't enjoy the conversation between them. "I didn't know how to prime the water. That was my fault also. Someone needed to fetch a bucket of water. Seems I made a mess of Bella's kitchen, flour everywhere imaginable. Didn't want her to have to clean the floor as well as go to the well." She put her finger to his lips, "Before you say the words, I offered to clean the floor. Believe she thought I would make an even bigger mess if she allowed that to happen."

Annie sighed one more time. "I've never been asked to clean much. It's not my best attribute. Cleaning. I'm better at other things."

That fact was true. He wanted to enlighten her as to her best attributes. There were many. Didn't believe she would appreciate the sentiment at this time.

"Let's go back to what happened afterward. I got there right when he kidnapped you, yet I wasn't able to catch up to you. I picked up the tracks right away. He didn't make any attempt to hide his trail."

Pushing her face against his shoulder, she ran her hands along his chest. When she lifted her head to speak again, her eyes glittered with the moisture that was hiding there. "He rode hard for at least an hour. After that he slackened the pace to give his horse some rest then he would ride hard again repeating the process. Even in the darkness, he knew where he was going."

"You didn't fight him?" Deke expected her to make the kidnapping attempt so difficult he would want to get rid of her.

"He held me across his thighs, head down. The gray matter in my head pounded so hard I could barely think let alone fight. Thought for some time I'd vomit on his boots. If I struggled too much, I would have found myself beneath the horse, trampled. He wasn't waiting around to get caught. He had a destination in mind where he was going to hand me over to Peter for money. I don't think it was Denver City."

"The bastard!" His fist came down hard on the floor.

"After about four hours, he stopped long enough to put me in front of him. He kept riding and riding. He gave me food to eat along with water to drink. It wasn't much. The man never stopped. It didn't seem he needed to rest. He wasn't human."

"I had to wait out the night. You say he traveled all night?"

"Yes. All night as well as into the afternoon of the next day. When Belt found him, he'd dismounted to look at something. What he could possibly see on solid rock is beyond anything I understand."

Into the night they continued to talk. Deke wasn't certain he held her cooperation in the palm of his hands. She was an independent little woman. Was used to passing her life the way she pleased. Maybe Annie didn't belong in the mountains. Perhaps she would be better off in the city.

In the city where there were street signs.

Deke knew having tasted her, explored her lovely body, he could never let her go. He would have to do a better job teaching her. The night passed. He slept fitfully. The morning would bring more turmoil. Peter along with Adair would have to be seen to. They would be arrested tonight if the posse made it back to Denver City, if the men were still in town.

"If they were gone, he didn't know what he should do. Race after them? Haul them back for a trial? In retrospect, he thought he should let them go. If he did, they would have their way with some other poor innocent. Someone they could coerce more easily than his Annie.

When the first rays of sunlight filtered through the bedroom window, he rose and dressed. Striding downstairs, he called for a bath for Annie along with breakfast then hot coffee. He met Maria at the foot of the steps.

"The little miss is fine this morning?" she asked while she bustled ahead of him leading the way to the kitchen.

Bella was there with a tray of food along with the coffee. "You going into town?"

Nodding Deke lifted the lid on one of the platters. "Smells good. I'll take this up to the room if you get that bath water for Annie. "Yes, need to make certain Bentley along with his pal are long gone or arrested. Annie will be with me. Want her by my side today. Until I know she is safe, I don't want her out of my line of vision." As long as there was a threat to her, she would stay with him.

Bella chuckled, "She's a feisty little thing. Don't ever set Maria and me to babysitting her again." She was shaking her finger at him. "She's too big a handful for the likes of two old women. We're not good at that job. She can get into a lick of trouble before I can even blink. She doesn't know how to cook or clean. Suppose our little doc only knows doctoring. We'll all be well takin' care of, that is for certain."

Deke agreed and disagreed with her. She knew how to do many things very well. If there was any trouble going on today, he wanted to be standing beside her. Hell, if he'd been five minutes earlier two days ago, nothing would have happened to her. He couldn't keep his eye on her all the time. Eventually, he'd have to let her out of his line of sight. He prayed Bentley and Adair would be long gone by then.

"I'll get that hot water up to her," Maria told him. "You go on take that food. She's going to need something more to eat. She was near starvin' to death last night when she got home."

"Will do that as soon as I speak with Levi."

He continued to the barn. Pye was munching his feed. Levi hopped down from the loft to see what he could do. Deke looked at that loft remembering the lovemaking. He would never forget her astonishment at being tossed into the snow or her indignation. When he brought her to the loft for the afternoon picnic, she'd been so very passionate. He wanted a repeat performance. As soon as the furor died down, he'd get Bella to make them another picnic. Would like to visit the lake again too. The summer after the weather heated up would be perfect for that visit.

"What can I do for you?" Levi pushed his hat back on his forehead, a piece of hay stuck between his teeth.

"Get Pye along with Briar ready. Annie and I are riding into town. Need to see if Bentley has left."

God, he didn't know what he would do if Bentley was arrogant enough to remain in the town. He tugged in a long breath of air holding the oxygen in his lungs for a few seconds. He told himself Taylor would have arrested him if he was still in town. He wanted the man to go to federal prison.

On the other hand, he didn't want Annie to have to see him in court, to testify against him. They needed to put the man along with his pals behind them. The man needed to be punished. His conflicting emotions surprised him. This confusion in his muddled head was something new to him. He wasn't used to indecision.

"Want me to go with you?" Levi asked as he rocked back on the heels of his riding boots. "Don't mind. Always can use an extra set of eyes and ears."

"Would like you as well as Angel to ride with us. Saddle the horses. We'll be ready in about an hour."

He felt as if his stomach was in his throat waiting to see what was happening in town. The sensations now weren't as bad as when he watched Annie disappear into the forest with a man he didn't know. When he understood she might end up in a townhouse in Boston if he didn't catch the man, both his fury and terror were in the forefront of his head. He said a silent thank you to Belt.

He turned, ready to go back to the house. When he entered the master chamber, Annie was in the tub. It was the same scenario he encountered last night. He restrained himself while he poured a cup of coffee. To get his mind off the image of Annie naked in her tub, Deke whistled. It seemed she wanted his attention. Her voice was soft and whiskey smooth.

"What? You don't want to share my bath this morning?" she teased, her smile flashing the prettiest white teeth he'd ever seen.

Deke was pleased she was in a good mood. If her ordeal was having a lasting effect on her, she wasn't showing the stress. He brought a second cup of coffee to her. Stepping back a bit from the vision in front of him, he gazed on her.

"I would like nothing better than to get into that tub with you," he told her in all sincerity. "If I did, we wouldn't be getting anything accomplished today. We're riding into Denver City with Levi and Angel."

"Was that a we I heard? You're not going to leave me behind while you do manly things to protect me?" she asked as she rose from the water then wrapped a towel around her.

She drank some of the coffee before setting the cup on a table. He watched her mesmerized by her fluid grace. Her long, slim legs rose to meet the towel. She provoked him, teased as she understood what the sight of her clothed only in a towel did to him.

"You heard right," he murmured wishing they could be newlyweds, could spend the day making love, talking. Besides the very tender erotic places on her body that he wanted to seduce, he had several other spots that would help quench his thirst for his wife.

"I will hurry. Wouldn't want to hold anyone up."

"Won't take you anywhere with me until you eat." He laughed

softly remembering another conversation, one she didn't like at all. "You are eating for two now."

The damp towel she'd been wearing only a moment ago hit him in the face. He held the cloth to his nose. Caught the scent of his wife along with roses from the fragrant oils she poured in the tub.

She didn't say a word. He saw the glittering of her eyes. Needed to taunt more thoroughly.

"I see a bit of bulge on your belly," he told her wishing he could see exactly that. He could barely wait to see his wife increasing from his seed.

Annie gasped then looked at herself. "You cad. You do not."

Her back to him, she strode to the armoire.

"Have you been sick at all?" he asked thinking there was a lot he needed to learn about his wife as well as pregnancy.

He would ask her for a book or two. Certainly, she must have something he could read.

Shaking her head, she slipped her chemise over a slightly damp body. The fabric caught on her pink nipples. "No. It's a bit early for morning sickness. Though I suppose it can happen any time and can last however long." She lifted her shoulders stepping closer to him to grab a slice of warm bread. She drank from her cup of coffee again.

After she dressed, they finished eating. When they reached the barn, the horses were saddled and waiting for them. The mountain air was crip this morning. The day would be warm. Clouds dotted the horizon. Deke smelled a thunder storm brewing. They might have to stay the night in town. That would be fine with him. All he needed was a big bed and Annie in his arms.

~ * ~

In Denver City, they tied the horses at the sheriff's office. Taylor was inside shuffling through the wanted posters. The man who abducted Annie was in one of the two jail cells. He looked up, a lazy grin spreading across his face. He appeared to not have a care in the world. He should at least be concerned with Annie. He abducted her. Didn't he?

Deke set his hat on the coat stand while he pulled out a chair for Annie in front of Taylor's desk. Annie sat. Deke turned his chair around, straddling it then placing his forearms on the top. "He talking?" Deke asked looking pointedly at the man resting negligently in the cell.

"Man's name is Charles Wells. That's about all I've gotten out of him. You want to try?" Taylor asked as he set the paperwork aside. "He isn't a wanted man. That's about all I know. No wanted posters with his name or picture to be found. Got the newest ones just two days ago."

Deke looked at Annie as if he expected her to ask questions. She lifted her shoulders slightly realizing she didn't have any ideas about what to ask that she hadn't already asked him. He never even told her his name. "No, I…don't believe he'll say anything more now than he did before."

Taylor was asking her while he rummaged through one of the drawers of his desk. When he looked up, "You want to make a statement as to what happened? We'll need that information in order for me to hold him. We didn't catch you with him. It could be his word, if he decided to talk, against yours."

"If it's necessary."

She relived this once this morning. With Deke's interrogation, she recounted everything to him. Doing so again wouldn't be pleasant. She would do whatever she had to. The man needed to be brought to justice.

"It is," Taylor said reaching into his desk for paper and pencil then bringing them out. He pushed them over to her.

"Is Bentley still in town?" Deke asked, his voice hard.

"He along with Adair were gone when we got back last night with Mister Wells." Taylor looked to the cell when he said the man's name. "You want to talk yet, Wells?"

"I'll talk to the little lady over there," Charles said his voice soft, his grin almost a leer before changing to something softer. "Decided I don't want to take the entire brunt of this conviction. I was misled. Thought the lady was a wife. Peter Bentley's wife to be exact. Was told she ran away. He only meant to retrieve what he deemed was his. However, I've heard that scenario before. Seems to be a common thread with the man."

"My wife," Deke volunteered harshly. "What the hell do you

mean, a common thread?"

"As I said I was misled, lied to. Mr. Bentley was paying me to bring her to him. Said she wouldn't come on her own. Also told me she wasn't quite right in the head." Wells pointed to his temple. "You know, a bit touched."

"He said what?" Annie sat up suddenly listening more intently than before. She sucked air. "I'm…"

"You can be a bit strong-willed," Deke added with a hoot of laughter that sent her eyes to crossing.

Charles sat back on his cot, his hands behind his head as he seemed to survey her. "Your little woman told me she could pay me more than Bentley if I let her go. Should have taken her up on the offer. I wouldn't be in here if I had. A man needs to learn from his mistakes."

"I could have. You said your word was your bond," Annie told him her hands fisted on her hips. Her indignation clear. "Now that you're in a pack of trouble you want to side with the law? What happened to your word?"

"I do. Can lead you to Bentley and his friend if the incentive is right."

Charles still looked too relaxed, too arrogant, and certain of himself. His legs were crossed at his ankles. He was a big man, strong. His shoulders were broad, his thighs incased in the buckskins were well-muscled. His hair was the same color as his short-cropped beard. His eyes glittered golden-brown. His hair was rakishly long.

"Where are they?" Taylor asked. "You can get out of this if you give them to me."

"Figured as much," Charles sat up then strode closer to the bars. "I'm a lawman as well. If you grab my saddlebags, you'll find my papers along with the star I could wear if I wished. You all understand why."

Annie gasped, outraged by his claim. Her fists clenched even tighter. She wanted to slap the arrogant beast. He didn't help her. "How dare you?" She stood, knocking her chair to the floor. "How dare you?"

"Sorry, ma'am just doing my job. That was to bring in Bentley. Was contacted by the Boston authorities. They wanted to catch the man in the act so to speak. They were going to be there when I handed you over to the men."

"No! You were actually going to give me to Bentley!"

For a moment his arrogance vanished from his face. He looked a bit contrite then that too vanished.

"Be where?" Deke asked seemingly unable to remain quiet. "Where were you going?"

"You...!" Annie began still outraged by the revelation Mr. Wells made.

Taylor was walking toward his desk, reading the papers, the star in his hand. He looked up, "A federal marshal. Not just any lawman, I see."

He stood his hands on the bars. "Guilty as charged. I had to wait to say anything until I felt certain no one else was involved. Can you let me out now?"

"You...!" Annie sputtered again. She was pointing at him, her finger shaking with the indignation she felt. "He should be charged with kidnapping. I don't care what the ruse was. Don't care if he's a federal marshal! He gave me the worst headache of my life!" She shifted her feet, tugging in a deep breath of air.

"Now, I'm sorry about that. Understood you weren't coming along willingly. Had to get out of there fast since your man got home before I suspected he would. Thought we would be long gone by the time your husband returned from town. Didn't mean to hurt you in any way."

His hands rose in a gesture of apology that softened Annie's heart.

"What are we going to do about Bentley?" Taylor asked seeming to wait for answers.

"Send a message to the law in Denver City. It will take those two a good week to make it to the settlement if that's where they are headed," Charles told them while Taylor unlocked the cell door. "He'll be watching for the men. Had a chance to talk to the sheriff there before I led your friends out here."

"You're positive they'll be apprehended?"

"Not too certain they'll survive the journey," Charles said with a knowing smirk. "I escorted them here. They are two green horns if I ever saw any. Another posse would be in order, just to save their fool necks.

Once we catch them, I'll escort the pair back to Boston for trial."

"You won't need me?" Annie asked, suddenly afraid she'd find herself on her way to Boston. She didn't want to leave Deke.

"No, a written statement should be enough, especially since they didn't succeed in abducting you. They've been under the eye of the law for a long time. Bentley and Crawford are wanted for more than kidnapping ladies. There are allegations of fraud as well as embezzlement surrounding their names. Bentley was rumored to be part of a diamond heist."

Deke stood behind her. His hands rested on her shoulders gently massaging the tension. "When do you need the written statement?" Deke asked.

"Tomorrow morning will be soon enough. Who was the half breed who knocked me out cold?" Charles asked, turning his attention to Annie.

"A friend," Annie told him wishing Mr. Wells had the power to give him his freedom. "A friend who took exception to you kidnapping me."

Taylor handed Charles his gun belt. He accepted it fastening it on his lean hips. "Can you get that posse ready by tomorrow afternoon. That should give those two enough time to get lost," Charles laughed, his amusement clear.

"Want to come along?" Taylor was questioning Deke.

Deke looked to Annie. When he returned his gaze to Taylor, he shook his head. "We're going to check out her old office and apartment above. Annie might want to share some of her time between the ranch and the town. Tonight, we just want to have time alone with no more worries or difficulties.

"Only until you find a new doctor." She did smile at Taylor who gave her the option. "No one will visit my office unless they are dying. We both know that for the sad fact that it is."

She held out her hand for Deke. He pulled her to her feet. "I'll make certain there are enough supplies in the office. If not, I'll send in an order. There should be though. Don't believe Mr. Crawford did any doctoring. Wonder if the man is a doctor."

Once out of the sheriff's office they strode down the street. Deke's arm was firmly planted around her shoulders. Leaning into him she soaked in his warmth. All she wished for now was a normal, well-ordered life.

"I don't want to share my time with you. Want to spend the rest of our days together at your ranch. This dream I had was always a dream. Father tried to dissuade me with relevant facts. Think I had to prove to myself I could be accepted at medical school as well as pass the courses. I've done all that. There is nothing more for me to prove."

"You certainly have."

"What now?" Annie asked reveling in sweet thoughts about tonight.

"I've plans," he murmured bending so close she felt the whisper of his words across her neck. His fingers tightened on her shoulder. "Do you want to make love on your bed? Or perhaps the kitchen table. We could put furs in front of the fire."

"You never change."

She liked the idea that he might have designs on her body even when they were old and gray…and she never wanted him to change.

"Is that good or bad?" he asked moving a bit away from her so he could look into her eyes. His were dark, blue-black a certain sign he wanted her now.

"Depends," she murmured skipping away from him then turning so she was backing up. She was happy, content. Annie wanted to race him to her office. She wanted to smooth her hands along the heat of his naked chest and back then to other parts of him as well.

"On what?" he queried picking up his strides, keeping a small distance between them.

"Look at you two?" Pauli called out merrily as she watched them from outside the saloon. She waved. "Love birds, if I don't say."

"You're right, Pauli," Deke laughed at her as he continued the pace. "We'll be closing the curtains in that upstairs room."

"You don't have to. I would enjoy the show."

Her trilling laughter followed them down the road.

The show? Annie knew Pauli watched her kissing Deke before. Ever since that first kiss, he'd been careful to keep anyone from seeing them together. He was possessive as well as protective of her.

Deke caught up to her, sweeping her into his arms. His mouth captured hers. When their lips parted, "Nobody is going to watch you except me. You can bet on that."

With that said, he picked up his pace. Raced up the stairs to the apartment above. Found the door unlocked as if the rooms waited for them. She'd not thought of requesting a key from Taylor. Had not expected the place to look just as she left it after the marriage. During the interim, nothing changed.

He set her on the bed. In a few seconds his clothing littered the floor. From where he stood, three long strides got him to the window. The curtains were closed. He leaned against the frame of the window studying her.

"Pauli probably saw you naked."

He smiled wickedly at her.

She wanted to know what he was thinking.

"What are you waiting, for my Annie girl? I want you just as naked as I am. If you recall, I'm not a patient man."

To Annie it didn't seem as he meant to do anything except watch her. Earlier, he said as much. "You," she whispered softly, holding out her hands to him. "I'm waiting for you."

He closed the distance. On the bed he quickly turned her, unfastening then stripping her of everything she wore. She lay on her stomach. His lips followed the path of her spine, tiny teasing kisses, laving, nipping. Her hips arched, her backside rising to meet his lips. She wanted to turn over. To touch him as he touched her.

Heat enveloped her. Magic shot through her until she moaned softly. His teeth grazed across her bottom then along her inside thigh. Against her flesh his lips were hot, soft as well. He knew just how to charm and seduce. He lifted her.

"You have the most delectable little butt I've ever seen or tasted." He bit lightly once then twice. His hands squeezed the naked flesh. "I like your backside as much as I love your frontside."

Tempest soared. Fires rose within her. "Deke…" a tiny mewl of pleasure, a soft sound, feminine cries followed.

She moaned. Heaved. He journeyed down her leg, stopped at the tender spot behind her knee. Heat and tempest joined together then roared to life when he lifted her, when his lips found the slick hot folds between her legs. He suckled. She cried out.

Annie wanted to touch him, return the tempest along with the enchantment and magic he ignited. She needed to hear him groan with his man's pleasure. If he'd allow her, she wanted to sightsee with her mouth and fingertips the length of his rock-hard body. It was not to be.

"My sweet," he murmured as he flipped her over again. She lay upon her back. His hands cupped her breasts, teased her nipples.

His mouth seized hers in a deep hard kiss. She met his kiss with her tongue, touching upon his, rubbing. He kissed her and kissed her hard. Her lips tingled with the pleasure. When he released her lips from his, he reared up to look at her. His eyes were so dark they appeared very nearly black. His jaw was tense. His knees braced her legs apart.

"I want you now," she told him, her hands roaming across his chest, touching upon the curling hair she found then his small nipples that hardened just as hers did.

She was amazed at how he responded when she touched him.

"After I've kissed every inch of you. Then and only then can you have your wicked way with me."

His mouth tugged on the tip of her breast then the other, back again. He couldn't seem to decide where to stay. "I covet all of you. There is not one part that I don't want to taste. All of you needs my ardent attention."

After that he kissed her navel, her belly. He parted her legs wider. With his hands he lifted her so he could easily close his mouth on the tender, sensitive place between her thighs. He kissed then suckled until she was writhing with the pleasure he so easily seduced. Tiny ripples of pleasure splashed through her. The sensations not enough to send her over the edge.

He looked at her. "Are you ready for me, Little Darlin'?"

"Please..."

Slowly, he eased his sex inside her. She felt the size of him along with the pulse of his blood. He was steel-hard. It seemed he meant to torture her. With infinite patience he finally impaled all of her. He stopped. Pushed damp tendrils of hair from her face. She arched. Twisted, trying to tug him deeper. Heaved and moaned. Wanted him to move within her passage.

With deliberate confident strokes, he began to travel within her. The rhythm was pure torture. So slow, each force measured, calculated to bring more mercuric heat to every part of her. Slow in then slow out he continued his tender assault.

He was her enchantment.

"You are magic to my soul," he murmured the words as he withdrew as slowly as he thrust into her again then again.

No warning for her...his pace changed. Now he shoved harder and faster. Harder still while he continued to tantalize her with the erotic placement of his lips, teeth and tongue. He suckled on her breasts, nipped at the tips. He kissed her mouth, dueling with her tongue while his fingers played with her breasts, tugging on her nipples.

Heat spiraled higher. She moaned softly in the back of her throat. He groaned as her body rose to meet his time and again. The uncontrollable pulsing of her core left her breathless. She clung to him, her nails biting into the hard muscles of his arms. She cried out. Her body reached that point where she could no longer think could only feel the sweetness of their union. Wave after wave of ecstasy shot through her for a moment blinding her with the sweetness.

Above her, Deke cried out. The muscles of his face strained as he pumped into her. She felt the heat of his seed fill her. He collapsed on top of her. His weight blanketed her. Annie ran her hands along his back stopping at his buttocks. He was hard muscle everywhere.

Rolling over, he brought her with him. She nestled against the great wall of his chest while she ran her fingertip down the middle of his chest to his naval. She wanted to touch his length to cup him in her hands. Next time, perhaps she would be able to seduce him as he did her.

His knuckles brushed gently along the column of her neck. He trailed a calloused fingertip along her collarbone stopping where her pulse still raced. "Are you glad that Peter and Adair will be caught?" he asked while one of his hands idly ran the length of her back.

"They will be caught. I pray with every breath in my body. When they are captured, will we receive a message?" she asked hoping that dispatch would come soon.

"I believe that Charles knows as much about tracking as anyone. Those two will be captured before they reach Fort Laramie. Odds are they will be ever thankful to see Charles Wells even though he is a federal marshal. Prison will be better than lost in the woods at the mercy of whatever wild animal might find them."

"You don't think they can find their way?"

Her hand rested on his chest.

"Could you?"

She laughed softly as he kissed the tips of her breasts. "I do know what part of my anatomy will guide me if I'm trying to move in a northward direction," she assured him. "My nose will always point north."

"No, it is the pretty tips of your breasts that will point the way."

She punched him on the chest. "You will always think…" she cut the following words off not wanting to push the conversation.

"What about the south?" He turned her over, placed a kiss on her bottom.

"Hmm…why don't you tell me?" Her body quickened. He turned her over again.

"Your delicious little backside if you need a reminder."

"I don't."

He rose then pulled her with him. "Are you hungry?"

"Famished. We don't have food."

"I'll see what the special is at the saloon. Unfortunately, the wine has been sent to my ranch. I could bring a bottle from the saloon if you'd like."

Epilogue

They sat by the lake. She was due anytime now. He told her they shouldn't take the chance. However, she felt no pains yet. Annie understood that today she wouldn't have the child. He made her promise that she would tell him the moment she felt a contraction.

Deke leaned against the trunk of a tree holding her. She pressed against his back. His hands settled on the hard ridge of her stomach. She sighed softly, relishing the soft breeze that rippled through the trees overhead.

This day at the end of February was unseasonably warm. The beauty of the day was the only reason she'd been able to talk him into an excursion. He said they would stay only long enough to eat the picnic Bella made for them. After they finished the meal, they would return to the ranch.

He pulled out a piece of paper handing it to her. "Read it."

She looked at him, a weary expression on her face. "What is it?"

"From Charles Wells."

"You had this…?"

"Since this morning. Taylor sent his deputy with the missive. I wanted to wait for the perfect time to give the letter to you. You will be pleased, I'm thinking."

Annie read. She looked to him. "Thank you."

"I didn't do anything. Wells found them lost, riding in circles. They were starving as well as cold. We knew that would happen."

"Yes, when he reached Boston with the two men they were immediately brought into custody. All the charges against the men stuck. They will be in prison for a very long time."

"Good," her voice sounded strained. There was a long pause while she seemed to catch her breath. Very calmly she told him, "I've started labor."

His breath caught in the back of his throat. For what seemed an eternity, his heart stopped. Now the organ thundered in his chest. "Can you ride? You told me not to worry. Hell!"

His voice was shaking. Nerves he didn't know he possessed stretched to the breaking point. For her sake he needed to stay calm.

"I'll have to ride now, won't I? Not much of a choice since the little one just decided it was time to see the world."

"No, you can ride in front of me. Don't want you to fall off."

She grimaced bending over for a moment. His heart lodged in his throat.

"If you wish."

She looked at him. Smiled.

The grin didn't look real. He understood she would never agree if she wasn't in pain. She gathered what was left of the picnic into the basket. He scooped her into his arms. He was frantic to get her home then send Levi for the midwife she didn't want.

"I wish," he muttered. "Why didn't you tell me sooner?"

She laughed softly. "Until I told you, I didn't know. The babe won't be born for quite a few more hours. As of this moment, I've only had two contractions. They were both weak." She patted him on the cheek. "It will all be fine."

He didn't like the feel of this situation. The lack of control galled him. He liked to orchestrate the events in his life. In seconds, she was in front of him, her horse following behind. At this pace, it would take them an hour to reach the ranch. "I should never have agreed to this nonsense."

He found himself swearing silently as they rode so very afraid for her. He was about to become a father. It was all very real.

"There was no way to know. You need to relax," she told him, a hint of laughter in her voice. "First babies take hours and hours."

He didn't see how he could possibly relax until this child was born and he knew they would both be fine. The contractions were about twenty minutes apart. He knew each time she felt pain.

When they rode into the yard, he bellowed for Levi or Angel to take the horses. With Annie in his arms, he slipped from Pye then headed for the house yelling at the top of his lungs.

"Bella! Maria!" Striding through the house he was first met by Maria.

"I can walk!" She hit his chest, smiling as he grunted. "It's good for the labor if I walk."

She was laughing outright.

He'd been like an angry bear all the way back to the ranch. His fright was for Annie. He recalled what she told him about the birth of Belt's child. What if something like that happened to her. She wouldn't be able to fix the problem. She seemed to be able to read his mind.

"Our babe is turned. I can tell the head is in the right place," she spoke calmly. "You have nothing to worry about. Even if it wasn't, I could give you a quick lesson in what to do. You've more experience than you realize."

His Annie was acting too calmly for him. Why wasn't she frightened or nervous. No, he didn't want her to be nervous or frightened. He wanted her to be just as she was. Trying to ease his fears he walked up the steps to the master room.

"I'll get the bed ready," Maria said. "Set your little lady down. Let her walk. She knows what she is talking about. Remember, she is a doctor as well as an intelligent woman."

He didn't want to set her down. Wanted to hold her. He found that when the bed was prepared, he was pushed from the room.

"I'm staying," he told the women.

He wasn't about to be left out of this. He had to be with her.

Over the course of the night, Deke found he didn't sleep. When she finally did give birth and he heard his daughter cry out, he said a silent prayer. The babe was cleaned then given to Annie to examine and feed. Amidst screams from the little one, the tiny girl finally found the nipple she'd been searching for.

"Isn't she beautiful?" Annie asked looking at him.

"Yes," he said but he only had eyes for his wife. "You're beautiful. You are both beautiful."

A daughter, he had a daughter. He would see that she never wanted for anything, especially love. He would see that when she grew, she would never come to harm.

"What are we going to name her?" Annie asked as she smoothed the top of the babe's head.

The little girl had pure white hair along with powder blue eyes. Eyes changed color sometimes. He hoped they stayed that beautiful shade of powder blue just like her mothers.

"Let's think on it overnight," he murmured unwilling to make a decision such as this one right away. "We'll have to find a name that suits her personality."

"Just how do you think to do that. She is only minutes old," Annie said indignantly. "Suits her personality?"

He felt a bit sheepish at the words he spoke. "I have no idea."

He walked the room with his daughter. She let out a loud very unfeminine burp. They laughed.

"Don't be thinking along those lines," Annie warned as she finally sobered.

"What lines?" he asked smiling as they both knew that he understood. "Do you want more children?"

"Only after this one is big enough that she can feed herself as well as walk. If you're thinking I might want to practice medicine, you're wrong. I don't need that in my life."

"I love you, Annie. You're my magic."

He sat down beside her on the bed as he watched her close her eyes. He wanted to hear her say the words he'd been waiting for since the moment he met her. "Well?"

She opened her eyes. "I do love you Deke, so very much. I love you with all my heart."

"Am I your magic," he asked placing a gentle kiss on her forehead.

"Oh yes, you are magic to me Deke Sullivan. So is your kiss," she added softly. "Deke's magic kiss."

Chasing After Still Water

Missouri 1836

Still Water Runs watched the wagon train move lazily along the rutted-out road. They'd been on the trail five days now. The train of wagons was over fifty miles west of Independence where they had begun the long journey to a new life. For the benefit of the people he scouted for, he was called Stephen Wilkes. That was the name he would go by until he reached Lakota territory. He breathed in the clean prairie scented air, eager to reach Fort Laramie where he would head north into more rugged country. This would be his last trip to the lands of his people. With the help of the Earl of Blackmore, he bought property in England, land that adjoined the earls. While he was eager to see his mother, he was also excited to begin his new life.

Wiping sweat from his forehead, he thought of Chauncey. Thought of the kiss they shared behind the church the day his friend, the Earl of Blackmore, wed Lyssa Andrews for the third time. This one was actually their second kiss. Chauncey didn't know anything about kissing. Now, he was leaving her behind. While his friend the earl found love with a white woman, he doubted if the miracle would happen a second time. Before he left, he told her to find someone else. She argued. He stood his ground. The notion gave him reason to smile. When he lightly cupped her breast in his hand, lazily roamed across the tip with his thumb, she gasped then jerked back, her eyes so wide they reminded him of the blue saucers the earl used with his tea cups. She was untried, innocent in every way.

When he took an intimacy he had no right taking, she ran her sweet tongue across her bottom lip. The tip was a lovely pink color. He wanted to be the man to teach her how to kiss as well as how to please him. The timing was all shot to hell. Slow and measured, he'd brought his hand up to her chin. Holding it lightly with his hand, he ran his thumb across the dewy softness he found there wishing he dared hope for more.

He didn't.

He understood the differences in their way of life. She would never fit his expectations for a wife. She was everything he wasn't. She was cultured. His life until England was primitive as well as savage. She was pure white. He fought against the white settlers encroaching on land that didn't belong to them. Killed some when he had to defend himself.

"I'm leaving tomorrow," he told her regretting his decision for an instant. He wasn't the man for her. If he stayed and courted her, she would eventually come to hate him. Still Water Runs understood he needed to be harsh with her. "I'll be back when I'm good and ready. Not a minute sooner. Don't wait for me. Find a nice man who is white who lives in your way. Marry him. Have white children."

"Where are you going?" Her query was hesitant as well as curious. She touched his thumb with her tongue. She wasn't listening to him. "I would go with you." After that she set her small white hand on his chest. The nails were clean, nicely manicured. If she traveled with him that would change all too soon. The nails he looked at now would become ragged, dirt would settle in them. Where he was traveling would not suit this delicate woman.

Unable to help himself he touched her lips with his once more. Unable to help himself, he kissed her again, drawing her closer to him with his hand on the small of her back then sliding the palm lower to cup her adorable backside. If he took her here behind the church, she would be willing. Her father would have his head as was his right. He reminded himself he was leaving. She would find someone more suitable. At the thought deep raw pain sluiced through him.

Her fingers shaking, she touched him, responded to his ill-advised advance, meeting his tongue with hers. Rising on the tips of her toes, she wound her small hands behind his neck. She wasn't a short woman but she didn't come to his chin. He needed to find a female who was sturdier.

Deep and low in the back of his throat, he groaned his voice hoarse. She drew back, looking at him, questions in her vibrant sapphire blue eyes. Eyes that were darkening with the rising passion he seemed to be generating in her.

Once again, he cupped her small breast in his hand, smoothed the hidden tip with his finger, wishing he dared move the tiny sleeves of her gown lower so he could see her breasts, touch as well as suckle. He wanted to discover the color of the tender buds that even now were responding to him, hardening with each pass of his finger. Once more he needed to remind himself that if he did what he was thinking, he would ruin her for another man. He had no business here. Nothing good could come from this.

When he looked at her bosom then back to her eyes, she looked embarrassed. She cleared her throat softly before she spoke. "They are not very big, nothing like Lyssa's. I would that I were larger…men like…"

He chuckled understanding what she spoke of. Lifting her chin, he kissed the tip of her nose, after that her forehead. Besotted with the woman, he couldn't stop the grin. "A man doesn't need more than a mouthful."

"A mouthful?" She blinked a few times as if mulling over his statement. "I don't understand what you're saying."

An innocent would never understand. She was so damn sweet, too tasty for the likes of him. "Yes. I'd like to taste you. Would you like that, Chauncey? Would you like my mouth to discover your flavor? What do you taste like? Your lips taste like mint along with the sweet red Bordeaux you drank a few minutes ago. They intoxicate me. What about the rest of you?" He fell silent watching the changing expressions on her lovely face.

"Intoxicate? The rest of me?" Again, she blinked a few times before running one hand along his chest where she now stared.

Chuckling, he asked, "Are you a little parrot?" He was enjoying himself immensely. He'd never been with an innocent. Even in his formative years, the women who came to his bed were experienced.

Chauncey was delicious.

"Parrot?"

He laughed again while he ran his fingertip down her nose. He wanted to kiss her again. They needed to return to the celebration before someone, her father, came to look for her. It was necessary for him to voice his thoughts. "Come along, little parrot, we need to get back to the festivity before anyone misses us."

"No." Her body tensing, she held her ground her lips formed into a thin line. Her chin tilted at an angle he was slowly beginning to understand that particular expression. "I want to know where you are going? Why are you leaving tomorrow?"

Leaning against the church, he tugged her back into his arms. Stephen spread his legs, cradling her next to his arousal, wondering if she felt how much he wanted her. He imagined it wouldn't hurt to tell her what she asked. There was nothing she could do about it. "Lakota territory. This might be my last chance to see my mother. She grows older. Don't know what I will find when I reach the home of my people. When Kane returns to England next summer, I'm hoping to be with him or close on his heels."

Once more, her hands rested on his chest then higher to wind around his neck. She ran her slender fingers through his hair. "I'd like to go with you." She stared at him as if the request was something he would agree to.

"No." Lakota territory was no place for a white woman. "No, as I said before it's too dangerous. You need to find a man to love. Someone who can return that sentiment whole heartedly." He did need her to wait for him. Wished to pursue this relationship to see where it might lead. He would never ask or hope for her to wait for his return. She was of marriageable age.

She was white. He wasn't full blooded Sioux, nor was he considered a half-breed as Kane was. There were hints of white man in his blood. He'd heard that his grandmother had been forced by a white man, a trapper. His lighter skin coupled with green eyes was the result. Both his parents were Sioux. Just as Kane was a breed, so was he. Stephen imagined that was why they'd become such friends. They understood the vulnerability. Neither were accepted completely in either world.

"I would be no trouble. I can ride and shoot. Know how to use a knife. Enjoy sleeping under the stars. My biscuits are almost as tasty as Amorica's. You would never regret bringing me along with you. I would do whatever you told me." Her plea seemed heartfelt as well as sincere.

While he wanted to laugh, he also needed to make her understand the seriousness of this mission of his. He didn't even know how he'd be received at his destination. "A woman who doesn't belong is always trouble." No, he amended to himself. All women were trouble. He didn't understand them. He smoothed hair from her face letting the tips of his fingers travel along her cheek then down her throat to her throbbing pulse at the base of her neck. He needed to kiss her there, explore and sightsee all of her.

Chauncey bristled at his words. He saw determination in the set of her jaw as well as the simmer in her eyes. "I would go with you. I'm never trouble. You should understand I'm not like most women."

No, Chauncey Lakeland was unique to herself. He should have never kissed her. "You barely know me…" He rubbed the back of his neck. It was so true. They'd known each other for twenty-four hours. He felt an immediate connection with her he'd never known with another woman. He wondered if she could ride like Lyssa Andrews. He prayed then that she couldn't. If she could not, he wouldn't have to chastise her when she put her life in danger. "You would have to obey me. Jump when I said jump. I would never stand for a woman who would gainsay my orders and, in the process, put herself in danger."

"Enough to know, I want to be with you." She straightened her shoulders. "I would do everything you said."

Somehow, he didn't believe her words. Her entire life, he felt certain, she'd been pampered and allowed to do whatever she wished. Life could never be that way where he was headed. "Such a determined little thing," he murmured softly, staring at her stiff back as she walked away from him. He didn't know what she was going to do. Now, she turned and was walking back to him.

"You're leaving in the morning?" she asked. "From Independence?"

"Yes, I'm the head scout for the wagon train. I've a job to do along the way. After that I'll head my own way." Perhaps he told her too much. Bloody hell, she was a woman. She wouldn't just up and leave her home, her family to follow him.

Would she?

No. Women did stupid things, foolish things when they took a notion into their woman's brain. She was walking away from him again, her skirts swinging around her delicate ankles, her back stiff as if she was determined. He groaned again. He wanted to understand what she was thinking.

Those memories happened weeks ago. Now he was well past Independence. She didn't follow him. Thank all the different Gods ever worshipped.

"Terrell," Stephen nodded to the wagon master as he was jerked away from his musings and back to the present by the company of the other man. He'd been lucky, he supposed. Chauncey stayed put as he told her to do. She would find a white man. She would marry then have children. It was all good. His memory would be like dust in the wind.

When he reached Independence there was no sign of her. He half expected to see her sitting on one of the wagons, guiding the oxen as well as horses down the long trail. He'd only met about half of the hundred or so people heading west on the Oregon Trail. She was not among them. Paranoid that she might have tracked him here, he'd scrutinized every woman.

As a single woman she would never be allowed to be part of the wagon train. It just wasn't done. Families had to look out for their own, wives needed to be certain there were no extra women to tempt their men. Chauncey was tenacious. If it was something she wanted badly enough, she would find a way to maneuver all obstacles out of the way to get what she wanted. He grimaced uncertain once more. Something quivered deep in the pit of his stomach. Looking at the expression on Terrell's face, he felt certain trouble brewed.

"Stephen," Johnathan said as he too watched the wagons lumber past them. "So far, no problems. Though we are less than a week out. What do you think of the people? Of the progress?"

Stephen leaned on his saddle horn as he studied the landscape below him. "No problems. Don't expect too many. Unless the weather changes to something nasty. Of course, eventually it will. We're making good progress." He wondered what question Terrell was asking him. His voice was vague yet imploring. There was something the man wasn't telling him.

Terrell tipped his hat back, seeming to want to say something to him. Stephen saw the tension in the set of his jaw, the weariness in his eyes when he looked at him. The man looked to the end of the slow-moving train then back to him.

"Spit it out, Terrell. What's eatin' at you? If here is something you want to say, say it. I'm not a man to play guessing games." This was unusual for the wagon master. He usually spoke his mind with no hesitancy. The difference gave him pause.

The man stared at him hard, brought his hand up to swipe dusty hair from his forehead. He cleared his throat, his Adam's apple bobbing. "Just wonderin' why you camp down with me. Doesn't seem logical."

Stephen shook his head, raising an eyebrow to the bright blue sky. How to answer the question slammed in his head. Caution before coming to an answer seemed appropriate. "Why do you ask?" He needed to know what else was on the tip of this man's tongue or in his mind that he wasn't telling him. Wished to know what was behind the question.

"Well, you see, that's just the thing," he paused looking down the valley then along the length of the lumbering wagons. Sweat beaded on his forehead.

"Terrell?" Stephen never appreciated solving puzzles when the answer could be spoken with no coercion. That was what this was rapidly becoming a puzzle. "Spit it out. If it's something I've done wrong tell me. We'll correct it."

The man's eyes darkened. "If I had a pretty little wife, riding solo in this long train with every man gaping at her, wanting to make her his, I'd be spending my nights with her all cuddled up and warm keeping her away from prying eyes. Making certain everyone knew who she belonged to. Don't understand what's gotten into you leavin' her all by herself." He held up his hands, "I know it's none of my business."

Wife?

He was shocked to the bottom of his soul. Deep in his chest his heart thundered. He approached this statement from a different vantage point. His first reaction was to deny the existence of a wife. His second was to shake her so silly that she'd never defy him again. He told her to stay put, to find a husband and have kids. She told him she wanted to go with him. He told her to find a white man and marry him. Stubborn minx.

Ah hell...

He had no idea how to answer the man. They were now too far out from Independence for him to return her. He didn't want her here. In danger. All he could do now was to acknowledge her then protect her with his life. His next instinct was to throttle her.

"Thought I should stay alert. If I cuddled up with my wife," he almost chocked on the word, wishing he dared do that very thing. "I might be otherwise engaged if you needed me." He thought that excuse to be a fine one. By the look on Terrell's face, it wasn't.

"You're our scout. A damn fine one. You would know if danger threatened us at night. You ride the trail every day. Think you should see to that pretty little woman before some man believes she's fair game. Every single man is talking about her, about her long legs and the curvaceous butt she shows in those britches she wears. If I were you, I'd insist she wear a dress. Get her out of men's clothing would be first on my agenda. Go on now, go spell her for a while. I bet those skinny arms of hers are sore from all the driving she's been doing. Don't want her hands calloused."

"Thank you. Believe I'll do just that." Stephen whipped his horse around then started down the hill toward the wagons. He was both eager as well as furious to see Chauncey. He wanted to yell at her then make love to her. The one he could do, the other he needed to keep in the back of his head. Taking her innocence was out of the question. He damn well wasn't going to ruin her chances of a decent marriage.

His wife.

She didn't have any idea what she'd done by proclaiming herself his. If he wished to do so, he could say the words and in the eyes of the People she would be his wife. The words would never suit her father. Nonetheless, in this situation the most fortuitous route might be to accept her as his wife, treat her as his wife. Furious emotions overrode eager ones to see her to hold her in his arms again, to kiss her, to have her in every way. The calm façade he was attempting to show slipped away as he drew nearer. His hands shook. His heart raced.

He galloped down the line of wagons nodding to people he didn't know, greeting the ones he did know with their name. His blood seemed to boil under the hot sun. When he reached her, he saw the look of surprise on her sweet features. After she smiled at him, he was bowled over by the sheer power of it. His body hardened just as it had the day of the wedding when he kissed her, touched her small breasts hidden beneath the fabric of her gown. She was lovely. Beneath his breath, he swore.

Her smile faded. "Still Water Runs?" Now that she had time to register the fierce look he slanted her, she didn't seem so pleased to see him. "I can explain."

Stephen bet she could. "Call me Stephen." He paused as he searched his head for the right words. "Or husband." His voice was harsh but not as harsh as he wished the tone to be. He was so damn pleased to see her. He automatically took some of the sting out of his voice. It was her smile that did him in. Her smile that robbed him of his anger. Her smile that sent all his senses to a boiling point.

"Stephen. What can I do for you?" she spoke sweetly, her head tilted flirtatiously to one side. "I would…" She stopped suddenly her gaze riveted on his eyes.

She was too certain of herself, too damn secure in what she was doing. He was pleased there was a moment of doubt no matter how brief that moment turned out to be. "Tonight, after we eat, I guess you'll find out."

The paleness of her face satisfied him. She ran her tongue along her lips. "I don't understand what you are implying. Are you eating with me tonight?"

"Scoot over." He landed on the seat beside her before tying the reins of his horse to the wagon. "I'm driving for the next hour or so. You need to rest. Have you been doing all the driving since we left Independence?" He took over, holding the reins with one gloved hand. "Let me see your hands."

Chauncey was sitting on them, shaking her head. "No. No, I don't think so. You don't have any right to demand anything of me."

"Don't want to have our first lover's spat over your hands. Let me see them." He was seething. As her white husband, he had every right to ask her anything and expect her obedience. As her Sioux husband, she had no rights at all. She was his to do with as he pleased.

"You can't expect me to do whatever you ask." She held them out, grimacing when he turned them over. "I can take care of myself."

He damn well could expect that of her. He cursed softly when he saw the broken blisters, the redness of her hands, the beginning of calluses. "As your husband, I've every right. In case you forgot, as your husband you are mine to do with as I damn well please. I should leave you at the next fort."

"But you won't." Her chin was up in the air, reminding him of her spoiled upbringing. "You would never leave me to fend for myself."

"You gambled on that fact. Didn't you?" His lungs swelled with the hot air he breathed in. "I'm going to thrash your pretty bottom until you can't sit. After that…well hell…" He couldn't do that. Idle threats got a man nowhere except into trouble he couldn't climb out of. What was he thinking?

"But you won't," she told him again, the sweetness of her smile sending heat straight to his groin. "You would never hurt me. I know that about you. Otherwise, I wouldn't be here," she said with a certainty she couldn't possibly know.

"Five days, Chauncey. How did you keep me from seeing you for five days?" His mind traveled over all the days searching for her. She would have been right up front and center when he traveled the lines looking over the train, assessing varying the abilities of the people. How had he missed her?

She lifted the shoulders he'd touched lightly that night. They were covered now. They still looked fragile. He stared at her britches. Seems he should have noticed her butt in the air. Ah, but he might have thought she was a man. Shaking his head, disbelief prevalent. No, he would have never looked at her curves then believed her male.

"You never looked at me. When I saw you riding this way, I'd turn to find something in the wagon." In a gesture that drove him crazy, she lifted her shoulders in a feminine movement that left the softest parts of her moving. "Made sure you never saw my face. What did you expect? I knew if you saw me too soon, you might find a way to send me home."

The little devil understood he would be angry with her as well as annoyed. She was right on all her assumptions. Now she flirted with him, testing him. Yes, if he'd discovered her a day or two out, he would have taken her back to Independence. Damn, but how on earth would he have gotten her home? He couldn't have left her alone to find her way back to the ranch even though it seemed she navigated her way to Independence with little to no trouble. Inside, he was both seething with fury as well as with anticipation. He understood that even with a desperate fight with himself, he would eventually succumb to her sweet charms. He was only a man. His emotions were mixed. He both wanted her with him while needed to send her home in order to protect her from himself from the elements he had no control over.

Her father would be worried sick, her mother…

His fury mounted at her selfishness. At the moment, he was too angry for words. He slapped the reins on the horses urging them forward to catch up with the wagon in front of them. To flay her with words would not be nearly enough. She sat next to him, stiff as the wooden brake next to his leg. He couldn't bear to look at her. If he saw any hint of victory in her face…he didn't know what he would do.

"Can I ride your horse?" she asked sounding sweetly, innocent. "You know I'm very good with them. Can ride just like Lyssa."

He turned to her, astonishment in his eyes. She must know the answer would be negative. The diversion wasn't going to work with him. "No." Breathing in deeply he reached for an inner peace that seemed to elude him the last few minutes. He needed to find a significant as well as successful way to deal with Chauncey.

"I don't see why? Give me a reason I can understand," she continued the discussion instead of taking his answer at face value. She would argue just to keep the conversation from her and this circumstance that was founded in foolishness. The smile of hers doomed him.

He stiffened, guarding his decisions. Practical actions as well as speech were the only way to proceed with her. "You don't have to understand my reasons." He sipped in hot scorched air asking the gods above for patience as well as endurance to maintain his decisions. It would be far too easy for him to give in to her.

Terrell was riding beside the wagon, grinning as if he'd done him the greatest favor in the universe. After he tipped his hat at them, he spoke, "You two lovebirds enjoying a few moments of togetherness? It's about time, Stephen here helped you with your burden."

Wouldn't say enjoying was what they were doing. She leaned into him, pressing herself against his arm. He felt her breasts. Heard the soft inhalation of air. Imagined how she would feel pressed against his length.

"Oh, yes," she purred sweetly, looking up at him that angelic smile of hers firmly in place. "It was nice of you to tell my husband he could be with me. I so appreciate the fact. Driving the wagon can be taxing work. My delicate hands have suffered. My arms are sore." To put emphasis on her words, she rubbed her arms.

Her acting skills were fine. If she kept insisting he was her husband, he would have to show her what husbands did with their wives. No, he wouldn't do anything to hurt her, even though she deserved a good shock. Even if he scared her, she would have to stay with the train. There was nowhere for her to go. There was nowhere he could leave her and feel she would be protected until he returned. His was a stalemate of her choosing.

Damn the woman.

He grinned at Terrell, dipping his head slightly, smiling as if he meant to do just what Terrell suggested. "I intend to enjoy the next hour then the rest of the evening with my wife. If you need me, you know where to find me. I'm going to be with Chauncey until tomorrow morning." He set his hand on her upper thigh, squeezed lightly then moved his finger closer to the apex.

She squirmed then tensed, her face flushing a soft pink. The color became her. He wondered what she would look like in the throes of passion when he gave her a woman's pleasure.

Terrell hooted while he grinned from one ear to the other. "See you're starting the loving early. Don't get too distracted. We've still got a few hours to go before we can rest for the evening meal. One can only do so much with his wife when he's got to keep the team of horses moving along."

He could do a great deal with his wife, including seducing her until she was panting with her need to discover what came next. "Never get too distracted now do I, sweetheart?" He leaned closer. His hand around her neck to hold her still, he kissed her. Ran his tongue along her lips, pushing for her to open for him. He didn't know what he would do if she did what he silently asked. At this instant her mouth remained closed tight against him. He'd embarrassed her. She retaliated. Good, she deserved a bit of humiliation after what she did.

Stephen watched the wagon master ride down the column of wagons, holding his breath along with his raging thoughts. He had so many questions to ask, he wasn't at all certain where to begin. He needed to understand what she told her parents. He felt certain it would be one fine tale. Lyssa and the way she sought out Kane came to mind. She was audacious, bold as well as blunt. Form the get go, Kane didn't stand a chance in hell against Lyssa's wiles. He groaned understanding Chauncey might be just as forward.

After several minutes ticked by, he turned to her. In a smooth drawl he learned from some of the guests at the wedding feast, he asked, "What did you tell your daddy? Did you tell him you were following me into Indian territory? He'll be mighty pleased to hear where you're headed. Do you have any idea what he'll do to me when I do bring you home? Scalping would be too good for the likes of the man who deflowered his daughter." He wondered what kind of an excuse she gave him for her absence.

She stiffened as she sent him a ferocious scowl. Her chin rose a notch as her breath hitched into her throat. After smoothing her hands along her pants, she began to speak. "Suppose I knew that question was coming. In truth…it's none of your concern. Didn't tell him I ran off to be with you. If you're afraid he will come for us, don't be. My daddy is expecting me to be in London with Aunt Ella, the duchess. Told him I thought I deserved a season. Wanted to find an earl to marry just as my cousin did."

"Supposed you must have told him something outrageous. He won't believe you longer than he can check out your sorry story. So, tell me. What is it you said that won't have your daddy showing up here with his shotgun? He could catch up to us without a blink. A man alone or accompanied by his son can move a hell of a log quicker than a wagon train."

"No, he won't. I promise you that."

"You're so certain. Know that I will hand you over to him as soon as he arrives. You've done this up all nice and tight. Chauncey, I don't appreciate being put in the position as your guardian or your fake husband. I won't be either." He didn't see how he was going to get out of this conundrum she created.

She did grin then, flashed him her pretty white teeth with a broad smile. She touched his chest with the palm of her hand. "Not my guardian. My husband, yes. Since that kiss, I thought of little else besides being with you. I want adventure. I want to see other parts of the world. I want to learn what it's like to be with a man. Not just any man, you."

He gritted out trying to push down the raging anger. Where Chauncey was concerned right now, he wanted to shake her or make love to her. "I'm not your damn husband! I'm not ever going to be. Get that notion out of your pretty little head. If you can do that, we'll deal so much better together. We've a long road ahead of us. Unless Aric does show up to bring you home, I'm all you've got to depend on. You have to trust me as well as what I tell you to do. In your case, there are no decision you are allowed to make. If your father does turn up, hope he paddles your pretty little backside until you can't sit for at least a week."

"Everyone believes you are my husband. I told the Murphys in the wagon ahead of me and the Whites in the one behind me. We share a campfire at night. Mr. Terrell obviously knows who you are. A young lady named Beth who is riding with the Whites knows. Soon the entire train will know who you are to me. You won't be able to deny the fact."

He groaned understanding that for the duration of this trip he was to be her husband. He remembered how her lips felt beneath his. How his fingers closed over her breast. How he felt when he slid his hand across the tightened bud. He wanted to discover how all of her would feel beneath him. How he would feel inside her. He wanted to see her naked with her legs spread wide just for him.

If he was going to return her unscathed to her parents, he would have the devil of a time. She set this in motion. To his dismay, he didn't want to find himself forced to marry the little piece of baggage. That was a lie. It was the other things that were important. Chauncey wasn't the type of woman a man dallied with. If he made love to her, he would have to marry her. A different choice for them would never be possible.

"Want to know if your daddy is going to show up here." The wagons were slowing now, forming a circle for the evening. He concentrated on what he was doing, still hoping for an answer. Her silence told him this wasn't a topic that left her feeling comfortable. Hell, he didn't feel comfortable with any part of this situation.

"I left daddy a message he would find at a later date, well after I'd been gone for at least a day." She grinned at him as if that was all that was necessary.

"Yes." He needed to encourage her to tell him everything. This was something he needed to know. What she told her father could not be left to chance. It seemed to be what she hoped for.

She cocked her head to the side for a second lifting one shoulder as she did so. "Told him where he would find me." She told him nothing more. Once again, the silence stretched long and thin around him. He felt his gut clench.

Stephen groaned again. He would be dodging bullets in a few days. He'd be a dead man. Once the story she conjured was out in the open, he didn't expect to live. "I don't believe any of this. I'm saddled with a wife I don't want. Can't even use her as a good wife should be used to slake my lust." Inside, his gut contracting, he fumed wondering how he was meant to keep his hands from her delectable little body.

When he turned from her staring at the landscape then to her, she spoke. "You must not have heard me. Told him I went to London. That I missed my cousins. Wanted to meet an earl like Lyssa did. Everyone wants a title. You know that don't you? Of course, you don't. Thought that maybe the duchess would help me. Also told him I left with Tira and Jamie."

He snapped his fingers. "Just like that Aric is going to believe you set sail for London without discussing the adventure with him along with your mother. How stupid do you think your daddy is?" He couldn't stop shaking his head at her stupidity. Your father will ride as fast as possible to town where he'll discover your lies. He will find out no ship took you to England. You never went with Tira and Jamie. What then? What will he think happened to you?"

"No, I said I went with Tira to Baltimore then Uncle Jamie would find a ship for me." She insisted as if this plan was unstoppable.

"Are you truly that stupid?" he bit out, frustrated beyond belief. "I'm not going to be back to the east coast for a year, possibly more depending on what happens on this adventure as you call it. "How long do you think it will take him to discover you didn't go with Tira and that Jamie didn't find you a ship? That you're not in London. That Ella never received you safely so she could chaperone you for a season? Well?"

She sat back, a wilted look on her usually bright features. "They are going to worry about me. It's obvious, they will wonder where I am." She brightened, surprising him. The little minx had something up her sleeve.

"Does anyone know where you went? It would be nice if you told someone…anyone…your brother." He was annoyed as well as frustrated beyond anything he could have ever imagined. He pinched the bridge of his nose, rubbing gently. Nothing eased the pain that was growing in his head.

"No, I guess…" she sounded meek, perhaps even defeated.

Stephen didn't think the defeated look would last long. She had this way of bouncing back despite the magnitude of her difficult situation. "You didn't think farther than the end your pert little nose."

He didn't have anything more to say. Neither did she. The wagons were circled. He hopped down, helping her, his hands around her tiny waist. He untied Spirit. Without another word to her, he mounted then raced away from the campsite, away from his supposed wife. For as many moments as he could tie together, he needed to find a bit of peace. He needed to think about what he intended to do with her. By showing up here, Chauncey became his responsibility.

Heaving, spent, Stephen pulled up Spirit. He stopped. The cliff overlooking the wagons gave him a view he didn't care to examine. He saw the men and women, going about the evening, fixing dinner, talking about the day or days so far, sharing their hopes as well as their dreams of starting a new life in the west. They were all risking their lives in hopes of a better future. All but Chauncey. She was here on a whim, treading on other's lives just for herself. He would have to figure out some way to deal with Chauncey. She didn't leave him much room to maneuver. Terrell believed them married. In front of some of these people, he would have to act the besotted newlywed. He had to do it without taking her innocence.

He dismounted. Sat cross legged as he set his mind to a new course. A place he'd not anticipated a few hours ago loomed in front of him. The difficulties of this new journey plagued him. The protection of this woman was at the forefront of his mind. He needed to return her safe to the bosom of her family. He would make her write a letter to her family. Aric Lakeland deserved to know where his wayward daughter ran off to.

She was beautiful.

Full of life and love.

Her sense of humor filled him with joy.

If she continued with this tactic, she would indeed become his wife in more ways than one. He knew now he would take her with him, all the way to Lakota territory, all the way to meet his family. Once she was within the circle of his people, she would be his. They would insist. There would be no turning around, no changing of the circumstance. He would not walk in a backward path. Until then, if he could find the way, he would keep his hands to himself. He didn't want to bring a pregnant woman on this dangerous path. Wouldn't risk a child or the woman.

He had to maintain his distance.

Stephen would have to make certain she understood. She would have to believe he didn't want her for his wife. That she would have to pretend until neither could pretend any longer. Until she slept with him on his furs in his lodge, he would not make love to her. He drew in a full breath of air, filling his lungs with the fragrant scent of the prairie, realizing he wasn't going to stand a chance of doing so.

Would she persevere in this scheme? He imagined that would be left up to the gods.

He wanted her more than he'd ever wanted another woman. He closed his eyes, feeling the wind speak to him, feeling the sounds of the ending summer fill him with hope.

This Sioux warrior couldn't take a white woman for a wife. Black Thunder took Lyssa Andrews as his. He was a damn earl. What did he, Still Water Runs, have to offer a white woman? Nothing. She was used to being a pampered child of an aristocrat. Well, he did learn that Aric Lakeland was a bastard. Unlike her father, at least he knew who is parents were. Confusion swamped him. Changing emotions ruled his head. He imagined he would allow fate to take its course.

Ah, the complexities of life. His stomach rumbled with need. He hadn't eaten since this morning. He would see what his wife had in store for him for dinner. She told him she could cook. Her biscuits were the tastiest. Could she cook over an open fire? That remained to be seen.

There was much that remained to be seen.

~ * ~

Standing beside her wagon, her hand shielding her eyes, Chauncey watched Still Water Runs race away. He ran from her. Coward. Perhaps he didn't. Discovering her left no choices for him. That was a lot for a man to absorb.

Five days out she'd been discovered. Every time he rode by the wagon, she held her breath while her heart raced, ducking to hide her face or pulling her hat down. With each new breaking of the dawn, she felt renewed hope that he would not be able to send her home.

He was angry, more than furious. Livid might describe Still Water Runs. She'd understood that would be his reaction from the first moment she put her plan into motion. A second message was left for her mother to find. The letter told them in truth what happened to her as well as why. She needed to make certain both her mother and father understood this was her decision. Still Water Runs had no idea what she planned. No one could have changed the fact she fell so in love with the man, her heart stopped at the thought of him going away. She couldn't allow him to leave for a year or more without her. If this decision of hers created problems, she would deal with them.

"How are you doing?" Beth asked placing a hand on her shoulder, her eyes searching. "I see he's discovered you. Mr. Wilkes doesn't seem pleased. What are you going to do now?"

"Imagine I'm relieved at the discovery. The worry along with the fear of the unearthing of my presence are gone. The weight is lifted from my shoulders. As to what I'm going to do, I don't have the foggiest notion. Suppose I should start dinner." She imagined what she would do would depend on Still Water Runs. No, Stephen, he wanted her to call him Stephen. She would have to take her cues from him, one moment at a time.

"Beans and bacon and biscuits?" Beth asked with a tiny laugh as she walked with Chauncey to the campfire. "We need some meat of some kind. Rabbit would be nice. I hear rattle snake can be tasty."

"Yes," Chauncey mused, she did have bacon along with beef jerky she purchased in Independence. She'd eaten very little of the stores, saving it for Still Water Runs when he discovered her. Perhaps she would make this meal a bit more mouthwatering by adding the bacon to the beans. Suppose she should start to think of him as Stephen. She did like that name.

Stephen Wilkes was a nice name. Unofficially and without benefit of clergy, she was now Mrs. Wilkes. A small giggle of pleasure left her. She wished she could see him again as she did that the first time she saw him, his chest bare while he raced beside fifty of the finest race horses money could buy toward the Andrews' ranch. Beth observed her for a moment with a strange look in her eyes but she didn't ask any questions. After a few seconds she looked away.

Entering into the back of the wagon, she pulled out her apron tying the strings around her waist. Next, she gathered the other items she needed to put on the fire she shared with the Murphy's and the Whites. Every once in a while, she straightened. Her hand on the small of her back stretching to stare into the space outside the wagons realizing she was searching for him. He left almost two hours ago to race off his anger. He might not return to the wagon. Stephen could very likely spend the night under the stars. She thought he would return. Believed he would protect her by complying with her lie. She needed to tell herself the falsehood was small. After all, the untruth only affected them.

Still Water Runs was not a man who spoke untrue. She forced him to do that. It was necessary for her to get what she wanted. A pang of guilt flooded her. She brushed the sentiment aside.

What did she know about men? Nothing.

Now the biscuits were cooked and cooling near the fire. The beans with the added bacon were also finished. She dished up a bowl for herself before grabbing a biscuit from the pan. Disconsolate, she sat down on the hard ground, leaning against a wagon wheel. She imagined she deserved the abandonment. He would come home for food. Wouldn't he? Probably not. He spent the last five nights eating somewhere else.

At this point, he couldn't denounce her. Of course he could. If he did, she would be set aside at the next tiny settlement or fort. She would have to wait for her father to retrieve her in disgrace. She was lost in thought, miserable thoughts, debilitating thoughts. What would she do if he left her somewhere. She pulled in a long, deep breath of smoky air telling herself to stop feeling sorry for herself. She needed to tell him she posted a letter to her father the day they left Independence.

"Got enough for me?"

She jerked to attention. Her gaze roamed up long legs ever higher up to meet his sizzling green eyes. He came back. She swallowed the surprise. Cleared her throat. "More than enough. Would you like me to dish up a bowl?" He was here, asking for dinner. That was a good sign. Wasn't it? She would proceed now as if everything was fine. She smiled at him.

Stephen didn't appear too pleased. "Don't need you to wait on me. Point me in the right direction and I'll dish myself up some of whatever it is you made. Would you like more?"

"The food is by the fire, beans with a bit of added bacon and biscuits on the side. The bowl is in the back of the wagon along with a spoon I set there for you. Truly, though, I can get it for you. You must be tired. You've been at work all day."

He shook his head then nodded. Holding her breath, she watched him, his long lose strides eating up the short distance. After he dished up, he sat down beside her, their shoulders touching. In the chilling night air, his warmth penetrated through the flannel of her jacket. She held her breath waiting for his thoughts. She wasn't at all certain how to deal with the man. He was always so stoic and calm. This afternoon he showed more emotion than she ever remembered seeing before. His green eyes blazed at her, simmered then when he studied her, his gaze heated her.

After several bites, he spoke, "Either I'm famished or your biscuits are better than Amorica's. I wonder…well the beans are good too. You added bacon. Yes, you said that. Thank you, it's better than what I've been eating the last five days."

"Yes," she agreed happily not knowing what to say to him. His compliment directed toward her food was sweet. The conversation was unimportant. He held her future in his large hands and he was speaking of biscuits. Eventually, he would get down to specifics concerning how he felt about her behavior.

Between mouthfuls of food, he began to question her. He reached for a third biscuit. "What is in your wagon? I trust you had good advice when you went shopping for the long trip." He wiped his bowl clean of sauce with an extra biscuit. He set down the bowl, drank a long swig of his coffee. "We can save the rest of these for breakfast. We're heading out early, the break of dawn I believe. Well, as close to that time as possible. Need to make it to the river by mid-afternoon."

At his revelation, excitement ripped through her. "River? A bath?" she asked in anticipation of feeling clean again. The tiny bit of water she washed with now didn't give her that same luxurious clean feeling she so loved. She pulled her shirt away from her sweat-sticky body. "Heavenly."

Immersed in water.

He chuckled softly at her question. "Only if I go with you. Heard there is a nice pool about fifty yards from where we will pull up. Everyone is going to want a bath though. We should go a bit farther for some privacy. This morning when I rode ahead, I spotted a pool with a nice little waterfall. No one will go that far away." He stared at her with those green eyes of his that could tug every bit of truth from her.

The horrible man continued to laugh when he witnessed her surprise. "Go with me? You can't be serious." He would see her naked. Without any clothing. You're supposed to be married, you ninny. She groped for meaningful words. Found none. Repeated herself. "You don't mean that."

One raven eyebrow arched speculatively. "Yes, wouldn't leave you alone to bathe anywhere except your home. This isn't a place where women are safe without a man." He paused for a few seconds while he stared into the night sky that was now twinkling with stars. "Or my home."

She didn't say anything. Chauncey was mulling his words over in her head. Was he accepting the fact that she called him her husband? She didn't know. It seemed he hid his emotions beneath a blank façade. She couldn't read him.

He would do as he pleased. She learned as much from talking with Lyssa. A woman had little control over her life once they wed. That wasn't something she was used to.

"Are you staying the night here? At my…our wagon?" Her voice wobbled with the confusion and mixed feelings soaring through her head.

She wanted him in her bed, holding her kissing her.

Silence hugged them until he finally spoke. "Don't have a choice," he said, taking her bowl from her. "You've taken all my choices away from me. I will sleep with my imagined wife." He rose, taking her bowl from her hands.

There was hot water simmering over the shared cook fire. He poured some in his bowl, swirled it as he walked to the wagon. "Soap?" he asked. He didn't sound angry just calm. Resigned.

She didn't know what to think. Her heart raced. The air she tried to breathe was filled with confusion.

"In the left-hand corner."

Still Water washed and rinsed the bowls setting them in the back of the wagon. He stared inside appearing to make a mental note of what she purchased. She knew she did well. The wagon was full of supplies, mostly of the edible kind. One valise with a minimum amount of clothing sat near the front. It was just enough to fit into her saddlebags when they left the train. His silence unnerved her, rattled her to her core. She didn't dare watch him though she wanted to see what he was about. At this moment he was inside the wagon, going through her things, her purchases. A twinge of panic drowned her. She wasn't a frivolous white woman as he suggested. Nor was she delicate. All her life she worked the ranch with her parents. She didn't care about wearing the highest fashions. Clothes were needed for work, practical clothes. Over the years she found men's clothing was easier to work in than women's clothing.

What would he think about her purchases?

When he sat down beside her again, her body shook with the tension she felt vibrating from him into her. His large hand settled on her leg, rested there while she felt heat rising to heat her cheeks. For a few seconds, he stroked her leg. Flames rushed through her. A different kind of trembling seized her. She swallowed hard, tried to concentrate on the fire in front of her instead of the one within her.

He continued in this vein, his voice bland when he spoke. "You cannot wear these or any britches any longer. It's not appropriate for my wife, my woman to wear men's clothing. Did you bring a skirt or a gown?" he asked. His hand settled at the top of her thigh. He waited for her to answer.

Chauncey didn't want to allow him to dictate to her. He didn't have the right. She felt his touch as if the contact seared her. Burned through her clothing. "I don't..." she began intending to deny him. "I can't..."

"You will obey me, your husband, in this. You cannot flaunt your delicious feminine butt nor the delightful curve of your hips to all the young bucks who are traveling with us. I won't have you showing all your curves to men, other men besides me. You are known as my wife now among all the people on the train. I've acknowledged you, accepted the lie you created. You will behave in the manner suitable to a real woman not a woman wishing to ape a man. Now, you are my woman." His voice was so calm, casual as if he spoke of what he ate for dinner.

She understood his anger, the fury he seemed to hide. Didn't agree with his demands. "That's your final command." A slow shimmer of rage shuffled through her, eager to find a way out. She wasn't used to being told what to do, how to act, what to wear or not to wear. She wanted to toss what was left of her coffee in his face.

"You set yourself up for this," he reminded her stroking her again, now resting his hand as if he owned her on her belly. He spread his fingers as if testing for something. He still didn't show emotion in his voice or his actions.

"I did," she admitted, shivering with a rush of feelings she didn't understand. The feelings were nice though. She wished for a kiss, after that another one. His head rested on the wheel. His breaths were slow and even. He pulled her across his thighs.

"This is for all of our spectators. There are people watching us. Did you know that? We seem to be today's gossip. The couple who were married. The couple who had not been together for five days." He stroked the length of her back. His hand wrapped around her. One fingertip exploring along her side until he was close to her breast. She felt the pressure of his hand lifting her breast from beneath. She sucked in air, startled by the contact. Butterflies danced and played in her stomach.

"Wh-where are you sleeping?" She thought of the pallet inside the wagon. Most of the people slept in tents or beneath their wagons. Filled with supplies there was not enough room for families to sleep in the traveling homes. She was small. The space was just enough room for her.

Not for Still Wa…Stephen. His thumb taunted her, teasing her, brushing across the hardened tip of her breast. She inhaled a stiff breath of air. This was what she wanted. Wasn't it?

"With my wife. You like this. Admit it to me." He stood, setting her back where she'd been, holding out his hand until she placed hers in his warmth. "Come, we leave early in the morning. You will need your sleep. I won't be able to drive the wagon for the majority of the day. I have to scout ahead then report back to Terrell."

She realized then that all the bedding was beneath the wagon; her pallet the blankets, the pillows. He would sleep with her tonight. The realization of his words hit home.

He would sleep with his wife.

What to do?

Sleeping with him was what she wanted.

This was real, very real as well as frightening. *It's what I wanted.* She didn't know how a woman slept with a man. With his big warm body beside her, she didn't think she would get a moment of rest. Her mother and father slept together. "I…" She slid her tongue along her lower lip, holding back as he tugged on her to tag along behind him. She stumbled. He cursed then held her closer.

"This is what you wanted. Is it not? To sleep with your husband was the reason for your foolishness. Wasn't it? Am I wrong? Did you have no idea what marriage entailed when you embarked on this foolishness?" His voice was gentle, soft as well. She heard the huskiness of desire that she associated with her father when he wanted her mother in the bedroom. He wouldn't let this go.

"Yes." She could never deny the truth. "Yes, I wanted this. I just don't comprehend what this entails. I'm eager as well as frightened to learn what you expect." Her steps still lagged though. She saw that he also set her nightdress out for her. She looked at him surprised. Her mother and father always slept naked. She knew the earl slept with Lyssa naked. She sucked in a deep breath of air, relieved for the moment. She felt as if he gave her armor to sleep in. Stephen was offering a momentary reprieve.

"Change then meet me beneath the wagon."

She watched him sit on the pallet to remove his shoes. He put them inside the wagon. After that he removed his shirt. Her gaze riveted on him. She waited for him to remove his buckskins. He unfastened them. At that instant he looked at her. He grinned showing a wealth of even white teeth. She ducked inside the wagon fumbling with the buttons on her shirt.

When she looked up, he stood at the end of the wagon watching her disrobe. Well, watching her fumble with the buttons on her shirt. "A dress would not give you so much trouble." Nonchalantly, he leaned on the back of the wagon, still staring. "Do you need help, Chauncey? I wish to go to bed before the sun peaks itself over the horizon."

"I, of course I don't. I can undress," her voice wavered slightly. She turned her back on him. Finished with the buttons. Her shirt slipped to the floor. She felt the coolness of the night air against her skin. Heard the soft curses. In haste, she reached behind her for the nightdress. Found it then slipped the fabric over her head. Heaving a silent sigh of relief, she slid her pants down her legs.

She was brushing her hair when she heard him again.

"What is keeping you?" he asked from behind her. He sounded impatient, exasperated.

The smile on her face widened, "Getting ready for bed. What does it look like?" she asked putting as much sugar into her voice as possible. "I always brush my hair one hundred strokes before I go to bed."

Once more she heard his soft swearing. Couldn't understand all the words, only a few. She should not want to make him angry.

"Now, Chauncey! You've tried my patience to its limit. If you are not in bed in the next five seconds…" The threat was unspoken yet very real.

She didn't hear the end of the threat. Didn't want to. Dropping the brush, she was out of the wagon and beneath the covers he set out in less than five.

"That's better," he mumbled as he slipped under the covers pulling her close. "It's the way a good wife should be, compliant."

She bristled. *Compliant? I'll give him the opposite.*

The length of him was against her back. His hand rested with possession on her belly, touched her hipbones. She didn't know what he wanted of her. She whimpered when his lips brushed softly against her nape. His teeth grazed lightly where his lips had been a second before. He cupped her breast in his hand, holding the tiny mound with gentleness. Against him she stiffened, heated at the magic his tender caresses brought to her.

When his hand fell away, she turned in his arms. His eyes were closed, his lips parted slightly with the breath he inhaled and exhaled.

He was asleep.

Chauncey didn't think she would be able to sleep. For minutes-upon-minutes, she stared out at the darkness, glimmering stars, the silver moon. As the moon passed across the dark sky, the campfire died down to smoldering embers. While the sentries patrolled the area, they added wood. The moon now sat low on the horizon.

The swat to her bottom woke her. "You're lazing away the day, Mrs. Wilkes. Time to rise. I heated the coffee you made last night."

In front of her, he sat on his haunches holding two cups of coffee. She wanted to rage at his boldness. When the blanket slipped to her waist, she realized the gown was unfastened. Her eyes widened when she saw he stared at her breasts. With as much haste as she could muster, she pulled the fabric together, wondering when that happened and why she wasn't aware. Startled by the revelation, she gazed at him questioning without speaking the words.

Touching her cheek with the back of his hand, he smiled. It was a masculine all-knowing grin, "You were sweet last night. I thank you for your first time."

His words shook her, her eyes widened even more, she gasped in a tiny puff of air. "My first time? The first time for what?" She didn't understand what he was talking about. White-knuckled her fingers held the gown together.

"I'm going to have to scout ahead this morning. I'll return around noon so I can spell you at the reins. A woman so breakable as you should not find herself driving a wagon all day. Terrell has no problems. This land is as safe as it can be. No hostiles will attack us. If we stop for any reason, don't leave the wagon until I speak with you."

Even though she had no intention of exploring in the moment as it presented itself, she bristled at his command. She wasn't stupid or foolish although he accused her of those traits. By coming here, she followed her heart. Despite his obvious dislike at having to acknowledge her as his wife, she would do the same again.

As she watched his back, he vanished, mounted on his big stallion. She observed the tiny bits of dust the hooves raised. They would be underway soon. Still Water Runs harnessed the horses for her. It was the first time she didn't have to do this herself. The night was spent in his arms. He thanked her for her first time. Confused…she would remember if he made love to her. What she did recall was that he fell asleep first. Tonight, would be another night. She could ask him.

Less than thirty minutes later the wagons started to move. Chauncey thought about the bath, the clean water along with the soap. She had trouble keeping her emotions in check as the day grew hotter. Sweat slid down her body, all of her body. Though she would not have believed the fact if Steven told her, she was cooler in the gown. She wore no petticoats or corset. All she had on was her gown and her chemise even foregoing pantalets. When she lifted her skirt to mid-calf, the breeze caressed her legs then her thighs.

He would most likely not approve of her choice of clothing. She didn't care. He could rant all he wanted. She would dress as she pleased…to be comfortable. There were no young bucks who looked at her with lustful thoughts. Tapping her finger on her chin, she did recall Percival Mahoney stopping by each day with a word or two. Several times, he offered to drive the wagon for her. His eyes didn't roam very far. They always seemed riveted on her bosom. Maybe Stephen had a point. A mouthful was enough to appease a man.

Beth liked the boy. She practically swooned the day Percival took off his hat then spoke to her. Chauncey chuckled to herself remembering, wishing Beth would have a young suitor.

"Can I ride with you?" Beth stood by the side of the wagon looking up. She looked wistful, as if she needed her for something. Clearing her throat, she began to speak. "Need conversation. Thought after the night with your husband, you might want to talk. I've been there before. It was your first time? Wasn't it?"

What she needed to know is if Stephen made love to her. Asking Beth wouldn't do her much good. Beth would know less than she did. Wouldn't she? Beth was only about seventeen. Not that much younger than her.

"Wouldn't mind a bit of conversation. Climb up."

A few minutes later the wagons lumbered down the trail. She was heartily exuberant they weren't going all the way to Oregon. These families all gave up so much for this journey. To her this excursion was an adventure in the making. To people like the Murphys and the Whites, it was a change in their lives. One they hoped would be for the better.

Beth looked at her with wide dark eyes. Gently, she touched her arm. "Was he good to you last night. I mean…he didn't hurt you, did he?" The girl was looking at her toes, her face pale. "I was afraid for you. I didn't hear anything though. No screams of pleasure or pain. That seems odd."

The girl just gave her a wealth of questions. She was confused. "Yes, he was nice and he didn't hurt me. He ate then we went to bed. That was all." Chauncey didn't know what else to say to the girl. "Why were you afraid for me?"

"Promise you won't say anything," Beth began solemnly, her voice soft with a small tremble. "The Whites rescued me from a work home. I was sold to a man and woman who wanted me to service the husband because the wife didn't want him anywhere near her. Lived with them for three years before the Whites came along. They must have bought me from the other people. Though they don't demand much of anything from me. I still have to pay for my room and board."

Chauncey's blood froze. "Demand? What did they demand, Beth? Service? I don't understand."

After shaking out her skirt, Beth began, "Sex. The men always wanted sex. After the first time I learned to stare at the ceiling and lay as still as I could unless he wanted me to touch him. Is that what you did last night? Drift off to a place where you wouldn't feel?"

Her breath stuck in her throat. "Does Mr. White want sex too?" She would have to tell Stephen. She promised Beth. She couldn't tell a soul. Chauncey didn't know how she could keep this secret. Beth asked too much. Even though she sounded matter of fact, Chauncey denoted hurt in her voice.

"Yes. Most nights it's over fast. I don't feel anything anymore. The first times though, before I learned to relax and keep my mind blank, what the men did to me hurt. I always screamed. Some liked me to yell. Now when it's done, I just curl up inside myself."

"Why are you telling me this?" Overwhelmed with the information, Chauncey wished she could right this problem. Still Water Runs would tell her it was not up to her to fix anything concerning Beth.

Beth touched her arm, moisture glistening in her eyes. "I want to help you if you need it. Men can be cruel and hurtful. I know how to help you get through with the sex without too much pain."

"Stephen isn't cruel. He's a very nice man." It was not difficult to defend Stephen. He was a nice man. She didn't believe he would ever treat her as Beth described.

"I know. I don't see any meanness in his eyes. Yesterday he was angry with you. Everyone saw that when he raced away from the wagons. He had to be furious with you for some reason. What was it?"

Chauncey lifted her shoulders, knowing she could never tell Beth everything. "I can't say. He would be angrier if I spoke of it." She understood he wanted to get away from all of this unscathed. Forcing a marriage on him had never been her intent, though by her actions that was exactly what she was doing. The romantic that she was, she thought he was in love with her. When he kissed her that first time, she fell in love with him. He didn't reciprocate the sentiment.

One kiss means nothing to men. She recalled Jess telling her brother that very thing. Men, her brother, Kane, they all kissed many girls. They didn't love any of them. She'd been a fool. This might be the biggest mistake of her life. In this case, there was no going back.

"If you want to ask anything, my offer stands. I'll answer any questions. Just tell me when you wish to talk."

Chauncey didn't believe she'd be asking Beth anything. At the moment, all she wanted was to stay away from Stephen. She didn't think he would allow her the privilege of keeping distance between them.

~ * ~

Aric Lakeland stomped through the house. He'd ridden to Baltimore. Dust covered him. Filled his mouth as well as his nostrils. Conversed with Jamie Lundin to discover his daughter lied to him. She didn't go to London to visit cousins. She didn't even go to Baltimore. Her name didn't appear on a ship's manifest.

Where the hell was she! His fist landed hard on the wall.

"Sit down, Aric. I'm certain she is fine. We have to believe that or we'll go crazy worrying about her." Ravyn plied her needle in the new stitchery she worked on. "You will drive yourself crazy if you keep pacing. What exactly did Jamie tell you?"

"That she didn't do as she said. She's not in Baltimore. Not in London." He rubbed the back of his neck, swearing softly beneath his breath. When he looked up to gaze at his wife, "Where the hell is she?"

"Lyssa believes she is with Still Water Runs. It seems she was enamored of him though we didn't notice. She says they shared a kiss or perhaps more behind the church the day of her wedding." She set her work on her lap to meet his gaze. "Do you recall that I hid in a trunk so I could stay with you rather than find myself sent back to London?"

He swore again. The memory didn't ease his worries. "You think she is that in love with the man. She barely knows him. He's headed for Indian territory. She's in danger."

"The man is Sioux. He will protect her."

Ravyn's words didn't calm him or soothe his stretched nerves they just made him angrier. "He will try. There are no guarantees. They will come back wed in the way of the People. Do you think they will find some backwoods traveling minister to wed them? When they return next year, we will wed them here. I won't have it any other way. If they haven't married in some way, there will be hell to pay. I'll recognize any marriage before I bring out my shotgun."

"That is quite magnanimous of you, dear." She rose. Walked to him then wrapped her arms around him.

"You won't change my mind with a tiny bit of loving," he said even as he turned to kiss her.

"I wouldn't dream of doing so. They will not have a bastard for a child."

"No, they won't," His fingers tightened on her shoulders. When he saw her look of pain, he let her go unable to figure out what it was he should do.

"I would not accept that either. Chauncey will do the right thing.

She will insist they wed."

"He's a man, Ravyn. I doubt if he instigated this. If he doesn't want to marry her, no one will be able to force him to do so."

"No, he most likely did not instigate this. We both understand our daughter is single-minded."

"Admit it, Chauncey is willful."

"Used to getting her way in everything. She is spoiled. We did that to her."

Aric pulled her closer, felt her warmth, knew what he wanted to ease his mind. "I will send Slade after her. He will find her."

She touched his jaw with her fingertip in an attempt to soothe. "We do not know where they went. We cannot send Slade into Indian territory on the off chance that he will find her. We could be sending our son to his death. Have you thought on that?" Ravyn asked gazing at him with loving eyes.

"No, don't know how they will travel or in which direction." He understood what she wanted, accepted the fact that in this situation they were helpless. There were too few choices to be made.

"We will wait." She pulled his head closer, her mouth raised expectantly to his. Running her tongue along her bottom lip she asked for a kiss, for renewal of love.

He understood she was just as frightened as he was. He kissed her, let his lips explore the woman he loved. Tugged on her bottom lip so she would open for him to sightsee. Heat filled him. All-encompassing love touched his heart. The kiss was long and slow. When he stepped back from the deepness, from the magic he knew his answer would not make her happy. It would have to do. They would have to find a way to come to terms with his need to run after his daughter then haul her home as if she was a recalcitrant child. "I don't believe I can."

"You have no choice," she murmured softly touching secret places in his heart. "You will have to trust Chauncey. She is an adult woman with needs you can't possibly understand."

He groaned when her exploring hands dipped beneath his buckskins, held him, stroked his swelling length. The warmth of her small fingers never ceased to arouse him. He saw Still Water Runs with his daughter. Imagined him making love to her. She was innocent. He was seasoned in every way a man could be. The man was older, would want her beneath him. He should understand what was right. Still Water Runs was still a man, a very virile one at that.

Saw her belly swelled with Still Water Runs child. His stomach twisted with the notion he failed to protect her. "She is an innocent, romantic at heart. Chauncey has no idea what she has gotten herself into."

"I imagine she does," Ravyn whispered. "Maybe not everything," she amended softly. She may be innocent but she has needs just as all other women. "Still Water Runs and Chauncey…he will treat her with respect. I'm certain of that fact. He is like Kane."

He withdrew from his wife to stride around the room, stopping every once in a while, to swear then to stare outside as if he would see her striding to the door. "I would know where she went. A father needs to protect his daughter. I failed." He gripped his fists tighter, wishing to hit the man who would take advantage of his daughter.

"You understand it is our daughter who made the assumption he would welcome her with open arms. Still Water Runs is most likely innocent in this deception of hers. He didn't want her to go with him. The man would never put her into danger. Escorting her into Indian territory would do that very thing. He is caught in a situation he no longer controls."

Aric turned on her, his fury simmering to the point where he thought he would burst. He wanted to ride hard. Needed to rescue his daughter. He didn't know where she was even though he was reasonably certain as to where she was headed. "Don't understand why you defend that man."

She laughed softly, setting her hands on his chest. "That man…reminds me of you twenty years ago."

Aric snorted, displeased with her confession. "Still Water Runs isn't anything like me."

"You were stubborn to a fault. Thought only you knew what was good for me. Intended to send me home even though I pleaded with you to let me stay. I wonder if Chauncey is pleading with her man even now."

Ravyn chose not to continue the argument. After the short diatribe she fell silent. To Aric, it seemed obvious she decided he was right and she was wrong. The front door opened. Booted feet that had to be his sons strode quickly through the house.

"Father! I've news!" When he entered the parlor, they stepped apart. Slade grinned as if he knew what they'd been doing.

His son was too observant. Hell, he was a young man now. Aric knew Slade wasn't celibate. "News?" Awkwardly, they both stepped forward. Aric's hand was stretched out to take the paper from Slade's hand.

He handed it over. "A letter from your lost daughter. I didn't read it," Slade quickly said as he watched.

Aric's brows drew together. He swallowed the gut-wrenching fear ripping through him. For several seconds he held the envelope in his hand while his breath hitched. Ravyn hand fluttered on his arm. It had been five days since they left…a lifetime.

"Would you like me to read it to you?" Ravyn asked, her voice soft. "Or Slade."

He tugged in a deep breath of air as he slowly opened the envelope then stared at the paper in front of him. Tears filled his eyes. It was just as he feared. Aric looked up then began to read quietly.

Dear Mother and Father,

The first bit of information that you should have is that I'm safe. The second is that I did this on my own. Still Water Runs played no part in my decision. You see, I love Still Water Runs. He doesn't know my feelings yet. I didn't want him to leave me for the year he said he would be gone. Don't come after us. You might catch up to the wagon train but I won't leave. You would only embarrass yourself and me as well. If you send Slade, well, even though he's my big brother, he's too young to be traveling through Indian territory by himself, a place he knows nothing about. You wouldn't put his life at risk. I know you.

As for me, I'm a grown woman. I can make up my mind. You no longer have a say in what I do. I'm writing this from Independence Missouri. I took the train here. Now, we are going overland by wagon train. Still Water Runs is a guide and a scout for the train. Here he is known as Stephen Wilkes.

No, Stephen doesn't yet know I'm here. I'm hoping he won't for a few more days. The more time we are out of Independence the less chance he has of taking me back. I've told everyone he is my husband. He will be furious with me when he finally sees me. Imagine, I deserve his anger.

I want him as my husband.

When he discovers my ruse, he won't hurt me. I know him well enough to understand he is a kind, gentle man. You see, he has no meanness in his eyes. I've seen that meanness before. If Still water…Stephen is my life. I love him.

Please forgive me. Please don't try to stop me in anyway. If you do, I'll never forgive you.

Love,

Chauncey

"He's a damn Sioux warrior. What does she mean there is no meanness in his eyes and that she's seen meanness," Aric asked letting the letter float to the floor. He turned to Slade in search of an answer. "What else has she told you?"

"It's Paxton," Slade said speaking softly. "He cornered her one day then tried to rape her. She made me promise to remain silent. That is what she was talking about. Because I was there. He left without getting what he wanted."

Nick's Tender Rogue
Naughty book One

Once a McClellan lass

Beautiful, naughty and audaciously daring, young Nickie Gray is a McClellan princess through and through—as wild and reckless as the most incorrigible of her male cousins. Now that she has reached a marriageable age, Nickie has set her amorous sights on a most unsuitable male—the notorious rake and womanizer known to all mamas on the debutante scene in London as dangerous. When her chaperone tells her all rakes are off limits, she finds the challenge one she sets her mind to.

Always a McInnis rake

Not expecting to find a ravishing woman throwing herself at him yet blatantly willing to accept whatever overtures she makes, handsome Collin McInnis is thrilled by the brazen escapades of this naïve creature and is willing to experience her high-spirited advances with no expectations of commitment. On the high seas, he is bested by a vivacious beauty whose love of freedom and adventure rivals his own...and by an inescapable tidal wave of passion that threatens to engulf them both.

Dream About Lyssa
Naughty book One

When Lyssa Andrews sees the earl sitting behind his desk scowling, she knows she will someday put a smile on his face. The handsome brooding earl isn't playing the same game. He resists her outrageous comments and questions until she is ready to give up. Lyssa didn't come to London with the intent to find a man. Now, though, she is willing to chance love with the stodgy earl of Blackmore.

Raised by the Sioux when his father sought adventure then fell in love with a Sioux maiden, Kane has been betrayed once by a white woman. He isn't about to give his heart to another, especially one who is as white as newly fallen snow. Despite his best efforts, he can't deny Lyssa's intoxicating effect on him. Now Kane will risk his very life to protect the innocent beauty who has seduced him with her tender love.

Connal's Eternal Love
Sweet McKenna Book One

A few days shy of All Hallows' Eve Connal McKenna, Laird of Clan Chattan stands on the parapets of his castle. Bonfires line the hillsides while his clan prepares for the upcoming festivities. Drawn by the whispering of the wind, Connal McKenna feels a strange restlessness in his soul. Setting out to discover the wickedness that is calling to him, he discovers his mate. With gentle words and sensuous kisses, the auburn-eyed highlander conquers his mate, the beautiful, defiant Wynnie Adair who he comes upon during an evening ride. She must ultimately put her trust in the only man who can save her from the ruthless plans of her father and succumb to his gentle coaxing.

In Brady's Arms
Sweet McKenna Book Two

Forced to run from the only home she knows, beautiful, headstrong Lillian Townsends seeks shelter in the wild highlands where the McKenna clan live. Trying to avoid a betrothal contract signed by her stepfather to an aging lord, she is desperate to find a means to sidestep the inevitable, including a marriage to the oldest son of the laird. Lilly is enamored of the young lord who pursues her with unrelenting determination flashing his devilishly handsome charms. She is hard pressed to resist.

Besotted from the first moment Brady McKenna sees Lilly, he is determined to find a means to coax her into his arms and bed. With only the promise of carnal pleasure as his mistress, Brady relentlessly pursues the woman who has unwittingly forged a place in his heart. She is like no other woman, proud, defiant and enchanting. Despite his father's advice to stay away from her, he cannot. He boldly seeks her out and makes her his own.

Nobody but Walker
Sweet McKenna Book Three

The Highland Lass...

She was brought up, adored and loved by a doting mother and father ardently protected by her brothers. She was everything sweet and innocent until she was faced with betrayal and an unexpected and out of wedlock pregnancy. When she gave her love to a man who couldn't return her passion and commitment, she was left devastated and furious. Faced with the loss of her child if she didn't comply to his demands, Crissie McKenna followed him to Belfast then on to his country home to discover he was already married.

...The Irishman

Stunned to find out his one and only encounter with the woman he wanted to love forever created a child, Walker Endicott, Earl of Briarwood, claimed his child as his only heir. Walker threatened all her previously held values even while he thrilled her senses. From the moment he first saw her to the second she ran after him begging him to make love to her, his captivating masculinity held her fascinated. In his arms she would know tempestuous passion, bitter despair, and a soaring joy that would humble them both before the power of love.

Roby's Moonlit Night
Sweet McKenna Book Four

Once she'd been a pampered child with high expectations for her future blessed with love. Then she became an innocent pawn in a terrible game of greed and power. Now, with a noose around her neck, Pippa was to hang before she had the chance to unveil the men who drove her from her home, before she had the chance to live.

Roby McKenna was a man blessed with endless charm and wit. While he searched for his eternal love across the Atlantic in a new land, he would have to come home to find her. His silver blue eyes could sparkle with amusement or harden to steel gray with displeasure. He had all the women a man could want or need. As he grew older, mistresses were not enough. A quirk of fate brought him to the gallows, a spark of destiny made him claim the condemned Pippa as his bride.

Made for Houston
Sweet McKenna Book Five

Leah Kennedy is as wary of people as she is strikingly beautiful. However, the shocking death of her father that forever changed her girlhood has left her terrified of the very love she desperately longs for. Only in the untamed splendor of the Scottish crags does she feel safe from the feelings she stirs in men and the cruel mockery of Selkirk's villagers.

Debonair, well-educated doctor Houston Stuart has turned his back on social privilege along with professional honors to set up a medical practice in the lowlands of Scotland. There, serving those who need him the most, he hopes to forget the bitter memories and disillusionment that disturb his days.

Coincidence brings the cultured doctor and this fey mountain girl together. Something as bizarre as destiny disrupts the obstacle of birth and breeding, stubborn pride and fear which has kept them apart...as each seeks to heal the other's wounds with a raw passion neither can deny and all the odds against them cannot defeat.

Say You Love Kit
Sweet McKenna Book Six

Fascinated...

When the woman stepped through the door of the pub, the sun setting her fiery red hair glowing around her delicate features, Kit Stuart finds himself captivated by the sight. The moment he sees her he knows she will be his. Convincing the fire-haired lady of that fact isn't easy. After she calls out another man's name when he kisses her that night, he is instantly enraged as well as jealous. The road they travel is fraught with secrets that neither can tell. Trust is an elusive quality that neither can give.

Intrigued...

Forced to run for her life, desperate and afraid, Aila MacDuff willingly enters into the Kinnel Stones, a mysterious place where people disappear then appear magically in different times. At the first sight of Kit, she finds herself inexplicably drawn to him. She's been told to search for her mate and that she will know when she finds him. Aila doesn't know what this man's name is or what he looks like. Nonetheless, she is certain he will be similar to her mate from one hundred years earlier. Despite the fact she is falling in love with Kit, he can't be her mate. Her mate is a shifter. Kit is not.

It Had to be Riley
Sweet McKenna Book Seven

Her anger assured retaliation...

Shawna's only concern with the contemptable scoundrel she had been forced to wed was the return of her dowry. She had not seen her husband in three years, and now Riley Stuart furiously repudiated there had ever been a marriage. He even went as far as to tell his family he'd never seen her before this day.

... Her passion promised love

In the heather clad hills of the beautiful Scottish crags surrounding the small village so near to the Mckenna keep, the ferocity of her loathing yields to the intense hunger of unquenched longing. In the powerful arms of the dark and handsome husband she thought she reviled, Shawna shivers with the honeyed torment of awakened desire and powerlessly submits to the wild, enchanting ecstasy of burning passion. Together they abandon themselves to the exquisite pleasure of the love their hearts cannot escape.

My Sweet Broc
Bad Boys Book One

He's a bad bad boy...

Broc Wallace is a fun-loving rake who never thought any beautiful woman could melt his heart. He lives life in the present enjoying the camaraderie of his friends and the pleasures of his mistress. When Bliss races into his life, he is ill prepared to deal with her secrets or give up the tenor of his life. When the truth is revealed, he finds himself unable to forgive and forget the betrayal.

...but she's sweet for him

Bliss MacTavish knows she's playing with fire when she refuses to tell this bad boy her name. He tempts her with sweet whispers of seduction knowing her innocent nature will be unable to refuse all he yearns to give her. Deciding to follow her heart, she finds the repercussions more than she bargains for when she gives herself to this bad boy.

Crazy for Cam
Bad Boys Book Two

He's a bad bad boy...

Lord Cam MacEwen, Viscount of Rosehill, tries his best to be proper and court the lady of his dreams in the acceptable way. The feat proves impossible when the lady in question uses every means at her disposal to tempt him. He fights his jealousy for another man as well as the need to make her his own, finally giving in to her irresistible passion.

...but she's crazy for him.

Chelsea MacTavish wants the bad boy she fell in love with and kissed just before her eighteenth birthday. With feminine wiles and irresistible allure, the sensuous lady plans to best Cam at his game of hearts and make him forget his need to court her properly.

Falling for Flynt
Bad Boys Book Three

He's a bad, bad boy...

Fascinated by Hope's loss of memory yet haunted by her sultry beauty, Flynt is irresistibly drawn to the stoic miss—and into her troubles with the sultan who wants her for himself. When he discovers she is the sister of his best friend, his pride keeps him from pursuing her and making her his.

...but she's falling for him.

Raised in a harem but now penniless, alone and without her memory, Hope must discover a way to remember all that she has lost. She finds a way to continue with her life as a servant in Flynt's home. The first sight of Flynt steals Hope's breath as well as her heart. Can she overcome her fears and give herself to the man she fell in love with.

Dancing With Donal
Bad Boys Book Four

He's a bad bad boy...

Once a bad boy always a bad boy, Donal Chamberlin's carefree ways come crashing down around him when he meets the ravishingly beautiful Daryl MacTavish, the innocent little sister of one of his best friends. He is determined to win her heart as he sets his sights on marriage and an heir. His past gets in the way of his quest when a woman he once loved threatens Daryl's life.

...but she's dancing with him.

Daryl has seen the control her sister's husbands hold over them. She yearns for a life where she makes decisions for herself. No man will have power over her. But no man kisses her the way Donal does. No man can make her forget all her goals leaving her helpless to give up her dreams. Yet Donal is determined to dance through all the barriers she thrust in front of him, pursuing her until she says yes.

Loving Leslie
Bad Boys Book Five

He's a bad bad boy...

Leslie Stewart, Duke of Southcliff is stoic, set in his ways, a spy who is used to having his life well ordered. He expects life to continue on in this perfectly conventional fashion. He assumes his bad boy status while keeping mamas and debutantes at arm's length. An heir is needed but Leslie has every intention of finding a woman who doesn't covet his wealth and tittle. He is irresistibly drawn to the headstrong young lady who becomes more beautiful as she develops into a woman.

...but she is loving him.

When Leslie kisses Lacie MacTavish, she knows even at the tender age of fifteen this is the man of her dreams. Forced to wait until she comes of age, Lacie withdraws into herself. Now she is eighteen and Leslie has returned from a mission for the British Government ready to claim her as his bride. She refuses him and he must find a way to seduce her and in the process create a burning passion within her, which she cannot deny.

Pleasing Arie
Bad Boys Book Six

He's a bad bad boy...

Arie Demir has never been denied anything in his life. He takes what he wants. What he undeniably yearns for is the beautiful redheaded spitfire he sees in a restaurant in Glasgow. At every turn, she confuses him by disputing his power over her. Alison refuses to accept the fact he owns her. While Arie tries desperately with patience and tenderness to drive her wild with new sensations, his scorching kisses ignite the fires of her very soul to make her understand he is all she will ever want.

...but is she pleasing him?

Alison Fletcher never expected to find herself kidnapped and sold to a whorehouse then bought by a Turkish sultan to become his slave. She vows to never surrender to the arrogant man who believes he owns her. She is stunned by the magnificently handsome man who awaits her compliance. Unexpectedly, she finds Arie the lesser of all the evils. The hidden depths of his mesmerizing dark brown eyes hold her into their power; his muscular embrace makes her weak with desire. She is his to do with as he wishes.

Graham's Wicked Kiss
Bad Boys Book Seven

He's a bad bad boy...

Graham Chamberlin is stunned to find three young boys dangling from the trees lining the drive to Runningmead Manner. On further inspection, he is astonished at their obsession to protect a young woman who has been brutalized by her pimp. The woman he discovers hiding in a third-floor attic room is gravely injured. He takes the silver haired stowaway under his wing. Clearly, Graham's new guest is a lady with many secrets. He is determined to unlock all the mysteries surrounding her.

...But she can't resist his wicked kiss.

The years since Ria left the convent where she was raised have been a nightmare. Her secrets are dangerous—as is the powerful man determined to find her. Handsome Graham Chamberlin is clearly a gentleman with secrets of his own, but staying with him could mean the difference between life and death for Ria. With each passing day, her handsome host turns Ria's convalescence into an increasingly sensual escape. Now her greatest challenge may be imagining anything less than a future in his arms.

Feeling Etienne's Love
Bad Boys Book Eight

He's a bad bad boy...

Etienne Dubois is the son of a wealthy vineyard owner who craves the excitement of putting his life on the line. Working with the French government and as a confidant of King Charles X give him reasons for living. An encounter with a beautiful young woman in a plush bordello in Paris has him rethinking his roguish ways. Etienne never expects to become a father especially from one encounter with an innocent prostitute who whispers his name and has him rethinking his well-ordered life.

...But she can't help feeling his love.

Elisa Moreau, the only daughter of Angelique Moreau, the owner of an exclusive bordello in Bordeaux, France, has loved Etienne Dubois since she was six. Unfortunately, until an unexpected encounter at a brothel in Paris puts the two of them in the same room, Etienne doesn't even know she exists. Confused but wanting Etienne and this chance meeting to never end, Elisa gives herself to the man who has held her heart in hands for what seems like her entire life

All I Want Is Link
Bad Boys Book Nine

He's a bad bad boy...

Merry Stewart is wildly unpredictable. Left alone to run wild over the Bordeaux and Scottish countryside she becomes impetuous and daringly bold. Over the years, she's found she can bedevil her softhearted brothers into allowing her exploits to go unnoticed. As a young woman she has learned she can do as she pleases when she pleases. Now, Merry has set her amorous sights on the Duke of Weston—a man she has never met but has every intention of marrying. No other suitor will satisfy her—especially not the exceptionally striking, horse breeder, Devlin Mathews.

...she's the woman of his desires.

Posing as commoner Devlin Mathews to escape a potentially fatal confrontation, Devlin is enthralled and infuriated by the audacious, duke-hunting dark haired vixen. Bedeviled at every opportunity, he finds dealing with the tiny she-devil exasperating as well as intriguing. Without revealing his true identify, the infamous rogue pledges to thwart Merry's plans to wed the man of her dream-never imagining the bewitching strategist would turn out to be the only woman he would ever dream of marrying.

Devlin's Angel
Bad Boys Book Ten

He's a bad bad boy...

Merry Stewart is wildly unpredictable. Left alone to run wild over the Bordeaux and Scottish countryside she becomes impetuous and daringly bold. Over the years, she's found she can bedevil her softhearted brothers into allowing her exploits to go unnoticed. As a young woman she has learned she can do as she pleases when she pleases. Now, Merry has set her amorous sights on the Duke of Weston—a man she has never met but has every intention of marrying. No other suitor will satisfy her—especially not the exceptionally striking, horse breeder, Devlin Mathews.

...she's the woman of his desires.

Posing as commoner Devlin Mathews to escape a potentially fatal confrontation, Devlin is enthralled and infuriated by the audacious, duke-hunting dark haired vixen. Bedeviled at every opportunity, he finds dealing with the tiny she-devil exasperating as well as intriguing. Without revealing his true identify, the infamous rogue pledges to thwart Merry's plans to wed the man of her dream-never imagining the bewitching strategist would turn out to be the only woman he would ever dream of marrying.

Needing Gill
Bad Boys Book Eleven

He's a bad bad boy...a man with no heart.

Gil Allemand wants to be left alone, especially by the beautiful outcast who's invaded the vineyard where he meant to wallow in his grief. She has a ton of impudence and brazenness, a talent for trouble, and a child who brings back memories better left in the dark recesses of his mind. Yet Jenna's feisty spirit might just be heaven-sent to save a hard, inflexible man.

...she's a desperate young mother.

Jenna Bonnet's bad luck has taken a turn she never imagined. With twenty-five silver francs, a mare that can't walk up the hill to the chateau that is her five-year-old son's birthright, a son she is desperate to keep alive, she's come home to a village that despises her. However, this single-minded young widow with a shocking past has learned how to fight. She'll do anything to keep her child alive—even take on a man with no heart.

Just For Michael
Bad Boys Book Twelve

He is a bad, bad boy...

Michael Flannigan has burgeoning ideas the moment he meets the woman who has inherited Mayfair. Clare will fit into his big plans quite nicely. Mayfair Plantation is his heritage. Even before the Revolutionary war Flannigans owned this land. No woman is going take what is his. Realizing the only way he can possess the land that is his birthright is to marry the impulsive woman who waltzes into his life, he sets his sights on making her his, slowly seducing her until she unwittingly falls into his scheme.

...but she is determined

When Clare Carter-Brown returns to Mayfair Hall in Virginia after several years absence, she intends to claim her inheritance. Bypassing Leslie Hall, she moves into Mayfair without a chaperone intending to take over from the manager. Michael objects to her tactics. At every turn, he adeptly points out her failings. As the fires rage around them they find a love that burns more fiercely than either could ever imagine.

Foolish for Piper

The pickpocket...

Piper has spent her life surviving the streets of St. Giles Parish in London, a den of iniquity and crime. Masquerading as a boy she escapes the whorehouses the young girls are sent to as they come of age. The day she encounters Brett MacLachlan begins the same as every other one. When she picks his pocket, she has no idea her life is going to change irreversibly.

...and the mark

Handsome aristocrat Brett MacLachlan has come to London for his amusement only to find his world turned upside down by a thief and her dog. From the moment he spots her, Brett knows there is something intrinsically wrong. In his arms, Piper discovers passion and joy. Yet secrets of her past haunt her, and a scar will tell the true tale as well as her identity.

Taylor's Destiny

She traveled to another time and place to change destiny...

Enjoying a day of sailing, Taylor Maxwell never expected after a suffering a concussion she would wake up in another century. A resilient independent woman in the twenty-first century, the blond beauty is ill prepared for life in the 1800s. Her first sight of the naval captain who rescues her makes her heart stop, giving her hope for her future.

His life is transformed by a woman who appears from nowhere...

Born to a life of ease, Reid Stewart defies the dictates of those born to aristocracy and chooses a life of adventure in the navy and as a spy for the crown. When he discovers a nearly naked woman on the bow of small sailing ship, his heart warms. His love for Taylor and his need to protect her from a man who pursues her might cost him his life as well as hers.

Caitlin's Duke

She played a fiddle in an Irish pub...

Caitlin O'Shea Is the most beautiful woman Roc Leighton has ever seen. With her blue violet eyes and long black hair she captivates him. In turn he mesmerizes Caitlin. Caught in the power of his gaze as he watches her, she is wise enough to know he desires her but will never give his heart to her. Caitlin has vowed to never be any man's mistress.

And fell in love with an English Lord...

Roc knows the first time he watches her play the fiddle and dance around the pub, she will be his next mistress. Despite her protest, he will find a way to convince her that her place is with him. While Caitlin's determination to keep her vows, fate takes a cruel turn and she is forced to seek refuge with Roc.

Catching Meara
Book One in the McKenna Clan Series

Meara Thorton was a feisty, world-class computer hacker—cornered by the FBI and shockingly given the chance to be their newly acquired technical analyst. Brilliant and intuitive, yet aching with the loss of everyone she has cared about, her restless heart led her to discover a love she fought and a world she didn't know could possibly exist.

Sweet Sexy Sadie
Book Two in the McKenna Clan Series

From the first time Sadie's eyes met those of Brody McKenna in the hot Sierra Madre Mountains, theirs was a potent attraction—not gentle, slow, and easy, but hot, hard, and all-consuming. The daughter of a dysfunctional family, Sadie had dreams no man could wrench from her with hot sex and an all-consuming passion. She'd challenge this alpha male with all the strength she possessed. But her red hair, fiery temperament, and indomitable spirit obsessed Brody...and he knew he had to find a way to show her he was more than he appeared and convince her to make a life with him.

Sweet Misbehavin'
Book Three in the McKenna Clan Series

Cast adrift after fleeing the home of Jokul, the ice demon, Atantsi, a firestarter, grew to womanhood as she moved through time to keep the demon from finding her. Though stubborn and courageous, she was ill prepared to use powers she had not been taught. Her first sight of the intoxicating Carr McKenna left her breathless, and her second encounter gave her hope for a future she never thought she had.

A playboy, a second son and a shifter, a man who thought his life would be carefree, Carr McKenna was shocked to discover the woman he'd paid as an escort is a firestarter who is running for her life. He is the leader of all the McKennas around the world and that he has multiple powers. His passion for Margo and the need to defend her might cost him his life as well as hers.

Sweet Talkin' Sugar
Book Four in the McKenna Clan Series

Lyonesse McKenna, was dreaming, or was she? From the instant Lyn saw Deacon McClain across a black jack table in a crowed Las Vegas casino the unmistakable attraction sent Lyn's senses flying into overdrive. Her family of shapeshifters believed in soul mates. She'd always been skeptical yet she couldn't help but question the way her heart sped when he looked at her.

When Deacon appeared in Las Vegas he knew his first job was to save Lyn from a Sea Demon, but the next order of business was to convince her he would someday mean more to her than she'd ever expected. But her stubborn nature and unbendable spirit consumed Deacon...and he had to chase away all the demons real and imagined in order to win her heart.

Sweet Surrender
Book Five in the McKenna Clan Series

Ripped from her family at the top of Infinity Cliff, Kimi McKenna finds herself thrust somewhere into the future. Dark elements threaten to destroy the earth unless Kimi can work together with the white witch to stop the destruction. Confused by her mate's role in the conspiracy, she refuses to acknowledge the connection. But amidst raging fire and attacks on the people she is coming to hold dear, she allows Maska O'keefe into her heart.

Maska O'keefe has loved the beautiful shapeshifter for years. Unable to save her life years ago, he vows to watch over her as he is given a second chance to convince her that even though he is a witch and not a shifter, they are indeed soul mates. Kimi's divided loyalties between her family and the cause she is now a part of will determine their relationship. Only the part she plays as the messiah can bring this to a conclusion in the final battle.

Sweet Dreams
Book Six in the McKenna Clan Series

For Cas Doyle finding the shifter of her dreams was a matter of life or death. She walked into the Red Neck Bar and Grill in Cactus Junction with a hope and a prayer he would be there and she would recognize him. What she needed was for him to take her home and take her virginity. Cas never thought to be a one-night stand. She had no choice.

Guy McKenna knew eventually he'd find his soul mate. He didn't expect the reality to happen this night. When he saw her he knew. She was dressed provocatively, enticing him to an extreme he never felt before. What he didn't know was if he could convince his protective family that Casidhe Doyle was indeed his soul mate.

Dakota's Bride
The first book in the Lakota/Pinkerton Series

When Emma St. John received her brother's letter imploring her to escape her stepfather's vengeful scheme and to trust Dakota Barringer with her life, she was willing to chance it. But the handsome, brooding riverboat owner Emma found in Natchez a danger of another kind. For Emma soon found herself surrendering to an unrelenting desire.

Raised by the Sioux when his parents were killed, Dakota had been betrayed once before by a white woman. He wasn't about to trust another, especially one claiming that her stepfather, a powerful U.S. senator, had framed her as a murderess. But he couldn't let Emma's intoxicating effect on him. Now Dakota would risk his very life to protect the innocent beauty who had seduced him with her tender love.

My Angel
The second book in the Lakota/Pinkerton Series

A BEAUTY IN BUCKSKINS

When her father decided to send her to a finishing school back East, Angela Chamberlain refused to be confined to stuffy drawing rooms. Instead, the daring spitfire who could shoot like a man and ride like the wind longed for a life of adventure and romance—and she knew exactly who could give it to her. Devil Blackmoor was a hired gun with a dangerous reputation. But Angela was willing to go to the ends of the earth to capture the handsome devil's heart.

A DEVIL IN DISGUISE

He'd come to America looking for excitement, but Devil Blackmoor got more than he bargained for when he encountered a beautiful rebel who answered his kisses with a wild innocence that touched his very soul. Yet standing between them were more obstacles than either ever dreamed. For Devil had strapped on a gun for the wrong man. And that made Angela his enemy. Now he'll have to choose between his duty and the woman he loves more than life.

The Locket
The third book in the Lakota/Pinkerton Series

The year is 1894. Seeking revenge for crimes against his family, Misha Petrovich follows a path that leads straight to Ariel Cameron's boarding house in Mist Harbor, Oregon. A family heirloom in Ariel's possession leads Misha to believe she is guilty. The locket has been handed down to the oldest girl in the Petrovich family for generations. Ariel is innocent of wrong doing, but her father is not. Misha is torn by his feelings for Ariel and his need for restitution against her father. Knowing that the relationship between them is fragile, Misha does everything in his power to protect Ariel's father. His efforts are to no avail when her father is shot. Ariel comes to realize Misha's steadfast courage and determination to protect her and her father despite what has happened to his family. Ariel's love and devotion heals Misha's heart.

The Talisman
The fourth book in the Lakota/Pinkerton Series

Running from a marriage that lasted one night, Dr. Moriah McKeown discovers the land she has settled on is coveted by determined and lawless men. Yet the proud young woman who once vowed never to abandon her home has second thoughts when her adopted children are threatened. Her only recourse is to enlist the aid of a dark, dangerous gun for hire.

Haunted by the past and a betrayal he will never forgive, Ian Civanovich uses his fast gun and his reckless courage to forget the faithlessness of a woman in his past. He will trust no female—nor will he rest until the threat hovering over Moriah McKeown is put to rest.

Forever His
The fifth book in the Lakota/Pinkerton Series

Struggling to come to terms with the part she played in Jacob St. John's death, Etta Barringer resigns from Pinkerton Agency and seeks peace and solace in a Rocky Mountain Cabin.

Jacob has vowed to discover the reason Etta has betrayed him, sold him out to his enemy and left him for dead.

Isolated in their cabin, they discover their love for each other and learn to trust. But the trust is shattered when Jacob learns she is married to his sworn enemy; the man who left him in the desert to die.

Allura's Secret
Twelve Dancing Princesses Book One

Allura McClellan is horrified by her father's decision to take out an ad in the Times awarding her to the man strong enough and smart enough to win her hand and uncover her secrets. She's an intelligent young woman who takes great delight in the freedom allotted to her by her father. She's well aware that marriage would effectively curtail the adventures she's shared with her sisters and cousins.

Hunter Gray is nothing like the other men who've arrived to vie for Allura's hand in marriage and everything that goes along with it. However, he is the first to refuse to concede defeat and pursue her despite her attempts to disguise her true appearance. It's her temperament that is of more concern to him than her looks. Hunter has worked all his life with the hope of someday owning his own land. Now that it looks like there's a very real possibility that everything he's ever wanted is within reach nothing is going to deter him – including Miss Allura's disagreeable disposition.

Amorica's Wager
Twelve Dancing Princesses Book Two

Amorica Hepburn was sent to London to find a husband. Finding a man was the last item on her agenda. With her two cousins, Amorica wagers she can dissuade her suitor before the others. Despite her efforts she discovers a chemistry that cannot be denied. Suddenly she is the arrogant man's wife, pledged to a marriage neither desire. But swept off to his ancestral home above the Dover cliffs and into his strong embrace, Amorica is soon possessed by a raging passion for the husband she had vowed to despise...

Damian Andrews couldn't afford to trust the emerald-eyed spitfire who happened upon his secret. Amorica's hatred of all men of his kind only inflames the war that rages between them. Still, he can not control the intense desire his stubborn bride inspires, or make her surrender to his will until he has conquered the headstrong beauty on the battlefield of love...

Ravyn's Marriage of Inconvenience
Twelve Dancing Princesses Book Three

A REGAL BEAUTY

When the duchess decides to wed her to a wastrel and a fop, Ravyn Grahm takes matters into her own hands and declares her engagement to another man. Instead of fessing up and telling her great aunt what she has done, she goes through with the pretense. Ariec Lakeland is the bastard son of an earl and has a dangerous reputation. But Ravyn is willing to do most anything to keep the duchess from discovering the lie.

A DEVIL-MAY-CARE SMUGGLER

He'd bought land in America, looking to put down roots and end his life of adventure, but Ariec Lakeland got more than he bargained for when he encountered a beautiful heiress who made a promise she didn't want to keep. But the promise could not be undone and standing between them were more obstacles than either ever dreamed. Ariec had made plans to spend the rest of his life in America and that was at odds with Ravyn's plan of living in England and running her father's estate. Now, he'll have to choose between his dreams and the woman he loves more than life.

Christel's Sunrise
Twelve Dancing Princesses Book Four

He Made Her An Offer...

Life has thrown Christel McClellan some experiences that could have devastated a less determined woman. Beautiful, self-assured and fiercely independent, she is trying to forget the loss of her stillborn child. But is the child alive?

She Couldn't Deny...

Life is carefree for Ryder MacLaren who loves to see what is on the other side of the sunrise. Laird of Clan MacLaren, he is wealthy, handsome and happily unencumbered...until stunning Christel McClellan enters his life. When he hears her story, he believes the child she thought dead has been sold to a wealthy buyer.

Storm's Passion
Twelve Dancing Princesses Book Five

SHE MADE A PROPOSAL...
Life strikes Storm Graham a shattering blow when she learns her father has bartered her to a man she detests. Storm is beautiful, self–assured and fiercely independent, and refuses to be a pawn in her father's schemes, yet she can find no way out of this bargain made in hell. Going on the offensive she asks the wealthiest man on the eastern coast of England to marry her, never believing she might fall in love.

HE TRIED TO REFUSE...
For Hadden Johnston life has provided everything he ever wanted, including a sanctuary for homeless children. He is wealthy, handsome and happily unencumbered...until stunning Storm Graham marches into his life and proposes a marriage of convenience. Yet this type of marriage to a woman who inflames his senses is far from acceptable. If he's going to be tied down, he will move heaven and earth to have this woman warming his bed.

Gotta Have Fayth
Twelve Dancing Princesses Book Six

A regal beauty with raven hair and piercing blue eyes, Fayth Graham is unwilling to parade herself in front of the wealthy Lords of England during the season. Seeking a means to dissuade any man wishing to wed her, she seeks a way to ruin herself for marriage. When she unexpectedly meets a man with sparkling gray eyes and an infectious grin, she decides this is the man who will keep her from agreeing to obey.

He returned from six months at sea, looking for a few nights of pleasure with a willing lass, but Jarret Kinsley got more than he bargained for when he met a beautiful debutant who responded to his kisses with a wild innocence that touched his heart. Yet the obstacles looming between them might rip them apart. Both had vowed never to marry, so when consequences of their dalliances got in the way, Jarret would have to choose between the life he's always desired and the woman he loves more than life.

Ella's Pleasure
Twelve Dancing Princesses Book Seven

A WHISPER OF PLEASURE
Ella Hepburn was an auburn haired debutant from the harsh Scottish coastline—a wild innocent to be seduced and tamed. A spirited beauty, she captivated Drake Montgomerie's jaded heart—while succumbing to the smoldering desire she felt for her unyielding suitor.

A WHISPER OF DANGER
In Drake Montgomerie's glittering world of money and privilege, young Ella discovered passion and desire could overcome everything she'd been taught to resist—entangling Drake, the heir apparent, in a lethal coil of aristocratic family intrigue. But grave peril would only nurse the sparks of a love that knew no limits and a magnificent ecstasy that would not be denied.

Eveleen's Seduction
Twelve Dancing Princesses Book Eight

A WHISPER OF SEDUCTION
A brutal attack on Eveleen Hepburn's cherished island off the Scottish coastline leaves her shattered and bewildered. Learning a man she once trusted can kill as easily as he can breathe even though the deed saves her life, creates questions that need answers. An innocent beauty, she enchants Logan Maxwell's cynical heart—giving in to the raging passion she feels for her mysterious suitor.

A WHISPER OF INTRIGUE

In Logan's Maxwell's world of espionage and privilege, young Eveleen discovers truths about herself she never expected, and a need for passion and love can overcome all her fears if she learns to accept certain truths. She finds herself entangled in a lethal battle for land that was once owned by French nobility, taken from them during the revolution and sold to Maxwell. But grave peril would unleash the flames of love that simmers, creating a magical union that cannot be refuted.

Tavia's Deception
Twelve Dancing Princesses Book Nine

WHISPERS OF DECEPTION

When her father decides to send her to London for her season, Tavia Hepburn resolves to see the world instead. The raven haired beauty decides to disguise herself as a lad and find employment on a ship bound for Barcelona as a cabin boy. But she never bargains on finding passion and love to a red haired sea captain who rescues her from certain death.

WHISPERS OF MURDER

For James Macmurra, the world is black and white until he meets a young debutante, who turns his world upside down. He's unable to deny Tavia's intoxicating effect on him. In a match tense with obstacles, unwillingness to divulge secrets, and unforeseen peril, irresistible desire and passion grows into undeniable love. James would risk his life to shelter and protect the innocent debutante who seduces him with her sweet love.

Larena's Fascination
Twelve Dancing Princesses Book Ten

WHISPERS OF FASCINATION

Fiery, free spirited Larena Graham never wanted to marry a duke.

She is thrilled to be in love with the fourth son of an aristocrat, Gavin Broon. But when it seems Gavin ignores her, she set her sights on politics and bettering human life. Unsuspecting intrigue and a plot against her, she continues her dangerous plans despite Gavin's wishes.

WHISPERS OF TRUST

Gavin has every intention of properly courting the beautiful Larena until he must leave the city in order to put his affairs in order. Returning to London, he finds the woman he means to make his own is embroiled in political protests that could lead to a prison ship. Larena must learn to trust the handsome Scotsman whose most pressing mission is to protect her and keep her from harm.

Tira's Education
Twelve Dancing Princesses Book Eleven

WHISPERS OF EDUCATION

Learning how to build ships is Tira Hepburn's only dream until she meets Jamie Lundin and her world is turned upside down. With her raven black hair and vivid green eyes, she tempts Jamie and pushes him to defy his vows. She never bargains on finding an irrevocable love and a passion to a man who cannot fulfill her dreams despite his burning desire for her.

WHISPERS OF A BARGAIN

Arrogant and self-assured Jamie is brought up short when Tira captures his heart. All his carefully made plans are put to the test when he decides to teach her the art of ship building if she will spend a week with him alone on his ship. He is unable to deny Tira's intoxicating effect on him. When Tira leaves him behind unwilling to live with him without the benefit of marriage, he races after her. Jamie will risk everything to shelter and protect the innocent debutante who seduces him with her sweet love.

Aidan's Love
Twelve Dancing Princesses Book Twelve

Whispers of Love

Aidan McLellan has loved since she first set eyes on him as a young girl. Spontaneous, wild and eager to grow up, Aidan haunts his waking thoughts day and night, insinuating herself into his life. With her fiery red hair and sparkling sapphire eyes, she seizes Blade's heart even while he tries to resist the innocent child until she becomes a woman.

Whispers of Courage

Blade has waited what seems a lifetime to claim the woman who captures his heart as a little girl. Claiming his inheritance before his younger brother takes what is rightfully his, Blade must convince Aidan of his sincerity after years of avoidance and wed her before his father dies so he can return home, securing his rightful place. Everything is put to the test when his life as well as Aidan's is threatened by the man who once called him brother.

Don't Hustle Letty
Good Girls Book One

She's a good girl...

As tempted as Scarlett was, she had too many secrets to let someone enter her world—secrets that would send any reasonable man to the farthest ends of the earth. Bobby was far from reasonable and despite her desperate attempts to hold him at bay, he would not let her past destroy their future. With her escort service, Scarlett used men and their insatiable lust for women to capitalize on the means to survive and prosper. She vowed to never wed, to never put herself in the control of a man.

...nonetheless he has other ideas.

Lord Robert Munroe, with his newly acquired title of marquis goes to Scarlett's for training on how to comport himself. The marquis, better known as Bobby, knows how to pick a pocket as well as get into a bloke's home to steal them blind. What he doesn't know is how to be a gentleman. When he sets his sights on the prim Miss Scarlet, Letty, to his way of thinking, he decides she is the woman he wants to call his wife. He tempts all that she is with sweet words and tender coaxing until she is unable to refuse all he hopes to give her.

Only Caro's Baby
Good Girls Book Two

The Scheme

Genius botanist with theories of inherited traits, Caroline Kenworth desperately wants a baby. Finding a suitable father won't be easy. Caroline's super-intelligence makes her feel pushed aside, unwanted as a woman. As a bluestocking she is determined to spare her child the suffering that plagues her life. Which means she must find someone very special to father her child. A person very...well...ignorant.

The Target.

Duncan Murray, the Earl of Downsberry, well known for his lack of intelligence as well as his rakish ways with women, seems as if he is the flawless man to fulfill the role. His amazing good looks and Scottish brogue are misleading. Caro learns too late that this debonair earl is a lot smarter than she first thought—in addition he's not about to be used then abandoned by any woman who has schemed to steal his sperm.

The Detonation

A dazzling solitary woman whose desires to learn what it would be like to become a mother... A man who is in control of all he does never allowing anyone to usurp his role will settle for nothing less than surrender... Can lust coupled with physical attraction drive two strong-minded yet vulnerable people to a completely unforeseen love?

Only Caro's Baby
Good Girls Book Three

She's a good girl...

Born a bastard, Honey McRae is taunted and bullied by her half-brother most of her life. Branded with a tattoo of the Saber and the Rose by the men's association, she is desperate to be free and escapes the country estate where she was held prisoner. Resigned to a passionless life devoid of men, she fights the nightmares that haunt her. Despite her past fears, she accepts the fact she will never be able to give herself wholly to the man she loves. Until that man, bold and breathtaking, decides he will find a means to woo her into his arms.

Nonetheless...

Stolen at birth and sent to live in the bowels of London, Billy–once a pickpocket and thief–discovers he is actually the Duke of St. Aubries. He is determined to win the woman he fell in love with the first time he saw her, the lady with a tattoo on her breast, a woman who has been cruelly used. He disputes her notion that men are only capable of inflicting pain...instead he binds her to his heart with his gentle and patient loving.

Betsy Be Good
Good Girls Book Four

AN ENGLISH ROSE

Sweet Betsy Darling, the oh-so-prim and innocent tutor for children born of rich aristocrats, is a woman on a mission—she has but a short time to lose her standing as a respectable spinster. Arriving in Glasgow with skirts flying, parasol pointing, and plump mouth issuing demands, she understands only one thing will save her form losing all she holds dear: complete and utter disgrace.

A BRAW HIGHLANDER

Known throughout the city as a bad boy with more money than he needs, Evan Murray has lost his temper one too many times, and now he's suspended from teaching at the university he loves as well as Halstead & Family the financial firm owned by his family. An apology which he refuses to issue is one of two things that will restore his career. The second is his complete and utter respectability! Now he's been coerced into escorting the bossy, parasol toting Miss Betsy Darling, and she's hell-bent on chasing down a tattoo parlor, dressing in skimpy clothing and worse…lots worse.

Twelve Days to Love

When Archer Steele shows up at Calanthe Durand's failing plantation with an alligator over his shoulder, Cali thinks she's never seen a more handsome man. During the war she had to defend herself and her servants from both union and confederate soldiers. Independent and self-sufficient, she vows to never marry.

But Archer Steele has different ideas. The first time Archer sees Cali in town, he feels an instant attraction. He decides he will do everything and anything to convince the beautiful Miss Durand he is worthy of her love. During the weeks leading up to Christmas, he gives her twelve gifts in hopes she will fall in love with him. Yet they are faced with challenges they must overcome before Cali can commit to a marriage.

Door to Heaven

Jessica Lawrence is the stepdaughter of a woman born in the twentieth century transported back in time to the year 1868. An acclaimed suffragette, she raises Jessica to believe in the equality of women. Jess Law believes everything she was taught, and when the time is right she becomes a private investigator. Courageous and impetuous, Jess finds danger in her quest to save all women from white slavery. Her passionate mission results in a wedding to Roc Newman, a man she knows can steal her heart...

Roc can't trust the sapphire-eyed spitfire who invades his home in search of secret papers and knocks him flat with her karate moves. Jessica's refusal to obey his wishes serves to inflame the war between them. Still, he cannot control the intense desire his reluctant bride inspires, or make her surrender her independence, until he has conquered the headstrong beauty on the battlefield of love...

Rebel Heart

HER REBEL SPIRIT DEFIED HIS OUTSIDERS SOUL...She was velvet and silk, eyes the color of a summer storm and amber hair. Victoria DeMontville, because of a promise and a codicil to her father's will, was forced to marry one man to protect her from another. She hated Cameron Savage with a fierce passion. But to hold on to her genetic research and find a cure for the deadly Signe virus, she must pretend to love the enemy at her door, come with weapons of fire to melt her icy heart...

HIS OUTSIDERS TOUCH IGNITED RAGING PASSIONS... He wore a mask, disguised as the Phantom, a true legend come to life. Even as war and debate over new genetic research engulfed them all, he would find his greatest adversary in the beauty who'd branded him an outsider and barbarian, the woman he was born to possess, his soul mate.

Safari Moon

Solo St. John, a wildlife photographer, is preparing for a trip to Alaska. Suddenly, Solo finds women of all sorts invading his privacy, his home and his office, all cooing nonsense words and blatantly throwing themselves at him. Solo doesn't know why, and he has no idea how to rid himself of the persistent women. He finally decides to beg a favor of his best buddy Nyssa Harrington.

In love with Solo for the past ten years and knowing he doesn't return her feelings Nyssa doesn't want to talk to Solo. She knows if she accepts his phone call, she will not be able to resist the temptation to hope again.

Straight to Heaven

Running from demons, Alexandra McMurdie stumbles into Forbidden Ground where up is down and elements of nature are contested. Though a strong independent woman in the twenty-first century' she is unprepared for life in the 1800s. Her first site of the formidable James Lawrence makes her heart skip a beat, giving her cause to reconsider her desperate need to find a way home.

Born with a silver spoon, James' life was torn apart during the War Between the States. Moving west he vows to put the life he once knew in the past. When he discovers a half-frozen woman near Gold Hill, his heart begins to thaw. His love for Alexandra and his need to keep her from a man who has pursued her through time might cost him his life as well as hers.

A Valentine's Anthology

The Lending Library-a fantasy by Christie L. Kraemer
Faeries try to fit into the human world when the forest where they make their home is destroyed by a mysterious enemy.

Chasing Rainbows-a contemporary romance by Genene Valleau

An eccentric aunt, an inventive uncle, a mother who wears poodle skirts, and a brother who wears pearls provide a hilarious backdrop for the courtship of a young woman who yearns for a "normal" family.

The Gift-an historical romance by Christine Young

A man and a woman on opposite sides of the Civil War get a second chance at love after one final battle returns soldiers to their war-torn homes to rebuild their lives.

A St. Patrick's Day Tale
Christine Young, C. L. Kraemer, Genene Valleau

Tumble through time...

...to Ireland in 1817, when tensions are high between Protestants and Catholics and fae people guide the fate of villagers. A lovely Catholic lass stumbles upon the weakly ritual fisticuffing between Irish lads. She falls into the lap of a handsome young Protestant. Family ties, grudges, and two conniving faeries threaten their budding love. But the faeries outsmart themselves when they hijack a time machine that has mysteriously appeared in their forest and are whisked to...

...Eugene, Oregon in the 20th century, amid a property feud between the local faeries and night elves. The conniving faeries from Olde Ireland try to stir up more mischief. However, a warrior gnome convinces the magic folk to control their own destiny, and forces the intruding faeries to take refuge in the time machine again, spinning their way toward...

...A modern day castle in western Oregon. An eccentric inventor is determined to reclaim his wayward time machine and save his beloved wife from her latest misadventure. If only they can travel safely past the black hole...

a May Day Anthology
Christine Young, C. L. Kraemer, Rosemary Indra, Genene Valleau

Highland Miracle — Christine Young

HURTLED THROUGH TIME, Sean Michael Sterling, landed in the midst of a May Day celebration he didn't understand, assuming the role of Laird Sterling.

ILLIGITAMATE CHILD OF NOBILITY, Reagan Douglas searches for a way out of her half brother's house.

Defying the Odds — C.L. Kraemer

The night elves on the hill aren't happy without their magic. They concoct a plan to punish those who were involved in the act that rendered them almost human. Meanwhile, Uther, the rogue night elf, has returned to woo the Librarian to be his eternal mate.

Love in Bloom — Rosemary Indra

When childhood friends reunite it takes two fairies and a matchmaking daughter to help them admit their true love for each other.

No More Poodle Skirts — Genie Gabriel

After drifting for years in the innocent age of the 1950s, a woman struggles to join today's world by finding a career and a new love, with some help from her zany family.

Once Upon a Christmas Moon
Christine Young, C. L. Kraemer, Genene Valleau

TWELVE DAYS TO LOVE

When Archer Steele shows up at Calanthe Durand's failing plantation with an alligator over his shoulder, Cali thinks she's never seen a more handsome man. During the war she had to defend herself and her servants from both union and confederate soldiers. Independent and self-sufficient, she vows to never marry. But Archer Steele has different ideas. The first time Archer sees Cali in town, he feels an instant attraction. He decides he will do everything and anything to convince the beautiful Miss Durand he is worthy of her love. During the weeks leading up to

Christmas, he gives her twelve gifts in hopes she will fall in love with him.

BOOTS AND BLADES
An ancient evil from the old country has arrived in the high desert of Oregon. Gnome children are vanishing then re-appearing, showing various stages of traumatization. Tiamoon, warrior gnome, will put her skills to use alongside Killian, a handsome warrior, also in need of a cause.

CHRISTMAS PAWSIBILITIES
With their world destroyed and their space ship malfunctioning, the dogizens of Planet Canid have little choice but to crash land on Earth. They face tortuous experiments at the hands of the Geeks in Green...or they can trust an eccentric inventor and his zany family to deliver the Canine Queen's puppies and help them celebrate new lives.